To those seeking adventure among the stars

Cover illustration: Dale Ziemianski
d-alien.com

Starship Deadfall is a science fiction action adventure in which you play as the main character. Unlike conventional books, you will read select paragraphs (references) and make decisions which will determine the story and what happens to you. All you need to play is this book, 2 standard dice and a pen and paper. It is easiest with a printed mission sheet and a pencil and eraser.

WWW.BIONIC-AGENT.COM

Publisher:

Inspiring Publishers

P.O. Box 159, Calwell, ACT Australia 2905

Email: publishaspg@gmail.com

http://www.inspiringpublishers.com

National Library of Australia Cataloguing-in-Publication entry

Author: Moodie, Dean

Title: **Starship Deadfall**/Dean Moodie.

ISBN: XXXX (pbk)

Cover illustration: Dale Ziemianski d-alien.com

www.bionic-agent.com

Subjects: XXXX

Dewey Number: XXXX

Quick Start

1. Decide which faction you will be aligned with. If this is your first time, the LWS faction is ideal.
2. Select a character from the list on the pages ahead (or randomize it if you wish). Write down the stats, weapons, items and ability for your character on your mission sheet.
3. Select a mission which goes with the character you just selected. Missions are specific to each faction. Write the details on your mission sheet.
4. Grab your dice and get comfortable.
5. Skip the detailed instructions and begin by reading the *prologue* on page 65.

Getting Started

In the Nuivairyiux Star system, there are 4 major rival factions. These are the Leading Weapon Syndicate (LWS), Space Designation Network (SDN), The Confederacy (Often referred to as Confeds) and the Xeno-Biological Research (XBR) faction. There are a few smaller, less known groups such as the Frontier Exploration Group (which are considered mostly neutral). Many small bands make up the bulk of the remainder population which will simply be referred to as non-Faction Aligned or NFA.

In Starship Deadfall you may choose from either LWS, SDN, Confederacy, or NFA (Non-faction aligned). This will be your faction alignment (Even though NFA is unlike the others and is not a faction in itself) LWS and SDN will provide longer reading times (and therefore longer adventure) to finish a mission.

Confederacy and NFA provide moderate length missions.

If this is your first time reading, it is suggested you begin with the LWS faction, but remember each time you play, you can start again with a different faction and character. Also note that the character (and therefore faction) you choose, if you complete your mission or at least survive, can be used in future missions in other Bionic Agent books. All details of your character will remain the same, all you need to do is replenish your vitality and then pick up the next book. Your character will continue to gain experience, items and the story will flow as scenarios unfold. In addition to your own development, you may change the course of events by achievement of your missions or tasks as well as the choices you make.

To start playing, you'll need a character and a mission. Your character is 'who you are' and stays the same throughout the game. Stats, items and weapons may change during game play. The information listed for your character is what you will write down on your mission sheet and begin with. Any changes made (e.g. swapping out a weapon) will be reflected by what you write on your mission sheet. A mission sheet is easily downloaded and printed out. To get by in a pinch you may simply use a blank piece of paper to record the information. To select a mission, check which faction you are aligned with and then select an appropriate mission for that faction. You must pick a mission which aligns with the faction of your character. If you do not, it will be impossible to complete your mission as you will be from a different faction and the story will not make any sense anyway. How you select both the mission and the character is completely up to you. For instance you may pick a random mission to start with. Let's say you choose Fugitive hunt. Then you simply need to pick a character from the Confederacy to play that particular mission. You can either randomize the selection or perhaps you'd prefer to just go with Moby as he is a good all-rounder which may be helpful if you are starting out.

As an alternative to selecting a character from one of those listed, you may also generate your own from scratch. See the section "Creating your own character" to do this. If you wish to play with the Collector of things mission, as a character who is non-aligned with any faction (NFA), then pick a NFA character, then do not collect any weapons or items. In Starship Deadfall as a NFA character for the Collector of things mission only, you start with only the clothes on your back - no items, no weapons and no armor

Mission Sheet

All of your stats as well as details such as notes and time are recorded on your *mission sheet*. To begin, fill in the details for your character. Printable versions of the mission sheet will be available online, though if you do not have one at the time, simply use a blank piece of paper to write down the details as needed. There are a multitude of items in the **Bionic Agent** series, so you will find some items are counted as miscellaneous items.

The mission sheet is shown on the following page. Printable versions of the mission sheet will be obtainable from www.bionic-agent.com

Name	Faction	Role

Vitality [max]	Close Quarter [CQ]	Ranged [Ra]
	Strength [St]	Agility [Ag]
	Perception [Pe]	Endurance [En]

Science [Sci]	Technology [Tech]	Biology [Bio]	Resilience [Re]

Code words

Weapons, items, armor — Details

Enhancements and additional items

Effects

Abilities

Time Passed — 1st TIER

☐☐☐☐☐☐☐☐☐☐☐☐☐☐
☐☐☐☐☐☐☐☐☐☐☐☐
☐☐☐☐☐☐☐☐☐☐

2ND TIER ☐☐☐☐☐☐☐☐

☐☐☐☐☐☐ IF TIME PASSES
FINAL TIER AGAIN TURN TO
☐☐☐ ⟶ 1000.

Consumables Quantity

Miscellaneous items

Carried items tally

Light items

Regular items

Creds

Chance
- 2   -1   0   +1   +2

Reference bookmark/Mission

Characters

Darion
(Leading Weapon Syndicate)

Stats
  Vitality 35
  Close Quarter 5
  Ranged 6
  Strength 7
  Agility 4
  Perception 4
  Endurance 6
  Resilience 4
  Sci 2
  Tech 4
  Bio 3

Weapons and items
  Laser pulse rifle
  Siege ram
  Med packs x 3
  High impact grenades x 2
  100 creds
  Coated multi alloy suit

Ability
  Ox and cart in one

Generon
(Leading Weapon Syndicate)

Stats
  Vitality 31
  Close Quarter 5
  Ranged 5
  Strength 5
  Agility 6
  Perception 6
  Endurance 5
  Resilience 5
  Sci 3
  Tech 5
  Bio 3

Weapons and items
  Dual auto pistols
  Utility socket
  High speed laser cutter
  Med packs x 3
  High impact grenades x 2
  100 creds
  Coated multi alloy suit

Ability
  Tech hoarder

Jaro "Skullcap"
(Leading Weapon Syndicate)

Stats
  Vitality 30
  Close Quarter 6
  Ranged 5
  Strength 5
  Agility 6
  Perception 5
  Endurance 6
  Resilience 5
  Sci 3
  Tech 4
  Bio 3

Weapons and items
  Laser pulse rifle
  Electro razor
  Med packs x 2
  Proximity explosives x 2
  150 creds
  Coated multi alloy suit

Ability
  Retaliation

Naldinn
(Leading Weapon Syndicate)

Stats
  Vitality 29
  Close Quarter 6
  Ranged 6
  Strength 4
  Agility 6
  Perception 5
  Endurance 5
  Resilience 5
  Sci 3
  Tech 4
  Bio 3

Weapons and items
  Laser pistol
  Electro razor
  Med packs x 2
  Stimserts x 2
  Proximity explosives x 2
  Scatter grenades x 2
  100 creds
  Coated multi alloy suit

Ability
  Close awareness

Vamoor "The shadow"
(SDN)

Stats
  Vitality 28
  Close Quarter 6
  Ranged 6
  Strength 5
  Agility 6
  Perception 6
  Endurance 6
  Resilience 6
  Sci 3
  Tech 3
  Bio 3

Weapons and items
  Knuckle lasers
  Proximity explosives x 4
  Stimserts x 4
  Ghost processor
  50 creds
  Reconstructing
synthesized polymer suit

Ability
  Stealth

Zotar
(SDN)

Stats
  Vitality 31
  Close Quarter 7
  Ranged 5
  Strength 4
  Agility 6
  Perception 5
  Endurance 5
  Resilience 5
  Sci 4
  Tech 4
  Bio 3

Weapons and items
  Short laser blade
  Utility socket
  Skewer launcher
  Proximity explosives x 3
  Med pack
  Stimserts x 2
  50 creds
  Reconstructing
  synthesized polymer suit

Ability
  Terminal hack

Phybose
(SDN)

Stats
   Vitality 30
   Close Quarter 6
   Ranged 5
   Strength 4
   Agility 7
   Perception 5
   Endurance 4
   Resilience 5
   Sci 3
   Tech 4
   Bio 4

Weapons and items
   Shock pistol
   Short laser blade
   Stimserts x 4
   Proximity explosives x 3
   Ghost processor
   50 creds
   Reconstructing
synthesized polymer suit

Ability
   Evasion

Demokkief
(SDN)

Stats
   Vitality 33
   Close Quarter 5
   Ranged 5
   Strength 7
   Agility 4
   Perception 5
   Endurance 7
   Resilience 4
   Sci 3
   Tech 3
   Bio 4

Weapons and items
   Laser pistol
   Med packs x 2
   Proximity explosives x 3
   High impact grenades x 2
   Ghost processor
   50 creds
   Reconstructing
synthesized polymer suit

Ability
   Brick wall

Vearoah
(Confederacy)

Stats
  Vitality 36
  Close Quarter 6
  Ranged 5
  Strength 7
  Agility 4
  Perception 4
  Endurance 7
  Resilience 5
  Sci 3
  Tech 3
  Bio 2

Weapons and items
  Breaker gun
  Shock mace
  Med packs x 2
  100 creds
  Combat armor

Ability
  Brick wall

Moby
(Confederacy)

Stats
  Vitality 33
  Close Quarter 5
  Ranged 6
  Strength 5
  Agility 5
  Perception 5
  Endurance 6
  Resilience 5
  Sci 4
  Tech 3
  Bio 3

Weapons and items
  Breaker gun
  Hammer fist
  Med packs x 2
  100 creds
  Combat armor

Ability
  Keen eyes

Bordall
(Confederacy)

Stats
  Vitality 30
  Close Quarter 5
  Ranged 6
  Strength 5
  Agility 5
  Perception 7
  Endurance 5
  Resilience 5
  Sci 3
  Tech 4
  Bio 3

Weapons and items
  Laser pulse rifle
  Shock mace
  Med packs x 2
  100 creds
  Combat armor

Ability
  Tracker

Tameepe
(Confederacy)

Stats
  Vitality 28
  Close Quarter 6
  Ranged 6
  Strength 6
  Agility 5
  Perception 5
  Endurance 6
  Resilience 5
  Sci 3
  Tech 3
  Bio 3

Weapons and items
  Laser pistol
  Shock mace
  High impact grenades x 2
  Med packs x 2
  100 creds
  Combat armor

Ability
  Negotiator

Joave "The Scavenger"
(Non Faction Aligned)

Stats
  Vitality 28
  Close Quarter 6
  Ranged 6
  Strength 4
  Agility 6
  Perception 6
  Endurance 4
  Resilience 5
  Sci 3
  Tech 4
  Bio 3

Weapons and items
  Laser pistol
  Med packs x 3
  Stimserts x 3
  High impact grenades x 3
  Ceramic plated vest

Ability
  Tech hoarder

Samell
(Non-Faction Aligned)

Stats
  Vitality 36
  Close Quarter 5
  Ranged 6
  Strength 6
  Agility 4
  Perception 4
  Endurance 5
  Resilience 4
  Sci 4
  Tech 3
  Bio 3

Weapons and items
  Punisher auto gun
  Short laser blade
  Scatter grenades x 2
  Med packs x 3
  Ceramic plated vest

Ability
  Strong arm

Gunnar "Smokin' barrel"
(Non-Faction Aligned)

Stats
  Vitality 33
  Close Quarter 6
  Ranged 6
  Strength 5
  Agility 5
  Perception 5
  Endurance 5
  Resilience 5
  Sci 3
  Tech 4
  Bio 3

Weapons and items
  Punisher auto gun
  Breaker gun
  Med packs x 3
  Scatter grenades x 3
  Coated multi alloy suit

Ability
  Enhanced leap

Naareiss
(Non-Faction Aligned)

Stats
  Vitality 30
  Close Quarter 6
  Ranged 5
  Strength 5
  Agility 7
  Perception 5
  Endurance 6
  Resilience 4
  Sci 3
  Tech 3
  Bio 4

Weapons and items
  Laser pistol
  Short laser blade
  Scatter grenades x 4
  High impact explosive
  Med packs x 4
  Ceramic plated vest

Ability
  Ultra runner

Abilities

Contortion

Requires an agility of 7 or more.
You are adept are dislocating your joints to fit into small spaces and holding difficult poses at any moment.
See text for specific details of using this ability.

Enhanced leap

Requires an agility of 7 or more.
Instant energy reserves for the legs and chemical insertion.
You may reroll the dice once for any jumping task, or follow text for use of this ability.

Upgraded

Requires an agility of 9 or more.
In addition to the bonus above, add 2 to the total of your roll for any jumping task or follow text for use of this ability.

Strong arm

Requires a strength of 7 or more.
You simply enjoy pushing things and people around.
Add 1 to your roll for any task which calls for your *strength* value.

Upgraded

Requires a strength of 9 or more.
Add 3 to the total of your roll for any task which calls for your *strength* value.

Keen eyes

Requires a perception of 7 or more.

Years of experience has given you the edge in spotting clues and things of significance.

See text for specific details of using this ability

Ultra runner

Requires an endurance of 7 or more

You are adept at running long distances and quickly.

See text for specific details of using this ability.

Upgraded

Requires an endurance of 8 or more and an agility of 8 or more.

See text for specific details of using this ability.

Undeterred

Requires a resilience of 7 or more and a perception of 7 or more.

Even when outnumbered your focus is on your mission.

See text for specific details of using this ability.

Ox and cart in one

Requires a strength of 7 or more and an endurance of 6 or more.

If you could carry more you would. So you do.

Ignore the first *heavy* penalty.

Upgraded

Requires a strength of 8 or more and an endurance of 8 or more.

Ignore two *heavy* penalties.

Frenzied fighter

Requires a CQ score of 7 or more.

Your close quarter fighting technique is just insane. Any close quarter combat you may do each of the following once only: Reroll a single 'to hit' die (the second result must be accepted). Double a single damage die. Ignore an instance of damage you may take, including any effect associated with the attack.

Upgraded

Requires a CQ score of 10 or more and an agility of 8 or more. You may do each of the actions listed above twice per combat.

Fury strike

Requires an agility of 7 or more and a CQ of 7 or more.

In any close quarter combat if this ability is not negated you may make two attacks instead of one in the first round of combat.

Upgraded

Requires an agility of 8 or more and a CQ of 8 or more.

Instead of attacking twice you may re-roll *any or all* of the dice you roll in the first round of combat, accepting the second results rolled. The choice to either reroll or to attack twice must be made before you start.

This ability may not be taken along with the *retaliation* ability.

Retaliation

If the enemy attacks first, then for your first attack of the combat you may *attack twice* in a succession.

Upgraded

Requires a CQ score of 7 or more and an agility of 7 or more.

For both of your two attacks you may reroll your to hit rolls. The second dice roll result must be accepted.

This ability may not be taken along with the *fury strike* ability.

The quick and the dead

Requires a perception of 7 or more
Unless this ability is negated you will always strike first in any ranged or close quarter combat.

Upgraded

Requires a perception of 8 or more and an agility of 8 or more.
In addition to the bonus above you may reroll all to hit dice in the first round of combat.

Brick wall

Requires an endurance of 7 or more and a strength of 7 or more.
Built like a brick wall you block opponents like one too.
Once per combat you may reduce incoming damage from a single attack by subtracting your strength score from the damage total. This is not considered defense and so may be used at any time unless this ability is specifically negated.

Upgraded

Requires an endurance of 8 or more and a strength of 8 or more.
If you also have the *Wrestler* ability then you may roll one die and add the result to your strength when determining the reduction from incoming damage.

Wrestler

Requires a strength of 6 or more.
In addition to using your weapons you enjoy body slams, head butts and the occasional pile drive.
Once per combat you may perform a wrestling move by substituting your normal attack and rolling 1 die to hit. If you roll 4 or more (this may not be modified further) you may use your strength value as the damage inflicted.

Upgraded

Requires a strength of 9 or more.
Decrease the to hit roll from 4 to 3 (this may not be modified further) and add 1 dice roll as well as your current strength value to determine your damage.

Evasion

Requires an agility of 7 or more.
You are just plain dodgy.
Once per combat instead of making a defense roll you may negate one full attack, including all damage and lingering effects for that combat round.

Upgraded

Requires an agility of 9 or more and a perception of 7 or more.
You may use your evasion feat twice per combat instead of once.

Stealth

You are adept at sneaking around and avoiding detection.
See text for specific details of using this ability.

Mystery man

You are highly skilled at concealing your identity and remaining unnoticed.
See text for specific details of using this ability.

Tech hoarder

Requires a tech score of 3 or more.
You have a specialty for identifying pieces of equipment which may be used to build or repair useful tech.
See text for specific details of using this ability.

Tech repair

Requires a tech score of 6 or more.
Can repair small items and gadgets.
See text for specific details of using this ability.

Upgraded

Requires a tech score of 8 or more.
Can repair minor and major pieces of tech.
See text for specific details of using this ability.

Terminal hack

Requires a sci of 4 or more.
You can hack any data terminal with relative ease
See text for specific details of using this ability.

Security analyst

Requires a tech of 5 or more and a sci of 5 or more.
You are well versed in finding chinks in any security set up. Also skilled in encryption and decryption.
See text for specific details of using this ability.

Medical expertise

Requires a bio of 5 or more
You have expert training in treating numerous types of disease and minor wounds.
See text for specific details of using this ability.

Paramedic

Requires a bio of 6 or more and a science sci of 5 or more.
You are experienced in treating all sorts of diseases and battle wounds in the field.
See text for specific details of using this ability.

Tracker

Requires a perception of 7 or more.

You are well adept at trailing anybody in all conditions, from a rain soaked wilderness to an urban identity trace.

See text for specific details of using this ability.

Got the lingo

You've got a language chip inserted allowing you to verbally communicate with ease, including extensive enunciation to drones and security networks.

See text for specific details of using this ability.

Explosives expert

Requires a tech of 5 or more.

You're damn good at making things go boom, but you are quite capable of diffusing bombs as well.

See text for specific details of using this ability.

Mithridatist

Requires a bio of 5 or more

You are immune to all but the most exotic of poisons.

See text for specific details of using this ability.

Available only to XBR or SDN factions.

Negotiator

You are adept at talking down potential hostiles and talking up yourself and allies.

See text for specific details of using this ability.

Available only to the Confederacy.

Got your back

You are skilled at maintaining awareness of your surroundings so you have allies well covered, but you also have your own back covered at all times too.

See text for specific details of using this ability.

Not available to SDN faction.

Close awareness

Your training and experiences have given you a distinct edge when it comes to perceiving happenings around you such as sneak attacks and multiple enemies or events surrounding you.

See text for specific details of using this ability.

Missions

Out of the following, select one mission which matches the faction you are aligned with and make a note of your choice:

Leading Weapon Syndicate [LWS]
Techno savage

Your mission is to board the starship and retrieve a new tech that is said to have been developed.

Leading Weapon Syndicate [LWS]
Proto-swipe

Your mission is to board the starship, find out what weapons the XBR are developing and steal any prototypes, plans or information regarding such developments.

Space Designation Network [SDN]

Disrupt and extract

Primary mission: Locate expert biological scientist Tuo Minkla and extract any data regarding his work. Eliminate him without leaving any traceable evidence.

Secondary mission: Disrupt and damage the starship beyond repair.

Space Designation Network [SDN]

Data thief

Primary mission: Break into the systems of the starships and extract data pertinent to the activities of the XBR faction.

Secondary mission: Disrupt and damage the starship beyond repair.

Confederacy

Fugitive hunt

Your mission is to locate fugitive Sjonn, a rebel wanted for crimes against the population of Phaeadron. You are to capture him and bring him in alive for the Confederacy to administer judgment.

Confederacy

Survey and Defend

Your mission is to assess the situation, report back details and help the XBR defend. The council will be looking to evaluate the incident in order to make the appropriate judgment. The following shall be typical of a sufficient report:

- Documented evidence of the incident or events surrounding the incident.
- Identity scans of any perpetrators.
- Incentive and intention of the perpetrators causing the incident

Non Faction Aligned [NFA]

Biohazard borrower

You are a plant on contract from another NFA to locate and smuggle out the central component of a bio weapon under development and get off the ship alive. The details given are few: you have been informed what you are looking for are toxic spores and they will be used to make a bio weapon known as LF-7.

Non Faction Aligned [NFA]

Collector of things

You have been working essentially as a slave aboard the ship for longer than you wish to remember. But you want out; and this may be your chance. Disable your bracelet, find anything of value on the starship and get off the ship alive.

[In this mission you will begin with no items or armor, regardless of the character chosen.]

Gameplay

Effects:

Effects are conditions that you will experience through your mission. If you are suffering shock or are badly wounded for example, these may have ongoing consequences which you will have to deal with.

There are two types of effects. The first is permanent. The second is lingering. A permanent effect is one you will endure until either the text says it may be removed or you take an action to remove the effect. An example is if you are carrying a large amount of equipment and are burdened with the *Heavy* effect. Until you cease to carry so much equipment (or somehow become capable of carrying so much) then you will have to endure the consequences of *Heavy*.

The second type of effect is a lingering effect. Any lingering effect will have the word *lingering* beside it, so you will always know which is which. These effects stay with you until they are "cleared". To clear a lingering effect, see below.

PERMANENT EFFECTS:

Heavy

This will be listed in the description of the item, usually as a restriction. If you carry an item listed as *Heavy* or have less energy tanks to the number of high energy items (even if you are not currently using an item) then you must deduct one point of *agility* for each *heavy* item. Note therefore that you may suffer from multiple instances of *heavy*.

Encumbered

If you are carrying 6 items or more on you, (this does not include what you carry in your hands, shoulder mount weapons, just items in your pack or on your belt) then you must endure an instance of heavy.

Overburdened

If you have **3** or more instances of *heavy* then you will become overburdened. In addition to the penalty to your agility, you will suffer a reduction to your endurance by 2 points. Note that just like the *heavy effect* when you lose the items causing the *heavy* effect, you lose the penalties and your stats are restored.

High energy

This will be listed on an item or weapon. You must have at least one energy tank to use any high energy items. Energy tanks act as reservoirs so during battles you can supply energy at the high rate required.

LINGERING EFFECTS:

Reduced capacity (lingering)

Your energy will run at a minimum while your reserves build up sufficient energy. Clears on a 3 or more. Until cleared you may not use any high energy weapons or items.

Burned (lingering)

Deduct 2 vitality. For each fail to clear the effect, deduct 2 vitality.

Stunned (lingering)

You are unable to use your weapons to your full ability for a moment. Do not apply any to hit modifiers.

Automatically clears after next combat round.

Shaken (lingering)

You have been knocked around and may not attack in the next combat round. Alternative actions may be undertaken. Automatically clears after next combat round.

Shocked (lingering)

Whilst recovering for the next combat round you will not be able to perform any action, including attacking. The individual may defend only. Automatically clears after next combat round.

Bleeding (lingering)

Deduct 3 vitality. For each fail to clear the effect, deduct 1 vitality.

Corroding (lingering)

For each fail to clear, deduct 3 vitality. Automatically clears on any fourth attempt to clear.

Poisoned (lingering)

Deduct 2 vitality. For each fail to clear the effect, deduct 2 vitality.

Infected (lingering)

For each fail to clear the effect, deduct 3 vitality. At the end of any combat, deduct 3 vitality. May not be cleared in combat.

Irradiated (lingering)

Deduct 2 vitality. For each fail to clear the effect deduct the result of a dice roll. May not be cleared in combat.

Grievous wound

Deduct 3 vitality and add the shocked lingering effect.

Critical wound

Deduct 5 vitality and add the bleeding lingering effect.

Crippled

Deduct 1 point from your stats based on the following table:

CRIPPLED TABLE

Dice roll	Deduct one point from the following stat. (Keep note of your maximum value however)
1	Close Quarter. You've suffered a debilitating wound to one of your arms.
2	Ranged. You've damaged a hand or arm, making it difficult to use any ranged weapon
3	Strength. You're hurting all over. It's tough to move let alone lift anything.
4	Agility. Your legs have taken a beating. Back flips are out of the question.
5	Perception. You've taken a hit to your head or neck, making it a challenge to remain sharp.
6	Endurance. You've sustained multiple injuries and will have to take it easy for a while.

At death's door

Apply Bleeding and suffer Crippled.

Annihilated

The individual is destroyed and may not recover unless the text specifically states otherwise.

How to clear a lingering effect:

Unless stated otherwise, the standard clear roll is 4 or more to clear on 1 die. Make a separate roll for each lingering effect you have. If you clear a lingering effect then remove the noted effect from your mission sheet.

In combat: The individual with the lingering effect will roll to clear at the beginning of their attack.

Outside of combat. Whenever time passes, make an attempt to clear any or all lingering affects you have. Note that each instance of Time passes will by default count as a failure to clear any lingering effect - even if you do not or cannot make an attempt to clear it. Note that some lingering effects are an exception and may not be clearable in this way. When this is the case the text will specifically say so, implying the lingering effect is such that it requires either an alternate action to be taken or simply a very long time for the effect to pass.

FIRING WEAPONS:

At various times you will engage in shooting. This may be a single shot at a target or it may be a combat. The text will give details as to what to do in this regard. To fire your weapon, follow the same procedure as a round of combat (detailed below). You will obviously need a weapon to fire; if you do not have one, you will be unable to shoot (though you may still be shot at) and details on what actions you may be able to take will be given in the text. Apart from actually having a weapon you will need to check the type of weapon which will be listed in the weapon description. Ranged combat is divided into either short ranged or long ranged. Likewise weapons will list their ability to be used at either short range, long range or both. Commonly pistols are limited to short range. Rifles and similar weapons listed as 'Ranged' can be used for both short and long range.

COMBAT:

Whether shooting it out or fighting at close quarters, the rules for combat are mostly the same.

You will begin by checking either your CQ scores (if it is a close quarter fight) or Ra scores (if it is a ranged/shooting fight). Then each combatant will take turns attacking their enemy. This is done by rolling one or more dice to 'hit' the enemy and for each hit applying damage.

To begin a combat:

Compare either CQ scores or Ra scores.

Result	Your CQ or Ra	Enemy's CQ or Ra
Reduce YOUR to hit rolls by 1	Higher	Lower
No change	Same	
Reduce the ENEMY's to hit roll by 1	Lower	Higher

- This is the basic modification table. A particular battle may negate this or weapons or skills may modify or negate values.
- A roll of a 1 is always a miss and a roll of a 6 is always a hit (unless circumstances or weapons change this)
- There is also high damage or *Annihilated* abilities for example if you have a CQ score of more than 3 higher than the enemy. (See the Domination table below)

Combat is divided into "combat rounds". Each combat round consists of you and each enemy listed making an attack, which may be defended against.

Under normal circumstances, the enemy will attack first. Sometimes you will attack first – for example if you surprise the enemy – details will be given in the text.

Each *Combat round* proceeds as follows:

1. Before either you or an enemy attacks, both you and the enemy will have the chance to clear any lingering effects. Most of the time this step will not be relevant, but when it is, make the necessary rolls. *Shaken* or *shocked* effects need to be cleared to ensure an attack may be made for example.

2. To attack, whether it be you attacking or an enemy attacking, roll to hit. Apply any modifiers, such as those from skills, having a lower or higher CQ (Close Quarter) or Ra (Ranged) score. For each hit, add the damage stated with your weapon. Note some weapons have specific instructions to roll to hit and what damage to apply. In this case follow those instructions.

3. The defender may now defend against the attack. Roll for *defense* to reduce the incoming damage. Note a defense roll may not always be available – for example if an enemy has no armor, they will simply take the damage. For the damage done, reduce the defender's vitality. If the defense blocks all incoming damage, then any lingering effect which is part of the attack will also be negated unless the text states otherwise.

4. Repeat steps 1 to 3 for the next individual involved in the combat.

5. Once all individuals have been through steps 1 to 3, then the combat round will end. Before completion, apply any lingering effects.

Continue combat rounds until either you or the enemy is killed (vitality reaches zero) or some other action is taken (example you *flee*). Alternate options will be given in the text – if none are given, you must fight to the death.

Defense

If you have some form of armor or a protective device, you may be entitled to a defense roll. You will only make <u>one</u> defense roll against an attack, even if you have multiple items with defense capability. When you suffer damage, either during combat or during the course of events you will often be entitled to make a roll for defense, potentially negating or minimizing the damage you would otherwise sustain. In some instances the damage will be such that no matter what type of defense you have, you will not be entitled to a roll.

In combat, you are entitled to a defense roll by default. Unless stated otherwise, after you have been hit, to see if damage is applied, roll for defense. The same is true for the enemy - if the enemy has a form of defense they are entitled to it by default; only a specific weapon or instruction will negate the ability to roll for defense. You will only make one defense roll per combat round. In other words, if for example you are faced with multiple opponents or multiple attacks in a given round, you will make <u>one</u> defense roll for the accumulated damage you are expecting to take for that round of combat. The same is true of the enemy if you are using a weapon which allows you to roll multiple attack dice. Add the damage together for that round and then make one roll to defend.

If you have multiple items that provide a defense roll, you may only use one at a time. That is, you will only make one defense roll using one of the items or armor that you have. Also note that you cannot wear more than one armor at a time.

Fleeing

At times combat can be tough and things may not be going your way. It is a smart move to turn and run if it means you survive the day. If given this option and you choose to do so, your adversary will get one free combat round to attack you. In this round you may defend as usual but will not have your turn to attack back. If you survive this, then follow the text as to getting out. If fleeing is not an option (some circumstances or enemies may prevent this) then it will be a fight to the death. If you have the option to flee and choose to do so before combat begins, resolve the first round with your enemy attacking you then follow the text to flee.

Further combat rules. At this point you could begin play. The following details events such as dominating combat, fighting without weapons, serious injuries and the like.

At any point during combat if the conditions are met you may apply the results of the *domination table*.

Before rolling on this table, note that the enemy may roll for defense if it can do so.

DOMINATION TABLE	You have a CQ or Ra score <u>more</u> than 3 points higher than the enemy:	You have a CQ or Ra score that is not <u>more</u> than 3 points higher than the enemy:
Your attack causes <u>more than 10</u> points of damage before any lingering effects damage	The enemy is *Annihilated*	The enemy suffers a *Critical wound*
You roll <u>2 or more</u> 6's when rolling to hit.	Apply double damage	The enemy suffers a *Grievous wound*

This table applies to both enemies and yourself.

WOUNDS TABLE Roll 2 Dice	More than 10 damage from any 1 attack (immediately)	Less than 10 vitality at end of battle
2	Suffer a *Critical wound*	*At death's door*
3	Suffer a *Critical* wound	Suffer *Crippled*
4	Suffer a *Grievous wound*	Suffer *bleeding*
5	Suffer a *Grievous wound*	Suffer *bleeding*
6	Suffer a *Grievous wound*	Suffer *bleeding*
7	Suffer *Shock*	Suffer *bleeding*
8	Suffer *Shock*	Suffer *bleeding*
9	Suffer *Shock*	Suffer *bleeding*
10	Suffer *Shaken*	No further afflictions
11	Suffer *Shaken*	No further afflictions
12	No further afflictions	No further afflictions

- Some items armor, abilities may modify the dice roll or negate the result.

RANGED COMBAT:

- If in ranged combat, you will need to note if it is a short ranged or long ranged combat. If there is no indication of which range the shooting is at, then you may default to short range. Some weapons such as pistols may only be used at short ranges. Others have such an attack that allows them only to be used for long range attacks. Check your weapon. If you cannot fire because your weapon is not suitable or you don't have a (functioning) ranged weapon, you may be in a bit of trouble. If there are no options in the text to *flee* or engage in close quarter combat or some other alternative action then you will be shot down.
- As a minor alternative action you may have the option to throw a grenade if you have one and choose to - the text will say if this is allowed.

CLOSE QUARTER COMBAT:

- If you have no close quarter weapon, then you can always fight unarmed. On one die, roll 5 or more to hit, 2 damage.
- Pistols may be used in close quarter combat unless specifically stated they may not for the particular combat you are fighting.

ALTERNATIVE ACTIONS:

- During combat you may perform alternative actions instead of fighting. These may include swapping out a weapon, taking some pills or using a device of some sort. Note that during combat ONLY MINOR alternative actions may be undertaken. To perform a minor alternative action you forgo your attack and instead perform your minor action. The enemy will still get their chance to attack you.

- Swapping out a weapon from your inventory is considered a minor alternative action. Simply exchange the hand held weapon for the item in your pack.
- Ammunition may be exchanged at any time and will <u>not</u> count as an alternative action.
- Outside of combat you may perform an alternative action at any time. If you perform a *major* alternative action, *time passes.*

Example of combat:

Enemy		
	CQ	4
	Vitality	12
	4+ to hit, 3 damage.	
	No defense.	

Firstly, compare CQ or Ra scores. As this is a Close Quarter combat we compare CQ scores. Your CQ score is 5. That means you will reduce your roll to hit by 1 point (to a minimum of 2+) Conversely the *Enemy* will increase his roll to hit by 1 point (to a maximum of 6). As you happen to be using a *laser pistol* in this combat (note that pistols can be used in close quarter combat unless stated otherwise) your 'to hit' value would normally be 5+ as listed for the *laser pistol* item. Since your CQ score is higher, this is decreased to 4+. So for the entire combat you will need 4 or more on a single die roll to hit the *Enemy.* According to his stats above, the *Enemy* would normally need 4+ to hit you, but we see from comparing CQ scores this will be modified to become 5+ in this combat. As there are no other specifics to this combat to be concerned about, we may begin. There are no specific instructions and your abilities do not help here so by default the *Enemy* attacks first. He rolls a 3. A miss. Your turn. You roll a 4, which counts as hit. For each hit scored, we apply the damage of the weapon we are using. The *laser pistol* causes 3 damage. As the *Enemy* has no defense, we may deduct the 3 damage from his Vitality. Battle continues. The *Enemy* rolls to hit, scoring a 5. You however are wearing armor, which grants you a 5+ roll to negate 3 damage. You roll for defense, rolling a 6. The damage that would normally be done is now reduced to zero, therefore there will be no reduction in your vitality. Battle continues in the same way until either you or the *Enemy* is reduced to zero vitality, unless the text has other instructions for what may happen in the combat.

Carrying items:

Whenever you pick up an item (or weapon) you will need a place to put it if you plan to carry it. Some items can be attached to your belt if you have one or others placed in your pack. The details of where an item actually is you do not need to be concerned about, but the number of items you are carrying at any given time you do. If you try to carry too much, this will slow you down and could get you into trouble.

You may add up to 10 items to your person (belts, pack, etc). The total of 10 items is what you are *carrying on you*. Holding onto a gun with your hand, wearing a helmet and having a shoulder mounted grenade launcher <u>do not</u> count towards the total. Lugging around a med pack and several grenades will count. If you are carrying 6 items or more, you will suffer *encumbered* (see Effects). Weapons may be placed either in their allocated position (e.g. in your left or right hand) or alternatively placed on your back. Weapons or items with the *heavy* attribute will add an instance of *heavy* regardless of whether they are in your hands, attached to you or on your back. Note that the *heavy* effect stacks, so each instance adds to the last. You will find it an hindrance to be carrying too much and trying to double up on weapons and the like. It is better to select your weapons carefully so that they suit you and to travel lightly, with the exception being if you have to take a long journey with few breaks and therefore will require more supplies. Lastly some items are small enough that they can be carried with ease. These are items with the *light item* attribute. Carrying 1 to 3 of this type of item counts as one normal item. Carrying 4-6 counts as 2 normal items etc. *Miscellaneous items* are considered *light items* by default.

Example of carrying items; you have 2 Stimserts, 1 Med pack and a short laser blade. If you were not carrying the laser blade in your hand and using it as a weapon, then you would be carrying 3 items. The Stimserts, being a light item only fill one slot of you belt/pack.

Example two; you are attempting to smuggle some weapons out and so are carrying an unusual amount of weapons on you. Your hands are full and what you carry consists of: A grenade launcher, 4 tactile grenades, an electro razor, two twin pulse rifles, a med pack and a heavy pulse rifle. The items take up eight "slots" in your inventory (with 1 light item spillover into the ninth slot from the grenades). You will suffer two instances of heavy — one for the heavy pulse rifle and one for having six or more items (encumbered). Note that the 4 high impact grenades takes up two slots. Note also that if you equip yourself with the grenade launcher, the additive ammunition will still take up slots until you actually fire them (or discard them).

Attachments:

Attachments are items which require some sort of device to plug into. These are usually tools or devices that will most often plug into an item known as a utility socket. When using attachments, only the utility socket itself will count towards the tally of items you are carrying. Any attachments you have plugged in will not count when working out how many items you are carrying.

Using grenades and explosives:

At various times you will be given the opportunity to use these, depending on the situation. It is important to note the difference between a grenade; which can be thrown at an enemy and a bomb/explosive; which can be planted at a specific location to destroy or damage something. In the item description you will note the *type* which states either *grenade* or *explosive*. Ensure you are using the correct item following the instructions in the text. You may also note for example there are both *high impact grenades* as well as *high impact explosives*. These simply share the same name as they use the same material to detonate and have roughly the same force when they explode; you cannot substitute one for the other. Likewise the grenade launcher uses additive ammunition (grenades) to fire, however these grenades although they have the same characteristics as regular grenades can only be used with a grenade launcher. Therefore note the distinction between having a grenade and having a *grenade as additive ammunition* to ensure you do not mix them up.

Additive ammunition and consumables:

Some items require additive ammunition. If you do not have any ammunition for these weapons, you will be unable to use them or will resort to the default weapon characteristics. The additive ammunition is kept on your belt or in your pack and therefore takes up slots in your inventory. You may exchange additive ammunition or load your weapon at any time; it does not count as an alternative action. Additive ammunition is the only ammunition that you will run out of. Unless stated otherwise for any other type of ammunition or weapon, you carry ample supply of ammunition or have the ability to recharge energy based weapons. Additive ammunition adds onto any effects and damage a weapon already does, unless the text specifically states alternatively.

Additive ammunition, grenades and explosives are consumable items by default. This means that once used, you lose them and should deduct them from your inventory. The same applies to any other item listed as 'consumable' - when it is used, reduce the quantity you have in your inventory.

Statistics:

Your statistics such as strength, agility and perception are not likely to change too much during your mission. Like abilities, there will be times when they come into play, some more so than others, depending on your choices and circumstances. It is smart to take on challenges that require stats which you are suited for and minimize taking on tasks if you are weak in any areas. You may lose points in any statistic, in particular if you are severely injured. Just like your vitality, you may not go beyond your maximum in any statistic when restoring lost points. Always make a note of your maximum should you drop below it. To increase any given statistic, that is, to increase your maximum, you are most likely to do this either via experience or physical implants. Note that if you are injured for instance and your current strength has been reduced from 6 to 5 and then you receive an augmentation which tells you to increase your strength stat by 1, then your maximum would now be 7 and you would currently be on 6. The text will say when to restore any lost points.

Discarding items:

You may discard items at any time whilst not in combat. Once discarded an item or weapon is lost permanently and may not be retrieved later.

Weaponized limbs and implants:

Some items utilize your whole arm or are implants. These items stay on you and may only be removed or exchanged via surgery. You cannot swap out these items for other items in your pack nor may you discard them outside of surgery. Note that attachments may be swapped out or discarded like any hand held item. Simply remove them from the socket and insert another if you choose. This counts as a minor alternative action if you are swapping the attachment out or as a discard if you are leaving the attachment behind.

Further notes:

Whenever you are instructed to deduct vitality outside of combat, then you will not be entitled to a defense roll by default. Often reductions to vitality are such that defense will be negligible or irrelevant; simply deduct the vitality unless the text states a defense roll is allowed.

Time:

Time is monitored by certain points in the text which say *time passes*. When this happens the time cycle is advanced. Cross off one box on your mission sheet for each instance of *time passes*. Manage your time carefully: you only have a finite amount of it and can easily waste it without achieving your mission.

As you cross off the boxes on your mission sheet you will note there are three tiers (levels) representing the amount of time remaining. This will become relevant when the text asks which tier you are in. If for example you have crossed off all the boxes on the first (top), second and third rows then you would be in the second tier. If you run out of time: you have crossed off all the boxes and then reach a point in the text where *time passes*, immediately turn to reference 1000.

As a rough guide, whenever you enter into a room for more than a glance, it will take time. Searching, waiting and moving long distances will take up time as well as performing major alternative actions such as using a med pack. Alongside your vitality, time is critical to both your mission and life.

Chance:

Chance represents those incidents which are outside of your control. Sometimes they may mean extra difficulty, other times a positive outcome. It is possible for your chance to lean one way or the other for a period of time, depending on events that may occur and the choices you make. In this way, your chance score acts as a modifier. You will begin with a chance score of zero and will be instructed when to change it. The score may become a negative or positive value. Whenever you roll for chance, which is done with one die, add your chance score to the result of the roll (unless the text states otherwise) and follow the instructions. You will notice the possible values on your mission sheet for you to circle. From this you can see the minimum value for your chance score is -2 (negative two) and the maximum value +2 (positive two). Any instruction to go outside these values is to be ignored.

Example of using chance; your chance score is -1 (negative one). The text says to roll for chance. The text says if you roll 4 or more then turn to a paragraph reference. If you roll 3 or less, turn to another paragraph reference. You roll one die and roll a 4. Since your chance score is -1, you will add that to the dice roll of 4, giving you a score of 3. You would turn to the 3 or less/second paragraph reference.

Tips:

- Keep focused on your mission or current task and try not to get sidetracked
- Be mindful of your vitality; if it is low, remain cautious until you can replenish it
- Use your time sparingly; it can easily be wasted if you are not careful
- Choose carefully when to use explosives and other consumables
- Pick your fights; some are best avoided and some are easier with the right weapon
- Maintain a map or clues to help you along the way

Creating your own Custom Character:

Instead of using one of the characters previously listed, you may create your own custom character. Choose which faction you will be aligned with and write this down along with your name on your mission sheet. Simply put "agent" for your role - this part is mostly relevant to NFA, and only in later books in the Bionic agent series. Now you are ready to generate your stats. To do this, begin with your vitality at 30, your sci, tech and bio stats at 3 and all other stats at 5.

You now have 3 points to spend in total, following these rules:

1. You may freely spend point(s) on the stats of CQ, Ra, Ag, St, Pe, En or Re.
2. For the intelligence stats of sci, tech and bio you may spend _one point only_ on any of these.
3. You may also deduct one point from either your sci, tech or bio score and add it to _any_ stat _once only_.
4. You may _deduct one point_ from any stat from either CQ, Ra, Ag, St, Pe, En or Re and put it into another of these same stats. You may do this up to three times.
5. You may spend any one point to add 3 to your vitality (once or twice only) <u>OR</u> you may deduct 2 from your vitality and gain one point to spend (once only).

Example 1:	Example 2:
Vitality of 28.	Vitality of 33.
CQ of 5	CQ of 5
Ra of 6	Ra of 6
St of 6	Ag of 4
Ag of 5	St of 7
Pe of 5	Pe of 4
En of 6	En of 6
Re of 5	Re of 5
Sci of 4	Sci of 2
Tech of 3	Tech of 4
Bio of 3	Bio of 3

Now select an ability from the previous list of abilities. You may choose any ability, provided you meet the criteria listed under the description for stats, faction etc.

Generating a random character:

As an alternative to freely selecting your stats, faction and ability you may randomize them. This may make things a little more challenging the more that is randomized, though you may turn out a worthy combination of stats and ability also.

Start with stats as above (5 for stats, 3 for intelligence, 30 for vitality)

Roll 2 dice. Take the higher value and deduct the lower value. (If you roll a double the result will be zero) Add the result to 30; this is your vitality.

Roll one die. If you roll 1-3, add one point to your CQ. If you roll 4-6, add one point to your Ra.

Roll one die. If you roll a 1, add one point to your CQ. If you roll a 2, add one point to your Ra. If you roll a 3 or 4, add one point to your St. If you roll a 5 or 6, add one point to you Ag.

Roll one die. If you roll a 1, add one point to your CQ. If you roll a 2, add one point to your Ra. If you roll a 3, add one point to your St. If you roll a 4, add one point to you Ag. If you roll a 5, add one point to your Pe. If you roll a 6, add one point to your En.

Roll one die. If you roll a 1 or 2, add one point to your Sci. If you roll a 3 or 4, add one point to your Tech. If you roll a 5 or 6, add one point to your Bio.

Select a faction at random or by choice.

Draw an ability from the deck. If the ability is unusable, redraw until you draw an ability which is compatible. Alternatively select the ability you prefer.

Once you have written down your stats and filled in the other vital details on your mission sheet and have an ability, you are ready to equip yourself.

- From the list below, purchase your weapons and items; you have 500 credits to spend.
- In addition, you start with 2 med packs.
- You will also have the following armor based on which faction you are aligned with:

Confederacy: Combat armor

Non Faction Aligned (NFA): Ceramic plated vest

Leading Weapon Syndicate (LWS): Coated multi alloy suit

Space Designation Network (SDN): Reconstructing synthesized
polymer suit

Additionally:

If you are with the SDN, add a *ghost processor* to your inventory.

If you are with the LWS, you already have a *utility socket*.

PRE-START SHOP

You may purchase any of the following items with your available credits, including multiples of the same item. Note: You will at the least need weapons to fight with in either close quarter or ranged combat.

Knuckle lasers	100
Skewer launcher	100
Laser pistol	100
Micro torch	150
Laser pulse rifle (LPR)	200
Breaker gun	180
Shock pistol	200
Dual auto pistols	200
Shock mace	100
Short laser blade	100
Electro razor	100
Hammer fist	180
Med pack	100
Stimsert	60
Scatter grenade	40
High impact grenade	50
Micro petard	40
High impact explosive	50
Proximity explosive	80
Utility socket	100
Continuous high speed laser cutter	150
Heavy rock breaker	200

Weapons

Ranged weapons:

Knuckle lasers

Miniature but powerful, attached to the fist knuckles are 5 lasers which may be used for short ranged directed attacks or at close quarters for that extra punch.

Type: Short ranged or CQ weapon, fits onto a free hand.
Manufacturer: Spectrum Corp
Availability: Production
Restrictions: None
Requirements: None
To use: As a short ranged or CQ weapon: On 2 dice 4 or more to hit, 2
     damage.

Skewer launcher

A lightweight arm attachment which slings piercing rods at close range.
Type: Short ranged weapon
Manufacturer: Spectrum Corp
Availability: Production
Restrictions: None
Requirements: Utility socket
To use: As a short ranged weapon: On 1 die 5 or more to hit, 3 damage.

Laser pistol

A common yet reliable pistol with self-recharging capability.
Type: Short ranged pistol
Manufacturer: Spectrum Corp and many others
Availability: Production
Restrictions: None

Requirements: None

To use: As a short ranged or CQ weapon: On 1 die 5 or more to hit, 3
    damage.

Micro torch

*Miniature tanks attached to the triceps feed the micro torch which fire from
a small barrel under the palm of the hand. Use it to fight or to cut through
impedances.*

Type: Short ranged or CQ weapon, fits onto a free hand.

Manufacturer: Spectrum Corp

Availability: Production

Restrictions: None

Requirements: None

To use: As a short ranged or CQ weapon: On 1 die 4 or more to hit, 3
    damage. Apply *Burned* lingering effect.

To use to cut through something: Roll 2 dice and score 9 or more to cut
    through.

Laser Pulse rifle

*This typical combat weapon is both readily affordable and reliable. It can
easily cut an unarmored man down with a single pulse.*

Type: Ranged weapon

Manufacturer: Spectrum Corp

Availability: Production

Restrictions: None

Requirements: None

To use: As a ranged weapon: On 1 die 4 or more to hit, 4 damage.

Modified Laser Pulse rifle

*As a commonly available weapon the laser pulse rifle is often the choice for
modifications including increasing the rate of fire or energy consumption.*

Type: Ranged weapon

Manufacturer: Spectrum Corp

Availability: Production

Restrictions: None

Requirements: None
To use: As a ranged weapon: On 1 die 4 or more to hit, 5 damage.

Breaker gun

Standard issue for Confederacy agents, the Breaker gun is a compact projectile weapon which fires small high energy capsules that discharge upon contact.
Type: Short ranged pistol, projectile
Manufacturer: Spectrum Corp
Availability: Production
Restrictions: None
Requirements: None
To use: As a short ranged weapon: On 1 die 4 or more to hit, 3 damage.
          Accepts alternative projectile shells.

Shock pistol

As its name implies the shock pistol delivers a high voltage shock to targets via EMF transmission to miniaturized projectiles.
Type: Short ranged pistol
Manufacturer: Spectrum Corp
Availability: Production
Restrictions: None
Requirements: None
To use: As a short ranged weapon: On 1 die, 4 or more to hit, 4 damage.
To use: In non-lethal capacity: See text for specific details.

Dual auto pistols

Fairly common especially among rebels, these pistols use a capacitive discharge method to propel small projectiles at a high rate of fire.
Type: 2 Short ranged pistols, projectile
Manufacturer: Spectrum Corp
Availability: Production
Restrictions: None
Requirements: Two free hands to use

To use: As a short ranged or CQ weapon: On 2 dice, 5 or more to hit, 2 damage.

To use: Assaulting: In the first round of combat only you may reroll any one die that misses (reroll only once). If this to hit roll is a 1 however, next combat round you may roll only 1 die to hit while you reload.

If for any reason you only use one auto pistol, roll only 1 die when attacking and you may not use *Assaulting.* Accepts alternative projectile shells.

Upgraded dual auto pistols

There are those that like to tinker with their equipment, attempting to squeeze out extra efficiency or performance even at the expense of reliability.

Type: 2 Short ranged pistols, projectile

Manufacturer: Spectrum Corp

Availability: After-market modified production

Restrictions: None

Requirements: Two free hands to use

To use: As a short ranged or CQ weapon: On 2 dice, 5 or more to hit, 3 damage. If ANY to hit roll is a 1 then next combat round you may not use assaulting and may roll only 1 die to hit while you reload.

To use: Assaulting: In the first round of combat only you may reroll any die that misses (reroll only once).

If for any reason you only use one auto pistol, roll only 1 die when attacking and you may not use *Assaulting.* Accepts alternative projectile shells.

Dual link pistols

Though light weight link pistols pack a powerful energy punch and are favored for their high rate of fire and conceal ability.

Type: 2 Short ranged pistols

Manufacturer: Spectrum Corp

Availability: Production

Restrictions: None

Requirements: Two free hands to use

To use: As a short ranged or CQ weapon: On 2 dice, 5 or more to hit, 4 damage.

To use: Assaulting: In the first round of combat you may reroll any one die that misses (Reroll only once). If this to hit roll is a 1 however, you may only roll 1 attack dice for the rest of the combat due to overheating.

If for any reason you only use one link pistol, roll only 1 die when attacking and you may not use *Assaulting*.

Punisher auto gun

Common amongst rebel groups and lone fighters alike, the "Punisher" gun as it is nicknamed is a reliable and versatile weapon.

Type: Ranged weapon, projectile

Manufacturer: Spectrum Corp

Availability: Production. Common

Restrictions: None

Requirements: None

To use: Single shot: On 1 die 4 or more to hit, 5 damage.

Burst fire: On 2 dice, 5 or more to hit, 3 damage. Accepts alternative projectile shells.

Hyper-Mag disc sling

Utilizing superconductive magnets to accelerate disc shaped projectiles at high velocities, the Hyper-Mag sling is both versatile and deadly.

Type: Ranged weapon

Manufacturer: Symbiotic systems

Availability: Limited production

Restrictions: None

Requirements: Attaches to forearm

To use: As a ranged weapon: On 1 die, 5 or more to hit, 6 damage. If you roll a 6 to hit, then roll again and add that to the damage. (Only once)

Stun pistol

A preferred weapon for the Confederacy, the stun pistol allows for disabling a hostile in order to extract information in the future.

Type: Short ranged pistol
Manufacturer: Resolute engineering
Availability: Production, Confederacy standard issue
Restrictions: None
Requirements: None
To use: As a short ranged weapon, damage mode: On 1 die, 3 or more to hit, 5 damage.
To use: As a short ranged weapon, stun mode: See text for specific details.

Twin Pulse rifle

Essentially a double barrel Laser pulse rifle, this weapon is a more efficient killer with only a slight increase in power consumption.

Type: Ranged Weapon
Manufacturer: Spectrum Corp
Availability: Production
Restriction: None
Requirements: None
To use: As a ranged weapon: On 2 dice, 4 or more to hit, 3 damage.

Laser blaster

The laser blaster is fearsome weapon, capable of delivering a massive amount of firepower sufficient to take down mobs, vehicles or heavily armored insurgents.

Type: Ranged weapon
Manufacturer: Spectrum Corp
Availability: Production
Restrictions: If not attached, counts as heavy.
Requirements: Replaces forearm as bionic limb if attached
To use: As a ranged weapon: On 3 dice, 4 or more to hit, 3 damage.

Grenade launcher

Intended for field deployment, the shoulder mounted grenade launcher is capable of lobbing various types of grenades over long distances.

Type: Long ranged weapon
Manufacturer: Resolute engineering
Availability: Production
Restrictions: Cannot be taken by SDN faction
Requirements: Shoulder mount.
To use: As a long ranged weapon: On 1 die, 3 or more to hit. Damage depends on ammunition type, requires additive ammunition (grenades) to fire.

Volatile Liquid sprayer

Considered a gruesome weapon by many, the volatile liquid sprayer spews out formulated chemicals which may either ignite in the atmosphere or upon contact with a solid surface.

Type: Short ranged weapon
Manufacturer: Chemplant Corp
Availability: Production
Restrictions: None
Requirements: None
To use: As a short ranged weapon: Contact ignition: Roll 2 dice. If either scores a 5 or more (do not apply modifiers to this) a hit is scored. A hit does 6 damage and applies *burned* lingering effect.
To use: As a short ranged weapon: Atmosphere ignition spray: Roll one die for each enemy in combat. On a roll of 4 or more, deduct 2 vitality and apply the *burned* lingering effect to the enemy the roll was made for

Close Quarter weapons:

Shock Mace

Standard issue for Confederacy agents, the Shock mace is a large bludgeon like weapon which not only shocks with an electrical burst upon contact, but shocks onlookers as well.

Type: CQ Weapon
Manufacturer: Resolute engineering
Availability: Production
Restrictions: Confederacy only
Requirements: None
To use: As a CQ weapon: On 1 die, 4 or more to hit, 5 damage.

Short laser blade

The short laser blade is a retractable hand held laser the size of a dagger or machete. Easily concealed, the blade is reliable and effective.

Type: CQ Weapon
Manufacturer: Resolute engineering
Availability: Production
Restrictions: None
Requirements: None
To use: As a CQ weapon: On 1 die, 3 or more to hit, 4 damage.

Corroder blade

Appearing as a copper colored dagger, the corroder blade upon inflicting a wound reacts with biological material to cause rapid degeneration.

Type: CQ Weapon
Manufacturer: XBR
Availability: New production
Restrictions: None
Requirements: None
To use: As a CQ weapon: On 1 die, 4 or more to hit, 4 damage. If damage inflicted, add *Corroding* lingering effect.

Electro razor

Though they may take multiple forms, the Electro razor is most commonly one or more electrified blades running along either the back of the hand or forearm.
Type: CQ Weapon
Manufacturer: Spectrum Corp
Availability: Production
Restrictions: None
Requirements: None
To use: As a CQ weapon: On 1 die, 4 or more to hit, 4 damage. A hand
is not required to hold this weapon.

Hammer fist

The hammer fist may appear as a crude, hand held brick of sorts, but in reality it is an effective piece of technology. Whatever is hit with the hammer fist not only takes the brunt of a hefty punch but the force of a magnetic burst sufficient to knock a civilian to the ground.
Type: CQ Weapon
Manufacturer: Resolute engineering
Availability: Production
Restrictions: None
Requirements: None
To use: As a CQ weapon: On 1 die, 5 or more to hit, 6 damage.

Manta stinger

Somewhat crude in appearance, the manta stinger is generally takes the form of a hand held prod of sorts. Retractable in length which is where the name originated, a 'stinger' can stab from a distance.
Type: CQ Weapon
Manufacturer: Numerous individuals
Availability: Common
Restrictions: Not available to Confederacy
Requirements: CQ of 6 or more
To use: As a CQ weapon: On 2 dice, 5 or more to hit, 3 damage. If
damage inflicted, add *shaken* lingering effect.

Paroxysm Flail

Type: CQ Weapon
Manufacturer: Unknown
Availability: Common on the black market
Restrictions: None
Requirements: CQ of 6 or more
To use: As a CQ weapon: On 3 dice, 5 or more to hit, 2 damage. Add
   shaken lingering effect if any of the 3 dice rolls is a 6.

Fists of flame

   Displaying intimidation, the fists of flame also work by setting alight opponents with a punch, grab or slap. Works especially well in winter.
Type: CQ Weapon
Manufacturer: Tanoma tech
Availability: Production but costly
Restrictions: None
Requirements: One free hand for fighting
To use as CQ weapon: On 1 die, 5 or more to hit, 5 damage. If a hit is
   scored add the *burned* lingering effect.
If both hands are free, decrease to hit the roll from 5 to 4 or more and
add one damage.

ARMOR

Combat armor

Type: Armor
Manufacturer: Resolute Engineering
Availability: Production for confederacy only.
Restrictions: Confederacy only
Requirements: None
To use: On a 4 or more will negate 3 points of incoming damage.
Boron-aramid composite.

Ceramic plated vest

Type: Armor
Manufacturer: Resolute engineering
Availability: Common though out of production
Restrictions: None
Requirements: None
To use: On a 5 or more negates 3 points of incoming damage.

Coated multi alloy suit

Type: Armor
Manufacturer: Resolute engineering
Availability: Production
Restrictions: None
Requirements: None
To use: On a 5 or more negates 4 points of incoming damage.

Reconstructing synthesized polymer suit

Type: Armor
Manufacturer: Unknown
Availability: SDN use
Restrictions: SDN only
Requirements: None
To use: On a 4 or more negates 4 points of incoming damage.

Xeno exo suit

Type: Armor
Manufacturer: XBR faction
Availability: Production
Restrictions: XBR faction only
Requirements: None
To use: On a 5 or more negates 3 points of incoming damage.

ITEMS

Med pack

Type: Consumable light item
Manufacturer: Omnimed
Availability: Production, common
Restrictions: None
Requirements: None
To use: Anytime not in combat or specifically unable to perform an action, you may use one med pack at a time as a *major alternative action*, adding 10 to the vitality of the treated individual.

Stimsert

Type: Consumable light Item
Manufacturer: Chemplant Corp
Availability: Production
Restrictions: None
Requirements: None
To use: Anytime not in combat or specifically unable to perform an action you may use one stimsert at a time, adding 5 to the vitality of the treated individual. During combat you may use up to three per combat as a *minor alternative action*.

Adreno

Type: Light Item for up to 3 doses. Consumable.
Manufacturer: Omnimed
Availability: Production, common on the black market
Restrictions: None
Requirements: None
To use: Prior to a close quarter combat or during (as a *minor alternative action*), you may take one dose of Adreno, granting you the

ability to reroll all to hit rolls for the next three rounds of combat.

Brutenide

Type: Light Item for up to 3 doses. Consumable.
Manufacturer: Chemplant Corp
Availability: Production, mostly via the black market
Restrictions: None
Requirements: None
To use: Prior to a combat or during (as a *minor alternative action*), you may take one dose of Brutenide, granting you the ability to deduct the total of two dice rolls from any incoming damage during the next three rounds of combat.

Scatter grenade

Type: Grenade, Light Item
Manufacturer: Resolute engineering
Availability: Production
Restrictions: None
Requirements: None
To use: 4 or more to hit, 4 damage or see text for specific details.

High impact grenade

Type: Grenade, Light Item
Manufacturer: Resolute engineering
Availability: Production
Restrictions: None
Requirements: None
To use: 4 or more to hit, 5 damage or see text for specific details.

Tactile grenade

Type: Additive ammunition only, Light Item
Manufacturer: Resolute engineering
Availability: Production
Restrictions: None
Requirements: Grenade launcher
To use: 4 damage or see text for specific details.

Groundbreaker grenade

Type: Additive ammunition only, Light Item
Manufacturer: Resolute engineering
Availability: Production
Restrictions: None
Requirements: Grenade launcher
To use: 6 damage or see text for specific details.

High impact explosive

Type: Explosive, light item
Manufacturer: Resolute engineering
Availability: Production
Restrictions: None
Requirements: None.
To use: 5 damage and see text for specific details.

Proximity explosive

Type: Explosive, light item
Manufacturer: Resolute engineering
Availability: Production
Restrictions: None
Requirements: None
To use: 7 damage and see text for specific details on use.

Demolisher bomb

Type: Explosive
Manufacturer: Resolute engineering
Availability: Production
Restrictions: None
Requirements: None
To use: 10 damage and see text for specific details on use.

Micro petard

Type: Explosive, light item
Manufacturer: Resolute engineering
Availability: Production
Restrictions: None
Requirements: None
To use: 4 damage and see text for specific details on use.

Siege ram

Type: Hand held item
Manufacturer: Anvil solutions
Availability: Production
Restrictions: Heavy
Requirements: Strength of 7 or more
To use: Roll 2 dice and score 6 or more to bust up something.
To use: As a CQ weapon: 1 attack die, 4 or more to hit, 4 damage.

Utility socket

Type: Item
Manufacturer: Spectrum Corp, Resolute engineering, Omnimed
Availability: Production
Restrictions: None
Requirements: One free forearm to add to.
To use: Insert up to 2 attachments of any sort.

Shoulder Utility socket

Type: Item
Manufacturer: Spectrum Corp, Resolute engineering, Omnimed
Availability: Production
Restrictions: Cannot take a *large* attachment.
Requirements: Shoulder mount.
To use: Insert up to 2 compatible attachments.

Ghost Processor

Type: Light Item
Manufacturer: Unknown
Availability: Select SDN issue
Restrictions: SDN only
Requirements: None
To use: See text for specific details.

Continuous high speed laser cutter

Type: Large attachment
Manufacturer: Spectrum Corp
Availability: Production
Restrictions: None
Requirements: Utility socket
To use: Roll 2 dice and score 8 or more to cut through.
As a CQ weapon: 1 attack die, 5 or more to hit, 4 damage.

Heavy rock breaker

Type: Large attachment
Manufacturer: Spectrum Corp
Availability: Production
Restrictions: None
Requirements: Utility socket
To use: Roll 2 dice and score 7 or more to bust up something.
To use: As a CQ weapon: 2 attack dice, 5 or more to hit, 3 damage.

Battering hammer

Type: Large attachment
Manufacturer: Resolute engineering
Availability: Production
Restrictions: None
Requirements: Utility socket
To use: Roll 2 dice and score 5 or more to batter anything.
To use: As a CQ weapon: 1 attack die, 4 or more to hit, 5 damage.

Bio scanner

Type: Attachment
Manufacturer: Omnimed
Availability: Production
Restrictions: None
Requirements: Utility socket
To use: See text for specific details.

ENHANCEMENTS

Brain stem interface

Type: Implant
Manufacturer: Omnimed, IPGB
Availability: Production
Restrictions: None
Requirements: None
To use: Usually required for further enhancements. See text for specific
details.

CNS (Central Nervous system) interface

Type: Implant
Manufacturer: Omnimed, IPGB
Availability: Production
Restrictions: None
Requirements: None
To use: Usually required for further enhancements. See text for specific
details.

Bionic heart

Type: Implant
Manufacturer: Omnimed
Availability: Production
Restrictions:
Requirements: None
To use: Adds 2 to endurance. See text for specific details.

Bionic eye

Type: Implant
Manufacturer: IPGB (Interplanetary group bionics)
Availability: Specialist production
Restrictions: None
Requirements: Brain stem interface
To use: Adds 1 to your dice rolls to hit for any ranged attack.
Infrared and Ultra-violet vision. Telescopic lens.
Benefits remain the same for one or two bionic eyes. See text for specific details.

Bionic arm

Type: Bionic limb
Manufacturer: IPGB (Interplanetary group bionics)
Availability: Production
Restrictions: None
Requirements: CNS interface
To use: Adds 2 to strength. This is one arm only. See text for specific details.

Discovered item tables

Table 1:

1. Dual link pistols
2. Dual auto pistols
3. Modified laser pulse rifle
4. Breaker gun
5. Shock pistol
6. Laser pulse rifle
7. Laser pistol
8. Micro torch
9. Punisher auto gun

10. Stun pistol
11. Hyper-Mag disc sling
12. Twin pulse rifle

Table 2:

1. Fists of flame
2. Manta stinger
3. Siege ram

4. High impact grenade
5. Corroder blade
6. Short laser blade
7. Micro petard
8. Scatter grenade
9. Continuous high speed laser cutter
10. Proximity explosive
11. Demolisher bomb
12. Paroxysm flail

Table 3:

1. Manta stinger
2. Shock pistol
3. Breaker gun
4. High impact grenade
5. Scatter grenade
6. Punisher auto gun
7. Short laser blade
8. Scatter grenade
9. Corroder blade
10. High impact grenade
11. Laser pulse rifle
12 .Proximity explosive

Prologue:

It was a time of relative peace in the Nuivairyiux Star system. The rivalry between the major factions was still present, but no conflict had been recorded for some time since the war time of last. Phaeadron was overseen by the Council which, with the enforcing of the Confederacy maintained the economic and structural stability of the star systems primary and most populated planet. Not all civilians accepted the ruling powers however; some chose to relocate to other moons or space stations while others formed groups and rebelled. Tensions grew, not just with these rebel forces which claimed no alliance with any of the well-known factions, but among all within the star system. It was as if the air in the room was running out; it was like an unspoken race was being run that no one spoke of and was never broadcasted to the masses. No, the peace was only temporary, for the divisions remained and from that conflict was inevitable. Conflict which would bring about a new war. A war which would dwarf the battles of the past and become unrecognizable in advancement.

Check your faction alignment (LWS, SDN, or Confederacy) and mission. On the following pages match your faction and mission with the text and begin.

LWS [Leading Weapon Syndicate] faction begin here, any mission:

'I'll tell you what I know, then I'll tell you where you are going,' said our commander. The other agents in the room shifted in their seats with some degree of nervousness. Everyone in the room knew this meant a new mission or a change of command, or both.

'We've received information that an XBR vessel is harboring a new technology that could make what we have look like sling shots. Now if that's the case, then we need to upgrade our sling shots agents.'

The commander paced across the deck as he spoke.

'The vessel in question is in orbit around Beutohn – a long way from their home turf. Which is why I'm talking to you now and that's where you'll be going.'

Munnik looked at you with a grin, brimming with excitement over a new mission.

'The launch will be at zero five hundred tomorrow. I cannot tell you any more than that, details will be given to you tomorrow when you are in flight. Keep the whispers to yourselves and hit 'em hard agents.'

Commander Denn then surveyed the room, anticipating any final questions or remarks.

'Any info on the nature of the tech?' Asked Pidge.

'I have no idea agent, I expect you'll know more than me on that one by tomorrow,' replied Commander Denn.

The agents sat silently as they contemplated what may lie in store for them. Seeing no further questions the commander began heading for the door.

'One more thing agents – After this mission you will all be assigned a new post and commander.'

With that the briefing ended.

A low hum was all that could be heard as the assault ship hurtled towards the XBR vessel.

A highly ranked agent appeared on the overhead holo projector. All twelve agents looked at the hologram and listened carefully.

'Greetings agents,' he began.

'For those that have not met me I am commander Ashkin and I will be directing this mission.

Firstly, take note of your bands – these indicate which team you are in.'

You looked down to see both arm and leg bands all faintly glowing light blue.

'If they change color, it's because I have changed them, and it will be done by necessity for the completion of the mission only. Stick with fellow team members at all times.'

You noticed that all the agents in this room have the same color as you. The other colors you determine will be in other rooms on the assault ship. The commander continued;

'We'll be going in hot. So keep your wits with you. The vessel is primarily a research ship. So we do not expect it to be heavily defended. That said, this mission will be no evening stroll. We have little data on the layout of the ship, which will make it easier for them to take up a defensive stance. All teams are linked, so wherever anyone goes, you'll all gain map data accordingly.'

You glanced at your visual display to double check it was receiving. It functions correctly, though there was no map data at the time.

'Our sources indicate that what you will be looking for is a weapon sizeable enough for 2 or 3 people to carry. It is expected to be within the central research facility. We know that it runs on an unrecognized fuel source, so for that reason do not attempt to tamper with it. Once located several of our ships are standing by to come and retrieve it. They are in standby as we do not want them forming part of the assault as they may be noticed by Confederacy eyes. Just find the weapon, then we'll get you out of there.'

'That is all agents. We are close to boarding. This is the way we lead.'

The hologram shut down and instantly Porz had something to say:

'Why'd he say 'we are close to insertion' – we all know he ain't on this ship.'

'He's a good commander though,' spoke Rumiq. 'I've had him before on a few missions.'

'Yeah well I get the naggin' this mission will be somethin' different,' replied Porz.

Little more was said as the agents kept intermittently checking their gear and readying themselves mentally for the attack.

Now turn to 100.

SDN [Space Designation Network] faction - any mission, begin here:

    As you ready yourself to enter the teleporter, you perform one final check of your armaments. Pulling up your holo-view in front of your eyes you do a last check of your mission brief. There is sure to be plenty of LWS and XBR agents around; hopefully you can avoid their squabbles and they eliminate each other you think to yourself. After enabling co-ordinate lock-on and closing down your holo-view you step into the teleporter. The machine is near silent as your body dips outs of physical existence and your surroundings change, bringing you back to materiality inside the XBR starship. There is no time to lose – you quickly step out of the teleporter and its cool air to the maintained climate of the starship.

    Turn to 500.

Confederacy faction - Fugitive hunt mission only begin here:

A break would have been nice you thought even before you had read the case file.

'Fugitive.' Grumbles Corporal Shapps. Looking at the synth-sheet you take a mental snap shot of the perpetrator's image and note the minimal details the confederacy has on him.

'Not much to go on as usual,' you respond, somewhat dissatisfied.

'I didn't think you'd like it either,' replies the corporal solemnly.

You glance up at his weathered face to see his sincerity. Merely a messenger on this one you thought.

'I'm aware you're overdue for time off too. But I need this case looked into and you need the creds,' he says, at the same time his dry lips strain to form his best efforts at a smile. He's right on both counts you think to yourself.

'Leave it with me,' you say. With that you extract a copy of the case file into your own data store and hand the corporal back the synth sheet. Folding the sheet and placing it in his pocket he turns to leave.

You set off to prepare yourself.

Close to an hour later you are in the process of issuing an investigation order to the starship's captain. He reluctantly obliges, asking you to report to him your findings before you exit his ship. The port co-ordinates are uploaded to your data store before the captain is called away from your interview by something seemingly important. He quickly wishes you well with your investigation and disconnects the com-link. Curious about such behavior you wonder what *is* going on aboard the starship. Grabbing your weapons you head to the teleporter and set it to take you to the starship.

Due to your time of arrival aboard the starship, the time remaining will be considerably limited for your mission. Mark off the entire *1st tier* of the *time passed* section on your mission sheet. You will only have the *2nd* and *final tier* of time remaining in which to complete your task.

Turn to 300.

Confederacy faction - Survey and defend mission only begin here:

A routine task like all the other times. Dropping off supplies to outpost Q4. You are looking forward to a well-deserved break from service. Lost in thought of how you plan to spend your time off, a bright flash out in the distance shakes you out of your trance. What was that? You wonder. Another flash. Checking your chart you note an XBR ship is in the vicinity of the flash. You decide to steer your small supply ship closer to take a look. As you near the origin of the flashes you begin to get a visual of the XBR starship.

You decide to ask them if everything is okay.

'We've been attacked by the Leading Weapon Syndicate'. Reports the captain.

'No doubt the Confederacy must consider this an unprovoked attack and a breach of peace regulations'.

'Something for the council to decide', you reply, not wanting to agree with the captain outright.

You've taken it this far, you had better report the incident to your superior you think to yourself.

Bringing up his image on your holo-view, the conversation is short and direct;

Cease other activities and board the ship, assess the situation and report back.

'I want to know why they are there, who exactly is there and have evidence I can bring before the Directors' he commands.

You'd like to protest, finish what you were doing and then go on leave, but what your commander says goes.

Gaining permission to board from the captain you steer your small ship towards one of the docking ports on the starboard side. Immediately you gain directions to the bridge to try to get a clearer picture.

'Take a look for yourself' says the Captain pointing to several holographic displays being monitored by crew members. 'We believe we have the situation under control, but that is hardly any reconciliation for such an act of war.' says the captain sternly as he moves to another side of the room.

Returning to the displays, you can see to some extent the damage done to the ship, and LWS agents, particularly in the loading bay assaulting crew and ship alike. You determine you will want copies of the vision you have just seen which you can obtain later, but for now you will need to get a closer assessment and see what you can do.

Taking one of the teleporters, you jump to sector E, the closest area to action.

Due to your time of arrival aboard the starship, the time remaining will be considerably limited for your mission. Mark off the entire 1st tier of the *Time passed* section on your mission sheet. You will only have the 2nd and final tier of time remaining in which to complete your task.

Turn to 300.

NFA [Non Faction Aligned] - Biohazard borrower mission only, begin here:

'Hey watch it,' blares one of the other loading bay workers. You wave back as you veer your cargo cart off towards a midsized transport ship that has just arrived. It's a job, but not really what you do. The loading bay driver is a cover for you being aboard an XBR ship. You've been given a contract by a man back on Phaeadron to steal a bio hazardous material and return it to him. Your contact had said the man was both reliable and had no faction affiliations. 'Let's hope so,' you think to yourself as you load up your cart. With your earplugs in you do not hear any noise, but you do notice the tremors and reverberation as the starship is jolted. You don't think too much of it and continue to load up your cart - the boss wants this one finished before the rotation. A short while later, having loaded your cart fully, you drive back down the ramp and head towards the back of the loading bay. You can't help noticing a number of red flashing lights, but being the new guy, you do not know exactly what they are signaling, aside from an emergency of some sort. Looking back over the loading bay you note a few people yelling out to each other and some rapid movements. Keeping your eyes to your driving you bring the trailer up to the supply elevator entry. Drawing your attention from your task you witness several armed agents storm onto the loading bay floor and open fire on anyone they can see.

Three guards suddenly rush past you heading towards the loading bay entry, towards the aggressors. You can see what is happening and realize it is escalating fast as more agents pour into the loading bay while workers and guards alike begin defending the ship. Realizing you are behind with what is happening around you, full throttle and the cart is careering towards port side. Wasting no time you yank open your personal locker and grab the weapons and items you have there. You head back to the loading bay floor.

Turn to 600.

NFA _[Non Faction Aligned] - Collector of things mission only, begin here:_

A flashing red light awakens you from your restful slumber. It's the whole ship alarm you note as you sit up in your bunk. 'Get up already, we're under attack', states a senior worker, standing dressed in the middle of the room with some authority.

'Attack by who?' blurts out another worker as he gets out of his rest pod.

'It's an LWS ship, but don't panic, our troops are already all over it'.

A status message appears on your labor bracelet:

"Report to Crew Schedule immediately" it states.

By the time you look back up from your bracelet the senior worker has already turned and is heading for the door.

'Hey check this out,' says Seyem quietly from the pod beside you.

You look over and he is holding a hand held obsolete video unit for you to watch. 'This is in the loading bay, 'bout a minute ago - I got it from Paiferin,' he says.

The video, though very short and with a number of glitches in it portrays an intense firefight between the crew of the starship and invading LWS agents.

'I bet this is bigger than they are telling us,' he states with vigor.

'You might be right,' you reply.

He grabs you by the shoulders: 'This could be our chance to get off this ship!' he exclaims.

You hesitate to reply, still in thought when he continues:

'All we need to do is defeat the database for the teleporters and we can jump off!'

'But what about these?' you throw back, holding up your labor bracelet.

'A strong negative field will make 'em useless, then you can bust them off - I've seen it done before.'

'You sure?' you ask.

'We gotta try - I ain't stayin' a slave for the rest of my time. Stay a fool if you want but I'm gettin' my brother and then I'm gettin' off this piece of junk of a ship!'

With that Seyem grabs a long zip bag with his items in it and races out of the room.

Other workers are also leaving the room to report for duty and the room is almost empty.

You look down at your bracelet once more with its bleak message telling you to report for duty at the crew schedule - then you think of smashing it to pieces and experiencing freedom once again.

Turn to 128.

1.

The drone has injected sufficient poison into your body to bring you to your knees. You try to fight it, struggling to move, your efforts are futile. Within moments you lose all ability to move your limbs and you can only watch as security enter the room to take you away to be interrogated before execution.

2.

Your destination is a neutral supply ship en route to Beutohn. You are simply glad it was available to save your life. For now it will take you down to Beutohn, the captain of the vessel content enough to allow you to stow away with some of the cargo. If you have the *Disrupt and extract* mission, turn to 31. If you have the *Data thief* mission, turn to 16.

3.

At the end of the corridor you reach a door which has failed to slide shut fully. If you have the *Contortion* ability, turn to 22. Otherwise you have no chance of fitting through the gap and must find a way through. Will you:

Try an explosive if you have one? Turn to 64.
Try your strength at pushing the door open? Turn to 139.

4.

The carcass of the deadly creature lies motionless at your feet. Having defeated the alien you move to the end of the aisle unimpeded where you can see the exit across from you. If you do not have it already written down, add the word "pet" to your mission sheet. You open the door with a manual button, entering the room. Turn to 55.

5.

With the other scientists fleeing the room while the battle was taking place, the room is now clear. You walk across to check the body of the scientist you took out. He has cards on him showing his identity. It's not Minkla. You eliminated the wrong man. Will you:

See if you can find Minkla's data on one of the terminals in here?

Turn to 67.

Not waste time and leave via the restricted surgical room?

Turn to 1284.

Rush to leave via the unmarked starboard door?   Turn to 317.

6.

Sweat pouring from your forehead, dripping onto the console while the ship shakes violently, you can only wait for the teleporter to find a lock. Without a lock you cannot jump to anywhere. You force the machine to rescan. Roll a die. If you roll a 1, turn to 270. If you roll anything else, turn to 56.

7.

While he is battered and down you attempt to arrest the fugitive. Roll 2 dice and add your *endurance*. Do the same for Sjonn, who has an *endurance* of 5. If your total is equal to or higher, turn to 971. If your total is less than Sjonn's total, he is not beaten yet; deduct 1 point from your capture tally and return to 54, continuing the fight.

8.

A right turn at another intersection and you can see the door to the teleport hub at the far end. You rush towards it as the ship shakes worse than before, an explosion elsewhere on the ship sending ripples through the floor and walls. If you have the word "slain" written down, turn to 35. If you do not have this word written down, turn to 24.

9.

[If you have the word "cast" written down, you do not have time to reenter the room, turn to 32.]

A particular type of keypass is required here. Try yours now, if it does not work, as the door has a number of security characteristics you choose another option. Return to 32.

10.

Having some familiarity with the type of implant device, you can tell the insertion gun has been previously used on a human going off the current setting. You are also aware of the prevalence of biological upgrades within the Xeno Biological Research faction. Will you:

Implant the loaded chip into your body? Turn to 65.

Leave via the restricted surgical room? Turn to 1284.

Leave via the unmarked starboard door? Turn to 317.

11.

Penetrating the gut of the agent, your last shot manages to put the enemy agent down on the floor. You don't have time to finish him off, the ship is in peril and you risk going down with it. You make a dash for it, sprinting to the far end of the corridor. Turn to 163.

12.

Having finished off the worker you turn to see what else is happening. You notice Zak preparing himself for a man running at him with a knife. With a strong elbow to the midriff Zak sends his attacker reeling, giving him time enough to throw him over the rails and down onto the loading bay floor.

'We'd better move' he says panting.

Looking up to the other side of the loading bay you see the fire fight there has intensified. It looks as though the red team is taking heavy casualties. Meanwhile fighting continues on the loading bay deck. You are tuned into the blue team's channel and you can hear that they are also doing it tough, but are bunkered in well enough for the moment.

Ahead on the walkway Zak has jumped on a large elevator platform. 'Jump on!' he yells as the elevator begins moving towards the loading bay floor. You move to get on. Suddenly a large energy blast hits the elevator platform. The body of Zak lies torn on what is left of the platform. Remarkably the platform is still functioning, continuing a slow descent to the floor.

Quickly you jump onto the platform and ride it to the loading bay floor, taking shots at XBR crew as you travel. The fighting intensifies as groups of fellow agents try to push through to the other side of the loading bay.

The XBR forces have increased their defenses, as a large number of guards, several XBR agents and a flock of airborne drones enter the arena.

Fight your way through by rolling a die three times.

For each roll of a 1 or a 2, deduct 3 vitality as you take incoming fire.

The battle continues with heavy casualties on both sides. It looks like chaos with the amount of smoke, laser fire and distorted messages through your com-link. You can no longer hear the commands of Ashkin either. The majority of the fighting surrounds a large crane in the middle of the loading bay, not far from where you are. Turn to 63.

13.

[If you have the word "billet" on your mission sheet, turn to 242 now.]

Time passes. Entering the room you see that it is a spacious office, possibly for three or four individuals. There is nobody here. You don't have time to start looking at the terminals but you do take a quick look around the room since you are already in here. There is a *med pack* attached to the wall which you may take if you choose. There is also a map of this level of the ship on the wall. You can see that in order to get to level 5 you will need to head towards the bow, then towards port, then towards the bow from your current position. A teleport hub is what you will require as it can teleport you off ship. There are none on this level and one is listed as being on level 5. Write the word "billet" on your mission sheet.

About to leave, you notice there is a locked cabinet in the corner. Will you:

Try to break into the cabinet?   Turn to 255.
Leave now?   Turn to 715.

14.

The injuries you just sustained are major. You are now *crippled*. Make a note of this fact and then roll on the *crippled* table. In your position you have to make a do-or-die effort to run for the end of the corridor which you do so without pause. If you rolled anything other than a 4 on the crippled table, turn to 163. If you rolled a 4 on the crippled table and have injuries to your legs, you will incur more attacks on you as you have been slowed considerably. Roll 3 dice. For each 4 or more, suffer 3 damage, though you may roll for defense. If you live through this onslaught, turn to 163.

15.

Looking around the teleport hub you can see it has areas of damage. You notice a nearby console sparking and part of the wall to your left blackened and smoldering. Out of the two main teleporters capable of off ship teleporting only one of them has a read out; the other is blank. Moving over to the one that appears to be working, you try to find a destination to lock onto. The system does not find one immediately as you had hoped, but continues to run through the scanning process. If you have no unmarked *time passed* boxes on your mission sheet, turn to 1263. If you can still mark off another box, then as *time passes*, turn to 50.

16.

Using the code words you have written down, can you create the word "breakdown"? If so, turn to 338. Otherwise turn to 1255.

17.

You are in a tough situation. If you try to run from where you are, the agent is highly likely to cut you down. You could possibly throw a grenade or you could sit it out. If you have a grenade and would like to use it now, turn to 135. If you plan to remain hidden, turn to 281. If you choose to keep fighting, return to 144.

18.

The slim-discs may be looked at by somebody with an old piece of technology which used to read them. If you know of Kinlac, then perhaps he may be able to help. If you do not know who Kinlac is, then try finding him. Now remember this reference and return to where you came from.

19.

If you have both a *mechanical spring-snap* and a *multi sensor* you have the means to quickly put together a *distraction contraption* as they are often called. Replace the other two items with this one (still a miscellaneous item) when you do. Once set the device will trigger when someone nears it and can be used to fire items like bearings or glass or to set off a grenade. Now return to your previous reference.

20.

From the wounds you just sustained you hit the floor, instinctively rolling to one side to avoid annihilation from your fearsome opponent. Roll a die to see the result of the injuries. If you roll a 1, turn to 14. If you roll a 2, 3 or a 4, turn to 66. If you roll a 5 or a 6, turn to 104.

21.

Through the loading bay door, you enter into a large hallway with multiple levels. It looks to be clear for the moment. Roll a die. If you roll 4 or more, turn to 33. If you roll 3 or less, turn to 650.

22.

The gap is a tight one, but after throwing your items through you push yourself between the metal edges with just some minor scrapes. Picking up your items you press on. Turn to 8.

23.

You are going to have to hack off his forearm to take his weapon. If you do this, add a *laser blaster* to your inventory. Though you now have a deadly weapon, you cannot use it whilst on the starship as it will need to be cleaned up and the dead agent's flesh removed. The weapon is intended to be used as you saw it; as a replacement for a lost or damaged hand and forearm. To do this will require surgery otherwise the weapon can be carried but with a penalty of being *heavy*. See the item description for details. Turn to 48.

24.

Roll a die. If you roll 4 or more, turn to 49. If you roll 3 or less, turn to 35.

25.

Happily he performs the exchange with you. Add 100 creds to your tally. The both of you now head back to the main room. You may not return to his hidden room to show him the items you just have traded. Return to 818 to finish any other dealings you may have.

26.

From out of the near darkness springs an obsidian black alien creature, ferocious claws and a vicious snarl vivify your senses. Face the terrifying beast under the dim light fronting one of the holding pens:

Specimen HK-01 CQ   8
                Vitality   28*
                On 3 dice 5+ to hit, 3 damage.
                3+ to negate 3 damage as chitin exoskeleton defense.

>If you have already fought the alien and have a *vitality* written down, then use that value.

>If the alien rolls 2 or more 6's when rolling to hit you and causes damage in that combat round, you will also suffer the *bleeding* lingering effect.

>If you choose to flee this combat, follow the normal rules for fleeing, make a note of the *vitality* of the alien and then turn to 92.

If you defeat the alien creature, turn to 4.

27.

You persist in trying to find a lock for the teleporter. Your time is surely running out as an explosion rips through the ship, fortunately nowhere near you. Roll a die. If the result is 4 or more, turn to 56. If the result is 3 or less, turn to 153.

28.

You engage the agent in a shootout. He takes up position alongside the wall, utilizing some of the support structures to conceal himself when not firing. Roll 3 dice. For each 4 or more, suffer 3 damage, though you may roll for defense. Retaliate by firing your own weapon at short range, with no modifications to the 'to hit' roll. If you cause any damage, roll for the defense of the agent: on a 5 or more, 3 points of damage will be negated. Start a tally of the *vitality* lost by the XBR agent. Repeat the process once more, taking your turn to fire at the agent after he has shot at you. If you have now reduced the agent's *vitality* by 10 or more, turn to 11. If you have not achieved this, you have two options: You may either continue the fight by turning to 34, or you may turn and make a run for it by turning to 38.

29.

As Melea is too wounded to help you in this combat, she leans against the wall outside the room where you left her, drifting in and out of consciousness whilst safely out of sight. Return to 41 and continue.

30.

To enter this room you require a standard keypass. If you have one, you will know how to use it. Otherwise will you:

Try the second door?	Turn to 510.
Keep moving?	Turn to 3.

31.

If you have either the word "slam" or "solid" written down, turn to 40. If you have neither of these words written down, turn to 223.

32.

There are three rooms here which you may investigate. Choose any you have not previously been in:

The first room on the left:	Turn to 90.
The second room on the left:	Turn to 9.
The room towards the end on the right:	Turn to 1242.

Alternatively you can keep moving to the end of the corridor:

Turn to 58.

33.

From up ahead flying down a ramp to your head height comes an airborne XBR drone. The drone bears one long laser combined with a deadly spearhead. You are going to have to take it out in order to get to the ramp up ahead.

XBR spear drone	Ra	4
	Vitality	10

4+ to hit, 3 damage.
5+ Agile flyer defense will negate all damage.

If you defeat the drone, *time passes* as you move ahead. Turn to 650.

34.

Deal another round of firing at the agent as you have just done: Roll 3 dice. For each 4 or more, suffer 3 damage, though you may roll for defense. Retaliate by firing your own weapon at short range, with no modifications to the 'to hit' roll. If you cause any damage, roll for the defense of the agent: on a 5 or more, 3 points of damage will be negated. If you have now reduced the agent's *vitality* by 10 or more, turn to 11. If you have not achieved this, you have two options: You may either continue the fight by repeating the process, in which case *time passes*, or you may turn and make a run for it by turning to 38.

35.

Reaching the door which opens automatically you stop in the doorway looking into the room. The room is not in the best of shape with some of the equipment damaged and exposed, sparking intermittently. Out of the two main teleporters capable of off ship teleporting only one of them has a read out; the other is blank. Moving over to the one that appears to be working, you try to find a destination to lock onto. The system does not find one immediately as you had hoped, but continues to run through the scanning process. If you have no unmarked *time passed* boxes on your mission sheet, turn to 1263. If you can still mark off another box as *time passes*, turn to 50.

36.

It looks as though out of the two teleporters capable of sending you off ship, one of them is still working; the other has no readout whatsoever. Quickly you try to find a destination lock on the functioning teleporter. Roll for *chance*. If the result is 4 or more, turn to 39. If the result is 3 or less, turn to 151.

37.

During the fight with the agent, the remaining scientists escaped. They are probably well on their way or even off the ship by now. The ship continues to shake amidst the turbulence. You need to get out:

Leave via the restricted surgical room: Turn to 1284.
Leave via the unmarked starboard door: Turn to 317.

38.

You turn and run, knowing that the other agent will fire at you mercilessly with the weapon attached to his arm. Roll 3 dice. For each 4 or more, suffer 3 damage, though you may roll for defense. If you have the *Evasion* ability, you may reroll up to two of the to hit rolls once. If you are wounded here, turn to 20. If you are unscathed from this attack, you race to the end of the corridor, turn to 163.

39.

The teleporter is having trouble finding a lock. You concede there may be nothing around. Phaeadron is likely out of the question given the location of the ship. Will you:

Keep trying to find a teleport lock?   Turn to 27.
Try to think of or look around for an alternative?   Turn to 79.

40.

Down the very bottom of the codewords section on your mission sheet, write the word "fracture". Though it does not happen instantly by the time you land you will receive payment for a successful mission. Add 500 creds to your total. Turn to 82.

41.

[If you have the word "fulcrum" written down, turn to 29.]

The agent has a gun attached to his right arm and is preoccupied, giving the impression he might be an easy target. You launch yourself at the agent whilst he is less than ready for you. You may attack first for this combat.

XBR agent Kylgren CQ 6

Vitality 20

On 2 dice, 5+ to hit, 4 damage.

5+ to negate 3 damage as defense.

>If you roll a double 6 when rolling for Kylgren's attack, he will instead try an alternate attack in which he will attempt to throw a small vial of liquid at you. Only if you have the *Evasion* ability may you dodge the attack by successfully rolling 4 or more on a single dice roll. Otherwise you will suffer damage equivalent to the result of one die roll plus 4. This damage cannot be negated by armor or any other ability. Should this damage reduce you to 10 or less *vitality*, Kylgren will try to finish you off - continue the combat. Otherwise if your *vitality* remains above 10 and Kylgren's *vitality* is less than 10, he will try to flee the scene. You may resolve one further attack against the agent before he will flee. If he manages to flee, turn to 87.

>If you need to flee this combat, follow the rules, then turn to 148.

If you kill the agent, turn to 113.

42.

From the now continual shaking of the ship, several of the containers have cracked open. Perched inside a container ahead of you, a frightened winged creature flies at you out of its broken prison, a dagger-like beak aiming for your head. Fend off the creature quickly.

Bafuiy creature CQ 4

Vitality 12

On 2 dice, 5+ to hit, 2 damage.

No defense.

Once you have shaken the creature off, you reach the door. Turn to 91.

43.

Time passes. Most of the room is a mess. There are broken pieces of equipment, smashed vials and bits of things all over the place. One thing catches your eye though. It looks to be an insertion gun sitting on one of the benches toward the starboard-stern corner. Picking it up you notice it has a chip loaded into it. The trouble is you do not know what the chip does. If you have a *Bio* score of 4 or more, turn to 10. Otherwise will you:

Implant the chip into your body?	Turn to 65.
Leave via the restricted surgical room?	Turn to 1284.
Leave via the unmarked starboard door?	Turn to 317.

44.

You turn and run as fast as you can. Not looking back you hope you can lose it by picking another aisle. Will you:

Head to your left at the end of the aisle?	Turn to 78.
Head to your right at the end of the aisle?	Turn to 126.

45.

You take up position facing Melea on the other side of the door. She waves her hand across the sensor on the wall and the double doors close. Only a moment later you can hear the sound of the two drones on the other side of the door. It is the familiar buzz of a scanner sweep. The room is silent with the team in position, the three men cowering under the table.

'Can they open that door' says Zak quietly but firmly to the men under the table.

None of the men answer.

Zak begins to repeat the question;

'Can they open th...' he stops himself short as two lasers begin cutting into the door from the other side.

'This could get ugly' Melea jokingly remarks.

Will you:

Change your position to behind the table ready for the drones when they enter?   Turn to 236.

Hold your ground and wait to see what happens next?Turn to 142.

Place an explosive on the door if you have one?   Turn to 97.

46.

You find the door is locked and requires a keypass to enter. If you have a keypass you can scan it now. Otherwise you cannot spare the time to break into a room which you do not know the contents of. Turn to 715.

47.

The agent has you pinned hard, there may be no means to escape his onslaught. If you have a grenade and would like to use it now, turn to 135. Otherwise the only other option is to wait it out, remaining hidden in cover. If you plan to do this, turn to 281. If you choose to keep fighting, return to 144.

48.

Turn to the reference according to the codeword you have written down:

Analog or Quaint:	Turn to 244.
Ardent or Extant:	Turn to 72.
Slant:	Turn to 37.
Fountain:	Turn to 5.
Slam:	Turn to 53.
Delete:	Turn to 15.

49.

Stopping in your tracks you see up ahead, standing in the doorway to the teleport hub XBR agent Kylgren. He is intentionally blocking your entry to the teleport hub, hoping you will go down with the ship. You take up cover behind one of the support structures on the side of the corridor. You are going to have to shoot it out; there is nowhere else to go and he will surely cut you down if you try to assault the XBR agent. Add the word "delete" to your mission sheet and turn to 144.

50.

At last the teleporter finds a destination. You do not hesitate to ensure you do not miss the chance; you leap onto the pad, initiating the sequence to send you far away in an instant. Turn to 2.

51.

Suddenly you notice one of the sign lights goes out - no something passed in front of it - you hear more footsteps. Something is approaching you...something big. Act now:

Face whatever it is heading for you?   Turn to 26.

Move quickly back along the aisle to avoid whatever it is?

Turn to 44.

52.

'Not creds. Something valuable you have.'

Kinlac looks at you beseechingly. 'You can see the items here, if you just choose one...' he says.

'You know I don't know what half this stuff does. It could be junk.'

Kinlac appears defeated. 'Very well,' he says, turning towards one of the shelves and grabbing a small device from a box. 'This I think you will find useful,' he says as he begins to show you how it works.

'It is used to reduce trauma - to slow things down so that medical treatment can be administered before you die. But it can only be used once.'

'How do I know it even works?' You ask.

'It will, but if you have changed your mind, you can take the creds instead.'

You have no doubt to suspect Kinlac is trading a dud with you and you just witnessed him take a dusty item from the shelf and start using it. You take the device off his hands. Since you have no idea what it is called if it has a name, simply add *Kinlac's device* to you inventory as a miscellaneous item. This item may be used once only. After it is used, remove it from your inventory. You may use it at any time, including during combat, with no penalty. If you have less than 10 *vitality* when you use it, add 10 *vitality*, plus the total of 2 dice rolls to your *vitality* score. If you use the device outside of combat, along with a *med pack*, then simply restore your *vitality* to maximum. Make a note of this on your mission sheet. You thanking Kinlac for the trade. You may not return to his hidden room to show him the items you have just traded. Now return to 818 and finish any other dealings with the man.

53.

With the other scientists fleeing the room while the battle was taking place, the room is now clear. You walk across to check the body of the scientist you took out. He has cards on him showing his identity. It is Minkla. You record his identity and death and check his pockets. There is a data store on him which you take. A quick check reveals it is loaded with research data. The ship shakes more, reminding you of the urgency of evacuation. Will you:

Search the room?	Turn to 43.
Leave via the restricted surgical room?	Turn to 1284.
Leave via the unmarked starboard door?	Turn to 317.

54.

Pushing open the door you find yourself in a small room with a ladder in one corner heading upwards. At the top of the ladder you see Sjonn - desperately trying to turn a valve to open a hatch on the ceiling in a bid to escape. Not wasting a moment you leap across to him up several rungs and grab one of his ankles, causing him to lose his footing. He tumbles down atop of you but quickly recovers, intent on escaping through the door you came in by. Right behind him you rip him away from the doorway as he tries to squeeze through and now have him cornered, forcing him to fight ferociously.

Fugitive Sjonn CQ   5

           Vitality   -

           5+ *dodge* defense to negate all damage.

>You may attack first in this combat.

>To fight Sjonn, you will need to subdue and capture him or at least prevent him from escaping. For this battle, follow the usual rules with combat rounds. For your own attacks, choose how you will fight by selecting one of the options below or fighting unarmed. Instead of deducting vitality from Sjonn, you will instead gain points which represent you gaining the upper hand in his seizure. Likewise, Sjonn will make moves from his own set of options with the results listed.

On your mission sheet, start two tallies: A "capture tally" for yourself and an "escape tally" for Sjonn. These tallies cannot go below zero.

For your own attacks:

You may either fight an unarmed combat round against Sjonn or select one of the options below. You may not perform the same option from the list below in a consecutive combat round. You may fight unarmed each combat round if you choose. If you cause damage (after defense rolls) then add 1 to your capture tally.

Alternative option to unarmed combat each combat round (Do not pick the same option twice in a row):

1. Use a *Shock pistol* if you have one: turn to 107.
2. Use a *Stun pistol* if you have one: turn to 214.
3. Use a *Shock mace* if you have one: If you cause damage, add 2 points to your capture tally.
4. Attempt to grapple him: Roll 2 dice. If the total is less than or equal to your *strength*, deduct 1 point from his escape tally and add 1 point to your capture tally.
5. Attempt to pin him: Roll 2 dice. If the total is less than or equal to your *agility*, add 2 points to your capture tally.

>If you have the *strong arm* ability, you may add 3 to your *strength* for the purposes of performing option 4: attempting to grapple him.

>If you have the *brick wall* ability, once during this combat you may totally negate one of Sjonn's attacks.

>If you have the *wrestler* ability, you may reroll (once per round only) your unarmed to hit rolls.

>If you have the *negotiator* ability, turn to 249.

Sjonn's attacks:

Roll a die each combat round to see what Sjonn will do. Note: Sjonn cannot improve his 'to hit' roll to less than 4+ even if you have a lower CQ score.

Dice roll:

1-3 Sjonn attempts to throw one of the implements in the room at you. 4+ to hit, 3 damage. If he injures you, deduct 1 point from your capture tally.

4-5 Using the piping in the room as a weapon, Sjonn attempts to either break a pipe and use the steam to burn you or push you against one of the burning pipes. 4+ to hit, add the *burned* lingering effect, deduct 1 point from your capture tally and add 1 point to his escape tally.

6 Sjonn attempts to knock you out with one of the implements in the room. 5+ to hit, 1 damage. If successful, add 2 points to Sjonn's escape tally.

>If your capture tally is 8 or more at the end of a combat round, turn to 7.

>Otherwise if Sjonn has 5 or more points as his escape tally at the end of a combat round, turn to 85.

55.

Time passes. The short room, devoid of lighting leads you to another door which again, with a push of a manual button opens for you. Inside the next room, you see that it is a laboratory and it is fully illuminated, aside from the odd light out. This lab is filled with benches and equipment, with some experiments just left as they are as people have evacuated the room. You make your way past several benches in order to get around to the other side. Turn to 171.

56.

Fortune is with you: within a short moment the teleporter finds a lock. You do not hesitate to ensure you do not lose your chance; you jump on the teleport pad and activate the machine. You are whisked away, traveling instantly. Turn to 101.

57.

Looking for a way out of this situation, you see few options. If you turn to run to the nearest door he will surely cut you down. There is however a bulky analysis machine atop a nearby bench. The machine has two parts to it; the top part being raised off the lower part with a gap in between. If you choose to roll toward this new vantage point, then you must forgo one of your attack rounds to do so. Once there however, Kylgren's to hit rolls will be increased to needing a 6 to hit you. Now return to 144 and fight.

58.

Reaching the end of the corridor you take a left turn based on the signage. The new corridor is long with a couple of rooms on one side, which you ignore, given the severity of the situation. If you have the word "slain" written down, turn to 163. If not, turn to 70.

59.

It looks as though out of the two teleporters capable of sending you off ship, one of them is still working; the other has no readout whatsoever. Wasting no time you try to find a destination lock on the functioning teleporter. The first scan returns a negative. You persist, forcing another scan. The readout suddenly changes; a lock has been found. Without hesitation you jump onto the teleport pad and activate the machine. You are out of here. Turn to 101.

60.

From one of the containers that has broken open an alien creature is running around the room at a frantic pace. The spindly looking little thing attacks ferociously with numerous tiny claws on four limbs.

Nargre alien CQ   5

            Vitality   17

            On 2 dice, 3+ to hit, 1 damage.

            5+ to negate all damage evasion as defense.

Once you have shaken the creature off, you reach the door. Turn to 91.

61.

The second drone takes aim at Melea. She is not quick enough and the drone shoots first. Fortunately for her the shot just misses and she has time to take it down. The ordeal is over as fast as it started. Without hesitation the three of you open the door again and head down the corridor. Turn to 134.

62.

Carefully and cautiously you move closer to the end of the aisle, all keeping watch for the slightest sign as you do so. You freeze momentarily as you hear movement. The end of the aisle is in sight not far away. Roll a die. If you have the *Stealth* ability, you may reroll the die once only. If you roll 5 or more, turn to 116. If the result is 4 or less, turn to 102.

63.

You don't know if it was a large battery or chemical container, but the crane and surrounding crates suddenly explodes into a massive fireball of blue flame. Shards of debris and bodies from both forces are flung across the floor. Roll for *chance*. If the result is 3 or less, deduct 5 *vitality* as you cop some of the blast.

The blast has all but cleared the room of fighters and noise, filling the room with smoke and dust.

You notice the few remaining LWS agents and XBR guards look for ways out or flee.

Now is your chance to get across to the other side and try to get through the main loading bay door.

Using your cutting tool or siege equipment, roll 2 dice and compare the result to the value needed for your item. If the result is equal or higher, you have broken through the door - turn to 21.

If you fail to get through, mark off a *time passes* box on your mission sheet. Try again by repeating the process, adding an extra 1 point for each previous try to the score for the work you have already done. You may continue trying with each additional try marking off a *time passes*.

If you do not have any cutting tool you may use your CQ weapon. You'll need to score 10 or more points of damage to get through. Each time you try, add 1 extra point for each previous try and mark off a *time passes*. When you get through, turn to 21.

64.

Remove the explosive from your inventory. Placing it on the door and setting it you quickly move away to let it do its job. A moment later the blast goes off and you are relieved to see the door largely destroyed, with the resulting opening easily wide enough for you to pass through. Turn to 8.

65.

Removing some of your armor to reveal some of your skin, you point the insertion gun at yourself and hit the button trigger. There is a slight burning sensation, but you feel fine. You do not feel any different for a moment then you begin to feel a little improvement as the chip does its work. You may now increase either your *strength* OR your *agility* by 1 point on your mission sheet. Additionally, increase your *maximum vitality* by 2 points. Now will you:

Leave via the restricted surgical room?   Turn to 1284.

Leave via the unmarked starboard door?   Turn to 317.

66.

You've just sustained some serious injuries. You now have a *grievous wound*. If this does not kill you, with no time to spare you pick yourself up and keep running, intent on making it to the end of the corridor. Turn to 163.

67.

Moving to the nearest terminal, you quickly begin searching for the data you are looking for. It is helpful the terminal has been left on and the information is readily accessible. The challenging part is the sheer volume of information about the research here and the need to sift through it to find what you are after. *Time passes.* It could take a while searching. Will you:

Continue searching the databases regardless?   Turn to 145.

Abandon the attempt and leave via the restricted surgical room?
                                                            Turn to 1284.

Quit now and leave via the unmarked starboard door? Turn to 317.

68.

As you move you begin to hear something. You reach the door safely and hit the button to manually open the door. Your heart pounds as something begins moving toward you fast, pounding the floor with heavy steps while the door is opening. As soon as you can fit through you push inside the next room and slam the button to close the door. The door closes relatively quickly but even in that instant you turn to see something large charging toward the door. Just as the door completely closes you hear a dull thud as the creature rams into the door from the other side. The door is solid and you expect it will hold - at least for long enough for you to get far away. Add 1 to your *chance* score. Turn to 55.

69.

There is nothing to gain by returning to this room, you decide on an alternative:

Try the second door if you have not already: Turn to 510.
Keep moving along the corridor: Turn to 3.

70.

[If you have the word "fulcrum" written down, turn to 80 now.]

Only part way along the corridor, you suddenly start taking fire, forcing you to dive against one of the walls for some cover. Roll 3 dice. For each 4 or more, take 3 damage, though you may roll for defense. Looking back, you see that it is an XBR agent and he is striding along the corridor from where you just came, his weapon trained upon your location. His whole forearm forms his gun and you see him fire again, hitting the wall as the three barrels dish out some devastating fire power. You're in a tough situation as running for it would leave you vulnerable and trying to take him on will be no easy feat and one you may not have time for anyway. Will you:

Fire back at the agent?   Turn to 28.
Make a run for it?   Turn to 38.

71.

You move past the next specimen pen. Then, you hear it. Several strong thuds above the background noise of the ship itself. They sounded like footsteps. Roll a die. If you roll an even number of 2, 4 or 6, turn to 62. If you roll an odd number of 1, 3 or 5, turn to 51.

72.

You now have the option to leave the room immediately or search the room. Will you:

Leave via the restricted surgical room?   Turn to 1284.
Leave via the unmarked starboard door?   Turn to 317.
Search the room first?   Turn to 43.

73.

In your peripheral vision you note nearby movement. A large grotty and plain clothed man has just climbed an access ladder and has his eyes set firmly on you. He is brandishing a large metal tool of some sort. You have time to fire a short range shot at him, then you will have to fight at close quarters:

Mechanical worker	CQ	4
	Vitality	14
	4+ to hit, 2 damage.	
	No defense.	

>Remember to roll on any of the appropriate battle tables.

If you defeat the worker, turn to 12.

74.

Look at the words you have written down. If you can form the word "skippet" by combining two of the words you have written down, turn to 122. If you can only form part of this word, turn to 247. If you cannot form any part of this word, turn to 321.

75.

Since you are not close enough, you lay low. Fortunately Melea is sharp enough with her reflexes and quickly shoots down the drone. All focus is on the task at hand. The three of you open up the door again and head down the corridor. Turn to 134.

76.

Taking careful aim at the agent, you send a shot his way, scoring a hit. He immediately ducks for cover as the scientists start running. Before starting the proceeding combat, resolve an automatic hit against the agent with your ranged weapon, allowing Kylgren to roll for defense. Add the word "slant" to your mission sheet and turn to 144.

77.

Time passes. The room has indeed been stripped of anything valuable, though searching inside one of the draws yields a bottle of *brutenide* which has enough for three doses. You may take this if you choose. Activating the terminal, you find the memory store or LMS as they are known as has also been wiped. If it were not erased securely however, it may be possible to recover data at a later point with the right equipment. If you choose to take it, add an *LMS* (Local Memory Store) to you inventory as a miscellaneous item. You now leave the room. Return to 32 and choose an option you have not previously taken.

78.

Roll a die. If you roll a 3, turn to 180. If you roll anything else, turn to 294.

79.

Time passes. Looking around and thinking hard, you draw the conclusion there simply is no other option. You perform another rescan for a possible lock. There has got to be something out there. Turn to 56.

80.

Maybe halfway along this lengthy corridor you begin taking heavy fire from behind you. You feel a laser beam hit your back, mostly absorbed by your armor, the remaining energy burning into your skin. Deduct 1 *vitality*. Melea takes a direct hit, the shot piercing her tattered armor. What little life was left in her body is extinguished and from the support of your shoulder she falls to the floor. She is surely dead and as you collapse with her also, you move across to hug a wall for some cover. Remove the words "Melea" and "fulcrum" from your mission sheet. Peering around one of the support beams at your attacker, you see it is an XBR agent, heavily armed with a triple barreled laser attached to his right forearm. He moves confidently down the corridor at a steady pace, looking to shoot you down. You're in a tough situation as running for it would leave you vulnerable and trying to take him on will be no easy feat and one you may not have time for anyway. Will you:

Fire back at the agent?	Turn to 28.
Make a run for it?	Turn to 38.

81.

'I like you because you bring me interesting stuff,' he says with a wry smile. 'Follow me,' he says, turning and walking towards the back of the room. Facing a board on the wall covered with tools, he lifts off one of the implements hanging up and pushes a small button which was behind it. You hear a click and notice the whole tool board swing open slightly. Kinlac shifts the tool board the rest of the way, revealing a doorway to a small room beyond. You follow him inside. There is a single workbench and shelves lined with dusty and unusual looking devices unfamiliar to you.

'I can decode them with this,' he says, brushing off a flat, rectangular handheld device.

Time passes as you watch as he goes to work. A short while later on his second attempt, the display of the device begins showing the contents of the first disc. You cannot make heads or tails of the schematics on display, but Kinlac obviously can, judging by his increasing grin.

'I need to get a copy of these right away,' Kinlac mutters.

You see what is happening. 'No,' you respond. 'They are not for free.'

'Ah yes, my apologies. What would you like for them,' he asks, hoping you will underestimate the value of the discs to him.

'Something of equal value,' you reply.

'I'll give you one hundred creds,' he states.

If you accept his offer for credits, turn to 25. If you reject the credits and insist on an item from his shelves, turn to 52.

82.

You have no need to report back the damage you did to the ship as the systems incorporated into your suit record your activities and relay the information back to Control. For each point of damage you caused to the ship, add 50 creds to your total. So for example if you did 3 points of damage, you have been granted 150 creds. Turn to 1300.

83.

You pause. Above the din of the ship and a low level grating sound nearby, you hear several thuds. It sounds like footsteps. Roll a die. If you roll a 1 or a 5, turn to 62. If you roll anything else, turn to 51.

84.

With the corporal out of the way, you source anything of use to you. You may take his *upgraded dual auto pistols* if you choose. Remove the word "filter" from your mission sheet and replace it with the word "deter". Roll one die. If you roll a 2, turn to 127, otherwise return to 590 and continue the reference.

85.

Bruised and beaten, Sjonn attempts to get away while you are down. If your capture tally is less than 5, turn to 862 now.

If your capture tally is 5 or more, test your resilience by rolling two dice and adding your *resilience*. If the total is 12 or more, you manage to recover in time; deduct 1 point from Sjonn's escape tally and return to 54 continuing the fight. If the total is 11 or lower, turn to 862.

86.

After a deep rest, you wake to find a video message left on your terminal. It is from your commander. You open it to see what he has to say:

'After consideration of your testimony and the information you provided, the Confederacy will be initiating a strike against the nearest

Leading Weapon Syndicate stronghold on Beutohn. This base of operations is largely unknown by most, in part because of the dense jungle there and also in part because they have actively tried to keep it hidden. However, we are aware of it and have a strike force en route. We will respond with the judgment of the council of the Confederacy for an unprovoked attack against another faction. For your part, we would like you to be part of the assault - no it is not an order due to your circumstances, but if you do help spearhead the strike I will ensure you receive full recognition for your part in all of this. For your mission just completed I have already given my commendations to the council and credits have been deposited for the evidence you obtained. Decide and respond agent.'

The video message ends.

You check to see your cred total. Add 300 creds to your total. Now you will have to decide if you will accept the mission or not:

If you do, continue your adventure as a Confederacy agent in book 2 of the Bionic Agent series: *Vault of carnage*.

If you decline the mission, you may finish delivering the supplies before returning to Phaeadron. In this case, continue your life as a Confederacy agent with book 3...

Whilst your mission here has ended and you have survived *Starship deadfall*;

If you have the word "footage" written down and have 3 or more identity scans, turn to 138. If not, turn to 1300.

87.

If you currently have no more unmarked time passed boxes on your mission sheet, turn to 270 now. Otherwise *time passes.* With the agent out of the way, you can search the room quickly. A large cabinet in the corner looks promising, and it happens to be unlocked as the agent was clearing out his things. Inside you find something wrapped up in cloth. Taking it out of the cabinet you strip away the layers to reveal a *paroxysm flail* which you may take with you if you choose. In a small box on the bench you also pick up 2 *stimserts* which may be useful.

Write the word "slain" on your mission sheet. You now leave the room. Turn to 32.

88.

Having wounded the agent he quickly withdraws back into the teleport room. Looking to finish him you rush to the door to find he has already jumped to another location. Replace the word "capacity" with the word "filter" and turn to 453.

89.

Add the word "slain" to your mission sheet. With the agent dead you take a moment to check his body. You find 2 *stimserts* he was carrying which you may take. There is also the weapon attached to his right arm. If you want to take this, turn to 23. Otherwise, turn to 48.

90.

A particular type of keypass is required here. Try yours now, if it does not work, as the door has a number of security characteristics you choose another option. Return to 32.

91.

The next room is a small preparation laboratory which you waste no time passing through. The corridor beyond turns once before bringing you to a junction. You head left, seeing the ramp which will take you to the next level and ultimately the teleport hub which you are trying to reach. The ship continues to shake, almost relentlessly now, destabilizing your movements as you go. Turn to 159.

92.

You sprint away, not looking back. Roll a die. If you roll a 1, turn to 1138. Otherwise, roll another die: If you roll 4 or more, turn to 78. If you roll 3 or less, turn to 126.

93.

Time passes. As the door of the decontamination room closes behind you, the automatic purging process begins. The air is sucked out through vents high in the wall whilst clean, filtered air is pumped back in. A bio scan lights up the whole room, engulfing you in a pale green glow. A short moment later the door at the other end unlocks and slides open. You step inside, finding yourself in an expansive darkened room. For whatever reason the lights are out in here, the only illumination at present which allows you to see anything at all is the light above you to the decontamination room as well as small sign lights you can see along one of the multiple aisles running away from you. Taking a couple of steps forward you reach the first sign light and see that it is for a room. It does not shine on the inside, but on the outside designating a specimen code for what the room contains. The room appears to be filled with these specimen holding pens, each aisle containing multiple pens. As you can only see the aisle you are looking down at the moment, it appears this aisle contains eight pens. As you are weighing up the situation you suddenly hear an ominous guttural sound echo around the room. Will you:

Head down the aisle you are in?	Turn to 168.
Head towards your left?	Turn to 149.
Head towards your right?	Turn to 120.

94.

Turn to 1245.

95.

Collecting your things you decide to head back into manufacturing through the maintenance tunnel. Do not return to the scrap compactor room in the future, you have found everything in this hidden room.

Will you:

Head towards the cabin?   Turn to 940.

Leave the area and return to upper deck via the ramp?

Turn to 796.

96.

If your *Bio* score is 4 or more, turn to 176. If it is 3 or less, roll a die. If your roll 4 or more, turn to 176, otherwise turn to 212.

97.

You quickly take out an explosive and place it on the door. Deduct the explosive from your inventory. Melea gets behind the table as you set the timer for a few seconds. The drones are close to cutting through as you rush to cover. Roll for *chance*.

If the result is 4 or more, turn to 150. If the result is 3 or less, turn to 348.

98.

Needing to stop momentarily as the ship shudders, you are taken aback as you see an object flying towards you, almost the size of your arm span. As it nears you see it is a sizeable drone, and it is well equipped with a variety of weapons.

Heavy drone	Ra	5
	Vitality	15
	See below for attack.	
	5+ to negate 5 damage armor for defense.	

>When the drone attacks, roll 1 die to see how it will do so:
1-2: On 2 dice, 3+ to hit, 3 damage.
3-4: On 3 dice, 5+ to hit, 4 damage.
5-6: On 1 die, 4+ to hit, 5 damage.
>If you need to or choose to flee this combat, resolve one combat round in which the drone attacks you, then after noting the current *vitality* of the drone, turn to 210.

If you defeat this formidable adversary, turn to 355.

99.

From your position you spot a large transparent container filled with a yellow liquid with tubes running out of the bottom of it stationed on a stand nearby. The stand is a tripod; if you shoot out the leg closest to the agent the stand should fall towards him. You decide to give it a shot. Some steady aiming does the trick, the leg gives out, causing the tripod to fall. Without support, the container falls toward the agent, shattering as it hits the bench, its yellow fluid splashing over the face and head of the enemy agent. He recoils in severe pain as the caustic substance eats into his flesh at a rapid pace. As his screams die down, you carefully make your way across to see the damage. He won't be identified by his face or iris that is for sure. Turn to 89.

100.

The room lights turn to a deep red. This you know signals battle mode. Seconds later a type of electrical fizz is heard – not loud, but unnerving none the less. An explosion elsewhere sends reverberations through the room. It came from outside the assault ship – you can tell the ship is still traveling. Another explosion and the ship rattles. Then only a moment later the sensations of a great force hits you. It is as if the ship has entered an atmosphere and you are encountering a tremendous gravitational force. But it is not an atmosphere, it is the XBR vessel itself that has been hit with the assault ship. The force continues and it is as if the attack ship is slowly pushing into the XBR vessel rather than colliding. The electrical fizz has escalated to a loud electrical cracking sound as the field on the front of the attack ship is eating into the XBR vessel. You suddenly think to yourself that when commander Ashkin said insertion, that is exactly what he meant.

Though it seems like everything is in slow motion, it does not take long before the assault ship has eaten far enough into the XBR vessel and come to a complete halt. The room lights turn white, brightening up the room and a siren sounds. The seat locks release and everyone is on their feet towards the door. You are fifth in line as you all quickly move out, single file.

From the wedged assault ship you and your team rapidly embark into a corridor with no lighting. Porz who is second in line throws down a hand held device which when it hits the floor lights up the whole corridor. Without hesitation the first in line fires his weapon blowing open the door at the end of the corridor. The team rushes through. You notice your visual display being updated as the map on it expands – the other teams are also on board. The next corridor is lit and a siren is sounding. Up ahead you see two men enter into the corridor from a room on the right. They bolt in the opposite direction to your advancing team.

'Rumiq take point,' barks commander Ashkin directly into your ear. Rumiq quickly moves to the head of the line and heads to the end of the corridor. Fourth in line Tubblurin enters a room on the left and seeks out a terminal. You follow him and take up a defensive stance at the door. The team spreads out, taking up positions and investigating rooms. Several unarmed people are discovered but they are left alone. A few moments later Tubblurin looks up to you and reports:

'Nothing here. It doesn't have the access. All I can tell is this is Sector F.'

'Move on blue team,' barks the commander.

The team regroups and meets at the end of the corridor. Being in search mode, the team divides in two, with half going left and half going right. Your new group, consisting of the odd numbers of the previous line all head left. No one is to be seen in this corridor – your team ignores the several rooms and keeps moving. You know time is against you.

The corridor ends and again your team splits up. Being an odd number again, you head left, now with two other team mates. This corridor turns to the right and Zak, your first in line takes a look around the corner. He signals silently that it is clear. All three of you move forward.

Half way up the corridor Zak finds a double door of interest. It has no security and so he walks straight in. Situated in the middle of the room is a large table with a hologram projected above it. Three men are at the table in discussion. They all freeze as your team enters.

'Get me a map of this ship,' orders Zak, pointing his gun at the man who was talking at the time.

'I.. I can't do that,' stammers the man.

'Yes you will if you want to keep your head,' rebuttals Zak, practically putting his gun in the man's face.

'No I mean I c-c-can't… I don't know if that's even possible.'

As Zak thinks twice your other team mate Melea has taken up position guarding the door while you keep your weapon trained on the other seated men. In frustration Zak turns to the hologram and begins manipulating the icons.

'We have incoming!' Yells Melea before she pulls back into the room.

'Two drones,' she barks as she moves to find cover. 'Flying – and they're moving fast.' Will you:

Take cover opposite to Melea on the other side of the door?

Turn to 45.

Take cover behind the table?   Turn to 170.

101.

At the receiving teleporter you are greeted by a short man with a bushy beard. He is the captain of the ship you are now on, which is a surveying ship traveling through the atmosphere of Beutohn. Apart from yourself he has received two other people which he says are crew from the XBR starship. They are resting with one of them wounded he tells you, so you decide to steer clear of them. The captain has decided to cut short his work to survey the forests of Beutohn and to return to Fenbannc; the main Confederacy colony situated on the moon. You ask the captain whom either seems disinterested in your alliance or turns a blind eye about using the ships com-link. He quietly agrees, allowing you to make use of the communication device to send a message to commander Ashkin. If you have the *Proto-swipe* mission, turn to 74. If you have the *Techno savage* mission, turn to 179.

102.

Rounding the end of the aisle you see the creature. You pull up and momentarily freeze at the sight, it's hulky, inky black form is chilling to behold. It moves carefully and intently, as if it is stalking you, making full use of the shadows of the room. Turn to 26.

103.

You make a dash for the door. Roll 3 dice. For each 4 or more, suffer 3 damage, though you may roll for defense. If you make it to the door alive, your next challenge will be to get the door open. Fortunately the circuit for the door is more accessible than most of the other doors you have encountered on the ship. To get the door open, continue the battle with Kylgren. During your turn to attack however, you may forgo your attack and instead work on the door. To work on the door, roll a die and add your *tech* score. If the result is 7 or more, you have opened the door and entered: turn at once to 1167. Make a note of this so you know what to do, then return to 144 and continue the fight using Kylgren's current *vitality* score.

104.

You're still in one piece and still breathing. No time to patch up the wounds here. You take off again, bent on making it to the end of the corridor by whatever means it takes. Turn to 163.

105.

Turning, you bolt down the corridor, taking a corner without slowing. The agent pursues. Test your agility by rolling two dice and adding your *agility*. If the total is 13 or more, turn to 1257. If the total is 12 or less, turn to 1212.

106.

Turn to the reference according to the codeword you have written down:

Analog:	Turn to 1145.
Quaint:	Turn to 121.
Ardent:	Turn to 99.
Extant:	Turn to 57.
Slant:	Turn to 47.
Fountain:	Turn to 17.
Slam:	Turn to 1158.
Delete:	Turn to 227.

107.

To use your shock pistol, roll to hit as normal. If you score a hit and Sjonn fails his defense roll to dodge the attack, deduct 1 point from Sjonn's escape tally and add 1 point to your capture tally. Sjonn will also be *shocked* for the next combat round. Now return to 54, remembering you cannot use your shock pistol in the next combat round.

108.

You have the feeling there could have been more you could have learnt of the happenings aboard the ship. None the less you are alive, having escaped the failing ship and you managed to score some vital data for Control. Now, for the time being on your way to Beutohn you wait as predictably there will only be a short down time before the next mission is issued. Add 100 creds to your total. Turn to 82.

109.

After exiting the lab, the corridor turns to the right, taking you in the direction towards starboard. The corridor is lengthy but fully lit and you can spot three rooms along here, each with a keypass scanner beside the door. Will you:

Stop to enter any of the rooms?	Turn to 32.
Keep moving to the end of the corridor?	Turn to 58.

110.

As if the constant alarm and gradual disintegration of the ship was not enough, stepping out of the teleport room is an XBR agent - and he has you in his sights. Will you:

Fight the agent?	Turn to 132.
Try to evade the agent?	Turn to 234.

111.

You fire at the scientists before they can leave the room. One is instantly killed and another wounded. The agent retaliates by bringing his gun to bear on your location. Roll 2 dice. For each 5 or 6, suffer 3 damage, though you may roll for defense. You will have to deal with the agent. Add the word "slant" to your mission sheet and turn to 144.

112.

If you hadn't been looking you would not have noticed you are beside a very short corridor on this side of the room. The tiny light of the manual open button was the giveaway. You do not however know where the door leads. If it is just a storage compartment you may be worse off. Will you:

Try the door?   Turn to 206.

Leave the door and continue to try to get to the other side of the room?   Turn to 123.

113.

If you currently have no more unmarked time passed boxes on your mission sheet, turn to 270 now. Otherwise *time passes.* The agent dead on the floor, you take a moment to search the room. There is a cabinet in the corner as well as draws and shelves, some of which are now bare. Fortunately the weapon cabinet in the corner is unlocked as the agent was grabbing his things to leave. Inside the cabinet you pull out and unwrap from some loose cloth a *paroxysm flail* which you may take with you if you choose. There is not much else here though you note one thing of significance. The dead agent's right forearm is a powerful gun which you could use. If you choose, you may cut off his arm and take the weapon, which is a *laser blaster*. You cannot however use the weapon whilst you are on the starship as you will need to remove the flesh still attached to it and clean it up. Normally this weapon is used in the fashion you just saw it - as a replacement for a hand and forearm usually lost in battle. Once cleaned up however it is possible to use it by rigging it to hold onto. If you do this once off the starship then the item counts as *heavy* - see the item description for details. Write the word "slain" on your mission sheet. You now leave the room. Turn to 32.

114.

Changing your position slightly to get a better view you peer over a cluttered bench to see the individual heading towards the starboard-bow corner with several scientists made obvious by their lab coats leading the way. Judging by the armor and markings you would say the individual is an esteemed XBR agent. Turn to 72.

115.

It looks as though out of the two teleporters capable of sending you off ship, one of them is still working; the other has no readout whatsoever. Quickly you try to find a destination lock on the functioning teleporter. Roll for *chance*. If the result is 4 or more, turn to 56. If the result is 3 or less, turn to 6.

116.

At the end of the aisle, you can now see the exit leading out of the room. There is no sign of the creature that lurks somewhere in the room which is somewhat concerning as it could be on the far side or it could be near, as a hunter ready to strike. You decide to move swiftly yet quietly towards the door while you have the chance. Choose to either be more cautious and watchful or quicker as you make your way to the door by using either your *perception* or your *agility* in this next test. When you have chosen which you will use (either perception or agility), then you may make a single die roll, adding them together. If you have the *evasion* ability or a *resilience* of 7 or more you may add 1 to the total. If the result is 9 or more, turn to 68. If the end result is 8 or less, turn to 164.

117.

Grab your cutting tool and begin working on the door. Roll 2 dice and consult your item for the result needed. If you manage to cut or break through on your first attempt, turn to 174. If you fall short, keep hacking away by rolling again. For this additional attempt, *time passes.* You may add 1 to the result of your dice roll for the work you have already done on the door. If you are through, turn to 174, otherwise continue to repeat the process; each attempt marking off another *time passed* box on your mission sheet and again adding an additional 1 point to your roll for the damage done previously.

118.

You have managed to free yourself from the slavery of the XBR starship on which you were held captive. Though you have no one to praise you, it is reward enough to claim your freedom and successfully escape the clutches of the XBR faction whom you deem illegally use slave labor which the Confederacy turns a blind eye to. Ultimately you want to get back to Phaeadron. However you may choose to lay low for a while on Beutohn.

If you plan to stay on Beutohn for a while, then continue your adventure by reading book 2 in the series: *Vault of carnage.* Otherwise If you decide to head straight to Phaeadron, there will be teleporters at the docking station for the supply ship. You will be able to teleport there easily enough. To do this, continue your life, unaligned with any faction and now free from any also by reading the 3rd book in the **Bionic Agent** series... Turn to 1300.

119.

Add the word "solid" to your mission sheet. You spin around and activate a stenciling tool normally used to mark tissue samples with circuitry using a laser. You ramp up the settings to put the laser at full power. You input a sequence for the stenciling device to run. It is ready to go and will start shortly. You spin the instrument around once more and direct the armature with the laser on it towards the scientist, pointing at his back but to the left side where his heart is. His data transfer is about to finish and he is jittery in anticipation. You are hoping he will stay still enough but if your plan fails you can always shoot him you think as you ready yourself. The arm of the machine jerks slightly as it makes a micro adjustment. It would normally fault out at this point as it cannot read the sample below it, but you have overridden that manually. The laser fires and the armature moves around within a space not much larger than your thumb. The laser cuts into the scientist, burning through his coat and skin and into his heart. Fortunately the laser burns a small hole in the front of his lab coat where the laser exited his body, but hardly continues into the room. With a short gasp hardly noticeable by the others in the room amongst the noise of the ship, the scientist slumps to the floor. You quickly crawl around the desk without being spotted to check the body and retrieve the data store which has now finished transferring. The scientist was MInkla. In a moment he will be noticed missing, so you keep on the move, sneaking around the port side of the room towards the bow.

Just as you are heading down one of the short storage aisles you hear someone call out. They have found the body. While they are distracted, you move swiftly to the starboard-bow corner to the door to the operating room. By the time they figure out what has happened you should be long gone. Turn to 1284.

120.

You decide to head to the right and select one of the aisles there to head along. Will you:

Pick one of the nearby aisles?   Turn to 1229.
Head right to the end and choose the last aisle?   Turn to 1155.

121.

From where you are, if you can reach the door you can still remain in cover even if you cannot open the door. It may be a risk getting there however. If you choose to make a run for it, turn to 103. If you do not want to risk it, return to 144 and continue the battle.

122.

Sending off your report to the commander, you can only wait to see a response when you return back to base. You'd consider the mission a disaster with the heavy casualties and numerous unanswered questions. There is obviously more to the picture you are not privy to at this point; more that you may need to find out independent of orders from your commander. Payment will still be received for your duties. Add to your credit total 400 creds. Meanwhile in the upper atmosphere of the moon Beutohn, the doomed XBR starship undergoes the final series of explosions which destroy the ship, sending countless fragments out to burn up upon descent. Turn to 287.

123.

Choose how to proceed. Will you:
Keep moving toward the end of the aisle?   Turn to 341.
Head back and try to get through along another aisle? Turn to 220.

124.

While hopefully pre-occupied you sneak around behind the man. Over the far side of the room there is a lot of talking going on which seems to serve well to detract any attention from you. You're now behind the man, only two bench tops away. From his armor he is an XBR agent. There is nothing for it; you launch yourself at him, catching him unaware. As the other occupants in the room disband in the ensuing chaos, you pummel your opponent and dig your weapon in.

Make two attacks with your close quarter weapon (or unarmed). Make a note of the damage done. The agent throws you aside and falls across a bench top while one of the scientists makes a futile attempt to attack you with his bare hands. The scientist is easily dispatched but in the meantime the enemy agent has taken up position across the room and opens fire. Add the word "extant" to your mission sheet and turn to 144, but deduct the damage you just did from the *vitality* of Kylgren.

125.

There is so much going on that you have yet to attract any attention to you. But your involvement in this mass battle is inevitable. Perform any preparatory action you need to and then roll one die and add your *perception*. If you score 8 or above, turn to 73. If you score 7 or less, turn to 130.

126.

Roll a die. If you roll a 1 or a 2, turn to 180. If you roll anything else, turn to 246.

127.

The ship shakes yet again: it seems you have even less time than you thought as the disintegration of the ship ramps up further. *Time passes*, now return to 590 and continue where you left off.

128.

With no weapon (you have no items whatsoever, regardless of your character) you will have to be careful and try to obtain one. Your other priority will be to disable the labor bracelet. Write the word "bracelet" on your mission sheet. You move to the door and check the corridor.

It is clear at present. Take either:

The corridor towards starboard and follow it around towards the bow: Turn to 465.

The corridor towards portside and follow it around towards the bow: Turn to 551.

129.

Opening the cell proves to be impossible - it functions on a timer or requires authorization to open the cell manually. Since the woman is infected you determine it may not be the best idea anyway.

If you have not already done so:

Head to the main terminal near the center of the room:Turn to 305.

Check the cells to see if any are occupied: Turn to 588.

Check the storage cupboards for anything of use: Turn to 455.

Alternatively leave the room: Turn to 451.

130.

You are busy seeking out targets on the loading bay floor. Meanwhile a large grotty looking man has climbed a nearby access ladder and is about to hammer you with a large metal tool of some sort. You are able to face him in close quarters just short of being clobbered:

Mechanical worker	CQ	4
	Vitality	14

4+ to hit, 2 damage.

No defense.

>Remember to roll on any of the appropriate battle tables. (At this stage it is likely you can only score a result on the *Domination* table if you are using a weapon which uses 2 attacking dice and roll a double 6.)

If you defeat the worker, turn to 12.

131.

Roll a die. If you roll a 1 or a 2, turn to 60. If you roll 3 or more, turn to 42.

132.

You begin taking fire from the agent at short range:

XBR *agent Nethit* Ra		5
	Vitality	24

On 2 dice, 4+ to hit, 3 damage.
5+ to negate 3 damage as defense.

>If you need to flee at any point, resolve one free attack against you as you make a run for it. Then turn to 105.

>If you reduce the agent's *vitality* to less than 10, turn to 88.

133.

Whilst you do intend to get back to Phaeadron eventually, since the ship is heading that way, you consider the possibility of staying on Beutohn for a short while; perhaps to pick up supplies before heading back out.

If you choose, you may spend some time on Beutohn by reading the next book 2 in the **Bionic Agent** series: *Vault of carnage.*

If you prefer to head to Phaeadron as soon as possible, there will no doubt be a teleportation hub at the docking station for the supply ship you are on. In this case, move on to book 3 in the series. Your *Biohazard borrower* mission is not yet over. Retain this mission even if you read book 2 next and take on another 'side' mission. You will not be able to complete this mission until you return to Phaeadron in book 3. Additionally it is also critical you retain any item specific to this mission that you are carrying as you have written it down on your mission sheet. Turn to 1300.

134.

Well lit and wide enough for 2 people to stand side by side, the corridor has several other single doors which you ignore. Checking your visuals you note the progress of the other teams as well as the indications they are encountering hostile situations. The corridor ends in a T-junction. Zak looks both ways and checks his visuals. 'This way,' he says plainly and you follow him to the right. The corridor is the same as the ones before – well lit and bleak. The team keeps moving at a rapid pace, a siren is still blaring in the background. Out of one of the doorways springs a uniformed man whom upon glancing at your team turns around and runs. Leading the way Zak neither shoots at him nor tries to chase him down. Just then you hear Commander Ashkin in your ear;

'Keep moving, you should soon reach the loading bay – we need you there immediately for support.'

With that Zak ups the pace. Another right turn at the end of the corridor.

Suddenly you hear the zing of a laser shot. You look back to see a pursuing drone and before you even have time to stop and turn around, Melea has responded with a laser of her own and taken the drone out. There is no pause, the team continues forward, turning left at the next intersection. Zak has stopped. A large double door lies in front of him. An explosion is heard emanating from the other side of the door. Zak signals you and Melea to take positions as he readies himself to open the door. You do so and he waves his hand over the sensor.

The doors slide open. *Time passes.* (Mark off the first time passed box on your mission sheet)

Looking inside you see the loading bay is a massive room filled with multiple levels, walkways and mostly of cargo, ships and containers of all sorts.

It appears you are on the second level with a walkway running left and right from the door. You can see several LWS agents of the red team on the opposite side of the level above you in a shootout with XBR crew further along their walkway. Down below on the loading bay floor you see more LWS agents – this time a mixture of two teams, both yellow and blue, scattered amongst the cargo and under fire from enemies on the floor to your left. Various other battles are taking place on other levels – this is a veritable fire fight. Zak is still surveying the situation. Will you:

Take a long range shot at the XBR guards on the level opposite and above you?   Turn to 279.

Try to take a shot at an enemy on the loading bay floor?

Turn to 312.

Wait for a call from Zak?   Turn to 183.

135.

Remove the item from your inventory. Grabbing the grenade, you lob it in the direction of Kylgren.

The grenade explodes, sending pieces of equipment flying. The grenade will do the base damage listed in the description. If you have thrown a *high impact grenade*, add 3 damage to the total. If you have thrown a *scatter grenade*, add 1 damage to the total. Additionally if your *chance* score is greater than zero, add another 1 point of damage. Deduct this value from Kylgren's *vitality*, ignoring his armor defense. His new position enables him to be ready for any more grenades: if you throw another grenade in this combat it will only do the base damage in the item description and the agent will be allowed his defense roll as usual. Now return to 144 and continue the fight.

136.

The scientists all start heading toward the restricted area, one after the other. You look to follow them but stay out of sight at least for now. What you hadn't planned for however is an XBR agent that you suddenly see get up from a concealed position over the side of the room and begin following the scientists. The agent will surely be a problem. Will you:

Fire upon all of the remaining scientists?   Turn to 111.
Aim for the XBR agent?   Turn to 76.

137.

Time passes. Once past the loading bay doors and safe in the loading bay hall you can slow down to catch your breath as you keep moving towards the end of the loading bay. There are a number of security guards all on the move heading towards the loading bay to help defend. Fortunately for you they have their orders and ignore you as a non-threat. Reaching the end of the hall you take a ramp which twists around and eventually brings you to a corridor which runs from port side to starboard.

Will you:

Take the corridor towards starboard?	Turn to 397.
Head towards port side?	Turn to 407.

138.

You have done exceptionally well with your mission and for the additional identity scans and thorough surveillance video data you have been awarded an additional 200 creds. If you have the word "judge" written down, turn to 333. If not, turn to 1300.

139.

Worth a try, you muster all of your strength to push the door open. Roll 2 dice and add your *strength*. If your *vitality* is 15 or more you may reroll one of the dice once only. If the result is 14 or more, turn to 233. If the result is 13 or less you will have to repeat the process and keep pushing. Each repeat will incur a *time passes* though you may add an extra 1 to the dice roll for the progress already made. When you are through, turn to 233.

140.

'All done,' Kinlac says boastfully with his characteristic smile. Gesturing towards the bench you see the laser cutter where you left it. Maybe not 'as good as new' as he claimed, but it is cleaner and with a quick power on, seems to be functioning fine. Your *high speed laser cutter* is no longer damaged and functions fine. To equip yourself with the item, you will require a utility socket to plug it into. You thank Kinlac for his work. Turn again to 818 if you have other business with Kinlac or turn straight to 451 to leave the room.

141.

The footsteps suddenly start again, increasing in tempo and loudness. Whatever it is, it is moving fast. Turn to 26.

142.

You do not have to wait long – in moments the drones have cut a hole large enough for them to enter.

They both fly in and Zak is quick to take the first one out. Roll for *chance*.

If the result is 4 or more, turn to 188. If the result is 3 or less, turn to 61.

143.

Add 1 to your *chance* score <u>if it is zero or less.</u> You hear movement. The steps are heavy and they are not far away - possibly toward the end of the aisle. Will you:

Run for it now?	Turn to 292.
Stay in the shadows for the moment?	Turn to 544.

144.

You are under attack from an XBR agent. He has you pinned with his formidable weapon - his whole right forearm is one triple barrelled laser gun.

XBR agent Kylgren	Ra	6
	Vitality	20

On 3 dice, 5+ to hit, 3 damage.
5+ to negate 3 damage as defense.

>You are pinned and therefore need to defeat Kylgren, but in the event of needing some way to escape the situation to avoid death, turn to 106.

If you manage to kill the agent, turn to 89.

145.

Time passes. There is much to go through, you have to check each group of files manually. A small fire started from the earlier fight has now increased in size across the other side of the room. Meanwhile the ship shakes more violently than before. Will you:

Push on searching the databases manually?   Turn to 211.
Get out now, leaving via the restricted surgical room? Turn to 1284.
Stop searching and leave via the unmarked starboard door?

Turn to 317.

146.

Time passes. At the end of the corridor you see there is a t-intersection with a sign indicating sector A. After a short distance you notice a putrid smell wafting through the air and upon finding a door on your left you open it to look inside. The stench fills your nostrils nearly causing you to vomit. The room opens up into a large sanitary facility which is a mess from spillages and broken tanks. You cannot stay even if you wanted to, the air thick with foul smelling vapors not fit to be breathed. Indeed most of this sector may be for sanitary and recycling purposes if the size of the room is anything to go by. You would guess there is no teleport hub in this sector either. Will you:

Continue along this corridor regardless?   Turn to 276.
Head back to the previous corridor?   Turn to 715.

147.

The plans are encoded on the disc and so may only be helpful to you if you are able to decode them. Second to that, if there are other discs, since this is labeled 1963, then you may need another disc for the information to make sense. If you find another disc, subtract the lower value from the higher and turn to the given reference for a clue (remembering the reference you are on). You may add the disc to your inventory as a miscellaneous item. Turn to 95.

148.

While the agent is off balance and against the wall you run out of the room and down the corridor to get away. It is more important that you stay alive and you know that if you don't get off this ship shortly, neither you nor the other agent will live to tell the tale. Turn to 58.

149.

You choose one of the far aisles and begin heading down carefully. The aisle appears like the others with only the signage providing minimal lighting. Aside from the background noise of the ship the room appears eerily quiet. Your senses pick up a low level fluttering from a pen you are passing on the left. Looking up at the next pen which appears to take up the rest of the aisle you see the illuminated signage designating the contents: HK-01. But the remarkable thing about this pen is you notice that the thick door is wide open. A vicious snarl rings through the room. You suspect that whatever was in that pen is now roaming around this room. Roll a die. If you roll a 1 or a 2, turn to 192. If you roll anything else, turn to 256.

150.

Deduct 1 from your *chance* score. Just as the drones have cut through and begin to enter, the explosive detonates. The timing is spot on and the ensuing blast destroys both the drones and the door. They may be thinking it was overkill but your team mates are pleased with the result also. After the smoke clears the three of your proceed down the corridor. Turn to 134.

151.

The control panel displays a defeating message: "No lock found". You make some adjustments to the scanner and try again; you have no other options here. Roll a die. If the result is 4 or more, turn to 56. If the result is 3 or less, turn to 153.

152.

In one of the draws you find a *photon grenade* which you may take if you choose. You leave the room immediately. Turn to 32.

153.

Time passes. Still nothing, no lock can be found. Using the control panel you force the machine to rescan, extending the range at the expense of a longer scan time. Turn to 56.

154.

Bringing your weapon to bear on the man across the room, you are surprised when he intuitively looks your way and reacts by ducking. Your first shot is a miss. This is clearly a well-trained individual; he rolls beside another bench and fires back at you, tearing up the place with some heavy firepower. Add the word "ardent" to your mission sheet and turn to 144.

155.

Another rattle courses through the corridor as the ship takes more punishment. Approaching you from the stern corridor is a corporal wielding auto pistols which he fires in quick succession.

Corporal Fullim	Ra	5
	CQ	5
	Vitality	20

On 2 dice, 5+ to hit, 3 damage.
5+ to reduce damage by 2 as defense.

>To begin combat the corporal will assault you, firing both his pistols aggressively until he nears you. In the first round of combat, Fullim may reroll both his to hit dice once if he misses.

If you defeat the corporal, turn to 84.

156.

Making use of the nearby teleport room you duck inside and jump to another sector. It looks as though you may have lost him as he cannot tell which area you teleported to. Remove the word "deter" from your mission sheet. Roll one die. On a 4 or more, turn to 604. On a 3 or less, turn to 525.

157.

You begin taking a look around the room starting with the work areas. There are scattered utensils and bits of something thick, gluey and dark green splattered about the place you find, lighting up small sections at a time with your built in torch. There is a small carry cage propped up on one of the benches which looks to be out of the ordinary. As you get closer you realize the door or side of the cage has been removed and then, in the blink of an eye something leaps out at you from inside. The small creature latches onto your arm and sinks its teeth into you. You recoil in pain before launching the little thing across the room and into a wall. Deduct 3 *vitality*. Roll a die. If you roll a 1 or a 2 you will be fine, if you roll 3 or above then add the *infected* lingering effect for the bite. You decide to get out of the room quickly. Turn to 280.

158.

Turn to the following reference according to the word you have written down:

"Deter":	Turn to 328.
"Filter":	Turn to 1285.
"Capacity":	Turn to 110.
None of these words:	Turn to 1094.

159.

At the top of the ramp you take a left at the intersection, the signs indicating the correct way to the teleport hub. You move fast as the ship does not seem to have long left. Fortunately the lights and teleporters are independently powered with their own ambient energy accumulators and the artificial gravity will likely be the last thing to go. You pass through a junction without letting up. There is no sign of anyone; perhaps there is no one else left aboard. Along the corridor you are in you spot two rooms with keypass scanners beside the doors, indicating they are rooms of importance. At the same time however, you may not have time on your side. Will you:

Try the first door?	Turn to 30.
Try the second door?	Turn to 510.
Keep moving?	Turn to 3.

160.

The clues you have gathered about the alien hybrid experiments may be valuable to you at a later date. Make a note of the number 531 and keep it recorded for future reference. For now though, return to your previous reference.

161.

As a Confederacy member killing members of another faction without a warrant is either frowned upon for the lightest of cases or results in an agent being marshaled and stripped of their rank and allegiance for the more severe cases. The Confederacy is in no way supportive of the XBR faction, however if reports are received by command of unjustified killing or harming committed by a trusted Confederacy agent, then you may have to deal with the consequences from your superiors.

For your previous action, if you have not done so already, begin a tally on your mission sheet: Dishonor: and start the tally at 1. If you already have a tally running, add 1 to the total. This tally is permanent - even if you complete your mission and begin a new one in a later book, retain this tally. Remember your Confederacy oath and note that the reputation of the faction is held higher than your position as an expendable agent. Now return to your previous reference.

162.

Entering the room it looks as though you are in a rest and recuperation room.

[If you have the word "reel" written down, turn to 69.]

You survey the room with haste. You have no time to use one of the rejuvenation cells and the place looks a mess as it has obviously been raided prior to people evacuating. Will you:

Perform a quick search through some of the mess?   Turn to 1253.
Leave and try the second door?   Turn to 510.
Head back into the corridor and keep moving?   Turn to 3.

163.

At the end of the corridor you race up a ramp that takes you up to the next level. The sign at the top points you in the right direction towards the teleport hub; you run hard, passing through a couple of junctions before finally reaching your destination. Having reached the door you look inside to see the room in a state of disarray. Some of the equipment is clearly damaged with smoldering readout panels and sparks shooting out of a control board on the wall. If you have no more unmarked time passed boxes left on your mission sheet, turn to 115. If you have 1 unmarked box remaining, turn to 36. If you have 2 or more unmarked boxes remaining, turn to 59.

164.

As you move toward the door you also hear something else move. Heavy footsteps reverberate around the room, an ominous thunder of something you know is after you. You reach the door. You hit the button to open the door manually and spin around to defend yourself while the door slides open. Something large with an obsidian black appearance charges toward you. The door is open, you spin around passing into the room, but as you do so, you feel something rip across your back. Roll 2 dice. For each 4 or more, deduct 3 *vitality*, ignoring your defense. Despite the wound you hit the button to close the door. You watch as the door slides shut, granting you protection as it crushes a clawed finger at the same time. A deep guttural sound can be heard followed by violent bangs against the door. You expect the door will hold - for now. Turn to 55.

165.

There may be more than one way to take out the scientist. There is a piece of lab equipment on a bench behind the scientist which could be made lethal with some tweaking. If you think you want to try this, turn 119. If you are not sure or plan to take him out with your weapon, turn to 1091.

166.

Covered in rags you spot an interesting item tucked away on a low shelf. Unveiling it you realize it is a *continuous high speed laser cutter* though a somewhat damaged one at that. You may take this item if you like, but note that it requires a utility socket to attach to and it is also damaged and unless repaired, unusable. Make a note that it is damaged for it also cannot be sold for any creds unless it is working. Write the word "wrench" on your mission sheet. You may investigate the starboard side by turning to 266 or leave the room by turning to 451.

167.

Reduce your *chance* score by 1 point. Passing some creepy looking creatures you make it to the door without incident. You head through into the corridor beyond. Turn to 91.

168.

Carefully you head straight down the aisle you are in. You are keen to simply get to the other side and get out of this room, but at the same time you are cautious, given how dark the room is and the sound you just heard which sounded like it was *outside* any of the holding pens. Will you:

Hold up, just for a moment?	Turn to 83.
Keep moving?	Turn to 71.

169.

Your shot misses your target, hitting the walkway railing. The agent hits the floor – hit by another shot that may not have killed him but he is down for now. Fortunately the agents are too engaged in a shootout with members of the red team to take aim back at you. That battle however is little compared to the chaos playing out on the loading bay floor. Turn to 183.

170.

You take up position behind the table. Melea takes up position beside the door, activating the doors to close while Zak is nearby behind the table. Only a moment later you can hear the sound of the two drones on the other side of the door. It is the familiar buzz of a scanner sweep. The room is silent with the team in position, the three men cowering under the table.

'Can they open that door?' Asks Zak quietly but firmly to the men under the table.

None of the men answer. Zak begins to repeat the question;

'Can they open th...' he stops himself short as two lasers begin cutting into the door from the other side.

'This could get ugly,' Melea jokingly remarks. Will you:

Wait, with your weapon trained at the door?	Turn to 236.
Grab one of the men to use as a shield?	Turn to 360.

171.

Inside the lab there appears to be something outputting a distinct sulfuric type of smell. Maybe it is an experiment that has been left unattended. On the nearest bench you can see work notes scattered across the surface and a broken beaker with a puddle of clear liquid around it. Will you:

Take a brief look at the notes?   Turn to 96.

Steer clear of mess and head straight to the door on the far side?

Turn to 109.

172.

Another scientist over towards starboard is motioning toward the restricted area, about to pass behind the translucent panel. His number you saw was 229. The scientist you saw earlier - 237 - has now begun moving in the same direction. Will you:

Take out the scientist 229 before he leaves?   Turn to 1245.

Take out the scientist 237?   Turn to 1091.

Wait even longer?   Turn to 136.

173.

Your movement has not gone unnoticed. Turn to 26.

174.

Busting through the door you move on, undeterred by any such obstacles. The corridor turns toward starboard, bringing you to a door on your left. You enter the room, a decontamination chamber. Turn to 93.

175.

Fortunately the door is not locked; a small wheel valve opens the hatch and you duck inside, slamming the hatch closed behind you. You take only a few steps down the corridor to find a series of containers all stacked from floor to ceiling, blocking the corridor. A simple test proves the containers are full of materials and you can now see that there are many of them in a line. It looks as though you are trapped as the narrow gaps between the containers is barely large enough for a child to pass through. If you have the *Contortion* ability, turn to 1169. If you do not have this ability, you see two choices:

Wait where you are and see if the drone passes by or leaves:

Turn to 309.

Take a moment allowing the drone to pass by then head back out:

Turn to 260.

176.

From what you can tell as the notes are quite sketchy since they were meant for the writer, the few tests that were being run were in relation to the duplication of muscle fiber activation of a specimen known as HK-01. The particular activation ability of the muscles of this specimen are unique as they will still fire even when depleted of an energy source or torn. You keep moving. Turn to 109.

177.

As you progress cautiously you hear another few footsteps, this time slower and not as loud. Roll for *chance*. If you roll 4 or more, turn to 219. If you roll 3 or less, turn to 141.

178.

Your keypass has worked. Turn to 13.

179.

Look at the words you have written down. If you can form the word "puppet" by combining two of the words you have written down, turn to 122. If you can only form part of this word, turn to 247. If you cannot form any part of this word, turn to 321.

180.

Time passes. The ship shakes yet again, another reminder that time is not on your side. Hopefully the shaking will help to throw the alien off your trail. Roll a die. If you rolled 4 or more, turn to 246. If you rolled 3 or less, turn to 294.

181.

Write the word "recover" on your mission sheet. The double doors open automatically for you and once inside you realize you are in a small training facility of some sort. The place is a mess and you notice two bodies on the floor and another slumped up against one off the walls. Upon closer inspection you realize it is Rumiq. He sits against one of the walls staring blankly across the room. You check his pulse and realize he is dead though his hand is still warm, so his death must have been recent. He has a large hole in his guts and is covered in his own blood. Closing his eyes you decide to leave the scene as there is nothing you can do. He had with him a *twin pulse rifle* which you may take if you choose. The signal on your visual display has now disappeared. Remove the word "Rumiq" from your mission sheet. Head to the exit and turn to 715.

182.

You find nothing here. Try again.

183.

Zak makes his call; 'We'll hold position and help clear a path for the teams on the floor.'

Each of you finds a position to fire from, using the doorway as cover. Zak is first to find a clear shot through the smoke and chaos. His laser beam cuts a man down from where he was trying to hide. You see an individual about to run between cover and seize the opportunity. Take a short range shot.

If you hit, turn to 228. If you miss or are unable to shoot, turn to 125.

184.

Now that he has turned around, you see the crew number of the scientist at the door. It is 229. He speaks to the man approaching him who just entered.

'The door won't open. We'll have to go through the operating room,' he exclaims.

'What are you waiting for then,' retorts the other scientist as he moves swiftly across the room. You catch a glimpse of his crew number: 231. The scientists are moving apart, with one heading towards the door to the operating room while the one that just entered towards the stern. You need to make a decision. Whichever target you choose, the others are likely to start running as soon as you kill one of them. There are also the other scientists over towards the stern. Will you:

Take out the scientist 229 heading towards the operating room?

Turn to 1245.

Take out the scientist 231 as he heads toward the stern side of the room?

Turn to 1063.

Let the situation play out further and sneak around the room?

Turn to 1153.

185.

Test your agility by rolling 2 dice and adding your *agility*. If your total is 12 or more, turn to 156. If your total is 11 or less the guard keeps up with you, requiring you to turn and face him; turn to 1034.

186.

Time passes. Traveling along the corridor towards port side you are on alert looking for danger. You don't know if there are LWS agents on this level or if an XBR crew member might suspect you or use some device to detect that you are not where you are meant to be. As if to answer your thoughts a uniformed man rounds a corner ahead and heads straight for you. You keep moving and give him minimal attention. He appears unarmed though in a hurry and fortunately only sends you are sharp look as he passes by. You reach the junction ahead. Turn to 407.

187.

Watching carefully from your crouched hiding place, you see little happening. As *time passes* with patience, something begins to happen.

You hear talking emanating from the far side of the room and then you see movement. The individual is leaving his position. Will you:

Open fire? Turn to 154.

Continue watching? Turn to 114.

188.

Without skipping a beat Zak fires another shot, taking out the second drone also.

'Looks like you don't even need us,' says Melea to Zak. A brief smile is shown by Zak which you note is a rarity for him. Then it is back to business and the three of you re-open the door and head down the corridor. Turn to 134.

189.

You enter into the room. *Time passes.*

[If you have the word "weave" written down, turn to 252 now.]

Inside you find yourself in a combination office and living quarters. Quickly you search, looking for anything of value. On the far side of the room you find a display cabinet. Inside there is a sealed box about the size of your head with a transparent top. You can see inside, through the window on the top; the box contains parts intended for surgical implantation. Whoever occupied this room previously was intending to upgrade their body. You may take this item if you choose, though you will have to take the box as it is to keep the contents of the box untouched. If you do so, add a *Brain stem interface* to your inventory as a regular item (as it is still in the box uninstalled). This item is an implant and as such to use it will require surgery to install. You look elsewhere in the room. If you have the word "solid" written down, turn to 1236. If you do not have this word written down, turn to 1187.

190.

Reaching another junction, you look both ways. Then you see it. A door at the end of one of the tunnels closing. Already drained you sprint to the door, the strenuous task taking its toll on your body. Deduct 2 *vitality*. The door you find is closed shut and the sealing valve spun to seal it. You'll need to spin it open, which will require strength as either the mechanism has deteriorated to an extent or the valve is partially obstructed in some way. Test your muscle by rolling two dice and adding your *strength*. If the total is 13 or more, you are quick to open the door, turn to 54.

If the total is 12 or less you take longer to get the door open and pass through:

In which case if you have the word "zero" written down, turn to 821, otherwise turn to 54.

191.

Write the word "scar" down the bottom of your mission sheet. Being alive is more important than completing your mission. Though you have not found the data as required by your mission, you live to fight another day. Control will surely have another mission for you soon enough as is the usual procedure, though you are wary of consistent mission failure and any consequences Control may administer. Turn to 82.

192.

Ever so gradually you edge closer to the far end of the aisle, all the while remaining fully vigilant. You hear movement from elsewhere in the room before it stops just as suddenly. You are almost at the end of the aisle, making slow, quiet and deliberate progress. Roll a die. If you have the *Stealth* ability, you may reroll the die once only. If you roll 4 or more, turn to 116. If the result is 3 or less, turn to 102.

193.

Though you have not managed to collect the spores you were looking for to meet your contract, there is no real loss. Your contact will surely see the difficulty of retrieval from a doomed ship or you can pick up a contract from somebody else and leave your previous contact to presume you dead within the XBR starship. All of that you can be concerned about later - for now you are safe and enjoying a short cruise down to the surface of Beutohn. Turn to 133.

194.

Beyond the door you reach another junction. The sign points you in the direction of the bow for the laboratory. After rounding the corner you find a thick door with an inset window. The small room beyond is clearly a decontamination chamber leading to the laboratory which you decide to enter. Inside the decontamination room you wait while the purging process takes place. The air is cleared and replaced with fresh filtered air. You are scanned by a faint beam that passes over your body. *Time passes.* Only once this whole procedure has completed do the doors on the other side unlock, allowing you to exit the room into the lab. Now inside the main laboratory for sector C via the portside entrance, you see that it is an expansive room consisting of several divisions. A massive amount of equipment covers the walls of the room as well as being positioned to form small islands and work areas within the room. With the amount of equipment, cabinets and shelving here you cannot see to the other sides of the room, but at the same time you can effectively conceal yourself and stay unnoticed. There are multiple people in here; you can tell this from yelling you can hear over the other side of the room. It sounds as though something has malfunctioned, possibly a door which has induced panic and concern. If you have the *Data thief* mission, turn to 245. If you have the *Disrupt and extract* mission, turn to 1296.

195.

Back at the crane you take a moment to catch your breath. There is no sign of the agents you fought earlier unless they are staying hidden behind cover. It looks clear, you decide to make a run for the rear loading bay doors.

Roll two dice and add your *endurance*. If the total is 10 or lower then deduct 2 *vitality* as a piece of shrapnel lodges itself in your back. You are not stopped however and you power on to the exit. Turn to 137.

196.

Your missed shot gives the drone a chance to fire back at you. It does not miss. One of its lasers cuts into your shoulder. Deduct 2 *vitality*. As you hit the floor as a reflex, one of your team mates shoots down the drone. Zak steps over to you to see the damage. 'Slap a medi patch on it and let's get a move on,' he says.

You do as he says and then catch up to them heading down the corridor. Turn to 134.

197.

The ship you are on will return to Beutohn. You will have the option of staying on the ship and returning to an LWS base situated on this moon. If you do, continue your adventure as a Leading Weapon Syndicate agent in book 2 of the **Bionic Agent** series: *Vault of carnage*.

Though it may be uncharacteristic as an LWS agent, you are technically between missions so if you choose you may make use of the teleporter to jump to Phaeadron. In this case, continue as an LWS agent with book 3… Turn to 1300.

198.

Time passes. Holding your position, you take the opportunity to evaluate what is happening. Whilst doing so, you also set your video link to record in order to collect some video data for future analysis. It seems the XBR are holding the LWS attackers off for now, especially as they have a central position behind a bulky container. LWS agents appear to be filtering in from the loading bay at the far end of the hall; each of them better equipped than the XBR guards. Write the word "judge" on your mission sheet for the footage taken. You now decide to move out. Turn to 257.

199.

For the capture of the fugitive, you are awarded 500 creds. Add the credits to your total. You have done well to complete your mission. Now turn to 1300.

200.

As you are sneaking across you are spotted by somebody else in the room over towards the stern. The individual is no weakling scientist as you soon discover. Add the word "quaint" to your mission sheet and turn to 144.

201.

After a deep rest, you awake to find a video message left on your terminal. It is from your commander. You open it to see what he has to say:

'After careful analysis of your testimony and the information you provided, the Confederacy will be initiating a strike against the nearest Leading Weapon Syndicate stronghold on Beutohn. We are aware of this base they have kept hidden and have a strike force en route. We will respond with the judgment of the council of the Confederacy for an unprovoked attack against another faction. For your part, we would like you to be part of the assault - no it is not an order due to your circumstances, but if you do help spearhead the strike I will ensure you receive full recognition for your part in all of this. The evidence you provided to us, though somewhat limited, is sufficient for this decision to be made and you have been transferred payment for your mission just completed. Decide and respond agent.'

The video message ends.

You check to see your cred total.

Add 150 creds to your total. If you have the word "footage" written down, add an additional 50 creds to your total.

Now you will have to decide if you will accept the mission or not:

If you do, continue your adventure as a Confederacy agent in book 2 of the Bionic Agent series: *Vault of carnage.*

If you decline the mission, you may finish delivering the supplies before returning to Phaeadron. In this case, continue your life as a Confederacy agent with book 3...

Whilst your mission here has ended and you have survived *Starship deadfall*;

If you have the word "judge" written down, turn to 333, otherwise turn to 1300.

202.

Heading down the corridor you soon come to another isolation door. There is a com-link panel beside the door which you try, but there is no response. You'll have to return to the junction and head towards the bow. Turn to 424.

203.

Your shot hits one of the XBR guards in the arm. The guard hits the floor – the shot may not have killed him but he is down for now. Fortunately the guards are too engaged in a shootout with members of the red team to take aim back at you. That battle however is little compared to the chaos playing out on the loading bay floor. Turn to 183.

204.

You are close to half way along the corridor and still no sign of whatever made the sound earlier. Aside from the background noise of the ship it is probably a little too quiet for your liking. Roll a die. If you roll a 1 or a 2, turn to 1224. If you roll a 3 or a 4, turn to 1248. If you roll a 5 or a 6, turn to 290.

205.

There appears to be a number of projects underway on the starship. Unfortunately this terminal can only list them, not provide any details. The main technological developments are bio-synthetic robots being manufactured in sector F followed by multiple genetic projects within the various laboratories which is nothing out of the ordinary for a Xeno Biological Research vessel. The bio-synthetic robots may be worth investigating, though if they are not weaponized in any new way, they too will be standard activity for the XBR faction. You may look up any research data this terminal may have access to by turning to 619 or if you feel you are finished with the terminal you may turn to 504. If you decide to search for other information, return to 487 and choose again.

206.

Time passes. You hit the button to manually open the door and are relieved to find it opens without a glitch. Inside the next room you quickly close the door behind you. The room you are in is darkened just like the previous one, the only illumination provided by a few small lights above the work areas on the side. It appears as though you are in a small prep room. Will you:

Take a look around this room?	Turn to 157.
Head straight to the exit on the starboard side?	Turn to 280.

207.

Forcing yourself into the narrow gap between the beam and the corridor wall, you manage an effective concealment for someone running past and not checking carefully. The agent passes you and turns at the next junction, thinking you have already rounded the corner. You take the opportunity to head back towards the teleport room in case he doubles back. Replace the word "capacity" with the word "filter" and turn to 453.

208.

Time passes. Heading down to the end of the corridor you reach a door which is closed. At the door a sensor detects your presence and the door starts to slide open. With a terrible grating noise it grinds to a halt, only partially open. Hitting a manual button on the side appears to do nothing to help. You are going to have to use some force to get through. Will you:

Use your strength to push open the door?   Turn to 237.

Use a cutting or demolishing tool to bust through?   Turn to 117.

Use an explosive if you have one?   Turn to 1123.

209.

Looking inside this room you see that it is a rest quarters, complete with numerous bunks and likely a hygiene room beyond the main room. Not wanting to waste time here you quickly leave. Turn to 363.

210.

Escaping this drone, could be more difficult than you imagined. You race down the corridor and take the corner quickly. The drone pursues: it is not as quick around the corners but accelerates to high speed along the corridors. Resolve one shot against you: On 2 dice, 5+ to hit, 3 damage. You may make a defense roll. Surviving this, you round another corner to the left. Now will you:

Duck into one of the rooms in an attempt to hide?   Turn to 1177.

Try a maintenance access hatch in the side of the corridor?

Turn to 175.

211.

Time passes. You continue going through the databases. You pick out a couple of files that may be Minkla's work, but you cannot say for certain. It is not nearly enough however. There must be more which you are determined to find. The fire has now taken over half of the room. Your searching has been in vain, if you don't leave now you'll be cooked alive if the ship doesn't self-destruct first. Abandoning the terminal, will you:

Leave via the restricted surgical room?   Turn to 1284.

Leave via the unmarked starboard door?   Turn to 317.

212.

The notes do not tell you much. Mostly because they are sketchy and because they are technical in nature. You move on, heading for the exit. Turn to 109.

213.

Write the word "recover" on your mission sheet.

The double doors open automatically for you and once inside you realize you are in a small training facility of some sort. The place is a mess and you notice two bodies on the floor and another slumped up against one off the walls. With the guidance of your sensor and a closer inspection you realize it is Melea. You check for a pulse and find she is still lightly breathing. She looks up at you with half closed eyes, uttering your name. You ask her what happened and she speaks a few labored words in response:

'My leg is broken. I'm done. The mission was a flop. There's no tech here. Somebody else wrecked the ship... the engines. It had to be a setup. The Confeds know what we've done.'

Her eyes close and she stops speaking.

You look at her mangled leg and also notice she is bleeding from the side of her body which her arm now covers.

If you do not already have it written down, add the word "pet" to your mission sheet. Will you:

Try to rescue her?	Turn to 1205.
Leave her and get moving?	Turn to 1265.

214.

To use your stun pistol, roll to hit as normal. If you score a hit and Sjonn fails his defense roll to dodge the attack, deduct 1 point from Sjonn's escape tally and add 2 points to your capture tally. Sjonn will also be *shaken* for the next combat round. Now return to 54, remembering you cannot use your stun pistol in the next combat round.

215.

You have managed to push open the door slightly, but it is not enough to get through yet. You continue to heave at the solid metal. *Time passes.* Roll 2 dice and add the result to your previous value. If your new total is now 16 or more, turn to 1164. If your running total is 15 or less, mark off another *time passed* box on your mission sheet and then turn to 1164.

216.

As you are not far into the aisle you decide to slip into one of the next adjacent aisles to get away from whatever made the call. Carefully you move along the aisle, keeping to one side and maximizing the use of the shadows. Hopefully the call of the animal acted as a distraction more than anything, you take the chance to capitalize on the moment by pushing ahead further down the aisle before slowing to listen and watch very carefully. Roll a die. If the result is 4 or more, turn to 219. If the result is 3 or less, turn to 177.

217.

Not far along you encounter some action. Ahead of you at a junction at the end of this corridor are two LWS agents using the corners for cover. To your side is an XBR guard engaged in a shoot-out with the agents. You notice the XBR guard has been hit as he is bleeding from his right thigh.

You'll need to get him to safety or fend off the LWS agents. Fight at short range.

LWS agents	Ra	5
	Vitality	30
	4+ to hit, 4 damage.	
	5+ armor negates 4 damage as defense.	

When you reduce the collective *vitality* of the agents to 15 or less, the remaining agent will flee the fight, getting away cleanly.

You leave the XBR guard to safely tend to his wound while you move on. Reaching the junction and ensuring it is clear, will you:

Head towards bow?   Turn to 238.

Head towards stern?   Turn to 357.

218.

If you have the word "clang" written down, turn to 239. If you do not have this word written down, turn to 243.

219.

You have made it quite far, almost to the end of the aisle in fact. You strain to hear any signs of the thing that is wandering around the room above the low level rumbling of the ship itself. Roll a die.

If you roll 4 or more, turn to 116. If the result is 3 or less, turn to 102.

220.

Carefully you head back to the start of the aisle, reaching it safely. *Time passes.* You choose one of the other aisles to head up in your attempt to reach the other side of the room. Turn to 246.

221.

As you have been here before you see little value in covering old ground. If you need to use an automated operating table, turn to 347.

If you do not have the word "flutter" written down you may begin hacking the main terminal. To do so, turn to 382. Otherwise you leave the room, turn to 451.

222.

Write the word "cast" on your mission sheet. While the ship is in evacuation mode, the bio scanner for this room has been disabled, which is one less thing for you to worry about. You open the door and are taken back by seeing another person in the room. He is armed and it only takes a moment for you to identify him as an XBR agent. It looks as though he was collecting items from several draws before you invaded his personal area. Will you:

Attack the agent?	Turn to 41.
Leave immediately?	Turn to 32.

223.

Write the word "scar" down the bottom of your mission sheet. You are thankful you are alive despite not being able to locate and eliminate the scientist. Knowing there may be repercussions for not completing your primary mission, you can only wait either way. You can expect another mission issued to you after a short down time, so you determine you will see things as they take course. Turn to 82.

224.

Turn to 1245.

225.

Turn to the following reference according to the word you have written down:

"Deter":	Turn to 271.
"Filter":	Turn to 155.
"Capacity":	Turn to 98.
None of these words:	Turn to 1204.

226.

The ships security is all inter-linked and this terminal can only list some of the security that is active at present. It has no means to change the security in any way. On this level is a security hub, the location of which is not disclosed; a drone hub located in sector J; numerous visual surveillance systems; biometric scanning at select locations as well as an active keypass system for personnel identification and isolation systems, mostly for the integrity of the ship itself. If you feel you are finished with the terminal you may turn to 504. If you decide to search for other information, return to 487 and choose again.

227.

You have to fight this one out or die trying. If you have a grenade you may use that in place of a regular attack. The damage done will be double that listed in the item description. Now return to 144 and fight.

228.

You manage to hit the unidentified individual directly in the head causing instant death. That will be one less to worry about. Melea and Zak are still taking shots at whatever targets they can find between the smoke and debris. Roll one die and add your *perception*. If you score 9 or above, turn to 73. If you score 8 or below, turn to 130.

229.

'That could be useful,' you think to yourself as you spot a *mechanical spring-snap* half way along atop a head-high shelf. You've seen before examples of crude devices used amongst rebels as a means to defend against unwanted intruders. You know you'll require a sensor of some sort to build the item. When you think you have both components, turn to 19, remembering the reference you are on to attempt to put the device together. Write the word "wrench" on your mission sheet. You may investigate the starboard side by turning to 266 or leave the room by turning to 451.

230.

There is nothing else of value in here you find. Turn to 32.

231.

'Back again so soon!' exclaims Kinlac with open arms, inviting you into his cozy little workshop. If you have the word "mend" written down, turn to 140. Otherwise, turn to 818.

232.

Time passes. You know you cannot wait forever as the ship is now in a critical condition. No sounds from outside can be heard. You decide to wait just a little bit more before opening the hatch. Turn to 260.

233.

If you have no more unmarked time passed boxes left on your mission sheet, turn to 270 now. Otherwise for the delay in getting through, *time passes.* You press on, keen to escape the ship alive. Turn to 8.

234.

Will you try:
To outrun the agent?   Turn to 105.
To hide somewhere?   Turn to 1183.

235.

The door unlocks. Turn to 527.

236.

All three of you are ready and waiting, with hardly a blink while the drones continue cutting through the door. You had figured maybe some armed personal to welcome you but not drones which not only are capable of cutting through doors to get to you, but do so in tandem.

It does not take them long to cut through as the hole they are cutting is only large enough for them to get through which is about the size of your head.

The cuts meet and the door fragment falls inwards. The first drone bursts into the room.

Zak is quick, he blasts it back into the wall before it gets a chance to shoot.

The second drone enters quickly behind.

Take a short range shot at the drone. If you have *The quick and the dead* ability, you may reroll once if you miss.

If you score a hit turn to 284. If you miss, turn to 196. If you are unable to shoot, turn to 75.

237.

You may be able to push the door open by having your back to the wall and using your arms and legs. Roll two dice and add your *strength*. If the result is 13 or more, turn to 1164. If the result is less than 13, remember the total and turn to 215.

238.

Taking the corridor towards the bow of the ship you find it soon swings around towards starboard. Ahead of you an LWS agent suddenly makes an appearance - the both of you as surprised as each other. Judging by the way he holds his side he is already wounded but he fights fiercely none the less.

Wounded LWS agent	Ra	5
	Vitality	12
	4+ to hit, 4 damage.	
	5+ armor negates 4 damage as defense.	

>If you choose to throw a grenade at him, since his movement is compromised you will kill him outright.

>If you defeat the agent you may take his *laser pistol* if you choose. Additionally you may take an *identity scan* of the agent which may be useful for your mission - in which case add 1 to the tally you have created on your mission sheet. Turn to 331.

239.

With the navigator out of the way you set yourself the task of getting into this terminal. As soon as you begin however the terminal crashes. It obviously wasn't security as the terminal would have shut down. You try a reset. Nothing happens. Unfortunate at the worst of moments. Reduce your *chance* score by 1. Write the word "defect" on your mission sheet and leave the room by turning to 543.

240.

You leave those two scientists and head across to another vantage point between the storage aisles. If you have the word "east" written down, turn to 172. If you have the word "last" written down, turn to 136.

241.

Looking in the room again you find it is still a mess - it has not been repaired in anyway and since it could be any moment when the crew turns up to investigate you do not plan to be around at that time. Turn to 465.

242.

As you have been in this room already, you decide not to spend more of your precious time in here. There are two rooms along this corridor you can try if you have not already. Alternatively you can keep moving. Will you:

Try the first room on the right?	Turn to 1057.
Try the second room on the right?	Turn to 46.
Head towards the bow?	Turn to 345.
Head towards the stern?	Turn to 146.

243.

'Just what are you trying to do there?' says the man half yelling.
You turn to see him barreling down upon you.
Will you:

Attack him?	Turn to 477.
Rush to the exit?	Turn to 267.

244.

Now will you:

Take a look around the room?	Turn to 295.
Leave via the restricted surgical room?	Turn to 1284.
Leave via the unmarked starboard door?	Turn to 317.

245.

Ahead of you are short aisles consisting of shelves lined with materials and many vials of substances all used for experimentation. At the end of the aisle you are in you can see some more of the room. Across towards the starboard-bow corner you can see a large translucent screen, behind which is an enclosed restricted area. From there, nearer the stern you cannot yet see them for there are some large instruments in the way spanning from floor to ceiling, but you can tell from their voices the source of the arguing is coming from that direction. How will you proceed?

Move closer to the starboard-bow corner to get a visual on the occupants here? Turn to 1215.

Head directly to your right towards the stern to investigate that side? Turn to 1186.

246.

Quickly you pick one of the other aisles, moving swiftly before slowing to remain unnoticeable whilst also concealing yourself as much as you can in the shadows. Roll for *chance*. If the result is 4 or more, turn to 304. If the result is 3 or less, turn to 143.

247.

Relaying a message to your commander of all you discovered, you'll have to wait to see the result as no reply will be returned to where you are now. Not until you return to base will you be likely to get any answers to the questions in your mind. Questions of why nothing could be found of the mission objective. Why communications were down so long. Why the attack ship was not available to jump to when needed. Payment will still be received for your duties. Add to your credit total 300 creds. Meanwhile in the upper atmosphere of the moon Beutohn, the doomed XBR starship undergoes the final series of explosions which destroy the ship, sending countless fragments out to burn up upon descent. Turn to 287.

248.

Luckily the door is unlocked and you slip inside breathing in deeply with relief. Following the tunnel you reach a junction with a ladder heading both upwards and downwards from your position. You decide to head up the ladder in an effort to both get further from the intruders and also to search for the hazardous material. At the top of the ladder is a large circular valve to open the hatch. Gripping it tightly you spin the wheel and push the hatch open. Climbing out of a recess you find yourself at a junction in a low ceiling tunnel. Not knowing exactly where you are to pick a direction and begin heading towards the bow. After a short distance you reach a ladder heading upwards with a sign beside it: "To Corridor EF-02". Realizing it will at least get you out of this cramped tunnel, you climb the ladder, open the hatch and look around. There is a corridor running left to right and it appears empty. Taking the opportunity you climb out of the tunnel and decide which way to proceed:

Head to your left (port) towards sector E?   Turn to 186.
Go to your right (starboard) towards sector F? Turn to 335.

249.

Using your expert negotiator skills you attempt to dissuade Sjonn from trying to escape and point to his inevitable capture. Whilst Sjonn is not going to give himself in by a long shot, you do succeed by reducing his fervor. Add 1 point to your capture tally. Now return to 54 and fight, you cannot use this ability again in an attempt to try to talk him down further.

250.

You move further along the aisle to get closer to the far end as well as put you at a greater distance away from whatever made the call. There is movement ahead of you and it is quick. Turn to 26.

251.

Heading towards the stern along another bleak corridor devoid of crew you see two rooms on the right side. Will you:

Turn around and take the corridor towards the bow? Turn to 345.

Try the first door on the right?   Turn to 1057.

Enter the second room on the right?   Turn to 46.

Keep moving towards the stern?   Turn to 146.

252.

You take another look around the room, but find nothing more from your earlier search. Now will you:

Try the first door if you have not already?   Turn to 30.

Keep moving?   Turn to 3.

253.

You continue up the aisle, weapon at the ready, fearless in the face of an unknown creature. Turn to 26.

254.

Peering inside the room, you see it is as before though the people have left. You see no point spending time in a near empty room. Turn to 397.

255.

Time passes. You blast the lock with your weapon. Though now unlocked, the latches at the top and bottom remain holding the door closed. You grab the door in the middle, squeezing your hand in behind the bowed metal and rip at the door. Eventually the latches snap and the door opens up. Roll 2 dice and compare the result to table 3 of the *discovered item tables* near the beginning of the book. This is the item you have found inside the cabinet. You may take it if you choose or leave it behind. Either way make for the exit fast: turn to 715.

256.

You make out something moving at the far end of the aisle. Though you can hardly see it in the near darkness, you suspect it can sense you. The steps are solid and the sound is loud - this creature is heading your way. Act fast:

Stand and fight the thing: Turn to 26.

Turn and run, heading to your left at the end of the aisle:

Turn to 78.

257.

You duck out behind the cover of a side support beam - one of many which run up the sides of the hall at regular intervals. A shot from a laser rifle melts into the beam you stand behind - almost at head height. Taking a glance you see where the shot originated from as you spot an LWS agent crouch back down behind a cargo cart. Getting involved in the action you attempt to take him out.

Secluded LWS agent	Ra	5
	Vitality	22
	5+ to hit, 4 damage.	
	5+ armor negates 4 damage as defense.	

>Fight this battle as a short ranged combat over three rounds only. If you kill the agent before the end of three rounds, turn to 1064. Otherwise at the end of the three rounds, turn to 1064.

258.

Remove either a *med pack* or *stimsert* from your inventory as you treat her. *Time passes.* You help her to her feet, her left leg being incapable of supporting her in any way. You brace her with your shoulder, encouraging her to move with you. She is alert enough though struggling on one leg and in considerable pain. Helping your allied agent along you make for the door leaving her weapon behind. Write the word "fulcrum" on your mission sheet and turn to 715.

259.

The door unlocks for you. Turn to 13.

260.

After waiting a short moment, you carefully open the hatch back up and peer outside. The drone is still there, patrolling the corridor, waiting for you! You are going to have to confront this killing machine. It is tracking you somehow, perhaps through detection of residual odor molecules which is the only way you can think of. The drone easily notices your exit from the hatch and immediately attacks. Use the *vitality* of the drone which you have noted down and continue the battle with the following stats:

Ra of 5, On 2 dice, 3+ to hit, 3 damage, 5+ to negate 5 damage armor for defense. The drone will make only the one type of attack for the rest of the battle. If you defeat the drone, you return to the corridor in which the encounter took place. Turn to 355.

261.

'Well I can only see so much at the moment. And we are in a low polar orbit around Beutohn.

The sooner we get out from the umbra of this crater for a moon, the better,' he states rather gruffly.

It certainly makes sense that an attack on the starship would take place during a phase when the vessel is cut off from Confederacy monitoring from Phaeadron. Now will you:

Ask for the location of the fugitive Sjonn?	Turn to 529.
Ask where the LWS attack is taking place?	Turn to 621.
Attack him?	Turn to 477.

262.

Thinking that if you alternate between browsing patient files and searching for information that is relevant, you may be successful in an attempt to evade detection by the terminal. Another prompt appears: "Identification required. Please scan your keypass or enter a clearance number".

Your guess is you won't get a second chance if you do not satisfy the terminal with its request.

Will you:

Immediately shutdown the terminal?	Turn to 504.
Try to think up something quickly?	Turn to 322.
Use a keypass if you have one?	Turn to 441.

263.

Time passes. Hoping to connect to the bridge in order to convince them to let you through, you try the com link. There is no response. You try another connection. You are on visuals so you presume you can be seen, assuming someone is actually watching. Another try and still nothing. You decide to abandon further attempts. Returning to the junction will you:

Head towards the bow?	Turn to 363.
Heads towards the port side?	Turn to 530.

264.

You shoot, killing outright the nearer scientist while wounding the second. You look to finish off the second to ensure he does not escape, but your plans are stopped short. Previously unaware of his presence, an XBR agent on the far side of the room raises his head above a cooling instrument. He fires at your location after he spots you. Add the word "slam" to your mission sheet and turn to 144.

265.

It turns out there is plenty of data which is open to the user of this terminal. The downside however is that the majority of the data pertains to engineering specifications and utility consumption. None of this information is helpful to you in anyway. Now will you:

Attempt to remove restrictions to the ships network? Turn to 380.

Attempt to update the platform to make the terminal perform better?   Turn to 537.

Attempt to connect directly to another terminal?   Turn to 659.

Use a *ghost processor* if you have one?   Turn to 868.

Quit trying to hack it and leave?   Turn to 743.

266.

Time passes. [If you have the word "tinker" written down, turn to 231.]

After a few rows of shelving you find the rest of the room opens out into an area with the appearance of a small workshop. To one side is a man bent over an item on the bench eying it with much attention. Surrounding him are various tools and all manner of bits and pieces both on the benches and in containers and on shelves. Sensing your entry into his domain he turns and looks at you with a grin.

'Take a look at this,' he exclaims as if you were already well acquainted.

Given his excitement and behavior you decide to play along and look closer at what he is up to.

On the bench in front of him is a small object half the size of his hand and it is rotating on the spot.

This does not seem to be anything amazing you think to yourself until he points a little light diode at the object and it spins itself apart into maybe 50 pieces.

'Neat' you say to him.

'Watch' he exclaims as if to stop you from retracting your attention.

Slowly, as if each piece is being pushed along, all the tiny fragments of the original object are moving towards each other and coalescing into the original object.

The man looks at you with his now familiar big grin.

'Fascinating. Oh I'm Kinlac, I don't recall having met you before. And what is it you are after?' he asks without interest in your identity.

You consider that Kinlac may be of help to you either now or in the future and so decide to leave your weapons alone whilst here.

Write the word "tinker" on your mission sheet.

[If you have the *Collector of things* mission, turn to 869 now.]

If you think Kinlac may be able to build or repair something for you, turn to 818. Otherwise turn to either 451 to leave the room or 383 to spend time looking at the shelves on the port side if you haven't already.

267.

The man is glad to see you leave. Check your mission sheet for any of the following words, turning to the associated reference accordingly. Note this reference as you will be returning here afterwards.

"Deter"   Turn to 368.
"Filter"   Turn to 442.

If you have neither of those words, nor the word "capacity" written down, write down the word "deter". Turn to 543.

268.

You sprint hard, making considerable ground quickly before slowing down and making use of the shadows. Roll a die. If you roll 3 or more, turn to 192. If you roll a 1 or a 2, turn to 173.

269.

Realizing you just walked in on their meeting, you quickly excuse yourself from the room and continue along the corridor on your mission. Turn to 397.

270.

As the starship continues to descend into the moon of Beutohn, it shakes even more than before, causing a series of explosions across the hulk of the vessel. In turn the structure fails catastrophically. You, not far from the teleport hub which would have been your escape route suffer a quick death as the starship undergoes a final series of explosions and melting of the framework leading to its ultimate destruction.

271.

As the ship creaks and moans from structural stress, from further down the corridor three XBR guards approach you. As they draw close enough, they begin firing their pistols. Taking up what cover you can find along the side of the corridor, you return fire.

Three XBR guards	Ra	4
	Vitality	28

On 2 dice, 4+ to hit, 3 damage.
No defense.

>If you choose to throw a grenade at the guards, for a successful hit, the grenade will inflict double damage (18 total damage for a cluster grenade). In addition, roll 2 dice and add the result as damage also. If you miss with your throw, there is still a chance of damage: Roll for *chance*. If the result is 4 or more, then roll 2 dice with the total being the damage done. If the result is 3 or less, then roll a single die and use the result as damage.

>If you reduce their collective *vitality* to 12 or less, the remaining guard will roll only 1 die for his attack round.

>The guards effectively have you pinned behind cover; you will not be able to flee from this battle.

If you defeat the guards, turn to 1220.

272.

Ripping the meshed grid off you have free access to the coils. You quickly smash them to pieces. The field is still active but it fails to function as before, allowing you to cut through the door and gain access. Turn to 509.

273.

You are beginning to leave sector F. As a controlled laborer you have been instructed not to leave this area. Your bracelet lights up and at the same time you receive a shock up your arm and through your body. Deduct 2 *vitality*. It may be best you head back to sector F whilst you have this bracelet on.

Will you:

Return to sector F?	Turn to 391.
Try to head further along the corridor?	Turn to 454.

274.

Roll 1 die. If the result is 4 or more, turn to 1293. If the result is 3 or less, turn to 1096.

275.

In a make or break effort to catch the fugitive you press on with everything you have left. Take your *vitality* and your *endurance* and add them together. Deduct two points for each item (excluding *light items*) you are carrying in your inventory (excluding weapons you are holding onto, attachments etc). Now deduct a further 10 points from the running total. Roll 3 dice. If the total of the dice roll is less than the running points total, turn to 190. If the total of the dice roll is equal to or higher, turn to 911.

276.

Time passes. Further along the corridor you see that the corridor ends by expanding out into a large open room. The room is filled with tanks that span from ceiling to floor as well as various sized pipes and walkways to get to the equipment. Your initial suspicions were correct: this whole area is used for sanitation and recycling purposes. It may be taking you further from any teleport hub by continuing this way. You decide to head back to the previous corridor. Turn to 715.

277.

Activating the memory scrambler, the interface loses communication with the door's security system, disabling the field and allowing you to open the door manually. Turn to 509.

278.

Using your honed skills you corrupt several specific programs which when activated through the network as they persistently are, disable the access restrictions normally in place for this particular terminal. You are in for now, at least until either someone detects what is wrong or the system scans the terminal for errors and forces a reboot. Turn to 972 to begin searching.

279.

You kneel down to steady yourself for the shot. Roll to hit, applying a -1 modifier for the range of the shot. If you hit, turn to 203. If you miss, turn to 169.

280.

The exit opens with the push of a button, bringing you to a corridor running from bow to stern. Being fully lit, you can see there is no one around. You are confident the route towards the bow is the right option. Taking that, you reach a t-intersection further along and after checking the signage decide to head towards port towards the lab rather than rest quarters. Turn to 171.

281.

Time passes as you bunker down in your concealed position. A few shots puncture the nearby equipment, letting you know the agent is still present. The firing stops. There is only the rattling of the ship. You hear a door open then close and decide to take a peek. There is no sign of anyone. *Time passes.* You get up and carefully look around. You make some noise to see if anyone responds. The room is definitely empty. Both the agent and remaining scientists have left. You had better do the same before the ship destructs. Moving quickly you approach the door. Turn to 1284.

282.

Adding another service delays you further as you have to wait for it to setup and begin; *time posses.* You are on edge knowing the terminal network is evaluating you, but not knowing what it is concluding.

Roll one die. If you roll a 1, turn to 472. If you roll anything else turn to 381.

283.

Answering the question with a direct 'no', you ask the man at the center if he knows anything of Sjonn, the person you are looking for.

'I do not know that person,' he replies quite plainly. Not wanting to waste time here, you move on. Turn to 397.

284.

All it takes is one shot – these drones have virtually no defense aside from their mobility. The drone is destroyed.

'Nice one,' comments Melea.

'Let's go,' says Zak.

The team re-opens the door and heads down the corridor. Turn to 134.

285.

You make a dash for it towards the rear of the loading bay. Sprinting hard, you hope the agents stay down, but they are sharp, and soon realize you are on the run. To see how many shots the agents take at you before you pass through the loading bay doors, perform the following test.

Roll one die and add you *agility and endurance* to the dice roll.

For each point <u>below</u> 14, deduct 2 *vitality*. Turn to 137.

286.

In contrast to when you were in here before, the room is brighter and it seems to be deserted.

Will you:

Search the room?   Turn to 306.

Leave?   Turn to 363.

287.

As an agent you may have picked up clues during your time aboard the XBR starship. There are instances where the information you discover or the things you encounter will make a difference later on - either simply for your current mission or for the overall turn of events. If you have some knowledge about the experiments taking place aboard the ship, you may know of a particular specimen. If you do, convert the name to a number. (To do this convert letters to numbers by taking A=1, B=2, C=3 etc then adding the numbers together) When you have done this, multiply the number by 8. The result is a reference you may turn to now before returning here. Now turn to 197.

288.

The information you have just obtained is quite helpful to you. Whilst it does not satisfy your mission as you are looking for technology, it may be worth reporting in the end. You have the sense there may be more pieces to this puzzle and if you are to complete your mission to the degree possible you may need to discover more of what is happening here. Now will you:

Head around the partition to the other side of the room?

                                                               Turn to 561.

Exit the laboratory?   Turn to 471.

289.

Time passes. Patiently waiting, you see more activity. Hearing the door and perceiving an outline only through the translucent panel, you note another individual entering into the lab from the restricted area to your left.

The scientist at the starboard door turns around to speak to the other individual, allowing you to see him better. If you have the word "east" written down, turn to 1061. If you have the word "last" written down, turn to 184.

290.

A deep guttural sound like the one you heard earlier reverberates around the room again. You spot movement. Or at least you see the shape of something at the far end of the aisle. Will you:

Head directly at the thing and take it on?	Turn to 253.
Stand completely still in the shadows?	Turn to 1133.
Turn and run back along the aisle?	Turn to 1256.

291.

Inside the room you see the makings of an infirmary. A man in plain uniform is busy at the far end of the room making adjustments to a control panel of some sort. He notices you but continues with his task. You realize you are out of place here and need to get to the Leading Weapon Syndicate (LWS) agents to fulfill your mission. You head back out of the infirmary and follow the corridor around towards the bow, reaching a solid isolation door. Turn to 361.

292.

Roll a die. If you roll a 6, turn to 180. If you roll anything else, turn to 1244.

293.

As soon as you place your hands on the door you are stung by an electric shock. Ripping your hand away in pain you can see the occupant of this room has booby trapped the door. Deduct 2 *vitality*.

You decide the smartest choice would be to leave it alone and move on. Turn to 711.

294.

Dashing into one of the other aisles, you then slow so you can conceal yourself within the shadows, avoiding the illuminated signage above individual holding pens. You have no idea where the creature is at this point. Roll a die. If you have the *Stealth* ability you may add 1 to the result. If you have an *endurance* of 5 or less, you need to ease your heavy breathing: add 1 to the result. If the end result is 4 or more, turn to 304. If the result is 3 or less, turn to 544.

295.

Taking a quick look around, you do not spot anything of significance. You do not have spare time to go searching the large databases on the terminals in here. You may have enough data for your mission already, a couple of data stores found in a draw will supplement what you already have. Now will you:

Leave via the restricted surgical room?   Turn to 1284.

Leave via the unmarked starboard door?   Turn to 317.

296.

You quickly determine that the terminals in this room, all being on the same link are not functioning presently. Will you:

Take a look at the holographic map?   Turn to 358.

Leave the room?   Turn to 543.

297.

Just as you are about to enter into the corridor someone exits a room further down and begins heading your way. Roll a die. If you have either *Stealth* or *Keen eyes* you may add 1 to the roll. If the result is 4 or more, turn to 422. Otherwise turn to 1076.

298.

Down on a bottom shelf you discover a used *micro torch*. Though the fuel tanks are only half full, a quick test proves it is still functioning. You may take this item with you if you choose. Write the word "wrench" on your mission sheet. You may investigate the starboard side by turning to 266 or leave the room by turning to 451.

299.

Time passes as you put on one of the fully sealed suits. Opening the door to the next room, you enter into a small cubicle used to cleanse the suit and purify the air. You head straight to the opposite door, waving your hand over the sensor and moving into the operation room itself the operation room is divided into four individual rooms, each with an operating table and instruments. There is nobody in here, but it looks as though the place was recently used and left without clean up as there are pieces of flesh on a mobile tray nearby and surgical instruments scattered across the benches. As you could potentially be seen through the window into the lab, you quickly move through into one of the back rooms. You spot a door in between the two adjoining back rooms and open it. A large open room, consisting of several workbenches and a collection of small carts used for carrying specimens to the benches or tables. There are two doors in this room. Will you try:

The door on the starboard side?	Turn to 1126.
The door on the stern side?	Turn to 1292.

300.

The starship's teleport hub is both spacious and elaborately equipped. Mostly automated, numerous detectors and monitoring devices adorn the walls and ceiling. The teleporters are divided in half intentionally as some are setup only for receiving whilst the others for departing – either off ship or within the ship itself. The room is presently vacated. There are two doors exiting from the teleport hub. Which will you choose:

The door on the port side?	Turn to 497.
The door on the starboard side?	Turn to 363.

301.

Nothing has changed in the room since you left as you accidentally pass too close to the automatic doors causing them to open again. Turn to 715.

302.

You push on in pain, despite the odds in a final effort to not let the fugitive escape. Add your *vitality, endurance* and *resilience* together. With that total, perform the following deductions:

If you have 8 items or more, deduct 7 from the total.

If you have any lingering effects or other afflictions, deduct 5 from the total.

For each instance of *Heavy* you are burdened by, deduct 6 from the total.

If you have a *crippling wound* or any specific wound to your legs, deduct 10 from the total.

For each item (excluding *light items*) you have, deduct 3 from the total.

Now roll 2 dice and deduct that from the total.

If the final total is 20 or less, turn to 911.

If the final total is 21 or more, turn to 190.

303.

As the ship is in evacuation mode, fortunately the bio scan has been disabled. The door opens for you.

Inside the vacant room you see that it previously housed someone of high rank, judging from the plaques and ornaments spread around the room. A bunk on one side and a terminal on the other round out the space. It looks as though whoever stayed here has cleared the room out of anything essential. Will you:

Search the room and check the terminal?   Turn to 77.

Save time and leave the room?   Turn to 32.

304.

There is still no sign of the creature as you continually check both ways. You move further towards the end of the aisle, doing so with senses on high alert. Turn to 192.

305.

The main terminal stands about waist height and with a flat opaque top it shows no sign of life; that is until you have been standing beside it for a second. A faint glow now covers the surface and several holographic elements can be seen floating above the flat top of the terminal. Will you:

Use the terminal to search the records of the infirmary? Turn to 414.
Use the terminal to search for a map of the starship?   Turn to 531.
Try to hack the terminal?   Turn to 318.
Alternatively:
Utilize one of the automated operating tables if you need to?
                                                        Turn to 401.
Check the cells to see if any are occupied?   Turn to 588.
Check the storage cupboards for anything of use?   Turn to 455.
Leave the room?   Turn to 451.

306.

Time passes. With nobody about you begin searching the draws and chests. It looks like anything important was taken with the crew members when they left. Seemingly fruitless and to reduce the risk of being discovered by returning crew members you decide to cease your search and head back into the corridor. Turn to 363.

307.

Half way along this corridor you find a large isolation bulkhead closing off the rest of the corridor. It is intended to completely seal off one part of the ship from the other in situations of emergency. As secure as it is, you also know it would take more time than you have to blow it open or cut through it.

Will you:

Try the com link on the wall nearby?   Turn to263.
Or return to the previous junction and:
Head towards the bow?   Turn to 363.
Heads towards the port side?   Turn to 530.

308.

Time passes. The crew were unarmed and have nothing of value on them. The room itself is almost bare - it is used more for meetings than anything else. Somewhat deflated you leave the room. Turn to 397.

309.

Time passes. You wait, giving ample time for the drone to have passed by searching for you. Then you patiently wait some more, just in case the drone paused outside the hatch door. Will you:

Take a look out the hatch now?   Turn to 1227.
Wait more before opening the hatch?   Turn to 232.

310.

The coils have a meshed grid surrounding them that you'll need to dispose of first. Roll two dice and add your *strength*. If the total is greater than or equal to 14, turn to 272. If the total is lower than 14, turn to 351.

311.

Moving with a steady pace along the corridor, from seemingly out of nowhere a man in a soiled uniform rounds the corner from the junction ahead and runs straight into you, pulling up just prior to collision. As you are armed he sees you as a threat and immediately tries to bash you with a solid metal bar.

Fight the man in close quarter combat.

Fleeing Loader worker	CQ	4
	Vitality	16

4+ to hit, 2 damage.
No defense.

After defeating the worker, will you:

Check his corpse for items?	Turn to 388.
Move on towards the bow?	Turn to 424.
Head towards the stern?	Turn to 202.

312.

You try to pick out a target on the loading bay floor, but it is certainly difficult as they are well hidden and move quickly between cargo and structure alike. Suddenly a piece of machinery close to the center of the bay is hit and explodes, releasing fragments and smoke into the air. You have yet to find a clear shot. Turn to 183.

313.

The man eyes you suspiciously with such a question. He looks you up and down closely and upon seeing you have a concealed weapon his eyes widen. You must act:

To attack him:	Turn to 477.
To run to the exit:	Turn to 267.

314.

[If you have the word "rose" written down on your mission sheet, turn to 286.]

Otherwise: If your time remaining is down to the *final tier*, turn to 209.

Otherwise, turn to 340.

315.

You soon realize waiting around is not going to get you in, but it is going to get you into trouble.

A security guard appears at the door to the armory and shoots at you with a small stunner. Roll one die. If you roll a 1 or a 2, deduct 2 *vitality* as the shot hits you, causing you to reel from an electric shock and hit the floor. You have a moment to pull yourself back up as the guard is advancing - you'll need to fend him off:

Security guard	CQ	5
	Vitality	16

4+ to hit, 3 damage.
No defense.

If you defeat the guard, you had better act before any of his friends arrive:

Use an explosive on the door:	Turn to 550.
Try a cutting or siege tool if you have one:	Turn to 339.
Quickly leave the room:	Turn to 392.

316.

Information regarding the LWS assault turns out to be very limited. The entire level below you (level 2) is on high alert with multiple sector isolations. The loading bay in particular is in lockdown. There is extensive damage to the side of the starship where the LWS ship lodged itself though presently, at least according to the data that damage is contained. There is no further information on casualties, additional warnings or reports on the reason or progression of the attack. If you feel you are finished with the terminal you may turn to 504. If you decide to search for other information, return to 487 and choose again.

317.

You move across to the door. It will not open - it is faulty in some way. The circuit for the door appears more accessible than many of the other doors on the starship so it may be a simple enough process to remedy the situation. Will you:

Try to get the door working?   Turn to 1213.

Instead try the starboard door towards the bow for the restricted area?   Turn to 1284.

318.

After discarding the main interface and delving into the second tier of the terminal's soft-structure, the terminal responds to your actions by querying your intent. It seems all main terminals are part of a quantum processing network, which means a degree of self-awareness. The terminal suspects what you may be trying to do. It also means it may take some time to hack the terminal and even if you do so, there is no guarantee you will find what you are looking for. Will you:

Continue to try to hack the terminal?   Turn to 382.

Or

Utilize one of the automated operating tables if you need to?

Turn to 401.

Check the cells to see if any are occupied?   Turn to 588.

Check the storage cupboards for anything of use?   Turn to 455.

Leave the room?   Turn to 451.

319.

Ahead, at a nearby junction an XBR guard spots you, immediately pulling back behind the corner structure and taking up fire. Take him out:

XBR guard Ra   4

         Vitality   17

         5+ to hit, 3 damage.

         No defense.

>If you choose to throw a grenade, a successful hit will cause double damage as well as the result of a single dice roll. If you miss with the throw, you may still cause some injury - roll a die and take the result as the damage done.

>If you choose to flee this combat, you may run in the opposite direction down the corridor. If you do this, the guard will get one free attack against you as you break away. Then add the word "flash" to you mission sheet and turn to 407.

If you defeat the guard, add the word "flash" to your mission sheet and take his *laser pistol* if you choose. Keep moving by turning back to 391.

320.

Double checking your 'goods' you see that the Buitonixum spores are still safely within their container. Now you will have the task of getting them to the contractor on Phaeadron you are in contact with so they can formulate the dreaded LF-7 bio weapon. Be sure to retain the spores, as you have it written now on your mission sheet. Turn to 133.

321.

Reporting back to your commander of the events of the mission, you can now only sit back and rest aboard the survey ship. What a mess you think to yourself. Still alive though, ready to fight another day. Payment will still be received for your duties. Add to your credit total 150 creds. Meanwhile in the upper atmosphere of the moon Beutohn, the doomed XBR starship undergoes the final series of explosions which destroy the ship, sending countless fragments out to burn up upon descent. Turn to 287.

322.

Roll two dice and add your *perception* to the result. If the total is 13 or more, turn to 377. If the total is 12 or less, turn to 396.

323.

Bringing up the main databases you are now attempting to retrieve normally restricted data from other parts of the network.

Roll one die. If you roll 3 or more, turn to 472. If you roll 2 or less, turn to 381.

324.

'I'm a navigator, I help with navigation,' he says gesturing towards the star map.

'That much is obvious,' you state reinforcing your position. He has no response to that. Now will you:

Ask of new technology that is being developed on the ship?

Turn to 458.

Attack him?   Turn to 477.

Leave now?   Turn to 267.

325.

You rip off the panel holding the manual release button to the wall. Inside a sealed box is a circuit board. Carefully, using a miniature laser cutting tool designed for small tasks such as this one you open up the box. You know what to do, but it takes time to perform the procedure as you bypass a certain section of the board by adding 3 jumper wires from a small coil of wire you have with you. *Time passes.*

A moment later the connections are complete and you test it by hitting the button again. This time the door opens for you. Leaving the panel, box and button dangling you head through the door. Turn to 194.

326.

As you have been here before and you notice nothing changed from when you left, you decide not to waste any more time here. You decide to leave, turn to 447.

327.

Looking inside the storage cupboards you find nothing of value to you. It looks as though the shelves have already been raided.

If you have not done so already, will you:

Head to the main terminal near the center of the room? Turn to 305.

Utilize one of the automated operating tables if you need to?

Turn to 401.

Check the cells to see if any are occupied?   Turn to 588.

Leave the room?   Turn to 451.

328.

As the warning light signaling necessary evacuation continues to pulse, from around the corner at the starboard junction steps a guard - and he has his eyes on you. Will you:

Stand and fight?   Turn to 1034.

Try to lose the guard?   Turn to 185.

329.

You sprint towards starboard side. Roll 2 dice and add your *agility*. If the total is 9 or less, deduct 3 *vitality* as a laser cuts across your arm.

Reaching the door, you test to see if it will open, not having considered the prospect it may be locked.

Roll a die. If you roll a 1 or 2, you discover in horror that the door is locked and you are going to have run back or be killed where you stand in the open. Repeat the agility test above and then turn to 195.

If you roll 3 or more, turn to 248.

330.

He gives you an intense look. 'Where did you get these?' He asks.

'Found them,' you reply not wanting to begin a long story. With the items you have, you will have made a note of a number if you are on the right track. Reverse that number. If you are not sure how to proceed, then Kinlac cannot or does not help you with the items you are showing him. Return to 818 and show him something else or leave him be.

331.

Following the corridor around as it diverges towards port side, a ramp leads down one level, which brings you to a large hall. The hall is multi story in height and spans perhaps triple that distance in length. Looking out from the open doorway into the hall you can see at least 5 XBR guards firing their weapons at LWS invaders to your left. Judging by the signs the loading bay must be nearby - it seems to be where the LWS agents are filtering through from. Will you:

Wait for a moment to evaluate the situation better?   Turn to 198.

Move out now and help the XBR defend?   Turn to 257.

332.

Time passes.

[If you have the *Survey and Defend* mission turn to 291.]

[If you have the word "clang" written down, turn to 703 now.]

[If you have the word "symptom" written on your mission sheet turn to 221 now.]

The double doors slide open as soon as you near them. Inside the infirmary you can see along one wall approximately 20 enclosed beds – otherwise known as cells. All of them are closed and you cannot see inside all of them; partly because the enclosures have a certain degree of translucency to them and partly because they span the length of the room and you would have to walk past to check them all. On the other side of the infirmary are three automated operating tables each with their own terminal, all empty. There are numerous cupboards scattered around the periphery of the room. There is also, slightly off set to the center of the room a main terminal on standby. Write the word "symptom" on your mission sheet. Will you:

Head to the main terminal near the center of the room?

Turn to 305.

Utilize one of the automated operating tables if you need to?

Turn to 401.

Check the cells to see if any are occupied?   Turn to 588.

Check the storage cupboards for anything of use?   Turn to 455.

Leave the room?   Turn to 451.

333.

For going out of your way to capture some of your own video evidence, you have been awarded an additional 50 creds. Turn to 1300.

334.

The rest quarters are of little interest to you so you decide to leave rather than waste time here. Turn to 590.

335.

Time passes. [If you have the word "bracelet" written on your mission sheet, turn to 273 now.]

Half way along the corridor you are in you find a door on the stern side. In the direction of the starboard side the corridor takes a ninety degree turn to the right. Will you;

Enter the room on stern side labeled"F009"?   Turn to 386.

Head in a starboard direction around the corner towards the stern?

Turn to 391.

Take the corridor towards the port side?   Turn to 467.

336.

Stepping quietly over to the nearest chest you crouch down to open it up. Fortunately it is not locked, it simply is closed with three latches. Undoing the latches you light up the inside of the chest with a small torch. Roll one die. If you roll a 5 or more, turn to 483. Otherwise, turn to 354.

337.

The words "Access granted" appear. Turn to 487.

338.

The information you have gathered is enough to satisfy your mission. Having already relayed it back to Control, you can only wait for what will be next. Combine both words to form "breakdown" and put the word on the bottom of your mission sheet. You can expect no praise; the usual sign of satisfactorily completing your mission will be an increase in your creds. No doubt there will be another mission issued after a short down time. Such is the way of the SDN faction, with efficiency being paramount.

Add 300 creds to your total. Turn to 82.

339.

Cutting into the door, you quickly realize the door is protected by a security field of some sort. You start slicing into the metal, but the field is drawing the power away, making it seemingly impossible to get through this way. You push on several times more but the door is solid and the field does not let up.

Use an explosive on the door: Turn to 550.
Attempt to bust into the wall to your left: Turn to 387.
Leave the room: Turn to 392.

340.

The door automatically opens as you near it. A dividing partition creates a very short passage for you to walk down before you can see the contents of the room. Reaching the end of the partitioned walls you peer into the room to see a number of bunks used for sleeping and rest. Personal draws and chests line the walls and sit at the foot of beds respectively. There are perhaps a few occupants sleeping in the beds.

Will you:
Take time to try to quietly search some of the draws and chests?

Turn to 374.

Leave the room?   Turn to 363.

341.

As you approach the end of the aisle, you see a dark form emerge from around the corner. Now you are too close to run and there is nowhere else to go as the creature blocks the only way out. Turn to 26.

342.

In between the faux maintenance work you are doing you begin to search the databases. You sense you are pushing it however. Will you take time and slow down searching and add another defragmentation service to the schedule? If so, turn to 282.

Or will you continue, aiming to find what you can and get out quick? Turn to 323.

343.

Returning to the teleport room you find it is an apparent disaster, with parts of the floor torn and pieces hanging from the walls, there is blood spread around from obvious fighting and most of the equipment looks to be in pieces. Fortunately a teleporter in the far corner appears to be properly functioning.

[If you have the *Survey and Defend* mission turn to 440 now.]
Otherwise will you teleport to:
Sector E?   Turn to 416.
Sector F?   Turn to 525.
Sector J?   Turn to 604.
Or leave the teleport room?   Turn to 649.

344.

Time passes. You sit down to work at one of the terminals.
[If you have the word "defect" written down, turn to 516 now.]

Will you attempt to hack the terminal?   Turn to 218.
Or search its databases for pertinent information?   Turn to 469.

345.

You take the long corridor towards the bow. Though there are several rooms along here, you decide to ignore them to save time. As you reach the intersection at the end you notice someone leave one of the rooms from where you just came. He begins heading toward you and looks to be an ordinary part of the crew - possibly an operational crewman from his uniform.

'Which is the quickest way to the teleport hub,' you yell out as he approaches.

'Left through the lab,' he responds helpfully, either not recognizing your allegiance or not being interested at this point. You take the portside route which in turn brings you to a laboratory which you enter. You can see the room is well lit and much of the workbenches and experiments, some of which are obviously still running are in disarray. Turn to 171.

346.

Looking out across the loading bay floor, it is apparent chaos. There is shooting going on all over the place, even on the walkways higher up; there is smoke, shouting, deafening explosions and strewn bodies. You have no interest in defending for the XBR faction nor saving the ship. However if the ship is taken over, that might mean you too as either prisoner or casualty. With how hot the firefight is becoming it looks like your best option is to get out of here as soon as you can.

Off to the side are two LWS agents with barrels aimed in your direction. You'll need to deal with them in order to make a run for it without being gunned down:

Treat the agents as one enemy in this short range combat:

LWS Agents	Ra	5
	Vitality	32

4+ to hit, 4 damage.

5+ to reduce damage by 4.

After 3 combat rounds, you have bought a chance to make a run for it as the agents hide in cover - will you:

Head straight towards the back to the loading bay hall? Turn to 285.

Run towards starboard where there is a maintenance tunnel?

Turn to 329.

347.

Laying down on the table you allow the automated scanners and robotic arms to do their work. *Time passes.* You may restore up to 30 *vitality*. If you currently have any of the following lingering effects, they will also be cleared: *burned, bleeding, poisoned or infected.* If you have the word "crippled" written down, you may restore one point only to any characteristic (such as agility) and if your characteristics are returned to their maximum/initial values then you may remove the word "crippled". Any other effect including specific versions of those listed above cannot be cleared using the operating table method here.

If you do not have the word "flutter" written down you may begin hacking the main terminal. To do so, turn to 382.

Otherwise you leave the room, turn to 451.

348.

Add 1 to your *chance* score. The drones have yet to finish cutting through the door when the explosive goes off. The door is blown into the corridor and a cloud of smoke remains. The three of you look up but have difficulty seeing through the smoke. It may not have been a wise choice to use explosives in such a close proximity. As if answering your collective thoughts about the drones, one of them enters the room, flying through the smoke. It shoots at you, but luckily being mostly behind cover you manage to duck down and avoid a potentially fatal wound. Zak takes the opportunity to shoot down the drone. All three of you wait a moment to see if the second drone survived. There is no sign of it, so you all proceed into the corridor once the smoke clears enough. Fragments of it lie on the floor aside the rubble. Zak leads the way down the corridor and you quickly follow. Turn to 134.

349.

Time passes. If you have the word "auto" written down, turn to 326 now.

The room you are in is filled with a main control console covered in various switches, buttons, displays and controls. Around the room and beneath the control console are a number of small storage compartments.

Write the word "auto" on your mission sheet. Will you:

Take a closer look at the controls?	Turn to 423.
Take a look in the storage compartment?	Turn to 375.
Leave the room?	Turn to 447.

350.

As none of the crew are neither armed nor prepared, you cut them all down with ease. Will you:

Search the bodies and room?	Turn to 308.
Or simply leave?	Turn to 397.

351.

The meshed grid is proving to be more robust than you anticipated. Using your weapon you hack at it and try to tear it away with your fists, which you eventually achieve, though you spend a laborious amount of time doing so. *Time passes.* With the mesh out of the way you smash the coils to bits which allows you to bust through the door unhindered by the security field which is now relatively useless. Turn to 509.

352.

Inside the room you notice a number of teleporters and supporting equipment. You have reached the teleport room for this sector. Seeing as you need to get to the action where the LWS ship has unloaded and have no need to return to the bridge just yet, you decide not to spend any time here. You make for the exit looking towards the bow for hostile activity. Turn to 497.

353.

It looks as though the drones are being controlled from elsewhere or perhaps from the network central. With you prying into the area, the system takes greater notice of your activities at the terminal. Turn to 687.

354.

Rummaging around in the chest you withdraw something worthy of a closer look. Roll one die. If you roll a 4 or more, turn to 549. If you roll a 3 or less, turn to 606.

355.

Remove the word "capacity" from your mission sheet and replace it with the word "filter". Roll 1 die. If you roll a 1, turn to 127. Otherwise, return to 590 and continue the reference.

356.

You spot a woman exiting a room down the corridor to your left, or closer to the bow. She stops short and spins around calling to somebody still in the room. You decide to avoid the crew and head towards the stern, away from them. The corridor turns toward starboard and you follow it around. There are rooms here also, but as you expect them to be either offices or living quarters you decide not to waste time searching. The ship shakes as you go, a constant reminder of the severity of the situation. You pass a junction and keep heading to the end of the corridor. The signage is pointing you towards the sector C laboratories which is where you are heading. At the end of the corridor a door opens via the push of a manual button. You've now entered sector C. Roll for *chance*. If the result is 4 or more, turn to 1266. If the result is 3 or less, turn to 1281.

357.

Halfway along the corridor you find a man slumped down on the side, his body cold and lifeless. Crouching to check his vitals, upon rising you hear the march of three XBR guards jogging steadily in your direction. They look at you and recognize your designation as they continue past you in the direction you came from. 'Action is this way agent,' one of them calls out. You decide to follow them towards the bow. Turn to 331.

358.

Looking closely at the map you can see Phaeadron with its three moons and clusters of orbiting satellites and starships. Relative to Phaeadron the XBR starship is in orbit on the far side of the largest of the three moons known as Beutohn. You can also see that the starship is in a dangerous low orbit, probably already descending into the upper atmosphere of Beutohn. If the ship crashes, it will be into the dense jungle landscape of this humid and hot moon. Will you:

Try to access a terminal?   Turn to 296.

Leave the room?   Turn to 543.

359.

You begin to perform a maintenance clean. Since the terminal is overdue for the tasks you are performing, you are perceived as maintenance personnel. You note a sensor continually scanning your biometric data which is a little unnerving, but you are well trained and also realize your only option here is to remain calm whilst you work.

[If you have the word "swoop" written down, turn to 472 now.]

Otherwise roll 2 dice and pick the highest out of the two dice. If your roll is 3 or more, turn to 342. If the highest dice roll is 2 or less, turn to 472.

360.

You grab one of the men as a shield. The drones continue to cut through the door. The man you grabbed has other plans than being your shield. He pushes you aside and leaps back under the table. At that moment the drones burst through the door. Both you and Zak are off guard due to the scuffle, but luckily Melea manages to shoot down the first drone. At the last moment Zak has kept hidden, but you on the other hand are open and unready which the second drone takes advantage of. A laser from one of the sides of the drone cuts into your shoulder. Deduct 2 *vitality*. Before it can fire again Zak blasts the drone, destroying it completely.

You slap a medi patch on the wound and the team re-opens the door and begins heading down the corridor. Turn to 134.

361.

Time passes. Noticing a panel on the wall of the corridor for a com-link you decide to make use of it to contact the bridge. One of the crew responds saying the door can be opened for you but once you are through it will be closed for security purposes and you will not be able to return the same way. Aiming to find the LWS attackers and to aid the defenders, you accept the conditions and after a brief pause the door lifts open slowly to allow you through. Moving ahead you reach the end of the corridor.

Decide on your direction:

Head towards starboard: Turn to 311.

Head towards port: Turn to 217.

362.

Roll one die. On a roll of 5 or 6, turn to 421 now. Otherwise, remove your explosive from your inventory and place it upon the door. The door is already compromised so this time around should be slightly easier. Roll 2 dice. If the total is equal to or higher than the value listed below, turn to 428.

Proximity explosive - 4

Micro petard - 7

Other explosive - 3

If you are using a demolisher bomb or high impact explosive, turn to 428.

If by some unfortunate turn of events you have failed a second time to blow open the door, you'd best try another option:

Use a cutting tool or siege equipment if you haven't already:

Turn to 435.

Head towards port side: Turn to 543.

Head towards starboard: Turn to 384.

363.

The corridor you are in runs front to back or bow to stern in the ship. It is presently empty. There is a door on each side of the corridor, diagonally opposite each other. Will you:

Open the door on the port side labeled "E002 Teleport hub"?

Turn to 400.

Open the door on the starboard side "E006" Turn to 314.

Head up the corridor towards the bow? Turn to 407.

Head down the corridor towards the stern? Turn to 384.

364.

You get the sense Sjonn is getting away. You are going to have to put everything you have into catching up to him. Roll two dice and to the roll add your *agility* and *endurance*. If the total is 10 or less, turn to 911 now. If you have the *Ultra runner* ability, add 3 to your total. If the total is between 11 and 18 inclusive, follow this procedure:

If you have the word "zero" written down, turn to 911 immediately.

Otherwise if you have the word "one" written down, change it to a "zero" now.

Otherwise if you have the word "two" written down, change it to a "one" now.

Otherwise, write the word "two" on your mission sheet.

If you have performed the procedure above or your total was 19 or more:

If you have the word "zero" written down turn to 302.

If you have the word "one" written down, turn to 275.

If you have the word "two" written down or no number words at all, turn to 190.

365.

Waiting for a moment, you sum up the situation and try to think of the best option for getting in. Concentrating intently you are shook up as an automated voice booms through to you from overhead: 'Verify your identity or leave immediately'.

It is a stern command and you must decide what you will do now:

Use an explosive on the door:	Turn to 550.
Try a cutting or siege tool if you have one:	Turn to 339.
Continue to wait:	Turn to 315.
Quickly leave the room:	Turn to 392.

366.

Fortune is with you: Alongside the man's belongings you find his *keypass* which may come in handy. If you take the keypass and have the opportunity to use it later, when you do so, add 132 to the reference you are on at the time. If the new reference does not flow on and make sense, either your keypass has failed or you are not using it correctly. With this acquisition you leave the room. Turn to 590.

367.

[If you have the *Terminal hack* ability, turn to 278 now]

Intending to hack the terminal, you perform a cursory check to see what the terminal shows it has access to. The terminal seems to perform sluggishly, which appears to be due to an outdated platform it is running rather than aged hardware, though the unit itself has clearly seen numerous cycles. It has limited access, mostly to technical details regarding ship equipment. You'll need a plan to proceed.

Will you:

Look at what data is openly accessible?   Turn to 265.

Attempt to remove restrictions to the ships network? Turn to 380.

Attempt to update the platform to make the terminal perform better?   Turn to 537.

Attempt to connect directly to another terminal?   Turn to 659.

Use a *ghost processor* if you have one?   Turn to 868.

368.

Replace the word "deter" with the word "filter" on your mission sheet, return to the previous reference and ignore the query for having the word "filter" on your mission sheet if the previous reference asks this.

369.

With ease you fool the terminal into thinking you are a technician, disabling the field and security to the door. Making use of the manual override feature you open the door and enter. Turn to 509.

370.

Keeping your head low as you sprint, weave and leap across the floor, you dodge incoming fire and obstacles alike, reaching a large crane near the center of the loading bay where you slide into position to take cover. Turn to 346.

371.

Falling short, you land at the far edge of the pool. A jolt is sent through your body, causing you to jerk yourself out of the water to cease the painful shocks. Deduct 3 *vitality*. Safely out, you take a moment to pull yourself back together; the electrocution shaking you up both physically and mentally. *Time passes*. Recovered, you move on reaching a junction and taking the portside path. Next you find a door on your right which clearly leads into a decontamination chamber. You decide to enter. Turn to 93.

372.

Inside one of the boxes you find an *RT data emulator* which you may add to you inventory as a miscellaneous item if you choose. Now:

Continue to search for a terminal?	Turn to 572.
Investigate the equipment within the main room?	Turn to 459.
Leave the room?	Turn to 465.

373.

Although the door has a keypass scanner equipped it is unlocked and you can push it open. Stepping into the room you see shelves littered with various forms of equipment. There are parts both large and small, tools and other unfamiliar items. A number of partitions also act as shelving for even more pieces of equipment. There appears to be nobody here from where you stand, and no sign of a terminal.

Will you search the rest of the room and look at some of the items?
Turn to 490.

Not spend any time here and leave the room? Turn to 451.

374.

Time passes.

Will you search the draws?	Turn to 430.
Or search the chests?	Turn to 336.

375.

Finding little of use to you in the storage compartments you are about to give up until you check the compartment directly adjacent the console. Inside you find a tiny bottle with a chemical commonly taken for the purposes of staying awake and alert. This may be helpful to you. As it will work similar to *adreno,* you may take this item if you choose - if so add one dose of *adreno* to your inventory. Now will you:

Take a closer look at the controls if you have not already?

Turn to 423.

Leave?   Turn to 447.

376.

There are no direct instructions on how to use the infirmary as it is trained knowledge for those that treat others, however there is information pertaining to the functions of the various pieces of equipment within the room. The cells are used for long duration treatment of illnesses as well as prolonged rest as a method of treatment or recovery from long voyages or extensive trauma. The operating tables are highly sophisticated and fully automated devices. They are capable of dealing with severe injuries in a short period of time. They do however have their limitations and often a biological technician is present to oversee the treatment process and guide the automation for complex surgeries.

If you feel you are finished with the terminal you may turn to 504. If you decide to search for other information, return to 487 and choose again.

377.

One of the recent patients happened to be a director of the medical facilities here and with a stroke of insight his clearance number flashes in your mind. You quickly enter the number into the terminal. A moment later the terminal responds, thinking you are the medical director. Now you may spend some time searching this terminal for any information that you may need or you may move on.

Search for information: Turn to 487.

Not spend any more time at the terminal: Turn to 504.

378.

Roll 1 die. If you roll 4 or more, return to 488 and continue reading. If you roll 3 or less, roll another die. Turn to the reference below according to the roll. Note that you will be returning here after you do.

1-3: Turn to 680.

4-5: Turn to 761.

After facing your enemy, add the word "spine" to your mission sheet and return to 488.

379.

Select which type of explosive you are using, remove the item from your pack and then roll 2 dice. If the total is equal to or higher than the value listed below, turn to 428.

If you have the *explosives expert* ability then add 2 to the dice roll.

High impact explosive - 7

Proximity explosive - 6

Demolisher bomb - 4

Micro petard - 9

Other explosive - 7

If your explosive or bomb fails to get you into the room, you may either try again by turning to 362.

Otherwise you abandon the door and either head towards port side; turn to 543 or head towards starboard; turn to 384.

380.

Attempting to remove the network restrictions directly resolves to be a hindrance. The system detects such a blatant attack to it in the short time and immediately shuts down the terminal and puts it into lockout. Add the word "swoop" to your mission sheet. You decide to leave quickly: turn to 743.

381.

Good fortune - your activities are still considered acceptable and you have gained access. Turn to 487.

382.

The terminal prompts you with not so much a warning, but a discouraging notification: "Your activities are now being logged".

You'll need a plan if you are to hack this terminal without being detected.

Will you:

Use the *Terminal hack* ability if you have it?　　　　Turn to 426.

Use a *ghost processor* if you have one?　　　　Turn to 445.

Browse patient records in between attempts to get past the second tier?　　　　Turn to 262.

Perform a maintenance clean of some disused files?　Turn to 359.

Abandon any further attempts to hack the terminal?　Turn to 504.

383.

[If you have the word "wrench" written down, turn to 446 now.]

Time passes. Looking the shelves up and down you see items of all sorts, the majority of which you have no idea where they originated. If you have the *Tech hoarder* ability, turn to 229. If you have the *Keen eyes* ability, turn to 166. Otherwise, roll one die.

If you roll a 1 or 2, turn to 298. If you roll a 3 or 4, turn to 515. If you roll a 5 or 6, turn to 418.

384.

The corridor intersects at a junction. Will you:

Head towards the bow?　　　　Turn to 363.

Heads towards the port side?　　　　Turn to 530.

Head towards the starboard side?　　　　Turn to 307.

385.

The words "Invalid keypass" appear. For whatever reason your keypass has failed. The terminal is now suspended, you will have to leave it and move on. Turn to 504.

386.

[If you have the word "social" written down, turn to 254 now.]

Though it is not locked, this door requires you to swipe your hand across a sensor to open it. This you do and upon stepping inside you see a circle of people all gathered around another man and a holographic projection. The man at the center of attention notices your entry:

'Are you here for the social integration training?'

Add the word "social" to your mission sheet.

[If you have the *Survey and defend* mission, turn to 269 now.]

[If you have the *Fugitive hunt* mission, turn to 283 now.]

Will you:

Answer 'yes' and join the group?	Turn to 457.
Attack them all?	Turn to 350.
Answer 'no' and leave?	Turn to 397.

387.

Finding the wall has a panel which has weak points at the joins, you smash it open. Inside there appears to be three coils all pouring off heat as well as a technicians control interface.

Will you:

Smash the three coils and circuitry attached to them? Turn to 310.

Try to access the technician's interface to disable the door and security? Turn to 420.

388.

Time passes. The metal bar he was using as a weapon is useless to you and the man does not appear to have anything else on him. Choose a direction to proceed:

Move on towards bow:	Turn to 424.
Head towards stern:	Turn to 202.

389.

A close inspection of the guards reveal a few items of interest. You may take one of their *laser pistols* and *electro razors* if you choose. One of the guards also carried a *med pack* which you may take with you also. Now return to 590.

390.

[If you have the word "bunker" written down, turn to 449 now.]

Time passes. The door opens automatically for you. Stepping inside you realize you are in a secure area: within a few steps you are surrounded by thick transparent shielding with a blast proof door inset into it. Behind the transparent shielding you can make out plenty of shelving and mounted on the walls several weapons. From this observation you deduce this must be an armory. There appears to be monitoring equipment yet no one around. You may try to open the door with a keypass, or you may:

Use an explosive on the door:	Turn to 550.
Try a cutting or siege tool if you have one:	Turn to 339.
Wait for a moment and see if anything happens:	Turn to 365.
Leave the room:	Turn to 450.

391.

[If you are allied with the LWS and <u>do not</u> have the word "flash" written down, turn to 319.]

The corridor splits into a t-intersection. You have three options:

Head towards the bow and round the corner to the left: Turn to 335.

Take the corridor towards starboard side:	Turn to 419.
Head in the direction of the stern:	Turn to 622.

392.

Wasting no more time, you make for the exit.

Check your mission sheet for any of the following words, turning to the associated reference accordingly. Note this reference as you will be returning here afterwards.

"Deter"	Turn to 368.
"Filter"	Turn to 442.

If you have neither of those words, nor the word "capacity" written down, write down the word "deter". Turn to 450.

393.

Though his shock mace cannot be used by you, the agent was also carrying a *high impact grenade* and 2 *stimserts* which you may take if you choose. Now return to 597 and continue the reference where you left off.

394.

'Either you are trying to rustle me or you're in the wrong place,' responds the man sternly as he nods in the direction of the door. Will you:

Attack the man?   Turn to 477.
Leave the room?   Turn to 267.

395.

At this point is an intersection. There is a corridor extending towards the stern which appears to have doors on both sides. Will you:

Take the corridor towards the stern?   Turn to 447.
Head towards the starboard side?   Turn to 711.
Head towards port side, following the corner around towards the bow?   Turn to 684.

396.

You are unable to think of anything in the time the terminal allows. The terminal is now in lockdown, you will have to leave it. Add the word "flutter" to your mission sheet and turn to 504.

397.

In the corridor, will you:
If you haven't already enter the room on stern side labeled"F009"?
                                                                   Turn to 386.
Head in a starboard direction around the corner towards the stern?
                                                                   Turn to 391.
Take the corridor towards the port side?   Turn to 467.

398.

You are now at a t-intersection. This corridor which runs front to back offers you three alternatives:

Head towards the bow?   Turn to 520.

Take the corridor directed to the stern?   Turn to 471.

Try the corridor heading port side?   Turn to 523.

399.

As the crew is clearly agitated you fabricate a few lines justifying how you ended up here thanks to some poorly issued orders by your superior. Whilst you hold them in their places with your tirade of nonsense you quickly scan the room with your eyes. You can see there is virtually nothing in here as the man rightly pointed out and certainly nothing useful to you. You sum up your story and apologize and leave the room, not wasting time and avoiding conflict. Turn to 497.

400.

Time passes.

[If you have the *Survey and Defend* mission, turn to 352 now.]

The teleport hub is a large room, divided into two halves. On the bow side are the larger teleporters which are configured for arrivals and departures to and from the ship. The other side has smaller, personal teleports which are linked only to other teleporters on the ship; allowing an individual to move quickly between sectors. It looks like a number of sectors, including the bridge, sector H and sector I are inaccessible via the teleporters at the present time. Will you:

Teleport to Sector F?   Turn to 525.

Teleport to Sector G?   Turn to 539.

Teleport to Sector J?   Turn to 604.

Exit the teleport hub via the port door?   Turn to 497.

Exit the teleport hub via the starboard door?   Turn to 363.

Alternatively you may teleport off the starship, ending your mission. This is a one way trip, if you choose to do so, turn to 900.

401.

The operating tables do not require any expertise or knowledge to operate. They will scan and function on their own for any wounds you may have sustained. It will however take time to allow the automated machine to do its duty. If you choose you may lie down on an operating table and begin the procedure. If you do this, mark off 2 *time passed* boxes on your mission sheet and you may restore up to 30 *vitality*. If you currently have any of the following lingering effects, they will also be cleared: *burned, bleeding, poisoned or infected*. If you have the word "crippled" written down, you may restore one point only to any characteristic (such as agility) and if your characteristics are returned to their maximum/initial values then you may remove the word "crippled". Any other effect including specific versions of those listed above cannot be cleared using the operating table method here.

After you have used the table or decided not to, you may, if you have not already done so:

Head to the main terminal near the center of the room: Turn to 305.
Check the cells to see if any are occupied: Turn to 588.
Check the storage cupboards for anything of use: Turn to 455.
Leave the room: Turn to 451.

402.

Peering inside you see that the room is a mess and the terminal severely damaged. There is no sign of anyone here, but you are sure there will be other guards on the way. You decide it best to keep moving. Turn to 450.

403.

You've cut through the door. Write the word "wide" on your mission sheet and turn to 527.

404.

You find yourself in a control room. Mostly the room contains various instrumentation for monitoring systems in this particular sector. It may be counterproductive to damage the controls here as you may need to make use of some of the systems such as the teleporters.

Leave the room by turning to 530.

405.

Facing the wall whilst bending down you act as if you are adjusting something to avoid being noticed. Moments later the person has disappeared - you cannot tell where to; they may have moved to one of the bunks. Beside you in one of the bunks a man stirs as he turns in his sleep. His belongings are piled on the floor at the head of the bunk. Will you:

Search his belongings?   Turn to 462.
Try to make it across the room to the door on the other side?
                                                           Turn to 480.
Leave the room?   Turn to 590.

406.

Looking over the area you find the woman that was here before has left. Her terminal is locked out, so you will not be able to access it. As far as you can tell there is nothing else of interest here.

Head into starboard section: Turn to 486.
Head into portside section: Turn to 538.

407.

You've reached a junction in the corridor.

[If you have the word "scrape" written down, but not the word "spine", turn to 607.]

Will you:

Head towards the stern?   Turn to 363.
Head towards port side?   Turn to 451.
Head towards the starboard side?   Turn to 494.

408.

Quickly you take up position behind a small mobile platform. With beams whizzing through the air in many directions, you spot an LWS agent in a central position and endeavor to take him out.

LWS agent	Ra	5
	Vitality	18

5+ to hit, 4 damage.

5+ to negate 4 damage as defense.

>This particular agent is also under attack from XBR guards. Each attack round, roll an additional die to represent fire from the guards. The guards will hit the agent on a 5+ and inflict 3 damage.

>If you choose to throw a grenade, any damage inflicted will be doubled.

When the agent is killed, turn to 627.

409.

In one of the cupboards you discover a *med pack* which you may take if you choose. Write the word "bottle" on your mission sheet. If you have not done so already, will you:

Head to the main terminal near the center of the room? Turn to 305.

Utilize one of the automated operating tables if you need to?

Turn to 401.

Check the cells to see if any are occupied? Turn to 588.

Leave the room? Turn to 451.

410.

Without even replying to the man you take up a choke hold on him and with the most minimal of gurgles he is asleep permanently. As no one seems to have awoken, you quickly return to searching the man's belongings. Roll one die. On a roll of 4 or less, turn to 482. On a roll of 5 or more, turn to 366.

411.

You scan some of the written notes on a pad nearby which fills some gaps in your knowledge of what is being done here. The plan is definitely to create a hybrid of some sort; something that can be used as a weapon or in conjunction with their agents in the field. The deep blue liquid is a highly corrosive substance when concentrated. Though it is not as planned, this is all valuable information to your mission. Write the word "skip" on your mission sheet. Rather than spend more time here you decide to leave the room. Turn to 471.

412.

Time passes. [If you are down to the *final tier* remaining, turn to 795 now.]

The automatic door slides open and you step inside. Within the moderate sized room, you see benches, some as high as your chest, cupboards and shelving alongside items and apparatuses all around the place. It is clear from the activity, including the bubbling flask on a bench to your right and the burettes and specimen jars on the shelves beside you that this is a laboratory. It is a large room and you cannot see beyond a large partition, but you do hear a female voice issuing instructions from over the other side of the room. Will you:

Enter further into the room?	Turn to 486.
Leave?	Turn to 471.

413.

From out of a draw you pull a small pouch. Roll one die. If you roll a 1 or a 2, turn to 562. Otherwise, turn to 606.

414.

Manipulating the relevant elements of the display you skim through the infirmary records. Most of the information you can only consider as trivial as it relates to surgeries performed, maintenance schedules and patient logs.

Will you:

Use the terminal to search for a map of the starship?   Turn to 531.
Try to hack the terminal?   Turn to 318.
Alternatively:
Utilize one of the automated operating tables if you need to?
                                                        Turn to 401.

Check the cells to see if any are occupied?   Turn to 588.
Check the storage cupboards for anything of use?   Turn to 455.
Leave the room?   Turn to 451.

415.

Firing ceases and you suspect you have defeated the agent. Seeing a shadow move at the end of the corridor, you edge closer to where the agent was. As you near his position you see a trail of blood indicating the agent has fled. The ship rumbles yet again; there is no time to pursue. Return to 597 and continue that reference.

416.

[If you are down to the *final tier* with the time you have remaining and have not already done so, turn to 1234, remembering this reference so you may return.]

You have reached the teleport hub in sector E. The room is vacant and has two exits to choose from.

Will you:

Take the port side exit?   Turn to 497.
Take the starboard side exit?   Turn to 363.

417.

Sprinting hard you are almost at the crane when you feel a sudden searing pain in your side. You've been hit and the pain brings you to the floor. Desperately trying to get out of the way of enemy fire you scamper the remaining distance to the cover of a large crane, clutching at your midriff. Deduct 3 *vitality* for the wound. You take a moment whilst under the protection of the towering crane. Turn to 346.

418.

Walking the lengths of the shelves you find nothing of apparent value. By the end you conclude it is all junk - bits of equipment that will not help you in any way. Write the word "wrench" on your mission sheet. You may investigate the starboard side by turning to 266 or leave the room by turning to 451.

419.

[If you have the *Survey and defend* mission <u>and</u> have the word "concede" written down, turn to 1071.]

[If you have the word "fresh" written down, turn to 596.]

A short way along this corridor you find a short side corridor extending in the direction of the bow. It looks as though there may be rooms at the end of the passage. Will you:

Stick to the main passage and head towards port side? Turn to 391.

Keep to the main passage and move towards starboard side?

Turn to 614.

Take the side passage towards bow? Turn to 450.

420.

The interface will still need some know-how to make it work for you. If you have the *Terminal hack* ability, turn to 369. If you have a *memory scrambler* device turn to 277. If you have neither of these, you will have to try to smash the coils; turn to 310.

421.

Flying down the corridor is a small drone. It locks onto you as a target and opens fire. Shoot the drone down in this short ranged combat.

| *Airborne drone* | Ra | 5 |
| | Vitality | 5 |

5+ to hit, 4 damage.

5+ Agile flyer defense will negate all damage

Now return to 362 and either set another explosive on the door or try an alternative option.

422.

Fortunately you spot the man before he sees you, giving you the chance to recess yourself against the wall at the bottom of the ramp out of sight. Watching as the uniformed individual passes, you head back up the ramp and into the corridor when it is clear once more. Turn to 208.

423.

Glancing at the control console you are overwhelmed by the complexity of it with many indicators, buttons and displays. For the most part it all appears to be automated so as not to require a user, except to perform maintenance or make adjustments manually. From what you can gather the system appears to control power distribution as well as utility monitoring among other things. As it is highly detailed it would take quite some time just to work out exactly what it does. As it controls an apparent great deal on this level it may also be under tight security you reason also. Will you:

Attempt to destroy the control console?	Turn to 518.
Take a look in the storage compartment?	Turn to 375.
Leave?	Turn to 447.

424.

Moving along, the corridor eventually swings around toward port. As you round the corner, you encounter an LWS agent crouched and waiting - she must have heard your footsteps. Roll for *chance*.

If the result is 3 or less, you have taken a shot from her laser pistol. Deduct 3 *vitality*. If the result is 4 or more the shot misses, burning into the corridor wall behind you. You rush her to duel her in close quarter combat.

LWS agent	CQ	5
	Vitality	20
	4+ to hit, 3 damage.	
	5+ armor negates 4 damage as defense.	

If you overpower the agent, you may take either of her weapons: a *short laser blade* or a *laser pistol*. Turn to 331.

425.

Your movement has not gone unnoticed. Across the room an enemy agent spots you sneaking around, immediately opening fire with a burst of searing laser beams. One of them cuts across your shoulder; deduct 3 *vitality*. You are going to have to fight this well trained adversary. Add the word "extant" on your mission sheet and turn to 144.

426.

Using your skills you locate the correct query registry and edit several values. Now the terminal will have no concerns with what you do or what files you access. You do however still have the task of actually finding any data that you are searching for. This you suspect will take some time as the databases on this terminal are quite large. Will you:

Take the time to search for information that interests you?

Turn to 487.

Abandon the terminal?   Turn to 504.

427.

Entering the room you find it vacant. There are several screens all showing distorted images you cannot make out. There are a few terminals in here, but as you move closer and try to activate them you find they are all inoperable. You decide not to spend more time here. Turn to 543.

428.

You've blown the door open. Write the word "wide" on your mission sheet. Proceeding into the room, turn to 527.

429.

You move across the room to access one of the terminals. As you start to sit down, the man bellows across the room; 'Did you not hear me? I said move it out of here!'

Will you:

Attack him?   Turn to 477.

Leave the room?   Turn to 543.

430.

Making only the faintest sound you step over to the nearest set of draws and delicately open them one by one. If you have the *Stealth* ability, turn to 413. Otherwise roll one die. If you roll a 1 or a 2, turn to 483. If you roll 3 or more turn to 547.

431.

There appears to be several types of drones numbering over a hundred located on this level. Their "nest" as it is aptly called is in sector J on the bow side. If you would like to try to disable the drones, turn to 353. Otherwise, turn to 468.

432.

Quite different to earlier when you were here you find the door is securely locked - apparently from the inside. Swiping your hand across the sensor the door still does not open - it tries to and then ceases with the sound of a mechanical jam.

Will you attempt to force the door open?   Turn to 293.
Leave it alone?   Turn to 711.

433.

As the automatic doors open you find yourself in a vast room filled mostly with a long production line. The production line snakes around the entire room and moves in a stepped sequence. Most of what is attached to the production line are humanoid robots at various stages of manufacture. There are also smaller devices or robots (it is difficult to identify them exactly from your vantage point) placed in between the robots every so often. You note several people in this room - all attending to the production line, mainly via the operation of production equipment. The closest operator looks up at you, but persists with his work regardless. It is likely the others either are too engulfed in their work to have seen or heard your entry.

Given the size, you realize it will consume quite a length of time if you choose to explore the manufacturing facility. Will you:

Explore the room?   Turn to 701.
Exit the room?   Turn to 488.

434.

'Well you are a little out of place here,' responds the woman after you greet her.

You ask of her work, to which she responds rather coldly: 'I do not answer to the Confederacy, you already know I am not obligated to elaborate on our operations here.'

[If you have the *Fugitive hunt* mission, you may ask of this: turn to 802.]

Otherwise you determine it best to leave the woman to her duties.

Head into the starboard section: Turn to 486.

Head into head portside section: Turn to 538.

435.

Using your cutting tool or siege equipment, roll 2 dice, deduct 1 from the total rolled and compare the result to the value needed for your item. If you are successful, turn to 403.

If you are unsuccessful, you may try again a second time, this time do not make a deduction from the total of the roll.

For any attempts beyond the second, add 1 to the dice roll total and mark off a time unit as *time passes*.

At any point you may abandon your attempt and either try an explosive if you haven't already (turn to 379) or move on:

Take the corridor towards starboard side: Turn to 384.

Take the corridor towards port side: Turn to 543.

436.

Trying to make sense of the scrawled notes, you piece together the following ideas:

An attempt to create a hybrid creature is underway. The creature or end result may incorporate three sets of genetic material in combination. One part of the text talks about what is commonly referred to in the notes as 'the beast', which seems to be persistently counter-resistant to the genetic material of the other creatures, whatever they may be.

Mulling over the scientists' notes is taking up valuable time.

[If have the *Proto-swipe* mission, turn to 288.]

Otherwise will you:

Head around the partition to the other side of the room?

                                 Turn to 561.

Exit the laboratory?   Turn to 471.

437.

Having dealt with the security you are now faced with getting through the door.

Try to hack the biometric scanner: Turn to 752.
Use a siege or cutting tool on the armory door: Turn to 773.
Leave immediately: Turn to 392.

438.

Reaching a junction, just as you are looking both ways, a waiting crew member jumps you with a burning hot blade. As you are thrown to the ground you feel the blade penetrate your armor and dig into your flesh. Deduct 3 *vitality*. Defend yourself against the assailant:

XBR crewman	CQ	4
	Vitality	18
	4+ to hit, 4 damage.	
	No defense.	

>You will need to defeat the XBR member in order to get past.

If you defeat the crew member, add the word "flash" to your mission sheet and take his *short laser blade* if you choose. From the junction will you:

Head towards the bow? Turn to 598.
Head down the corridor towards the stern? Turn to 497.
Take the corridor leading towards the starboard side? Turn to 451.

439.

Testing the door you find it is locked. You notice there is a keypad on the door itself. A little further up from the keypad you see that the door also has an unusual access hatch approximately at head height.

[If you are with the Confederacy, turn to 655 now.] Will you:

Try entering the access code if you think you know it? Turn to 706.
Attempt to hack the door open? Turn to 563.
Leave the door alone? Turn to 585.

440.

You look to explore a sector you have yet to so far:

Sector F?	Turn to 525.
Sector J?	Turn to 604.
Or leave the teleport room?	Turn to 649.

441.

You quickly take out the keypass you have. Insert the keypass by turning to the reference with the same value as the keypass plus this one (441).

If you cannot do this, you will have to abandon your attempts to hack the terminal; turn to 504.

442.

Replace the word "filter" with the word "capacity" on your mission sheet and return to the previous reference.

443.

Pushing through the next slightly open door, the tunnel ahead has widened. Just ahead of you a metal cage lies on the floor in the middle of the tunnel. It appears to have been thrown down from several that are stacked to the right side. The cage rattles and shakes. Something inside is trying to escape. As you approach, the creature breaks free and leaps onto you seeking to prevent you from putting it back into another cage. You have to fend it off so you can continue the chase.

Furrend Creature	CQ	4
	Vitality	14
	On 2 dice, 5+ to hit, 2 damage, causes *bleeding*.	
	No defense.	

> At the end of the fifth combat round and each combat round thereafter follow this procedure:

If you have the word "zero" written down, turn to 911 immediately.

Otherwise if you have the word "one" written down, change it to a "zero" now.

Otherwise if you have the word "two" written down, change it to a "one" now.

Otherwise, write the word "two" on your mission sheet. Now continue the combat.

If you defeat the creature, *time passes* as you race to catch Sjonn. Turn to 364.

444.

The same sound you heard earlier reverberates around the room again. Then you see what made it. Or at least you see the shape of something at the far end of the aisle.

Will you:

Head directly at the thing and take it on?	Turn to 253.
Stand completely still in the shadows?	Turn to 1133.
Turn and run back along the aisle?	Turn to 1256.

445.

After inserting your *ghost processor* and taking a mirror image of the processing architecture, you then run some algorithms on the mirror you just captured. The results indicate that this terminal at least has a rudimentary awareness due to its limited access to the network. So there is only so much you may learn from this terminal no matter what you do and at worst the terminal will flag security if it determines your activities are suspicious. You also note that it appears the terminal does not recognize any maintenance work as suspicious activity; perhaps as the terminal is overdue for a scheduled service.

Will you:

Use the *Terminal hack* ability if you have it?   Turn to 426.

Browse patient records in between attempts to get past the second tier?   Turn to 262.

Perform a maintenance clean of some disused files?   Turn to 359.

Abandon any further attempts to hack the terminal?   Turn to 504.

446.

Not wanting to waste time searching the shelves again, you decide on another option.

You may investigate the starboard side by turning to 266 or leave the room by turning to 451.

447.

You are mid-way along a corridor running front to back relative to the ship. There are doors on opposite sides of the corridor. Will you:

Try the door on the starboard side labeled "J078"?   Turn to 689.
Try the door on the port side labeled "J079"?   Turn to 570.
Head towards the stern along a long corridor?   Turn to 750.
Take the corridor towards the bow?   Turn to 395.

448.

Time passes. Entering the room you find yourself in a laboratory: you see bench tops with all manner of apparatus scattered about on them, shelves lined with specimens and substances.

[If you are down to the *final tier* of time, turn to 909 now.]

On a bench beside you two beakers being heated by small burners are bubbling away with a green liquid. On another bench further ahead you notice an elongated tube filled with sediment on the bottom and a crimson liquid swirling around. There is no sign of anyone here, though it is a large room and some of the benches and partitions block your view in areas. Will you:

Investigate the beakers with the bubbling green liquid? Turn to 674.
Take a closer look at the tube of swirling crimson liquid?

Turn to 502.

Move further into the room around the benches?   Turn to 723.
Leave?   Turn to 565.

449.

Time passes. Returning to the armory may not have been the best idea. Waiting inside the room you are faced with an enemy armed and ready just for you. Roll one die. If you roll a 3 or less, turn to 680, remembering this reference so you may return here. If you roll a 4 or more, turn to 761, remembering this reference. After having defeated your enemy you decide not to stick around any longer. Turn to 450.

450.

[If you have the word "bracelet" written down, turn to 568 now.]

You are at the end of a short corridor. There are two doors opposite each other. You may:

Take the corridor and head towards stern, rejoining the main corridor: Turn to 419.

Try the door on port side labeled "F013 Restricted area":
                                                         Turn to 513.

Try the door on the starboard side labeled "F014 Restricted area":
                                                         Turn to 390.

451.

The corridor you are in contains two doors half way along; one on the bow side and a double door on the stern side. As an alternative to trying the rooms there are junctions in both directions of the corridor. Will you:

Try the door on the bow side labeled "E011"?   Turn to 373.

Try the double door on the stern side labeled "E010 Infirmary"?
                                                      Turn to 332.

Head along the corridor towards port side?   Turn to 512.

Take the corridor heading towards starboard?   Turn to 407.

452.

Looking up the location of the ships bridge, you find it located in sector C on level 5. Since it is not even on the same level as you are on you check for the possibility of teleporting to the bridge. It is a restricted area and at present does not allow for teleportation to it without administration authorization at the receiving end. If you feel you are finished with the terminal you may turn to 504. If you decide to search for other information, return to 487 and choose again.

453.

Time passes.

[If you have the word "curb" written down and have not done so previously, turn to 343.]

You are in the teleport room for this sector. It is presently empty.

[If you have the word "fresh" written down, turn to 648.]

[If you have the *Survey and Defend* mission turn to 440 now.]

You may jump to select sectors from here. Will you teleport to:

Sector E?	Turn to 416.
Sector F?	Turn to 525.
Sector J?	Turn to 604.
Or leave the teleport room?	Turn to 649.

454.

As you move forward by only a few steps you see the bracelet light up again. Then without any notice another shock, this time much more powerful ripples through your body. Deduct 5 *vitality*. The shocking continues until you manage to stumble backwards towards starboard. You now realize you will have to get this bracelet off before you can continue. Head back into sector F by turning to 391.

455.

Time passes. [If you have the word "bottle" written down, turn to 327 now.]

There are quite a number of storage cupboards in each area of the room so you begin opening them up at a sharp pace and checking their contents. Many are filled with various drugs, chemicals, surgical implements and maintenance equipment. Roll one die. On a roll of 4 or more turn to 552. On a roll of 3 or less, turn to 409.

456.

It looks as though the man had nothing of value on him. Will you:
Study the holographic map if you haven't already?   Turn to 533.
Access a terminal if you haven't done so?   Turn to 344.
Leave the room?   Turn to 543.

457.

Time passes. Sitting in with the group you listen to the man in the center of the room speak. He talks about different groups and routines for the crew - nothing of concern for you, not that you are listening with your full attention. One of the other participants looks at you a little unsure, wondering about your attire.

If you have the word "filter" written down, turn to 564 now. Otherwise if you have the word "deter" written down, turn to 511. If you have neither of these, the training talk proceeds and you soon decide to excuse yourself from the room so as to not waste any more valuable time. Turn to 397.

458.

'I know nothing of that, it is not my area of expertise,' he retorts.
'Where can I find out?' You ask, pushing him for information.
'Whatever is being built will be in manufacturing in sector F,' he says matter-of-factly.
Now will you:
Ask him who he is and what he is doing if you haven't already?
    Turn to 324.
Attack him?   Turn to 477.
Leave now?   Turn to 267.

459.

Though there is much equipment in here and most of it functioning with elaborate colored displays none of it is helpful to you in any way. Now:

Continue to search for a terminal: Turn to 572.
Search the cupboards and boxes if you have not already:
                                                      Turn to 612.
Leave the room: Turn to 465.

460.

You've reached a junction.

[If you are allied with either the SDN or LWS and <u>do not</u> have the word "expire" written down, turn to 485.]

Here you may:

Head towards port: Turn to 699.
Head towards the bow taking a right hand corner at the end:
                                                      Turn to 585.
Take the corridor in the direction of the stern: Turn to 684.

461.

Taking up position behind the mobile platform rig you note Leading Weapon Syndicate (LWS) agents storming across the loading bay floor. Several shots pass by you, scolding the air. Narrow misses as they could easily have scolded your flesh instead. Realizing your position affords limited cover, you decide it necessary to make a dash for better defense. Make the sprint by testing your agility. To do this, roll 2 dice and add your *agility* score.

If the total is 10 or more, turn to 370.
If the total is 9 or less, turn to 417.

462.

Taking the opportunity you begin rummaging through the man's belongings. Your best efforts to remain silent are not enough however, the man intuitively realizes someone is into his stuff and his eyes spring open.

'Get your dirty hands off my things and get out, before I report you,' he says in a low scornful voice.

If you have the *Sneak* ability or you are part of the SDN faction, turn to 410.

Otherwise, turn to 506.

463.

Over at the corner of the room you find, surrounded by apparent scrap and practically hidden from view to the other side of the room a grimy looking terminal. Will you:

Attempt to hack the terminal?	Turn to 367.
Checks the items on the shelves?	Turn to 635.
Have a closer look inside the toolbox?	Turn to 657.
Leave the room?	Turn to 743.

464.

[If you have the word "trend" or "ranked" written down, roll 1 die. If you roll 4 or more, turn to 878.]

Otherwise turn to 565.

465.

[If you have the *Survey and defend* mission and have the word "concede" written down, turn to 669.]

The corridor you are in runs lengthways relative to the ship. There is a large door on the port side towards the bow end of the corridor. Towards the stern on the starboard side is another door of regular size. Will you:

Try the door on port side labeled "Manufacturing"?   Turn to 599.

Try to enter the door on the starboard side labeled "F002"?

Turn to 481.

Continue along the corridor heading towards the bow? Turn to 614.

Head towards the stern, following the corridor around the corner?

Turn to 590.

466.

Looking you up and down and momentarily staring at your armor the man greets you in a positive serving manner; 'I had not been informed the Confederacy was aboard our ship. What is it you need?'

How will you respond?

Ask for the location of the fugitive Sjonn?	Turn to 529.
Ask where the LWS attack is taking place?	Turn to 621.
Ask him what he sees on the map?	Turn to 261.
Attack him?	Turn to 477.

467.

Heading towards port side you find halfway along the corridor a large ramp leading downwards.

[If you are allied with the LWS faction turn to 791 now.]

[If you have the *Survey and Defend* mission, turn to 628 now.]

There are a number of rooms along this corridor, which appears to be the beginning of sector F from the room designations. Will you:

Take a look in some of the rooms here?	Turn to 658.
Keep moving to the end of the corridor?	Turn to 763.
Head back into Sector F?	Turn to 397.

468.

You suddenly notice something on one of the monitors. It is small and moving fast towards you. Placing yourself against the side wall you prepare to meet it if it enters the room. You hear the whoosh of air as it flies up to just outside the door. Then you hear a distinct hissing sound. A gas is filling the room making the air both toxic and difficult to see through. In addition an intense strobe begins flashing glaringly and a piercing siren adds to the assault. This drone is designed to immobilize and disorientate you and then poison you into a state of catalepsy.

You must escape the security room or perish from the toxicity. Roll one die and add your *agility*. If the total is 11 or more you have escaped from the gas quickly enough to avoid breathing any in. If your total is less than 11, then you will become *poisoned* before you manage to escape. Roll another die and add this to the total. If you still have not reached 11 or more, deduct a further 2 *vitality*.

Upon reaching the door you smash the drone which was still hovering in midair.

You quickly leave the area, heading to the end of the corridor and then taking a right turn towards port side where you reach a junction. Write the word "scrape" on your mission sheet. Turn to 391.

469.

It looks as though this particular terminal has very minimal information that is helpful to you, unless you plan to waste time looking through a database of supply routes and shipping information. Will you:

Attempt to hack the terminal?   Turn to 218.
Leave the room?   Turn to 543.

470.

In your attempt to disable the scanners you unintentionally cross two wires, discharging a capacitor and giving yourself a shock in the process. Deduct 2 from your *vitality*. Luckily though the short has also damaged the scanners enough that they are unable to perform their duty until repaired. You decide to move on before anybody arrives to investigate what has happened.

The teleport hub has two exits. Which will you choose:

The door on the port side?   Turn to 497.
The door on the starboard side?   Turn to 363.

471.

You are at the end of a corridor. There are two unmarked doors which you may try or you may leave this area via the corridor heading towards the bow.

[If you have the word "gaseous" written down, turn to 753 now.]
Will you:

Open the door on starboard side?   Turn to 721.

Try the door on the port side?   Turn to 412.

Head up the corridor towards the bow?   Turn to 398.

472.

Your actions have alerted the awareness of the terminal and it has detected your intentions. Immediately the terminal goes into lockdown, shutting you out of it completely. Add the word "flutter" to your mission sheet and turn to 504.

473.

Time passes. You were right and Seyem has yet to return; after searching diligently you discover, hidden beneath several other containers a dark, unmarked container you can tell is out of place. Opening it up you find what you were after. There is a *laser pulse rifle* in pieces which you can quickly assemble; enough smart bands and medications to form a *med pack* and also a *high impact grenade*. Where he managed to find these items or how he managed to get them you can only imagine, but they are yours for the taking now. Equipped and ready you make for the exit and head back to the corridor. Turn to 622.

474.

Time passes. [If your time remaining is down to the *final tier*, turn to 427.] Otherwise:

[If you have the word "starman" written down, turn immediately to 514.]

Entering the room you find a circular double platform, above which seemingly levitates a hologram spanning almost half the breadth of the room. The hologram is clearly a map; furthermore it appears to be of this section of the Nuivairyiux star system. On the other side of the hologram a man stands, intently studying the map. It seems like he may have noted your entry but does not remove his vision from the hologram. Glancing around the room you can see several screens displaying visual feeds from places you do not recognize, as well as a number of terminals, small tables and chairs. Write the word "starman" on your mission sheet. Will you:

Study the holographic map?	Turn to 533.
Meet with the man on the other side?	Turn to 591.
Access a terminal?	Turn to 344.
Leave the room?	Turn to 543.

475.

Flying rapidly towards you, a drone has you in its sights:

Airborne drone	Ra	5
	Vitality	5
	5+ to hit, 4 damage.	
	5+ Agile flyer defense will negate all damage.	

After the battle return to your previous reference.

476.

Functioning well, your Bio-mimic device does the trick and gets you in. Turn to 781.

477.

Although tall and of solid stature the man is unarmed and unready. Your attacks overpower him, expediently bringing him to the floor.

[If you are with the Confederacy, turn to 161 now, remembering this reference.]

Write the word "clang" on your mission sheet. Now will you:

Search his body?	Turn to 456.
Study the holographic map if you have not already?	Turn to 533.
Access a terminal if you haven't already?	Turn to 344.
Leave the room?	Turn to 543.

478.

Looking in the room again you find it is now empty as all the people have left. Taking a quick look around you see nothing new and nothing of interest. *Time passes*. Turn to 565.

479.

Stepping through the doors you find yourself in a well-lit and expansive galley. To your left are cooking ovens, utensils and cupboards, whilst on the right you see some vats and steam trays. You are about to move forward into the room when a door on the far right bursts open and a worker robot scoots in on four wheels. Navigating the path around the two island benches, it abruptly skids to a stop near you before prompting you:

'Do you require service?'

You return a plain 'no' as to have the robot move out of the way and continue with its duties.

If you are part of the Confederacy or do not belong to any faction (NFA), turn to 557. Otherwise, turn to 586.

480.

Time passes. Carefully you begin walking slowly across the room. The more bunks you pass, the more you see there are plenty of people sleeping here. Somebody shifts in their sleep. You freeze for a moment. Then you continue to head towards the door. Upon reaching the door you press it open slightly. The ambient lighting activates to a low level and you peer in. It is empty. Stepping inside you realize you are in a hygiene room. There is residual steam slowing being extracted by fans and droplets of water from recent usage. It does not take you long to realize there is nothing to be gained here. You decide to leave the room. Turn to 590.

481.

[If you have the word "stir" written down, turn to 241 now.]

Entering the room you look around to see apparatus containing clear liquid, pipes, filters and numerous other devices. There is a work bench to one side, as well as a number of scattered cupboards and boxes lining the room. It appears to be cluttered with the amount of items in the room, yet somewhat neatly organized at the same time. Your best guess is that the room serves the utilities such as water supply and possibly some repair work. Will you:

Explore the room further?   Turn to 508.

Not waste time here and leave?   Turn to 465.

482.

Amongst his items you find one that is of value to you: a single dose of *adreno* which you may take if you like. You decide to keep moving and leave the room. Turn to 590.

483.

Suddenly an alarm sounds and the room lights up in a dim flashing red. Instinctively opting for the smartest move you dash straight for the exit to avoid the waking occupants. Hopefully none of them identified you on the way out. Write the word "rose" on your mission sheet and turn to 363.

484.

The door is still securely locked; you decide to leave it alone than risk more trouble and time spent. Turn to 450.

485.

Roll a die. If you roll a 5 or a 6, turn to 1209. If you roll 4 or less, return to 460 and continue reading that reference from where you left off.

486.

As you wander around the workbenches you see much happening. There are experiments in progress, notes scribed on pads as well as various substances left standing on the benches. Will you:

Head around the partition to the other side of the room?

Turn to 561.

Take a closer look at some of the experiments in progress?

Turn to 542.

Take a look at the written notes?   Turn to 436.
Not spend any more time here and leave?   Turn to 471.

487.

Time passes. You have full access to this terminal and the limited access it has to the starship network.

What data do you seek?
How to use the infirmary: Turn to 376.
Important functional parts of the ship: Turn to 524.
Location of the ships bridge: Turn to 452.
Information about the LWS assault on the starship: Turn to 316.
Any information on the scientist Tuo Minkla: Turn to 555.
Technology being produced on the starship: Turn to 205.
Research that is happening on the starship: Turn to 619.
Any information on an individual named Sjonn: Turn to 574.
Information on the ships security: Turn to 226.

Alternatively you may close the terminal down and do something else or leave the room by turning to 504.

488.

The corridor you are in extends from port to starboard. There is a door here.

[If you have the word "scrape" written down, but not the word "spine", turn to 378.]

Will you:

Try the door on the bow side labeled "Manufacturing"?

Turn to 433.

Head towards port side rounding the corner?   Turn to 551.

Keep moving along the corridor towards starboard side?

Turn to 590.

489.

Something seems out of place in here. There are containers scattered about rather than being neatly organized. You can't quite put your finger on it, but a small little storage room like this could be used to either hide or hide something. None the less you find nothing out of the ordinary here, but have the nagging feeling the fugitive is in this sector somewhere. You decide to leave. Turn to 622.

490.

Where will you begin searching:
Shelves on the port side?   Turn to 383.
Shelves on the starboard side?   Turn to 266.

491.

Time passes. With gusto you begin hacking into the controls, smashing gauges and puncturing pipes. It will be a while before they fix this mess you think to yourself, and that is aside from the chaos and confusion that will result downstream. If you have not already done so, begin a tally on your mission sheet of the damage you have done to the starship. Add 1 point for the damage done to this room. Write the word "stir" on your mission sheet.

The deed is done and between the water leaking everywhere and sparks being flung around you had best leave the room; turn to 465.

492.

Time passes. Remove the explosive you intend to use from your inventory. You place the explosive on the door and arm it, quickly moving away.

A moment later, you expect the explosive to detonate, yet nothing has happened. Returning to the door you discover your explosive blackened and charred; it has been disabled, likely with an electromagnetic field of some sort. Worse than that however is your attempt to blow open the door has triggered an alarm. A strip light surrounding the door has begun pulsating red. Roll one die. On a roll of 4 or more, turn to 787. If you roll 3 or less, turn to 571.

493.

Seemingly thrown in a box as junk underneath a number of other items you find a partly full bottle of *brutenide* tablets. A little aged, they should still work none the less. There is enough for three doses remaining if you choose to take them. Will you:

Continue to search for a terminal?	Turn to 572.
Investigate the equipment within the main room?	Turn to 459.
Leave the room?	Turn to 465.

494.

[If you have the *Survey and Defend* mission, turn to 578 now.]

On the way you pass several disused or makeshift storage rooms. Option to:

Return to the junction and head towards port side:	Turn to 451.
Return to the junction and head towards the stern:	Turn to 363.
Follow the corridor leading you to sector F:	Turn to 335.

495.

Appearing the same as earlier, both bodies lay lifeless on the floor. You are risking being caught by returning here. Roll one die. If you roll a 1 or a 2, turn to 680, remembering this reference. If you roll 3 or above or have just returned to this reference, nothing else happens. Either:

Head into starboard section:	Turn to 486.
Or head into portside section:	Turn to 538.

496.

Looking a little more closely and applying your knowledge of biology and chemistry, your educated guess at what they are doing here is that for one thing there are plans to combine genetic material and create a hybrid of some kind. The other plan it seems they have is to create a concentrated form of whatever the deep blue liquid is.

[If have the *Proto-swipe* mission, turn to 411.]

Now will you:

Head around the partition to the other side of the room?

Turn to 561.

Take a look at the written notes?					Turn to 436.

Not spend any more time here and leave?			Turn to 471.

497.

You are in a corridor running from the bow (front) to the stern (rear) of the ship. Closer to the bow on the port side is a door. There is also a door on the starboard side. Will you:

Open the door on the port side labeled"E012"?		Turn to 575.

Open the door on the starboard side labeled "E002 Teleport hub"?

Turn to 400.

Head up the corridor towards the bow?				Turn to 512.

Head down the corridor towards the stern?			Turn to 543.

498.

Taking a quick look inside the room you find it is vacant and nothing of interest in here for you. You head towards the exit. Turn to 497.

499.

Roll one die. If you roll a 1 or a 2, turn to 1017. If you roll 3 or higher, turn to 943.

500.

The starship's teleport hub is both spacious and elaborately equipped. Mostly automated, numerous detectors and monitoring devices adorn the walls and ceiling. The teleporters are divided in half intentionally as some are setup only for receiving whilst the others for departing – either off ship or within the ship itself. The room is presently vacated. There are two doors exiting from the teleport hub.

An automated message fills the room: 'Unscheduled arrival, please validate your identity.'

Before you set off any alarms you begin with an attempt to disable the scanners.

Roll two dice and add your *sci* score to the result. If the total is 8 or more, turn to 536.

If the total is 7 or less, turn to 470.

501.

Entering the room you find it mostly empty: there are several shelves with a few items on each, but nothing else aside from that. Will you:

Search the room?	Turn to 734.
Leave?	Turn to 597.

502.

According to the notes lying on the bench nearby, the crimson liquid is a mutagen of some sort. You are not sure on any actual details of the liquid, but it does seem to swirl all by itself. The tube is currently sealed - you could if you chose to remove it from its stand and take it with you. If you do, it will count as a miscellaneous item, however it is large enough that it will <u>not</u> be a *light item* as miscellaneous items usually are. Now:

Investigate the beakers with the bubbling green liquid?	Turn to 674.
Move further into the room around the benches?	Turn to 723.
Leave?	Turn to 565.

503.

'Well if you need something repaired then take the first right and then the first left,' he says pointing towards the bow. Now will you:

Move around the other side and study the holographic map?

Turn to 533.

Access a terminal?　　　　　　　　　　　　　　　Turn to 344.

Leave the room?　　　　　　　　　　　　　　　　Turn to 543.

504.

If you haven't already done so, will you:

Utilize one of the automated operating tables if you need to?

Turn to 401.

Check the cells to see if any are occupied?　　　　Turn to 588.

Check the storage cupboards for anything of use?　Turn to 455.

Leave the room?　　　　　　　　　　　　　　　　Turn to 451.

505.

The uniformed man is quick to question your intent: 'Who are you and where are you from?' he asks directly. Will you:

Identify yourself?　　　　　　　　　　　　　　Turn to 559.

Claim to be a worker?　　　　　　　　　　　　Turn to 618.

Attack the man?　　　　　　　　　　　　　　　Turn to 477.

506.

Though you could easily silence the man permanently you see that you would be stirring up a room of possibly armed people which may not be the best thing to do right now. You decide to save your fighting skills and time and make for the exit. Turn to 590.

507.

From down the corridor you make out the armored figure of a Confederacy agent. As he nears you, he picks your identity, his steps turning into strides as he hurries toward you. Fend off the Confed' before he can beat you down:

Confederacy Agent	CQ	5
	Vitality	28

4+ to hit, 5 damage.
4+ to reduce damage by 3 as defense.

>The Confederacy agent is well trained at close quarters and is a tough opponent even without his standard shock mace. If the agent rolls a 1 when rolling to hit, he may still hit you with either a punch or an elbow. Roll another die. If the result is 4 or more, he will score a hit, causing 2 damage.
>If the battle lasts 5 rounds or more, *time passes.*
If you defeat the agent, turn to 393.

508.

Time passes. [SDN faction: turn to 567 now.]
You may choose to:
Try to find a terminal if there is one here: Turn to 560.
Search the cupboards and boxes: Turn to 612.
Take a closer look at the items and equipment within the room:
Turn to 459.
Leave: Turn to 465.

509.

Write the word "bunker" on your mission sheet.
You step inside a small chamber where the actual door to the armory awaits. Once inside the door closes behind you. Within the chamber there is a biometric scanner to your left that you will have to overcome in order to open the door to the armory.

If you think you know of a way to defeat the biometric scanner, then you may attempt to do so now.

If you are unsure, you have the following options:

Perform a scan on yourself: Turn to 698.
Try to hack the biometric scanner: Turn to 752.
Use a siege or cutting tool on the armory door: Turn to 773.
Wait and let it play out: Turn to 629.
Leave immediately: Turn to 392.

510.

To enter this room you require an executive keypass. If you have one, you will know how to use it.

Otherwise will you:

Try the first door?   Turn to 30.
Keep moving?   Turn to 3.

511.

Without warning 3 security guards burst into the room. They make no apology for their entry and do a very quick look around the room. With fortune your back is to them and they do not look carefully enough to identify you or notice your concealed weapon. The guards leave quickly enough, moving onto the next room no doubt. Remove the word "deter" from your mission sheet. You have to wait a little longer for the heat to dissipate while the man waffles on some more. *Time passes.* Eventually you excuse yourself and leave the room. Turn to 397.

512.

[If you are allied with the LWS and do <u>not</u> have the word "flash" written down, turn to 438.]

You have reached a T-junction. Will you:

Head towards the bow?   Turn to 598.
Head down the corridor towards the stern?   Turn to 497.
Take the corridor leading towards the starboard side? Turn to 451.

513.

[If you have the word "iris" written down, turn to 484 immediately.]

[If you have the word "scrape" written down, turn to 402 immediately.]

The door is securely locked. It looks like both a key pass and biometric identification is required. If you have a keypass and would like to try it here, follow the procedure previously given to use it, remembering this reference. Will you:

Try an explosive on the door?   Turn to 492.

Attempt to hack your way through the door with a suitable tool or weapon?   Turn to 546.

Leave the door alone?   Turn to 450.

514.

This time around you find the room to be clear of any crew. The holographic map and visuals are still as they were earlier. Will you:

Take a look at the holographic map?   Turn to 358.

Try to access a terminal?   Turn to 296.

Leave the room?   Turn to 543.

515.

Within plain sight you spot a *dynamo case*. Not sure what you may use it for now, perhaps you may find a use for it later. If you choose to add it to your inventory it will count as a miscellaneous item. Write the word "wrench" on your mission sheet. You may investigate the starboard side by turning to 266 or leave the room by turning to 451.

516.

The terminals are no longer working and still in need of repair. You decide to leave the room. Turn to 543.

517.

[If you have the word "forest" written down, turn to 611 now.]

[If you are part of the Confederacy and down to the *final tier* of time remaining, turn to 1120 now.]

What strikes you most as you enter the room are the sounds. Rather than the low murmur of the ship, you become receptive to sounds of insects and flowing water. Beyond the patch of grated floor on which you stand, there is what appears to be a small section of forest, inclusive of insects and animals and a small flowing stream. The forest contains no large trees or plants - they are all dwarves to fit within the confines of the room and in the same manner the stream would obviously flow from a fountain or pump hidden somewhere. Just inside this forest, seated on a chair pressed into the ground cover is a uniformed woman looking intently at the plants and shrubs.

She is yet to note your entry, so you may either leave unnoticed or sneak across and jump her.

Will you:

Move to attack her?	Turn to 593.
Greet her?	Turn to 647.
Leave the room?	Turn to 710.

518.

After the first strike at the console you realize your mistake. An alarm sounds and the door is covered in an instant by a drop down security curtain, locking you inside. Then you hear a sharp hiss as from four nozzles on the ceiling a gas pours out, filling the room. Eventually you will have to take a breath and when you do, the gas will knock you unconscious and put you on the floor; your mission and life ends here.

519.

You're looking at a blueprint for the layout of sector F. Directly across from the security room is the armory. On the monitors you can see no activity in there. Most of sector F is taken up by the manufacturing room. Aside from that there are living quarters, rest quarters and training rooms.

Quickly, you move on.

Roll one die. If you roll a 5 or a 6, then turn to 468 now.

To keep searching, return to 646. To leave now, turn to 774.

520.

Time passes. You've reached a junction. Which path will you take:

Head towards starboard side?   Turn to 608.
Head towards port side?   Turn to 710.
Head towards the stern?   Turn to 398.

521.

The alien has found you. Turn to 26.

522.

You have reached the lowest level of the engine bay. In the middle of the floor the 3 filaments extend into an inky blackness in the floor.

[If you are aligned with the SDN faction, turn to 902.]

If not, as there appears to be nothing here for you, you decide to head back up. Turn to 981.

523.

[If you are down to the *final tier* with time remaining, roll 1 die. If you roll 4 or more, turn to 158.]

You are approximately a third of the way from the starboard side end of the corridor you are in. There are doors on either side of the corridor opposite each other. Will you:

Open the door on bow side labeled "G007: Restricted"? Turn to 692.
Head towards starboard side junction?   Turn to 398.
Head along the corridor in the direction of port side?   Turn to 649.
Try the door on the stern side labeled "G008/G009"?   Turn to 676.

524.

It is difficult to find functional parts of the ship on their own as the information is setup from an engineering perspective with multiple layers detailing specific sub-systems of the ship. However you note on the level you are on which is level 3, entry to the engine room is in sector J; there is a main air filtration room also in sector J; a small control room in sector E; laboratory in sector G and water filtration in sector D.

If you feel you are finished with the terminal you may turn to 504. If you decide to search for other information, return to 487 and choose again.

525.

The teleporter has successfully brought you to sector F. Stepping off the tele-pad you make for the exit, looking outside down the lengths of the corridor, checking for hostiles. Turn to 551.

526.

As the security room has access to the database it is relatively easy to find what you need. Hacking through to bypass password entry you then proceed to remove the restrictions against your name. Now any biometric scanner will accept you. When you encounter a biometric scanner, add two hundred and twenty two to the reference you are on to validate yourself. Now return to 646.

527.

Time passes. [If you have the word "local" written down, turn to 554.]
[If you are allied with the SDN, turn to 581.]
Otherwise, turn to 404.

528.

As an avid collector of all things tech related, you know a useful piece of 'junk' when you see it. Inside one of the boxes you find an *RT data emulator* which you may add to you inventory as a miscellaneous item if you choose.

Continue to search for a terminal?	Turn to 572.
Investigate the equipment within the main room?	Turn to 459.
Leave the room?	Turn to 465.

529.

'I am unable to help you with that unfortunately. We have workers across multiple divisions and - I'm assuming you have clearance for this - I would not know where to start looking. Now I have a meeting in a moment so you will have to excuse me,' he says, gesturing towards the door.

You decide to comply and head for the door. Turn to 543.

530.

You are now in the middle of a corridor which extends from side to side. There is a door on the bow side. Will you:

Open the door with labels "E003" and "Technicians only"?

Turn to 556.

Continue along the corridor towards starboard side?   Turn to 384.

Head along the corridor towards port side?   Turn to 543.

531.

It appears as if the terminal has no map layout of the starship itself. The closest thing it does have however is a listing of recuperation cells like the ones here in the infirmary in various locations around the ship. The cells are linked back to this terminal in order to log usage. Of noteworthiness you see there is one located in a conservatory in sector G.

Now will you:

Use the terminal to search the records of the infirmary? Turn to 414.

Try to hack the terminal?   Turn to 318.

Alternatively:

Utilize one of the automated operating tables if you need to?

Turn to 401.

Check the cells to see if any are occupied?   Turn to 588.

Check the storage cupboards for anything of use?   Turn to 455.

Leave the room?   Turn to 451.

532.

All that you can learn about the armory from this terminal is that it is highly secure in the same way as the security room is. It is located across the corridor and looking at the monitors you see no signs of crew inside. Roll one die. If you roll a 5 or a 6, then turn to 468 now.

To keep searching, return to 646. To leave now, turn to 774.

533.

Looking closely at the map you can see Phaeadron with its three moons and clusters of orbiting satellites and starships. Relative to Phaeadron the XBR starship is in orbit on the far side of the largest of the three moons known as Beutohn.

[If you are part of the Confederacy, turn to 591 now.]

There is nothing more you note from the holographic map. Will you:

Access a terminal?   Turn to 344.

Leave the room?   Turn to 543.

Alternatively, if you do not have the word "clang" written down:

Meet with the man on the other side if you have not already?

Turn to 591.

534.

Time passes. Crouched at the bottom of the ramp you take a brief moment to get a better idea of what is going on. At the same time you set your video link to record some of what is happening. At present XBR forces seem to have the upper hand, commanding a central defensive position within the hall. The LWS agents do appear to be filtering in continually, however you know they are better equipped with both firepower and armor than the guards. For capturing footage here that may be of value to your mission, write the word "judge" on your mission sheet. You head out to assist the XBR crew. Turn to 408.

535.

Time passes.

[If you have been here before or are NFA, turn to 334 now.]

[If you have the *Fugitive hunt* mission, turn to 712 now.]

As you approach the doors slide open for you and you step inside. Dimly lit, from what you can make out as you slowly enter the room are a number of bunks located around the periphery. There is movement: a door at the far end of the room opens and a silhouette enters into the room you are in. A number of the bunks are also clearly occupied. Shall you:

Avoid being caught and leave the room?   Turn to 590.

Stay in the room and see if there might be anything of interest?

Turn to 405.

536.

A little tinkering with the inputs and the scanners won't register your presence in the room. Since there is no follow up, the initial identity check will not be flagged – it will reside in the system memory only. You decide to move out. The teleport hub has two exits. Which will you choose:

The door on the port side?   Turn to 497.

The door on the starboard side?   Turn to 363.

537.

Time passes. It looks as though the terminal could do with updating - the user seems to have been intent on running outdated versions of the soft-structure and unwilling to update each time an update has become available. The update is a slow but steady progression. Will you:

Whilst it is updating - try to access more of the network?

Turn to 499.

Wait until the update is finished and then try?   Turn to 601.

Or you may attempt to crash the update hoping you can access the network while the system is down by turning to 943.

538.

If you have the word "criteria" written down, turn to 865 immediately.

Otherwise if you have the word "induct" written down, turn to 892 now.

At the far end of the bench you notice a lab scientist working diligently with his experiments. His back is to you and he has yet to note your presence. Will you:

Attack the man?	Turn to 930.
Try to talk with him?	Turn to 820.
Ignore him and head towards the benches and exit on the port side?	
	Turn to 745.

539.

[If you have the *Survey and defend* mission <u>and</u> have the word "proceed" written down, turn to 1161.]

Arriving at sector G you find the teleport room here vacant. You move to the exit. Turn to 649.

540.

Looking at Melea's wounds you realize you'll need to do what you can and curb the bleeding in order for her to travel with you. If you have a *med pack* or *stimsert* you can and are willing to use on her, turn to 258. If you do not have anything that can help her medically or decide you cannot spare anything, you leave her be. Remove the word "Melea" from your mission sheet and turn to 1265.

541.

Tucked away, at least until your discovery, you find a *utility socket*. This you may take if you choose, noting that it may be useful later when you have an attachment to insert into it. Will you:

Continue to search for a terminal?	Turn to 572.
Investigate the equipment within the main room?	Turn to 459.
Leave the room?	Turn to 465.

542.

Time passes. Investigating some of the experiments in progress, you note one experiment has something to do with chromosome combinations whilst another experiment is about deriving a constituent from a deep blue chemical.

If you have a *Bio* score of 5 or more, turn to 496.

Otherwise, will you:

Head around the partition to the other side of the room?

Turn to 561.

Exit the laboratory? Turn to 471.

543.

Having reached the corner at the end of the corridor you find a door on the port side. Alternatively you may ignore the door and keep moving.

Open the door labeled "E014 Navigation B": Turn to 474.
Continue along the corridor towards the bow: Turn to 497.
Continue along the corridor towards starboard: Turn to 530.

544.

Waiting in the shadows, your heart pounds and sweat pours off you as the creature lurks within the room, fully capable of tearing you up should you make the wrong move. Will you:

Make a run for it? Turn to 268.
Stay still? Turn to 521.

545.

Mistaking you for a guard, the man remarks dismissively; 'We are fine here. Move along to check the other sectors.' Will you:

Attack him? Turn to 477.
Study the holographic map? Turn to 533.
Access a terminal? Turn to 429.
Leave the room? Turn to 543.

546.

Teeth grit and sweat pouring you hack into the door, determined to get into this room.

If you have the word "block" written down, turn to 852. If not, turn to 787.

547.

From out of a draw you pull a small pouch. Roll one die. If you roll a 1 or a 2, turn to 562. Otherwise, turn to 606.

548.

Time passes. After inputting the code you have recalled, you wait with bated breath for something to happen. A slight pause and then the door slides open. You step inside. A very small room - more like a booth is filled with mostly data stores, but also an older form of storage known as scribes. You cannot read the scribes but you can read the data stores and that is what you are here for. You quickly begin scanning neatly ordered stores for the most crucial ones you will upload. This takes time given then number of data stores in here, but it is critical for your mission. Next you scan the data stores you have selected and upload them to Control. *Time passes.* Write down the word "down" on your mission sheet. Whilst there is no response from Control, you are sure you have just achieved at least part of the requirements of your mission. You decide to leave the area. Turn to 977.

549.

You find a *universal timer*. You may take this if you choose by adding it to your inventory as a miscellaneous item. Write the word "rose" on your mission sheet and sneak out of the room by turning to 363.

550.

Taking out your explosive you place it upon the door (remove the explosive from your inventory).

Dashing to the door for cover you wait for the timer to hit zero and... Nothing.

Returning to the door you find the explosive blackened and charred - a security field on the door has nullified the explosion, rendering the attempt useless. You do however notice that to your left the wall is now emitting a considerable amount of heat.

Try a cutting or siege tool if you have one:	Turn to 339.
Attempt to bust into the wall to your left:	Turn to 387.
Leave the room:	Turn to 392.

551.

[If you are down to the *final tier* with the time you have remaining and have not already done so, turn to 1234, remembering this reference so you may return.]

You are in another bleak corridor with a door on the port side. The corridor extends towards the bow in one direction and looking towards the stern you can see a corner up ahead, veering off to the left. Will you:

Try the door on port side labeled "Teleporter"?	Turn to 602.
Head along the corridor towards the bow?	Turn to 622.
Take the corridor in the direction of the stern rounding the corner?	
	Turn to 488.

552.

In one of the cupboards you discover 2 *stimserts* which you may take if you choose. Write the word "bottle" on your mission sheet. If you have not done so already, will you:

Head to the main terminal near the center of the room? Turn to 305.
Utilize one of the automated operating tables if you need to?
Turn to 401.
Check the cells to see if any are occupied?   Turn to 588.
Leave the room?   Turn to 451.

553.

[If you have the *Collector of things* mission and do not have the word "road" written down, turn to 716.]

You have reached a junction. There are three paths to choose from:
Head towards the stern: Turn to 565.
Take the corridor heading towards the bow: Turn to 728.
Head along the corridor towards starboard: Turn to 649.

554.

As you have already damaged this room there is nothing more to be done here. The room appears the same as when you left it, nothing has been repaired. Turn to 530.

555.

Looking up information regarding the biological scientist, you find that his last recorded location was in sector C on level 4 (the level above the one you are on). Tuo Minkla works in the area, but also moves around to the other laboratories aboard the ship as a co-director. You note his crew number which is 237. Getting to level 4 might be a challenge as you also check the possibility of teleporting there, finding teleportation to other levels from the one you are on disabled. Multiple sectors within level 3 have also been isolated due to the LWS attack. If you feel you are finished with the terminal you may turn to 504. If you decide to search for other information, return to 487 and choose again.

556.

[If you have the word "wide" written down, turn to 527 now.]

The door is locked. It appears to be secure, though not military secure. If you have a keypass you may try that. Alternatively you may use force to enter this room or leave the door and move on.

Use a keypass if you have one: Turn to the reference by adding the keypass number along with this reference number (556). If the reference does not make sense then your keypass has failed; select another option.

Use an explosive if you have one:	Turn to 379.
Use a cutting tool or siege equipment:	Turn to 435.
Take the corridor towards starboard side:	Turn to 384.
Take the corridor towards port side:	Turn to 543.

557.

Having seen these common worker robots before, you are familiar with their operation and know that they are designed to be persistent until given the right instruction. The robot asks another question:

'Are you here to assist with preparatory duties?'

You respond back clearly: 'Inspection override.'

Instantly the robot continues on its way, reverting to programmed duties.

Unhindered by the robot, will you:

Investigate the room beyond?	Turn to 610.
Leave?	Turn to 622.

558.

You know that Seyem had mentioned hiding his "goods" in a cold store somewhere. You start to think whatever he had could be in here - provided he has not already taken it. Roll one die. If you roll a 1 or a 2, turn to 623. If you roll a 3 or more, turn to 473.

559.

You tell the man you are from the Leading Weapon Syndicate and are on mission here. His eyes widen but he does not make any moves.

It appears he is unarmed so perhaps he sees the situation. 'Well you could have killed me by now, so what is it you want here?'

Ask of new technology that is being developed on the ship:

Turn to 458.

Ask him who he is and what he is doing: Turn to 324.

Attack him: Turn to 477.

560.

Moving around the room you check the bench tops for any sort of terminal. The room is actually larger than first glance; you discover it opens up with a partition creating a t-junction of sorts at the far end of the room. The partition proves to be the back wall of a separate island room within the main room. This smaller room does not have a door, but rather an opening on the far side. Looking in you can see monitoring equipment but still no sign of an actual terminal. Now will you:

Continue to search for a terminal? Turn to 572.

Search the cupboards and boxes: Turn to 612.

Investigate the equipment within the main room? Turn to 459.

Leave the room? Turn to 465.

561.

[If you have the word "trend" written down, turn to 495 now.]

Otherwise; [if you have the word "sample" written down, turn to 406 now.]

Time passes.

Moving around the partition you stop as you see a woman towards the end of the bench facing away from you working. Partially hidden behind the partition, you consider your next move.

[If you are with the Confederacy, turn to 434 now.]

[If you are SDN aligned, turn to 589 now.]

Otherwise, turn to 584.

562.

Fortune is with you. Inside the pouch you find one of the crews' *keypass*. This may be quite handy for getting into some rooms. Add the item to your inventory as a miscellaneous item. To use your keypass, add 132 to the reference you are on when you encounter a keypass scanner. If your keypass works the reference you turn to will make sense and continue from where you are. With such a find you decide to leave the room to continue with the task ahead. Write the word "rose" on your mission sheet and turn to 363.

563.

You sum up the door and your options to bust through. Will you:

Try to cut a hole on one side to get through?	Turn to 756.
Smash up the keypad?	Turn to 809.
Try to break open the hatch?	Turn to 768.

564.

Without warning three security guards burst into the room. They make no apology for their entry and do a very quick look around the room. With fortune your back is to them and they do not look carefully enough to identify you or notice your concealed weapon. The guards leave quickly enough, moving onto the next room no doubt. Remove the word "filter" from your mission sheet. You have to wait a little longer for the heat to dissipate while the man waffles on some more. *Time passes.* Eventually you excuse yourself and leave the room. Turn to 397.

565.

[If you have the word "gaseous" written down, turn to 816 now.]

You are at the end of a corridor. There are two unmarked doors which you may try or you may leave this area via the corridor heading towards the bow.

Try the door on the starboard side?   Turn to 448.
Open the door on port side?   Turn to 616.
Head up corridor towards the bow?   Turn to 553.

566.

A small device you use, no bigger than your finger detects skin oils on several surfaces around one of the bunks which match with Sjonn's identity. Though there is nobody in here presently and no personal items of his to look at, you know he *was* here recently and is likely not far away. You leave the room. Turn to 590.

567.

As you look with greater detail at the quality of this room and the items it contains, you become more convinced the room serves as maintenance for the utilities aboard the ship. It does not seem large enough to service the entire ship, but you reason that it must serve at least this sector. Damaging this room would serve to create havoc here and elsewhere. Will you:

Cause some destruction here?   Turn to 491.
Leave the room?   Turn to 465.

568.

As you move further down this corridor you suddenly notice your bracelet light up and then a second later you are jolted as the bracelet sends a shock coursing through your body. Deduct 2 *vitality*. This shock however only serves as a warning for entering a restricted area. Will you:

Ignore the bracelet and continue towards the end of the corridor?
     Turn to 633.
Return to the previous junction?   Turn to 419.

569.

As you are about to leave an airborne drone appears at the doorway, buzzing incessantly. Without pausing it locks onto you - it must have been dispatched earlier with your position. Launching a volley of microspheres into the room, you dive for cover. Roll one die. If you roll a 1 or a 2, some of the microspheres make contact with your skin and burst, releasing a deadly bacteria. Double the result you rolled for the *vitality* you lose as well as add the *infected* lingering effect. The threat is not over yet though. As you are ducked behind a table the drone hovers in the doorway scanning for you. At the same time the whole room is becoming contaminated with whatever the drone shot into the room. You attempt to take out the drone with a well-placed shot. If you are able to fire your weapon and at short range, roll 1 die and add your *ranged* score. If the result is 10 or more, you hit the drone; turn to 594 now. Otherwise the drone responds by firing another round of microspheres, this time in a much more focused shot rather than the all-round spray of before. Perform the same test as above by rolling one die. If you roll a 1 or a 2 the bacteria has made contact with you. Double the result you rolled for the *vitality* you lose as well as add the *infected* lingering effect if you have not already. A short moment later whilst you are summing your options the drone suddenly takes off as quickly as it arrived. You can only presume it has either done its duty or is out of ammunition. Not knowing the sort of bacteria they are using has you concerned. If you are *infected* make a note that this infection is slightly different. You will be unable to clear this lingering effect in the usual way. Instead each failure will cause 1 point of lost *vitality* instead of the usual 3. You will have to find some other means to rid yourself of the bacterium before it cripples you. With this incident *time passes* and you now leave carefully avoiding any surfaces. Turn to 565.

570.

Trying the door you find it is locked. It looks as though a particular type of keypass is required to open this door. Inspecting the situation more closely, the door also appears to be heavily monitored. There is also a lockdown door at the end of the corridor which you don't like the looks of; if it closes it may prevent you from getting back to the teleporter or simply out of this corridor. For this reason it seems like too much of a risk to try to gain entry by force. If you have a suitable keypass, you may try it now.

If your keypass does not work or you do not have one, you decide to leave the door alone. Turn to 447.

571.

Security is quick to respond: within moments a sentry robot appears at the other end of the corridor. Its arm is a high powered laser gun, the barrel of which is now pointed at you:

Sentry robot	Ra	5
	Vitality	15
	5+ to hit, 6 damage.	
	4+ armored coating as defense will reduce damage by 5.	

>You are pinned at the end of the corridor and so must destroy the robot in this short ranged shoot out.

>As the robot uses the corner of the corridor junction for cover, any grenades thrown will do their stated damage only.

If you are victorious, write the word "block" on your mission sheet. Will you:

Use a cutting or siege tool if you have one?	Turn to 546.
Simply attempt to damage the door?	Turn to 664.
Leave it alone?	Turn to 675.

572.

Time passes. Looking at the various gauges, monitors and readouts you see quite a lot of equipment and information on display here, but no sign of a terminal. Will you:

Search the cupboards and boxes if you have not already?	
	Turn to 612.
Investigate the equipment within the main room?	Turn to 459.
Leave the room?	Turn to 465.

573.

Roll one die. If you roll 2 or more, turn to 337. If you roll 1, turn to 385.

574.

There is a man named Sjonn listed in the labor workforce database. He is stationed in manufacturing which is located in sector F on the level you are on now. There are no further details on him aside from his relatively short work history aboard the starship. If you feel you are finished with the terminal you may turn to 504. If you decide to search for other information, return to 487 and choose again.

575.

Time passes.

[If you have the word "tangle" written down, turn to 498 now.]

[If your time remaining is down to the *final tier*, turn to 498.]

You step into the room which appears to be a conference room - one in which there is a meeting taking place. Three men and two women sit around an octagonal table; their clothing a deep tan color. Upon your entry they all turn towards you; their meeting adjourned for the moment. Aside from the meeting the conference room hardly seems to have anything else of interest. You'll need to deal with the crew members if you plan to stay in this room since you have no invitation to the meeting.

'What do you think you are doing just barging in here?' Questions one of the men. Will you:

Attack them all?	Turn to 605.
Claim to be inspecting the room?	Turn to 625.
Apologize and leave the room?	Turn to 497.

576.

From up at the next corner an agent spots you, and opens fire with a pulse rifle. Reeling for cover along the side of the corridor you manage to avoid preliminary shots. Now you will have to deal with the LWS agent.

LWS *agent* Ra	6
Vitality	22

4+ to hit, 4 damage.
5+ to reduce damage by 4 as defense.

>If you choose to throw a grenade at the agent, the grenade will inflict base damage according to the item details. If you roll a miss; double damage if you roll a hit or triple damage if you roll a 6.

>If the agent rolls a 6 when rolling to hit you, he has thrown a grenade at you. Roll another die and add 3 to the result to determine the damage for the attack.

>If the battle lasts 5 combat rounds or more, *time passes.*

>If you reduce the *vitality* of the agent to 5 or less, turn to 415.

577.

Time passes.

[If you have the *Survey and Defend* mission, turn to 660 now.]

[If you have the word "thief" written down, turn to 617 now, remembering this reference.]

Inside, you find yourself in a familiar looking teleport room. Where do you plan to go?

Sector E?	Turn to 416.
Sector F?	Turn to 525.
Sector G?	Turn to 539.
Exit the teleport room?	Turn to 684.

578.

Looking to get to the battle that is taking place you follow the corridor some way towards starboard where you then come across a ramp on the bow side leading down. You take the ramp, which turns to the left twice and brings you to an expansive hallway. The action is clearly here; along this expansive multi-storey hall you see flashes of laser beams, smoke and scattered bodies with attackers and defenders alike hiding and moving from cover to cover. Will you:

Wait a moment and observe the situation?   Turn to 534.

Head straight in and find cover?   Turn to 408.

579.

The man seems to accept your story for now. 'Do what you need to do quickly as I have a meeting in here shortly,' he says gruffly.

If you have the *Got the lingo* ability, you may turn to 615 to use it now. Will you:

Ask him where you can find production?   Turn to 503.

Move around the other side and study the holographic map?

Turn to 533.

Access a terminal?   Turn to 344.

Leave the room?   Turn to 543.

580.

'His name sounds familiar but I have no idea where he might be,' he states. Will you:

Ask him where the ships data is stored?   Turn to 313.

Attack him?   Turn to 477.

Leave the room?   Turn to 543.

581.

This room holds key systems for the functioning of the ship in this area. Damaging the controls and monitoring equipment will serve your secondary mission. You turn up several dials overloading a power distribution grid and shut off heat dissipation sinks to cause a disaster elsewhere. To ensure nothing is fixed you bust up the panel and smash all the readouts.

If you have not already done so, begin a tally on your mission sheet of the damage you have done to the starship. Add 1 point for the damage done to this room. Write the word "local" on your mission sheet.

Leave the room by turning to 530.

582.

You feel you are making progress as you disable two of the clearance programs restricting complete access to the terminal. Those feelings are short lived however as the connection is severed from the other end. Another user has shut you out and will likely log the incident. Turn to 955.

583.

Searching through items is hardly conducive to your mission. You waste no more time in this room. Turn to 465.

584.

Somehow, intuitively perhaps, she notices your presence and turns around. You are forced to reveal yourself. She immediately goes on the offense, questioning your reason for being in here. Write the word "sample" on your mission sheet. Will you:

Attack her?	Turn to 834.
Try an excuse for being here?	Turn to 786.
Say you are leaving and leave via starboard?	Turn to 471.
Say you will be on your way and head into portside section?	
	Turn to 538.

585.

Along this corridor there is a door on the stern side. It also looks as though there are more doors further along the corridor towards starboard side. Will you:

Try the door on the stern side labeled "J065: Security only"?

Turn to 439.

Head towards port, following the corner around towards the stern?

Turn to 460.

Continue along the corridor towards starboard?   Turn to 597.

586.

The robot asks another question: 'Are you here to assist with preparatory duties?'

Again, in an attempt to shrug off the robot, you say 'No, I am here for another reason.'

As it persists by stating 'You are required to either return to the eatery or state your function here,' you decide to sidestep the robot and move around the island bench. The robot follows closely behind. You move again, now closer to a door on the right hand wall and again the robot follows you.

'Preparatory duties interrupted, please state your function,' it says in a monotone. Will you:

Smash the robot up?   Turn to 685.
Ignore the robot and enter the adjoining room?   Turn to 667.
Ignore the robot and leave?   Turn to 722.

587.

This might be an ideal chance to disable the biometrics for you. If you choose to attempt this, turn to 526. Otherwise return to 646.

588.

Walking beside the cells you peer into each one through their translucent covers. The cells are used for long duration recuperation. Each one appears empty, until you reach near the end of the row - there is one occupied. Checking the display at the foot of the cell you read the individual's details and their current health status. The individual is a middle aged woman in a deep sleep from a previously long voyage. Her health appears to be stable though the display still lists her as been infected with something of unknown origin. You may:

Attempt to open the cell: Turn to 129.

Alternatively, if you have not already done so:

Head to the main terminal near the center of the room: Turn to 305.

Check the cells to see if any are occupied: Turn to 588.

Check the storage cupboards for anything of use: Turn to 455.

Leave the room: Turn to 451.

589.

Aiming to avoid the alerting of any guards, you consider either sneaking past or performing a surprise attack on her.

To attempt to sneak past: Turn to 653.

To surprise attack her: Turn to 834.

590.

[If you are down to the *final tier* with time remaining, roll 1 die. If you roll 4 or more, turn to 225.]

You have come to the middle of the corridor you are in which extends sideways relative to the ship. A single door is located here on the stern side. Will you:

Enter the room on the stern side labeled "F004"? Turn to 535.

Head along the corridor towards port side? Turn to 488.

Or move towards starboard side following the corner to the bow?

Turn to 465.

591.

You walk around the other side of the hologram to stand beside the man. He is tall, bearded and dressed in a rather plain deep blue uniform. You are given a stern look from him.

Based on your faction alliance, turn to the following reference:

LWS:	Turn to 505.
SDN:	Turn to 624.
Confederacy:	Turn to 466.
Non-faction aligned:	Turn to 545.

592.

Time passes. The tables and chairs are all clean and neatly organized you find as you move between them across the room. There is some food remaining in the covered warmer and behind the bench top housing the warmer are refrigerated units with bottled drinks in them. Beside the refrigerated drinks is a set of doors. Looking around there is little else of interest - even the walls in here are one clean, smooth continuous surface. Will you:

| Stop and help yourself to a meal? | Turn to 634. |

| Walk around the other side of the bench and check the cupboards and draws? | Turn to 656. |

| Head through the doors at the back? | Turn to 479. |
| Leave the room? | Turn to 622. |

593.

Sneaking closer step by step you silently draw your weapon, preparing to pounce at her. Mere steps away you begin to leap when you feel the punch of an invisible wall which knocks you backwards. Of course! There is a containment field around the forest area to segregate the forest from the ship. Noticing the thump of your fall and discerning your attempt to jump her, the woman quickly activates a device on her wrist, calling security. You had better act fast:

| Look for a way past the field? | Turn to 740. |
| Get out of the room before security arrives? | Turn to 808. |

594.

Making a skilled shot, you hit the drone, though it is not enough to destroy it. It whirs and loses stability before retreating by flying away. Hopefully there are no more or it does not return. If you are *infected* make a note that this infection is slightly different. You will be unable to clear this lingering effect in the usual way. Instead each failure will cause 1 point of lost *vitality* instead of the usual 3. You will have to find some other means to rid yourself of the bacterium before it cripples you. With this incident *time passes* and you now leave carefully, avoiding any surfaces on the way out. Turn to 565.

595.

[If you have the word "draft" written down, turn to 432 immediately.]

[If you are with the Confederacy and into the *final tier* of time remaining, turn to 1016.]

Time passes. Entering the room you find it is dimly lit, though you can roughly make out the contents of the room. Mostly tools and workable materials, the room is neatly organized and well stocked. A small bench in the corner has a backlight and a blueprint on display. There is also an open toolbox on the floor nearby. Will you:

Check the items on the shelves?	Turn to 635.
Take a look at the bench in the corner?	Turn to 463.
Have a closer look inside the toolbox?	Turn to 657.
Leave the room?	Turn to 711.

596.

Returning to the corridor junction, you find the thick gas cloud of earlier persisting. Roll 1 die. If you roll anything other than a 1, you hazardously take in some of the thick green gas. Add the *poisoned* lingering effect, or if you already have this lingering effect, deduct 3 *vitality*. As vision is also impaired inside the persistent gas cloud, there is too much of a risk trying to get through it. *Time passes.* Either Duck away towards starboard: Turn to 614.

Or head towards portside: Turn to 391.

597.

You are now part way along a corridor running from side to side relative to the ship. On each side, opposite each other are two doors. [If you are into the *final tier* of time remaining, turn to 767.]

Will you:

Try the door on bow side labeled "J063"?	Turn to 501.
Try the door on the stern side labeled "J066: Aux emergency"?	
	Turn to 666.
Take the corridor towards port side?	Turn to 585.
Head towards starboard to a junction?	Turn to 670.

598.

Part of the way along the corridor you encounter an inset isolation door blocking the corridor. The bulky door appears capable of withstanding a great deal of punishment and is obviously meant to isolate one sector of the ship from another in emergencies.

[If you have the *Survey and Defend* mission, turn to 361.]

Faced with this near impenetrable blockade you decide not to waste time on the door and head back.

Head down the corridor towards the stern?   Turn to 497.

Take the corridor leading towards the starboard side? Turn to 451.

599.

The door opens for you. You have stepped into a large room filled mostly with a long production line. The production line snakes around the manufacturing facility and moves in a continually starting and stopping sequence. Most of what is attached to the production line are humanoid robots at various stages of their build. There are also smaller objects - likely equipment or robots you think breaking up the rows of robots every so often. You can see several workers operating equipment connected to the production line, though their distance and business has resulted in your entry going unnoticed.

Given the vastness of this area, you realize it will consume some time if you choose to explore the manufacturing facility. Will you:

Explore the room?   Turn to 757.
Exit the room?   Turn to 465.

600.

The situation intensifies as both the attackers and crew members engage in a fierce firefight. Flashes of laser beams followed by an explosion ripping through a small ship near the loading bay entry put your senses on high alert. You need to decide what you will do:

Drive the cart across to the middle of the loading bay? Turn to 672.

Take cover where you are behind a moveable platform rig?

Turn to 461.

601.

Time passes you wait patiently as the update finally finishes. Now that the terminal is on par with the other terminals in the network, there will be a short duration of re-mapping this terminal by the other terminals across the network. Whilst this is happening, you may have a quick chance to access normally restricted programs and databases. Turn to 972.

602.

Time passes.

[If you have the *Survey and Defend* mission, turn to 652 now.]

[If you have the word "bracelet" written on your mission sheet, turn to 683 now.]

[If you have the word "thief" written down, turn to 617 now, remembering this reference.]

Upon entering the room you see six teleport pads lined up against the back wall. There are two larger pads whilst the other four are the usual size for an individual. Other than that the room is rather featureless as it is designed for one purpose only.

You may leave the room by turning to 551, else you may teleport to another available sector:

Sector E:	Turn to 416.
Sector G:	Turn to 539.
Sector J:	Turn to 604.

603.

Making use of your security keypass you swipe it across the scanner and the light for the door illuminates green. The door opens and you step inside a small chamber where the actual door to the armory awaits. Once inside the door closes behind you. Within the chamber there is a biometric scanner to your left that you will have to overcome in order to open the door to the armory.

If you think you know of a way to defeat the biometric scanner, then you may attempt to do so now.

If you are unsure, you have the following options:

Perform a scan on yourself:	Turn to 698.
Try to hack the biometric scanner:	Turn to 752.
Use a siege or cutting tool on the armory door:	Turn to 773.
Wait and let it play out:	Turn to 629.
Leave immediately:	Turn to 810.

604.

You have arrived at sector J. Stepping out of the teleporter into the room which is absent of any crew, you head to the door, checking the corridor beyond before exiting. Turn to 684.

605.

The crew members are taken back by your audacity. Before they have time to get up and fight back you may have time to reduce their numbers. Roll one die, if the result is higher than or equal to your *agility* score, you will have time to take one short range shot before the nearest crew member is onto you. If the result of the roll is less than your *agility*, you may take two shots. If you have the ability *The quick and the dead* then you may take an extra shot regardless of the roll.

After taking any short ranged shots, take the first pair in close combat:

Process Administrators	CQ/Ra	4
	Vitality	20

3+ to hit, 2 damage.
No defense.

If you choose to flee the scene, follow the procedure and turn to 662. If you defeat the two process executives turn to 704.

606.

Examining your findings, you see that you have found a *ratcheted ring*. If you choose to take the item, write it down on your mission sheet as a miscellaneous item in your inventory.

Write the word "rose" on your mission sheet and quietly leave the room by turning to 363.

607.

Roll 1 die. If you roll 4 or more, return to 407 and continue reading. If you roll 3 or less, roll another die. Turn to the reference below according to the roll. Note that you will be returning here after you do.

1-3: Turn to 475.

4-5: Turn to 761.

After facing your enemy, add the word "spine" to your mission sheet and return to 407.

608.

You are in a corridor running from side to side relative to the ship. There is a door on the stern side of the corridor. Will you:

Try the door on the stern side with label "G012"?	Turn to 630.
Head along the corridor towards port side?	Turn to 520.
Head towards starboard side?	Turn to 815.

609.

Looking at some of the artifacts, you note that the majority of them are items with coded labels attached, which you imagine link them to files on some of the data stores. Unfortunately the items hold no value for you, so you quickly decide to do something else. If you have not done so already you may start searching through some of the data stores by turning to 631. Alternatively you may leave the room by turning to 523.

610.

Entering the room you find it is an extension of the galley. There are numerous food storages in here and an enclosed area on the port side appears to be a cold storage. You may:

Take time and search this room:	Turn to 661.
Spend time searching the cold storage area:	Turn to 702.
Leave these rooms and return to the corridor:	Turn to 622.

611.

Time passes. Entering the room again you take a brief look around. It is as before though there is no sign of the woman. Seeing nothing to gain by staying you make for the door. Turn to 710.

612.

Time passes. Looking in the boxes and cupboards you find many items - though to you it appears as junk. Some tools here, a collection of bolts in another box, a cupboard space littered with broken thermostats. You feel like you could waste all the time you have left in here. Based on your allegiance, turn to the appropriate reference:

LWS:	Turn to 645.
NFA:	Turn to 678.
Confederacy:	Turn to 583.

613.

Time passes. You reach the door you saw Sjonn going through and attempt to push it open finding it is jammed. It is not jammed completely but you find it is obstructed by something which you manage to reach in and clear out of the way. Having moved the small crate that was lodged in place you push the door open and give chase again. Ahead is another junction with no sign of the fugitive. You need to pick a direction fast:

To go left:	Turn to 742.
To go right:	Turn to 443.

614.

You've reached a junction in the corridor. Will you:

Head towards port side?	Turn to 419.
Head towards starboard?	Turn to 785.
Take the corridor in the direction of the stern?	Turn to 465.

615.

With some fast talking you explain to the man how you need to get a new part produced for a machine in the loading bay but are unsure where to go. He begins responding that there is a maintenance workshop down the corridor but you cut him off insisting you are meant to go to somewhere bigger where *all* the production takes place.

'Well that would probably be manufacturing I guess...in sector F,' he says, still pondering over exactly what you are needing.

Considering his information helpful and aiming to leave without giving yourself away, you thank him and make for the exit. Turn to 543.

616.

If you have the word "ranked" written down, turn at once to 784. If you do not have this word written down but have the word "vision" written down, turn to 478. If instead you have the word "learn" written down, turn to 751 now.

Entering the room you find yourself in a spacious expanse; and in it are several individuals busy with activity. As your presence is not yet noticed you conceal your weapons for the time being. To your left are scores of data stores filed away into walled sockets. Looking further into the room to your right you see a pair skimming through documents on the holographic projection above the table they sit at.

There is also a woman occupied with arranging a holographic matrix of elements midair near the corner of the room. There is also another man seated along the side wall. He is completely still, almost unnoticeable as a statue, save for the fact that he is wearing a pair of bulky projector goggles. Whatever he is watching has him enthralled. Write the word "learn" on your mission sheet.

From what you can gather the people in this room are all engaged in learning or research of some sort.

Will you:

Attack them all?	Turn to 741.
Interact with them?	Turn to 754.
Leave?	Turn to 565.

617.

From the trap you encountered earlier, you are afflicted with a unique viral compound. There is no means you have or readily available to cure the virus - you will simply have to allow it to run its course and for your own immune system to clear it in time. If you are down to the *final tier* of time remaining, roll one die. On a roll of 1, your body has cleared the virus - you may remove the word "thief" from your mission sheet. If you roll anything else, deduct 2 *vitality*. Whilst in the *final tier* of time remaining, for every instance of "time passes", perform the previous test - on a roll of 1 the virus is cleared, otherwise deduct 2 *vitality*. If you are in the *first* or *second tier* of time remaining, deduct 2 *vitality* and return to your previous reference.

618.

You claim to be a worker from the loading bay. If you are carrying either *high speed laser cutter* or a *siege ram* then turn to 579. If not, turn to 394.

619.

There is some research data listed - results from near ten studies conducted recently. Some of them involve using genetic material of alien species to experiment with - one in particular a specimen HK-01 is proving to be both promising and highly dangerous at the same time according to the conclusions. The data you can find does not indicate anything produced nor end intentions for the experimentation.

As they are inter-related you may look up any technology data this terminal may have access to by turning to 205 or if you feel you are finished with the terminal you may turn to 504. If you choose to search for other information, return to 487 and choose again.

620.

You move closer to the scanner. After a brief pause a light runs over your face. There is another pause as if the scanner is waiting for something. Yet there is no announcement for any other input from you, nor does there seem to be any other apparatus that requires a keypass, code entry or anything else. A pad to the side of the door illuminates a red hue before fading to black. Your guess is you have not been authorized. Thankfully no alarms are triggered either. Now will you:

Place an explosive on the door?	Turn to 642.
Try to cut or hack into the door?	Turn to 673.
Leave the door alone?	Turn to 523.

621.

'As far as I am aware the attack was on the level below us and it is now contained. To get there take the corridor towards the bow and follow the signage.' he says pointing towards the bow.

'Now I have a meeting in a moment so you will have to excuse me,' he says, gesturing towards the door.

You decide to comply and head for the door. Turn to 543.

622.

You are not far from the middle of the corridor. There is a single door here on the port side.

[If you are with the Confederacy and do <u>not</u> have the word "conduit" written down, turn to 858.]

You may:

Try the door on port side labeled "F006": Turn to 632.

Head along the corridor towards the bow where you can see a junction: Turn to 391.

Head along corridor towards the stern: Turn to 551.

623.

Despite a lengthy search you cannot find anything and suspect Seyem has already taken anything he had here. *Time passes.* Starting to feel the chill of the room you turn and leave, returning to the corridor. Turn to 622.

624.

With your weapon concealed and apparel with no unusual markings on it, the man after taking a glance at you has yet to suspect your identity.

'The sooner we get out from the umbra of this crater for a moon, the better,' he states rather gruffly.

Will you:

Ask him where you can find the scientist Tuo Minkla? Turn to 580.

Ask him where the ships data is stored? Turn to 313.

Attack him? Turn to 477.

Leave the room? Turn to 543.

625.

'An inspection? In here? There is almost nothing to inspect!' says one of the men in a commanding tone.

If you have the *Got the lingo* ability, turn to 399 now.

Taking another look around the room, you see he is right and cannot think of a reply in the moment. Will you:

Attack the crew?	Turn to 605.
Apologize and leave the room?	Turn to 497.

626.

You find nothing of value to you despite a careful search.

Continue to search for a terminal?	Turn to 572.
Investigate the equipment within the main room?	Turn to 459.
Leave the room?	Turn to 465.

627.

Now that the agent has been taken out, there is a chance to advance forward, which you do, taking up a new position behind a large support beam on the port side of the hall. You've been spotted by an agent much further down the hall on the same side, also hiding behind a beam. She maintains a watch, attempting to take you down if you move again.

Hidden LWS agent	Ra	5
	Vitality	20
	5+ to hit, 4 damage.	
	5+ to negate 4 damage as defense.	

>Fight three rounds of combat only. If you defeat the agent or at the end of three rounds, turn to 695.

628.

Since you were here earlier you see no value in heading back down the ramp again. You decide to head back into sector F to see what you can find there. Turn to 397.

629.

Waiting around does not help your cause - within moments a guard is on the scene and looking to capture or kill you:

Security guard	CQ	4
	Vitality	19
	4+ to hit, 4 damage.	
	No defense.	

>If the guard rolls a 6 when rolling to hit, unless your defense roll is successful, he will electrocute you in an effort to subdue you. If this occurs, you will suffer 4 damage and the *shocked* lingering effect.

If you kill the guard, turn to 437.

630.

The room you enter is quite small and lined with rows of shelves. It is clearly a small storage room. On the shelves are perhaps hundreds of items - most small, though a few large and many items in containers. There appears to be chemicals, powders, flasks, vials, test equipment and the likes which make up the items here. As soon as you step ahead to move further into the room, a sensor detects you and an announcement can be heard: "Please scan your keypass for the entry log."

You notice a keypass scanner to your side just inside the door.

Will you:

Scan your keypass if you have one?   Turn to 705.

Ignore the message and continue further into the room to view the items?   Turn to 762.

Leave the room?   Turn to 608.

631.

Time passes. Starting at a random point since there are scores of them you begin searching through the data stores. The majority are all current generation data stores, though there are some older disused storage devices also. Unfortunately any key information that may aid you could be on any type of storage medium. It could take seemingly forever to go through the stores to only potentially find information of value to you. You determine it would not be worth it. Turn to 523.

632.

Time passes. Opening for you, the double doors reveal what is clearly a kitchen and eating area. Rows of tables and chairs populate the bulk of the room while a kitchen area covers the far side with doors leading out the back. What you find remarkable however is that the room is completely deserted. There is nobody to be seen in here and no sign that anyone was here recently.

If you have not been in this room before, will you:

Head further into the room and search around?   Turn to 592.

Otherwise not spend any more time here and leave?   Turn to 622.

633.

Only a few more steps in and the bracelet lights up again, though this time with a shock severe enough to put you on the floor in pain. Deduct 5 *vitality*. The shock does not subside, until you manage to crawl back towards the stern, at which point the bracelet ceases administering its deterring shock. You'll need to remove this bracelet in order to enter any restricted areas as you imagine trying to crawl to the end of the corridor would be enough to kill you. You pick yourself up off the floor and return to the previous junction. Turn to 419.

634.

The food is free and you feel you could do with a snack. Taking out some of the food from the warmer you pull up a seat and begin eating. The food tastes reasonable and is still warm. Though you shovel the meal into your mouth at a moderate pace, it takes time to finish off the whole plate. *Time passes.* You now feel satiated and ready to get back to the tasks ahead. Add 5 *vitality.*

Now will you:

Walk around the other side of the bench and check the cupboards and draws?   Turn to 656.

Head through the doors at the back?   Turn to 479.

Leave the room?   Turn to 622.

635.

Looking at some of the items on the shelves you notice some interesting tools and pieces of equipment. Most appears as junk to you however and some items look like they have been taking up shelving space for years. Will you:

Pick out one of the more interesting items for a closer look?

Turn to 775.

Ignore the items on the shelves and take a look at the bench in the corner?   Turn to 463.

Investigate the toolbox on the floor?   Turn to 657.

636.

Tucked away behind a worn relay set you find a *Phyclo generator* which you may take with you if you choose by adding it as a miscellaneous item on your mission sheet. Now will you:

Move over to the corner bench and take a look?   Turn to 463.

Check out the toolbox on the floor?   Turn to 657.

Not spend any more time here and leave the room?   Turn to 743.

637.

Time passes. The door opens and you step inside. Before you is a well lit room with several tables and chairs. There is also a projector in the corner turned off, as well as a refrigerated cabinet on one of the walls filled with meals and beverages. It appears as if nobody is around. You can also see a door on the opposite side of the room. Will you:

Open the cabinet and sample some of the food and drink?

Turn to 814.

Enter into the adjoining room?   Turn to 803.

Leave?   Turn to 728.

638.

Write the word "tangle" on your mission sheet as you head to the exit. Turn to 497.

639.

You rush out of the cabin, making it half way towards the ramp before a laser beam cuts across your right thigh, sending you skidding across the floor. You scramble to a nearby piece of equipment to use as cover, putting pressure on the wound as you assess the situation. Deduct 3 *vitality*. Approaching is a uniformed man brandishing a laser pistol. You'll need to shoot him down before he reaches you as you're in no position to fight him hand to hand. This is a short range combat with no escape.

With the scattered equipment around, if you throw a grenade, it will do double damage for a successful hit, or base damage even for a miss as you are bound to hit him with some shrapnel.

Line supervisor	Ra	4
	Vitality	16
	5+ to hit, 3 damage.	
	No defense.	

If you defeat your attacker, you take a moment to pull yourself together (add 1 *vitality*) and head across to the ramp. On your way you may take the supervisor's *laser pistol* if you choose. Fortunately no other hostiles come down the ramp and you head back up to the level above, covertly skirting the portside perimeter towards the manufacturing facility exit. Turn to 796.

640.

From what you can tell much of the security on the ship is automated. There are drones on each level which are mobilized on demand as well as a reserve of guards stationed right across the ship. Monitoring and identity checks are common, with secure rooms like the one you are in often requiring keypass entry and/or biometric identification. Roll one die. If you roll a 5 or a 6, then turn to 468 now.

To keep searching, return to 646. To leave now, turn to 774.

641.

'What are you doing?' Calls out one of the scientists. You've been spotted sneaking up to the translucent panel. The others all react, immediately turning suspicious. You are going to have to deal with them as the first moves toward you boldly. Turn to 1107.

642.

Time passes. Remove the explosive or bomb from your pack as you attach it to the door. As soon as you try to do this, the security system on the door does something to your explosive. If you tried a proximity explosive, it partially explodes before it is disabled, hitting you with some of the blast. Deduct 4 from your *vitality*. The door is protected with some advanced security. Aside from disabling your attempt to blast it open, an alarm has been triggered. A strip light surrounding the door is lit up and is flashing red. There is no audible alarm, simply the flashing light. You decide to move on before any security guards arrive. Turn to 523.

643.

As if waiting just for you, 3 small drones about the size of your head hover centrally between the toroids. You know this spells trouble and you also note the tight space for any sort of fight as well as the drop down to a lower level from where you are. One of the drones performs a quick scan-sweep of your body and you note this drone is a little larger than the other two and carries a larger rod or "stinger" underneath it. They can outrun you so you are going to have to deal with them:

In this battle you may use either a close quarter weapon or a short ranged weapon as the drones will be darting in and out. You may also fight the drones in any order.

XBR Infector drone	Ra	5
	Vitality	8

5+ to hit, 2 damage. Adds infected lingering effect.
5+ to negate all damage as evasive defense.

XBR Disabler drones	Ra	5
	Vitality	14

5+ to hit, 3 damage.
5+ to negate all damage as evasive defense.

If you defeat the drones, write the word "create" down and then either:

Head up the stairway towards the platform: Turn to 864.

Follow the ringed walkway you are on around the toroidal structures: Turn to 912.

644.

You find the equipment in this room damaged beyond repair and the place a mess.

Not wasting time you return to the corridor. Turn to 447.

645.

You continue to search through the boxes and cupboards. If you have the *tech hoarder* ability, turn to 528. If you do not have this ability, roll one die. If you roll 4 or more, turn to 626. If you roll 3 or less, turn to 493.

646.

The terminal is active. [If you have the *Collector of things* mission, turn to 587 now.]

Otherwise roll one die. If you roll a 6, then turn to 687 immediately. If you roll anything else:

What will you search for?

Ship layout data:	Turn to 519.
Drone data:	Turn to 431.
Any info regarding the armory:	Turn to 532.
The security of the ship:	Turn to 640.
Leave now:	Turn to 774.

647.

Moving further into the room you greet the woman and she responds similarly after a delayed pause. There is no query of your purpose or commands from the woman, she instead remains silent, aware of your presence yet enjoying the controlled environment at the same time. Around the forest area as you draw nearer you see signs of a containment field as a small insect tries to fly through it, making minute light pulses with each collision. Likewise you will not be able to simply enter the area contained by the field. It may be best to converse with the woman for now you determine.

To converse, turn to the relevant reference based on your alliance:

SDN:	Turn to 965.
LWS:	Turn to 1011.
NFA:	Turn to 837.
Confederacy:	Turn to 720.

648.

Roll 1 die. If you roll 4 or more, return to 453. If you roll 3 or less, remove the word "fresh" from your mission sheet and return to 453.

649.

[If you are down to the *final tier* with the time you have remaining and have not already done so, turn to 1234, remembering this reference so you may return.]

You are approximately a third of the way from the port side end of the corridor you are in. You may:

Try the door on bow side labeled "Teleporter":	Turn to 453.
Head towards starboard side:	Turn to 523.
Make your way to the port side junction:	Turn to 553.

650.

You run up the ramp which leads you to the level above. A stretch of corridor spans from starboard to port. It looks clear.

If Melea is still with you, you decide it best to search separately. 'We should split up,' you say, knowing your chances of survival will be better if you do so. Parting ways, you determine which way you will head. Will you:

Take the corridor towards starboard?	Turn to 397.
Head towards port side?	Turn to 407.

651.

Looking over the body you discover two *stimserts*, and his *corroder blade* which you may take if you choose. On the floor nearby is a *laser pistol* which you may collect. The armor he was wearing is still intact and after checking you find it matches your size for fit. You may take this *ceramic plated vest* if you like also. If you have no armor you can put it on straight away. If you already have armor on and choose to change into the plated vest then this will count as a *major alternative action*, in which *time passes*.

Moving to the end of the tunnel you find the heavy door at the end securely locked. Sensing little point to trying to continue along this path you decide to return to manufacturing. Turn to 764.

652.

Upon entering the room you see six teleport pads lined up against the back wall. There are two larger pads whilst the other four are the usual size for an individual. Other than that the room is rather featureless as it is designed for one purpose only. You may leave the room by turning to 551, else you may teleport to another available sector.

Sector G: Turn to 539.
Sector J: Turn to 604.

653.

Roll one die. If you have the *Sneak* ability, add 2 to the result. If the result is 4 or more, choose which way you were heading:

Towards starboard: Turn to 486.
Towards portside: Turn to 538.

If the result is 3 or less, you are noticed and must attack her now:

Turn to 834.

654.

The words "Access granted" appear. Turn to 487.

655.

As this is a secure door, you decide it is best left alone as you see no reason to enter let alone break in. Turn to 585.

656.

Walking through the kitchen area, behind the bench you begin opening the cupboards and draws. It does not take you long to realize they contain nothing more than they are intended to; mostly cutlery, plates, cups and other utensils. You decide to leave the rest and try something else:

Stop and help yourself to a meal if you haven't already: Turn to 634.
Head through the doors at the back: Turn to 479.
Leave the room: Turn to 622.

657.

Bending down you inspect the toolbox a little closer. It is quite a bulky toolbox and appears to have undergone the rigors of a lifetime of service with scratches and bolts missing. The top compartment seems to have nothing of use to you. Opening up the second tier compartment you are suddenly hit with something; a minute dart has sprung forth from the open compartment and lodged itself in your neck. You suddenly feel weakened and a cold sweat runs across your face. Your extremities feel cold while your torso is feeling hot. Your concern now is you do not know what may have been in the dart. Looking at the gadget that fired the dart tells you nothing - all you can tell is the owner of the toolbox was intent on nabbing a would-be tool thief. Deduct 4 *vitality* and write the word "thief" on your mission sheet. *Time passes* as you recover.

You decide to leave the room in case the owner is anywhere near by or now knows you are here. Turn to 711.

658.

Time passes. The rooms here are all non-functional rooms; they look to be training or meeting rooms and you see nothing of value in the first two rooms you check out. Will you:

Keep moving to the end of the corridor?   Turn to 763.
Head back into Sector F?   Turn to 397.

659.

Time passes. You attempt to establish a direct connection. Roll a die. If you roll a 1 or a 2, turn to 843.

If you roll a 3, turn to 708. If you roll 4 or more, turn to 938.

660.

Inside, you find yourself in a familiar looking teleport room. From the limited areas available to teleport to, where will you go?

Sector F?	Turn to 525.
Sector G?	Turn to 539.

Report back to the bridge and leave the starship? (Ending your mission) Turn to 778.

Exit the teleport room? Turn to 684.

661.

Time passes. Inspecting the room you can see nothing in here that could be of value to you. The contents are exactly as intended - food stores and items meant for food preparation. You don't feel as though you are making progress with your mission here. Will you:

Search the cold storage area?	Turn to 702.
Exit and return to the corridor?	Turn to 622.

662.

Quickly you turn and run into the corridor. The crew members are unprepared for a chase after you. Write the word "tangle" on your mission sheet and turn to 497.

663.

There is a list of workers here, all cataloged according to worker number and crew number. The list does not detail names, ages or other personal information as it is more for skills and division allocation.

Intensely looking through files at the terminal you do not notice two guards have carefully reached the outside of the cabin. They sneakily make their way inside in an attempt to ensnare you, but your training keeps you aware at all times and you prepare to face them not a moment too soon.

Fight them in close quarter combat together:

Security guards	CQ	4
	Vitality	26

On 2 dice, 5+ to hit, 3 damage.
No defense.

If you defeat the guards, you find nothing of value on them and determine now would be a good time to leave. Turn to 639.

664.

Teeth grit and sweat pouring you hack into the door, determined to get into this room.

If you have the word "block" written down, turn to 852. If not, turn to 787.

665.

You sit down to work at the terminal. As soon as you begin searching for files or information that may help you with your mission, the terminal responds: "Restricted network access. Security code V5."

Most likely the network core has limited the files this terminal is capable of locating due to the LWS assault earlier. Since you have no idea how long the restrictions will remain in place, you decide it best to move on from here. Turn to 471.

666.

You find the door is locked. Alongside the door you find a familiar looking keypad requiring the correct number combination on the door itself. Will you:

Enter the access code if you think you know it?	Turn to 817.
Try an explosive on the door?	Turn to 845.
Attempt to hack through the door?	Turn to 744.
Leave the door alone?	Turn to 597.

667.

Entering the room you find it is an extension of the galley. There are numerous food storages in here and an enclosed area on the port side appears to be a cold storage. Will you:

Spend time searching this room if you have not already?

Turn to 732.

Leave the area?   Turn to 714.

668.

You note the production line has stopped and with the quietude spot movement of humanoid shapes on the far side. Feeling there is nothing more to be gained by returning here and that you will simply be wasting precious time, you turn back and head towards the stern. Turn to 796.

669.

Up ahead you spot an LWS agent. As he spots you also, the both of you hug the corridor walls for cover and begin taking shots at each other.

LWS agent	Ra	5	4+ to hit, 4 damage.
	CQ	5	4+ to hit, 3 damage.
	Vitality	18	

5+ to reduce damage by 4 as defense.

>If you throw a grenade, then double the damage inflicted.
>At any point you may charge at the agent. He will be entitled to one free short ranged attack at you, then after that, continue the rest of the battle at close quarters.

If you defeat the agent, turn to 749.

670.

Time passes. You've reached a junction. There are three ways you may go. Will you:

Head towards the bow?	Turn to 860.
Take the corridor towards port side?	Turn to 597.
Take the corridor towards the stern?	Turn to 730.

671.

Roll a die. If you roll a 4 or more, turn to 1166. If you roll 3 or less, return to 730 and continue with that reference.

672.

Driving at top speed you race across the loading bay. As you do so, a Leading Weapon Syndicate (LWS) agent springs in front of you, weapon in hand attempting to run between cargo containers for cover.

Making a split second decision, you attempt to run him down before he can react.

Roll 2 dice. If the total is 7 or more, turn to 758. If the total is 6 or lower, turn to 839.

673.

Time passes. You ready yourself by moving up close to the door. As you begin cutting at the door a field of some sort activates and you watch in surprise as the energy is drained away from your attempt. It seems to simply suck up laser and electrical energy or deplete any crude cutting device of its kinetic potential. Your attempts to cut into the door have also triggered an alarm which is indicated by a red flashing light. Wanting to avoid any guards and feeling like you are wasting time here, especially since you have no idea if there is actually anything that may be useful to you in the room, you decide to leave the door alone and move on. Turn to 523.

674.

Moving closer to the bubbling green liquid you now see three beakers, all being fed drip by drip by a glass tube connected to a container of clear liquid. You are a little too close though - the closest beaker has an unusually large bubble forming and as it rises to the top it bursts, splattering some of the green liquid onto your exposed skin. Roll for *chance*. If you roll 3 or less, deduct 4 *vitality*. If you roll 4 or more, deduct 2 *vitality*. After that painful lesson you decide to keep well away from that particular experiment. Will you:

Take a closer look at the tube of swirling crimson liquid?

Turn to 502.

Move further into the room around the benches?   Turn to 723.

Leave?   Turn to 565.

675.

Write the word "iris" on your mission sheet. You quickly leave the area, heading to the end of the corridor and then taking a right turn towards port side where you reach a junction. Turn to 391.

676.

Time passes. Swiping your hand across the sensor the door opens, revealing a data storage facility. From floor to ceiling the walls are covered with filing arrangements containing mostly hand held data stores. There also appears to be several artifacts secure behind cabinet windows. As you follow the snaking shelves around towards port side, you find they reach a locked door with no details or markings on it. Will you:

Start searching through some of the data stores?   Turn to 631.

Investigate the artifacts?   Turn to 609.

Try to gain entry into the adjoining room?   Turn to 718.

Leave the room?   Turn to 523.

677.

Continuing around the perimeter, you are now on the stern side. Will you:

Walk around the perimeter platform towards starboard then the bow?   Turn to 922.

Take the perimeter platform towards port then the bow?

Turn to 830.

Take a walk towards one of the toroids? (#3)   Turn to 981.

678.

Having known the man who works in here you know he'd have a stash in one of the cupboards somewhere. You perform a detailed search: surely there must be at least *something* useful in here. Roll one die. If the result is a 5 or 6, turn to 541. If the result is 4 or less, turn to 372.

679.

Activities for the sector cannot be seen aside from a current alert which is strictly monitoring crew movements. Now will you:

Search for layout data of sector H?   Turn to 733.

Attempt to hack the terminal remotely?   Turn to 582.

Alternatively you may disconnect from the remote terminal and try another option by returning to 367.

680.

A security guard has found you - he will need to be dealt with:

Security guard Ra		4
	Vitality	18
	4+ to hit, 3 damage.	
	No defense.	

After the battle return to your previous reference.

681.

Deduct a micro petard from your inventory as you place it on the door. Having it set, you move out of the way before triggering it. The muffled explosion sends a shockwave into the room, damaging shelves and cabinets alike. Panes of transparent panels shatter and numerous items fall to the floor. The door itself you find is damaged also. The lock has been blown apart. But the door does not budge. You suspect it may have a second locking mechanism which you were unaware of. Having wasted enough time here without any results you decide to move out. Turn to 523.

682.

To the left you notice several cans of liquid that obviously had been stacked previously toppled over onto the floor. You surmise that as he rounded the corner at full pace he must have brushed against the cans. You rush to the left; turn to 788.

683.

As you pass through the door entering into the teleport room, you receive a warning shock from your bracelet, causing you to stop still. Deduct 2 *vitality*. You know this area is off limits for you as a controlled worker. Will you:

Continue further into the teleporter room, ignoring the bracelet?

Turn to 736.

Leave the room, returning to the corridor? Turn to 551.

684.

[If you are down to the *final tier* with the time you have remaining and have not already done so, turn to 1234, remembering this reference so you may return.]

[If you have the word "linger" written down, roll one die. If the result is 4 or more, turn to 1206.]

You are now approximately half way along a corridor heading lengthways relative to the ship. There is a door half way along labeled "Teleporter".

Will you:

Open the door on the port side?	Turn to 577.
Take the corridor towards the bow?	Turn to 460.

Head towards the stern and follow the corner to your left?

Turn to 395.

685.

Hardly capable of defending itself, the robot does not put up a fight and with ease you send it to the scrap heap. Now it is no longer bugging you, what will you do?

Try the door to the adjoining room?	Turn to 610.
Leave and return to the corridor?	Turn to 622.

686.

Taking the initiative you rush him before he has a chance to prepare himself. Fight him at close quarters and you may strike first:

Manufacturing foreman	CQ	5
	Vitality	17
	4+ to hit, 4 damage.	
	No defense.	

If you defeat the foreman, write the word "driver" on your mission sheet.

Check your mission sheet for any of the following words, turning to the associated reference accordingly. Note this reference as you will be returning here afterwards.

"Deter"	Turn to 368.
"Filter"	Turn to 442.

If you have neither of those words, nor the word "capacity" written down, write down the word "deter".

You may:

Search the room:	Turn to 908.
Or return down the elevator and	
Go into the lunch rooms:	Turn to 883.
Head down the ramp to the lower level:	Turn to 822.
Head towards the stern along the portside wall:	Turn to 796.

687.

Without warning the terminal abruptly shuts down on you. Attempting a reset alters nothing. Turn to 468.

688.

The door unlocks. Turn to 527.

689.

[If you have the word "purify" written down, turn to 644 now.]

Time passes. As you enter the room you take in a breath of clean air - the reason becomes obvious; you are in an air filtration room. Crisscrossing the ceiling are large diameter pipes. On the walls are various pieces of equipment used to monitor and adjust the air quality. To the side of you there are several tanks filled with a type of green moss. Will you:

Take a closer look at the equipment and tanks?	Turn to 790.
Leave the room?	Turn to 447.

690.

You thank the senior man for his short discourse before turning to one of the terminals.

The senior man calls out: 'If you are planning to use that, I wouldn't bother... the terminals here have very little accessibility at the moment - probably something to do with the syndicate attack.'

Having no reason to doubt the man, you decide to move on. Turn to 471.

691.

Moving quickly you leave the cabin, checking for hostiles as you go. There is activity: the churning of the production line, an alarm going off and the grating of machinery; but no sign of any guards. Taking the ramp back to the level above you cut across the room towards the stern exit, avoiding any contact with any of the workers. Turn to 796.

692.

Looking closer at the door you see it is a secure door and that it is locked. There is a biometric scanner to the side which must be used to gain entry. The door appears to be reinforced and with security mechanisms in place. Simply moving your hand close to the door begins to make your whole arm feel weak. Will you:

Attempt a bio scan?	Turn to 620.
Place an explosive on the door?	Turn to 642.
Try a cutting or siege weapon on the door?	Turn to 673.
Leave the door alone and move on?	Turn to 523.

693.

Time passes. Letting the corporal live may prove to be a smart idea. His *electro razor* you may take from him if you choose and he also has a *high security keypass* which you may take. To use the keypass in the future, add 213 to the reference where you are required to scan your keypass. The result will be the reference you will turn to and if the text makes sense, the keypass has worked.

Moving over to the scanner for the door, you test the high security keypass. It works, a small light illuminates green and now the panel is insisting on a biometric scan. The corporal, barely conscious but alive more importantly will serve as your scan. Dragging him across you place his face in front of the scanner and lift up his eyelids. The biometric scanner does its duty and a moment later the panel lights green and the door opens.

You now leave the corporal to fall to the floor and rush inside. Waiting are two guards who were hoping not to meet you:

Security room guards	CQ	5
	Vitality	20

4+ to hit, 3 damage.
No defense.

>If you reduce the *vitality* of the guards to 10 or less, increase the to hit roll of the remaining guard to 5+. If you defeat the guards, turn to 990.

694.

Walking the platform around the perimeter you reach the bow side of the engine bay. Will you:

Head around the perimeter towards starboard, then the stern?

Turn to 922.

Head around the perimeter towards port then the stern?

Turn to 830.

Take a pathway towards one of the toroids? (#2) Turn to 912.

695.

There is no sign of the agent now - it is possible one of your shots took her out or she is simply laying low. You take the opportunity to further help the defensive forces. Will you:

Hold position where you are? Turn to 863.
Move to a better central position? Turn to 1064.

696.

Time passes. Jumping on the elevator you hit the controls and within a short moment you reach the entrance to the suspended office.

[If you have the word "driver" written down, turn to 949 immediately.] Otherwise:

[If your time remaining is down to the *final tier*, turn to 782.]

The door opens automatically for you and inside you see a man at a desk on the other side of the office. He turns to see who has entered. Surprised by your entry he questions with urgency:

'Under what authority are you here?'

He seems to be on his guard and you'll need a response. Will you:

Tell him you were sent by the captain? Turn to 776.

Attack him? Turn to 686.

Tell him you made a mistake and leave? Turn to 806.

697.

As the senior man seems willing to talk you query him on the creature they are studying. Showing enthusiasm he takes you across to the holographic projector table with his companion following behind. Manipulating the controls, he makes the display change several times before settling on the projection he was after.

'If you haven't seen the specimen, then this is it,' he says as he checks to see you are looking at the projection.

'Of course this is a simulated rendering of the creature living - we are yet to catch a specimen that is alive.'

Glancing at the projection you can see a large quadruped with scaly skin and jaws filled with gnashing teeth.

'Looks like a friendly fellow,' you say.

'Hardly,' responds the man.

'Remarkable indeed however. Take a look at the specimen's hunting ability. This sequence was rendered from infra-red cameras.'

A short movie begins to play on the holographic projector.

Narrating the movie, the man continues;

'You can see that even in full darkness from that distance the *delidus uumis* can keep track of multiple prey. Using the canyon walls it will create echoes that confuse the other animals it is hunting.'

'Impressive,' you respond as you note the time you are taking here. Will you:

Allow the men to continue their work while you access one of the terminals? Turn to 690.

Say goodbye and exit? Turn to 471.

698.

Do you have in your inventory a *Bio-mimic* device? If so, turn to 476. If not, it turns out getting scanned was not the best idea - your biometric identity is excluded from the system.

A siren sounds and whole room blinks red from flashing alarm lights. Quickly you smash the scanner in an attempt to shut it up, but the wailing siren and flashing continues. Hardly a moment later two guards are on the scene, bursting into the room to get you. Fight each one consecutively in close combat:

First Security guard	CQ	4
	Vitality	19
	4+ to hit, 3 damage.	
	No defense.	

If the first guard rolls a 6 when rolling to hit you, he will use his weight to slam you into the corner of the room. In this case the attack will inflict 4 damage along with the *stunned* lingering effect. For your next combat round attack you may only attack without your weapon - unarmed.

First Security guard	CQ	5
	Vitality	17
	4+ to hit, 4 damage.	
	No defense.	

If the second guard rolls a 1 when rolling to hit you, he will go into a rage for the death of his comrade, assaulting you with increased vigor. For the rest of the combat he will roll 2 dice to hit you instead of 1.

If you manage to defeat both adversaries, turn to 437.

699.

Time passes. The corridor extends for some distance before veering to the left. At the end you encounter a sealed isolation door. This door is solid enough to withstand some serious punishment. With the security in place you are also weary of trying to continue here as you could easily become cornered trying to get through. You decide it best to head back to the previous junction. Turn to 460.

700.

[If you have the word "pup" or "skip" written down, turn to 1250 now.]

Inputting a teleport lock onto the attack ship, you successfully teleport off the XBR starship. Back aboard the attack ship you head to the helm where you can check on what is happening. The ship itself has distanced itself from the XBR starship to remain out of sight and out of danger. According to the read outs the XBR starship is mal aligned and being pulled down by the gravity of Beutohn. As for other agents returning, you are the first to arrive, though there are still a few remaining on the ship according to the status monitoring. Without hesitation you contact Commander Ashkin. Upon hearing your report he makes the call for any remaining agents to be pulled out of the ship. Though there has been no success with the mission, the commander remains detached despite the heavy casualties sustained. Without further feedback on the mission or any future plans, he ends the communication.

For now, neglecting needed rest you continue to monitor the fate of the XBR starship and the status of your comrades. The XBR ship does not take long to be sucked into the moon and disintegrates in the process; flashes of light can be seen in the upper atmosphere as explosions take place. As for the other agents, it looks as though a few have returned through the teleporter. Add 100 creds to your credit tally. Turn to 287.

701.

Time passes. Shunting forward at systematic intervals the production line virtually fills the room, starting somewhere towards the bow and ending somewhere near the center. A motorized railing higher up appears to carry the robots that have reached the end of the production line to somewhere else on the ship on the next level above. Also of interest is a building or room attached to the port side wall about half way up. As for the rest of the room, the production line dominates your view, both making it difficult to see, but also aiding you to avoid detection. There is movement of several individuals as far as you can tell glimpsing minor bodily portions between the production line, and the clearly visible man operating a small mobile platform towards the starboard does not take a second glance at you. Will you:

Head along the port side wall towards the bow?	Turn to 961.
Head along the stern wall towards starboard?	Turn to 889.

702.

Time passes. Inside the cold storage area you find numerous containers filled with frozen food supplies. Nothing seems out of the ordinary, you open up some of the containers to find exactly what is listed on their lids.

[If you have the *Collector of things* mission, turn to 558.]

[If you have the *Fugitive hunt* mission <u>and</u> the *Tracker* ability, turn to 489.]

Otherwise will you:

Search the food storage room?	Turn to 661.
Exit and return to the corridor?	Turn to 622.

703.

Time passes. As you enter the infirmary through the double doors, you are confronted by 3 security guards, one of which turns towards you and points; 'There he is!' he exclaims. It is clear the guards intend to take you alive or dead.

Will you:

Attack them?   Turn to 789.

Run from them?   Turn to 849.

704.

Having seen two of their fellow crew cut down, two of the other three executives flee the room. A tall, aged man brandishing a short blade that crackles with an electric green charge remains with no intent on leaving.

Chief of processes	CQ	5
	Vitality	18

4+ to hit, 4 damage.

No defense.

>You may flee at any point by turning to 662.

If you defeat the chief, decide what you will do next:

Search the bodies: Turn to 739.

Inspect the room: Turn to 771.

Leave now: Turn to 638.

705.

Time passes. The keypass scanner accepts your entry, logging your attendance. Looking around, there are many items ranging from liquids and powders in containers to scales, a mixing device and glass tubes. If there are any items here you decide to take, you may do so:

A length of glass tubing

Purordurumn powder

Granular filter

Condenser funnel

Distiller filter

Anti-microbial cloth

Tunnel flask

Trimethylin liquid

Lanune Di-3 powder

Carrier vapor container (non-light item)

ETU scanner (non-light item)

Note that each miscellaneous item counts as a light item with the exception of the two last items above which will count as one item each for purposes of working out how much you can carry. Once you are done here, turn to 608.

706.

After trying the code you have to wait for a moment. Nothing happens aside from the display on the keypad saying "Entry denied". Now will you:

Try to force your way in?	Turn to 563.
Leave the door alone?	Turn to 585.

707.

Standing before the production line you sum up the situation for the ideal way to get through. The tricky part is that the production line moves in timed intervals. However the timed intervals are not the same as they depend upon which part is currently being worked upon further up the line. The majority of production is for robots which seem to move quickly, stopping for a few seconds only at a time and leaving little room between them. Their feet almost touch the floor of the facility and there is a guidance rail system on either side of the production line.

You could try getting past the robots:	Turn to 746.
Or wait for a better opportunity to come along:	Turn to 913.

708.

A successful connection to a terminal in sector H has been made. Will you:

Search for layout data of sector H?	Turn to 733.
Search for activity data of sector H?	Turn to 679.
Attempt to hack the terminal remotely?	Turn to 582.

709.

[If you have the word "planted" written down, turn to 987 now.]

Otherwise you make it to the exit without further incident. Turn to 730.

710.

You are now part way along a corridor running port to starboard. As one option there is a door on the bow side.

[If you are part of the Confederacy and down to the *final tier* of time remaining, turn to 1105 now.]

Will you:

Head towards starboard?	Turn to 520.
Take the corridor towards port side?	Turn to 728.
Try the door on the bow side labeled "G002"?	Turn to 517.

711.

You are now at the end of the corridor. There is a door here on the starboard side or alternatively you may continue around the corridor.

Try the door on the starboard side?	Turn to 595.
Head along the corridor towards port side?	Turn to 395.
Head up the corridor towards bow?	Turn to 730.

712.

You find yourself in a long room mostly filled with bunks; you are in one of the ships rest quarters.

If you have the *Tracker* ability, turn to 566. If you do not have this ability, you find nothing that might help you and the room is deserted; turn to 590.

713.

[If you are with the SDN faction and do <u>not</u> have the word "create" written down, turn to 643 now.]

Moving along one of the walkways, you can see further down than before. It appears the engine bay extends for one level below you, though the engine filaments go through the floor on the level below. As you approach the first toroidal structure, you reach an adjoining walkway which forms an outer ring, that will take you to the other two toroids. To your right, connected to the walkway you are on you can see a stairway which leads back to a platform on the bow side wall. Will you:

Head up the stairway towards the platform?   Turn to 864.

Follow the ringed walkway you are on around the toroidal structures?   Turn to 912.

714.

As you try to leave you find the robot blocking the doorway. Ordering it to get out of the way doesn't seem to help and it seems to be paused and waiting for a correct instruction or for you to do something. Leaving you with no other ideas or options you smash the robot up and then climb over the wreckage to get out. *Time passes.* Turn to 622.

715.

There are two rooms along this corridor you can try if you have not already. Alternatively you can keep moving. Will you:

Try the first room on the right?   Turn to 1057.
Try the second room on the right?   Turn to 46.
Head towards the bow?   Turn to 345.
Head towards the stern?   Turn to 146.

716.

Rounding the corner up ahead is an XBR guard whom upon glancing at you draws his pistol. 'You shouldn't be here,' he mutters to no one in particular. The guard fires a shot, narrowly missing you and you take the opportunity afterwards to rush toward him and fight him at close quarters.

XBR guard	CQ	4
	Vitality	15

5+ to hit, 3 damage.
No defense.

If you defeat the guard, you may take his *laser pistol* if you choose.

Add the word "road" to your mission sheet and choose which way to go at the junction you are at:

Head towards the stern:	Turn to 565.
Take the corridor heading towards the bow:	Turn to 728.
Head along the corridor towards starboard:	Turn to 649.

717.

After having collected some spoils from the armory you decide to get out now before you have company. Reaching the door to the armory which opens to the corridor, you are stopped mid step as a burst of energy flies by you, narrowly missing burning through your torso. Down the end of the corridor is a man crouched with a rifle - waiting for you to try to leave. He is known as Desmorr Tawr, a proficient XBR shooter and he is blocking your way out - you'll need to out shoot him to avoid being trapped when other XBR crew arrive.

Desmorr Tawr	Ra	5
	Vitality	20

5+ to hit, 5 damage.
5+ to reduce damage by 3 as defense.

Each combat round, Desmorr may attempt an alternative attack. To determine if he does when he attacks next, roll one die. If you roll a 1 or a 2, Desmorr will throw a small grenade at you instead of shooting his rifle. Roll to hit by rolling a die and consulting the following chart:

1: Miss
2: 2 points of damage.
3: 3 points of damage.

4: 4 points of damage.

5: Roll one die for damage result.

6: Suffer a grievous wound.

>You may try for a defense roll for any of Desmorr's attacks.

>If you choose to throw a grenade at Desmorr, a successful hit will cause base damage plus the result of one die roll. A miss will cause no damage.

>You must kill Desmorr in order to move on - there is nowhere to flee to here.

If you defeat Desmorr, turn to 859.

718.

The door is locked and appears to be reinforced. Additionally it is in such a position that there is not enough room for you to use a tool or weapon against the door and using an explosive will bring down at least part of the room you are in - (or destroy the data) meaning you will trap yourself in. A micro petard might do the job of destroying the lock without destroying the room. It seems like a risky option. The alternative is to type in the access code to unlock the door.

If you know the access code, type the number in by subtracting it from the current reference and turn to that result. Otherwise:

Try a micro petard (if you have one):	Turn to 681.
Start searching through some of the data stores:	Turn to 631.
Investigate the artifacts:	Turn to 609.
Leave the room:	Turn to 523.

719.

The raw materials list is long and detailed. Supply is derived from numerous contractors, some of which operate without registration in order to avoid the watchful eyes of the Confederacy. Aside from this you find no relevant information and nothing unusual about the materials themselves.

Busily searching the records at the terminal you do not notice two guards have carefully reached the outside of the cabin. One of them throws a stun grenade into the cabin, sending a piercing sound reverberating around the cabin and putting you on the floor in shock. They then launch themselves at you, giving you no time to prepare.

Fight them in close quarter combat together. The guards will attack first, regardless of any abilities you may have - you are still reeling from being stunned. In addition, for the first round of combat, roll 3 dice for their attacks rather than 2.

Security guards	CQ	4
	Vitality	24
	On 2 dice, 4+ to hit, 3 damage.	
	No defense.	

If you defeat the guards, you find nothing of value on them and determine now would be a good time to leave. Turn to 639.

720.

Explaining your position and purpose, the woman seems a little more receptive whilst still not overly concerned with your activities here. Discussing the LWS attack she mentions the robots being built in manufacturing which they are also building in other ships and bases. She believes the LWS faction would be after those - either blueprints or samples as they are always after the latest technology she states. Yes they seek out technology at every chance, but still some details of this story do not add up. The robot technology is not new; the LWS have no shortage of advanced robots either. The XBR faction is not known for advanced robotics, but are known for their biological weapons development, which the LWS does not pursue. And if the XBR faction really did have some new technology then why an attack on one XBR starship? Potentially starting a war, it would be better to strike at every location if that were the intent. Why attack just the one ship and risk Confederacy judgment? You wonder to yourself before you ask a question related to your mission. In response she says she does not know and so cannot help, and then refers you to the captain for advice. No better off you seem to have done all you can in here. Turn to 1030.

721.

Time passes. [If you have the word "hollow" written down, turn to 894 now.]

Entering the room you see several terminals and a holographic projection on one side. The projection appears to be charts of some sort as far as you can tell from where you stand. On the other side is seated two men with a number of specimen slides scattered across an illuminated desk.

One of the men glances to see your entry, but nothing more as his companion continues explaining something to him. Add the word "hollow" to your mission sheet. Will you:

Talk to the men?	Turn to 737.
Head over to one of the terminals?	Turn to 665.
Leave the room?	Turn to 471.

722.

You have no difficulty getting around the robot as it is merely constructed for work duties. You pass through the eatery and return to the corridor. Turn to 622.

723.

[If you have the word "criteria" written down, turn to 865 immediately.]

Otherwise [If you have the word "induct" written down, turn to 892 now.]

At the far end of the bench you notice a lab scientist working diligently with his experiments. His back is to you and he has yet to note your presence. Will you:

Attack the man?	Turn to 930.
Try to talk with him?	Turn to 820.
Move towards the door to the other lab section?	Turn to 561.
Head towards the benches and exit on the port side?	Turn to 745.

724.

Having defeated the manufacturing controller, there is bound to be some recoil. You notice the production line is still running, but probably not for too much longer and if security doesn't already know the damage you have just caused they will soon find out. Write the word "Insist" on your mission sheet.

Check your mission sheet for any of the following words, turning to the associated reference accordingly. Note this reference as you will be returning here afterwards.

"Deter"   Turn to 368.

"Filter"   Turn to 442.

If you have neither of those words, nor the word "capacity" written down, write down the word "deter".

A quick scan of the room reveals a number of cabinets and draws which may contain something of interest. Also the terminal that the robot was connected to is active and idling. Judging by the alarm that has just gone off you determine you'd best take one option or leave now:

Access the terminal: Turn to 841.

Search the room: Turn to 793.

Leave immediately: Turn to 691.

725.

Bleeding and exhausted Corporal Leggilis sits slumped against the corridor wall. In a last ditch effort he pleads with you to spare him, before adding a sneering little quip: 'You're still not getting into that room though.' Will you:

Let the corporal live?   Turn to 693.

Finish him off and then continue cutting your way in? Turn to 813.

726.

The keypass you have is validated. Now for the biometric scan. You'll need to get past it somehow.

If you have a *Bio-mimic device* and want to use it, turn to 1023.

If you are out of options you can either return to 515 and try an alternative for your attempt at entry or you may ignore the door and room by turning to 450.

727.

Rounding the corner ahead at high speed is a plain clothed individual; running at such speed he almost runs into you. Seeing the situation and looking to get past you, the man draws a blade with the intent to use whatever force required to pass.

NFA ex-crew	Ra	5
	Vitality	20
	4+ to hit, 4 damage.	
	No defense.	

If you defeat the man, with the time taken to fend him off and try to identify him, *time passes*. Return to 597 and continue the reference.

728.

You are now at a corner. There is a door at the corner or you may continue around the corridor.

Will you:

Try the door on the bow side labeled "G001"?	Turn to 637.
Head towards starboard side?	Turn to 710.
Take the corridor in the direction of the stern?	Turn to 553.

729.

You are not strong enough to push the door open fully - it slams shut with powerful magnets. Contemplating your next move, your thoughts are abruptly interrupted as the door opens and a large robot bursts out. It scans you within a second and obviously finding you are not authorized to be here, attempts to subdue you by administering a paralyzing shock to your body. You are brought to your knees as the shock causes you to lose function of your legs. Deduct 3 *vitality*.

Quickly you strike out at the mechanized arm which is sending jolts of electricity through you and lop it off in one clean swipe. The robot recoils, backing further into the room. You have a brief moment to get up and decide what to do:

Follow the robot into the room and take it on: Turn to 871.

Run back to the upper deck while the robot re-stabilizes itself:

Turn to 796.

730.

You are in a long corridor running lengthways relative to the ship. There is a large door on the port side.

[If you are allied with either the SDN or LWS and <u>do not</u> have the word "trawl" written down, turn to 671. Otherwise if you have the word "linger" written down, roll one die. If the result is 4 or more, turn to 1206.]

Will you:

Try the door on port side labeled "Engine bay"?   Turn to 770.

Continue along the corridor towards the bow?   Turn to 670.

Head along the corridor towards the stern?   Turn to 711.

731.

Fortunately as you have hacked the biometric scanning system of the ship, your entry will be considered valid.

The door opens and you enter. Turn to 781.

732.

Time passes. Looking around you can see nothing in here that could be of value to you. It is exactly as intended - food stores and items meant for food preparation. Feeling you have spent enough of your valuable time in here you make for the exit. Turn to 714.

733.

You find listings for all the rooms in sector H along with extensive information regarding connections, supply and equipment present.

There is a class Y research laboratory, numerous living quarters with amenities, a stock supply and a number of planning rooms. Now will you:

Search for activity data of sector H? Turn to 679.

Attempt to hack the terminal remotely? Turn to 582.

Alternatively you may disconnect from the remote terminal and try another option by returning to 367.

734.

To the rear of the room you notice something half covered with a piece of thin cloth. Unveiling what is underneath you find what appears to be a disused terminal.

[If you are with the Confederacy, turn to 1040 now.]

Will you:

Try to use the terminal? Turn to 844.

Investigate some of the items on the shelves? Turn to 780.

Leave? Turn to 597.

735.

With the robot at point blank range seemingly careening out of control you fire a final time, blowing apart the torso and bringing it to a halt.

If you are NFA, turn to 1055. If you are with any other faction, turn to 979.

736.

As you move forward, the bracelet begins increasing in output, sending a punishing shock through your body. Deduct 5 *vitality*. The shock is severe enough to put you on the floor in pain, almost unable to move at all. Rolling over, closer to the door, the shock begins to dissipate to your relief. As your ability to move returns, you move closer to the door. You need to get the labor bracelet off your wrist if you are to use the teleporter. You head back out into the corridor. Turn to 551.

737.

Approaching the men you throw out a question to grab their attention; 'What are we examining,' you ask as if you are part of the team or crew.

'Er well, it happens to be the salivary glands of a *delidus uumis*' says the man who was doing the explaining, somewhat taken by surprise.

Now it is your turn for surprise as you have no idea on the creature he just mentioned.

Noticing this he adds; 'Oh, the new species we recently found on Lumerion'.

You feign new understanding from this remark.

Will you ask of their findings related to this creature? Turn to 697.

Or tell the men to carry on while you:

Access one of the terminals: Turn to 665.

Leave the room   Turn to 471.

738.

The manufacturing plans tell you nothing you did not take note of on the way in; they are building bio-synthetic robots which you are aware the XBR faction has been doing for some time now - in several of their installations or vessels. Future plans are almost non-existent; much of the same with a minor possible alteration or improvement.

[If you have the *Techno savage* mission, turn to 1058 now, remembering this reference.]

Intensely looking through files at the terminal you do not notice a brutish looking guard lumbering towards the cabin. Storming straight into the cabin you are taken aback by his towering figure. His friends know him as 'Gummut the hauler' for his usefulness in lugging heavy items around. You know he plans to carry you out of the cabin either dead or alive. You leap to your feet and prepare for battle:

> *Gummut the hauler*   CQ   5
>   Vitality   23
>   4+ to hit, 4 damage.
>   No defense.

>If the guard rolls a 3 when rolling to hit you, he will attempt to crush you with a bear hug: Unless you can roll less than or equal to your *strength* score on two dice, you will incur 3 damage (you may roll for defense if you have any).

If you defeat Gummut, you decide to leave immediately before the rest of the guards show up. Turn to 639.

739.

On the chief is his *short laser blade* which you may take if you choose. Now will you:

Inspect the room?	Turn to 771.
Leave now?	Turn to 638.

740.

Time passes. Your attempt is futile: within a short moment two XBR Corporals are at the door with weapons drawn. You have no choice but to fight them:

> *XBR Corporals*   CQ   5
>   Vitality   24
>   4+ to hit on 2 dice, 4 damage.
>   5+ to reduce damage by 2 as defense

>As they block the exit you cannot flee this fight.

>When their *vitality* is reduced to 12 or less, roll only 1 die for the remaining Corporal's attack.

If you defeat the Corporals, you may take a high impact grenade and/or 2 link pistols if you choose.

Looking around the room, there is no sign of the woman whom was seated in the forest.

You see no point spending more time here. Write the word "forest" on your mission sheet and turn to 710.

741.

Drawing your weapons you launch yourself into the pair skimming through documents. Unarmed and unprepared the crew members do not stand a chance. Flitting to the other officers you cut them down in turn; their only response a state of shock before meeting an untimely demise. Looking upon the corpses you notice the woman who was using the hologram has the insignia of a ranked officer. The rankings are unfamiliar to you, however her death may not go unnoticed. Write the word "ranked" on your mission sheet.

[If you are with the Confederacy, turn to 161 now, remembering this reference.]

Now will you:

Investigate the room?	Turn to 811.
Search the bodies?	Turn to 842.
Leave?	Turn to 569.

742.

You run towards the door a short way along the length of the tunnel. You find it is sealed closed. Sjonn could not have come this way otherwise he would still be on the other side of the door sealing it closed from the other side. You double back, re-doubling your efforts also.

If you have the word "zero" written down, turn to 911 immediately.

Otherwise if you have the word "one" written down, change it to a "zero" now.

Otherwise if you have the word "two" written down, change it to a "one" now.

Otherwise, write the word "two" on your mission sheet. Now turn to 443.

743.

Write the word "draft" on your mission sheet. You leave the room, turn to 711.

744.

Time passes. If you are using a cutting tool, ram or similar piece of equipment, follow the instructions for the item to get through the door. If you fail, you may continue to work your way through, adding 1 to the dice roll for each successive attempt. For each successive attempt *time passes*. If you are using a close quarter weapon to break through the door, treat the door as an opponent with a vitality of 8. All dice rolls to hit become 2 or more to hit. For each 'combat round' after the first, *time passes*.

If you break through, turn to 799.

You may quit at any time by turning to 597.

745.

On a bench beside you two beakers being heated by small burners are bubbling away with a green liquid. On another bench further head you notice an elongated tube filled with sediment on the bottom and a crimson liquid swirling around. There is no sign of anyone here, though it is a large room and some of the benches and partitions block your view in areas. Will you:

Investigate the beakers with the bubbling green liquid? Turn to 674.

Take a closer look at the tube of swirling crimson liquid?

Turn to 502.

Move towards the benches towards starboard?   Turn to 723.

Exit the laboratory?   Turn to 464.

746.

You anticipate the next pause in the line. This could be a tight squeeze. Test your agility by rolling 2 dice and adding your *agility* score. If you have the *Contortion* ability, you may add 3 to the result. If the sum total is 12 or higher, you get through just in time. If the total is 11 or lower, when the production line moves forward again you are pushed into the guide rails on the other side, causing a sprain (Deduct 2 *vitality*). Having reached the other side, you may either head towards the stern along the port perimeter or take a nearby ramp to the level below.

Head further down port side:	Turn to 961.
Take the ramp to the lower level:	Turn to 822.

747.

The robot bears down upon you. At short range, fire for three rounds, with you going first.

Overseer robot	Ra	4
	Vitality	15

5+ to hit, 0 damage, see below.
4+ to negate 5 damage as defense.

The robot will attempt to paralyze you with a high voltage array. If the robot scores a hit on you, roll one die. If you roll 4 or more, turn to 801 immediately. If you have a *resilience* of 6 or more, the dice roll needs to be 5 or more, for you to become paralyzed (turn to 801). If you roll lower, continue as normal; the attempt to subdue you has failed. If you survive three rounds or reduce the robot's *vitality* to 0, then turn to 735.

748.

You see this as an ideal place to place a bomb or explosive.

[If you have the word "planted" written down and have a bomb/explosive to use, turn to 1069 now.]

To prevent any possibility of reigniting the filaments, two bombs exploding simultaneously at both ends of the filaments would be required. The actual placing of the bombs is also a little tricky. The challenge however is to place it close to the filaments for maximum damage, but at the same time you do not want to get too close as to absorb some of the ionizing radiation. If you have an explosive or bomb (grenades or petards do not count) and want to use it here, remove it from your inventory and roll one die. If you roll a 1 or a 2, deduct 3 *vitality* for the dose of short term ionizing radiation. If you plant a bomb or explosive, write the word "planted" on your mission sheet as you carefully set the timer. You now head back down. Turn to 851.

749.

Checking over the body of the dead agent, you discover a *med pack* and a *laser pulse rifle* which you may take if you choose. Additionally you may take an identity scan of the agent - if you do, add one to an identity scan tally written on your mission sheet. Remove the word "concede" on your mission sheet and replace it with the word "decide". Now will you:

Try the door on port side labeled "Manufacturing"?   Turn to 599.

Try to enter the door on the starboard side labeled "F002"?

Turn to 481.

Continue along the corridor heading towards the bow? Turn to 614.

Head towards the stern, following the corridor around the corner?

Turn to 590.

750.

Heading towards the stern through a rather long corridor you in time reach a solid isolation door. The door clearly has some security measures in place and is designed to keep anything from passing through to the other side. Rather than risk it, you decide to head back to the previous junction. Turn to 395.

751.

Returning to the room you find the previous occupants have all left - no, you spot the man in the corner with his headset on. Again he is still engrossed in whatever he is watching. Will you:

Attempt to communicate with him?   Turn to 879.
Leave the room?   Turn to 565.

752.

Since you will not have the deprogrammer ability you cannot hack it directly. Power will shut down and the door will remain closed - you will have to cut through to get in.

Time passes. The biometric system is not an easy thing to hack. In fact it proves to be beyond difficult if it is at all possible. With your attempts though, power is shut off from the system with the door still securely shut. With the scanner inoperable, you now are left with two options:

Use a siege or cutting tool on the armory door: Turn to 773.
Leave immediately: Turn to 392.

753.

From beneath the door on the port side you can see a thick grayish gas seeping out. Surely the room will be filled with the stuff you think to yourself and so decide it best to avoid that room entirely.

Will you:
Open the door on starboard side?   Turn to 721.
Head up the corridor towards the bow?   Turn to 398.

754.

Time passes. Will you:
Take a look at some of the items around the room?   Turn to 877.
Greet the pair looking at documents?   Turn to 804.
Talk to the woman over in the corner?   Turn to 917.
Try to communicate with the man along the side wall? Turn to 779.
Leave the room?   Turn to 565.

755.

After your response, the scientists look at each other before turning back to you with one of them nodding his head. The scientists split up and you move in further as the scientist whom nodded earlier beckons you forward before asking the name of the substance.

As you begin to tell the technician what you are after you feel something hit you in the back, pushing you forward onto a bench. Deduct 2 *vitality* for the hit. Getting back to your feet you find both the scientists armed with crude weapons from around the lab advancing on you. It seems you are not trusted given you are inside a hazardous laboratory without any protection suit. Fend off the technicians as a single pair:

Lab technicians	CQ	4
	Vitality	22

5+ to hit on 2 dice, 2 damage.
No defense.

If you defeat the technicians, you set about exploring the room to learn more. Will you:

Check out the equipment?	Turn to 905.
Check out some of the substances?	Turn to 1001.
Open up the substance repertory?	Turn to 1020.
Leave the room?	Turn to 866.

756.

Time passes. If you are using a cutting tool, ram or similar piece of equipment, follow the instructions for the item to get through the door. If you fail, you may continue to work your way through, adding 1 to the dice roll for each successive attempt. For each successive attempt *time passes.* If you are using a close quarter weapon to break through the door, treat the door as an opponent with a vitality of 8. All dice rolls to hit become 2 or more to hit. For each 'combat round' after the first, *time passes.*

If you manage to cut through, turn to 827. You may leave the door alone at any time by turning to 585.

757.

Time passes. Moving further into the room you reach the production line which has paused for a moment before shunting forward once more. The working equipment, shunting production line and various other sounds create a cacophony across the room. You cannot simply pass through the production line and it would be impractical to do so anyway. Will you:

Head along the production line towards the stern?   Turn to 881.
Head along the production line towards the bow?   Turn to 910.

758.

Steering sharply you manage to smash into the agent and knock him to the floor. Looking over your shoulder he doesn't get up and you bring the cart to a screeching halt. Amongst the smoke and frenzy of activity you spot a large crane nearby which you determine would make excellent cover. Jumping out of the cart in one swift move you take up position beside the towering crane to defend and assess the situation. Turn to 346.

759.

Climbing down the ladder you reach the bottom and begin along the tunnel as before. Following the tunnel around you eventually reach the end where a securely locked door prevents progress. You sense you are only wasting time down here and not making any progress with your mission. *Time passes.*

Return to manufacturing by turning to 920.

760.

Looking through the cupboards, sorting through the various chems that are kept here in an attempt to find something useful, you do not notice someone enter the room. Previous training kicks in though and you catch the assailant attempting to sneak up on you. Armed with a crude blade the woman lashes out at you, slashing and stabbing away; and you are forced to fight back.

Vicious Crew member	CQ	4
	Vitality	16
	5+ to hit, 2 damage	
	No defense	

Once you have fended off the crew member you finish searching: roll 1 die. On a roll of 1, turn to 872. If you roll 2 or more, turn to 898.

761.

Waiting for you is an XBR corporal armed with an electrified blade.

XBR corporal	CQ	5
	Vitality	20
	4+ to hit, 4 damage.	
	5+ to reduce damage by 2 as defense.	

If you defeat the corporal, return to your previous reference.

762.

As you step forward again, the keypass scanner illuminates red and on each side of the room barriers drop down from the ceiling, enclosing all the shelved areas. It looks like the only way to access the contents of this room is with a keypass. Damaging the barriers or blowing things up is likely to damage the supplies here. If you are in this room for a particular purpose, take the words which are the reason for you being here and count the letters. Multiply the value by 60 and then turn to that reference. If you do not think it may be worth your time to try to gain access to the supplies, you may leave - turn to 608. Otherwise you may try to obtain a keypass and return later.

763.

Deciding to keep moving to the next sector, despite there being rooms here you pass by them, round a bend and arrive at a junction. By the signage on the walls you are now in sector E. Turn to 407.

764.

Doubling back along the tunnel you reach the ladder and climb it back up the manufacturing level. Write the word "pipes" on your mission sheet and turn to 920.

765.

Continuing at the door, you are making slow progress around the thick plated door. Sure enough more security arrives to stop you. It is Corporal Leggilis, and he is far from pleased you are trying to break into his security hub. Fight one round at short range before fighting at close quarters for the rest of the battle.

Corporal Leggilis	CQ	5
	Ra	5
	Vitality	20

4+ to hit, 4 damage.
5+ to reduce damage by 2 as defense

>For each combat round after the *vitality* of Leggilis is reduced to 10 or less he will fight savagely, drawing a sinister looking dagger to use for a second weapon. Decrease his to hit roll from 4+ to 3+ and add *bleeding* as a lingering effect his damage will have on you.
>If you reduce the Corporal's *vitality* to 3 or less, turn to 725.

766.

Entering the lab you find things as they were when you left, aside from one obvious difference - the bodies are missing. Judging by the blood trails they have been dragged to the entrance and then lifted away. Not liking the situation and seeing no point going over your previous steps you decide to return to the corridor junction you came from. Turn to 520.

767.

Suddenly a shudder runs through the ship, forcing you to stabilize yourself and avoid toppling onto the floor. Roll 1 die. If you roll 3 or less, return to 597 and continue with that reference. If you roll 4 or more and have not done so previously, turn to the following reference determined by your faction alliance:

Confederacy: Turn to 727.
SDN or NFA: Turn to 576.
LWS: Turn to 507.

768.

You have only just begun to dig at the hatch on the door when all of a sudden it flips open and an aerial drone flies through into the corridor. Reflexively you duck, which is enough to save you from being hit in the face by the drone, but also enough to avoid being detected; the drone scoots by, heading down the corridor towards its destination. Seeing the function of the hatch now, you guess that was not the only drone in the room. You decide it best to move on rather than risk having to deal with more drones. Turn to 585.

769.

The door unlocks. Turn to 527.

770.

Time passes. [If you have the word "fatal" written down, turn to 1022 now.]

You have entered the engine bay. Expansive in size, the engine bay extends across three levels. Looking up you can see the ceiling high above in between a lattice of supports and walkways connecting to the engine filament structures. On the level you are on there are three donut-like toroidal units, each the size of a small room, surrounding the engine filaments which extend vertically.

An incessant hum fills the air, which slowly pulses dues to the energy generation in here. The platform you are on appears to extend around the perimeter of the room. Will you:

Take a walkway towards one of the toroidal structures?

Turn to 713.

Walk around the perimeter platform towards the bow? Turn to 694.

Head along the perimeter platform towards the stern? Turn to 677.

Leave the engine bay?   Turn to 730.

771.

Time passes. Looking around the room there seems to be little of interest to you in here. An assortment of charts and adornments mostly - nothing to aid you in your duty. You decide to not spend any more time here and make for the exit. Turn to 638.

772.

Time passes. The yellow powder has you curious enough to take a closer look. It can be difficult to tell much about a substance from appearances alone. The powder is a bright yellow with the odd black spec in it and does not give off any odor. To the side of the powder is a small voice recorder. You replay the last few notes made:

'Substance 3YX has provided none of the results expected. It does not dissolve easily, nor does it handle temperature variation to any large degree. Inadvertently we discovered 3YX is considerably volatile when dispersed and ignited. It shall be noted as volatile for this reason before we transfer our sample for electro-magnetic scanning.'

If you choose you may place the powder in a small container and take it with you. If you do, add 3YX powder to your inventory and count it as a miscellaneous item. Will you:

Look at another of the substances?   Turn to 952.

Attempt to open the substance repertory?   Turn to 1020.

Not spend time here and leave?   Turn to 967.

773.

The door is solid and thick. You now have the arduous task of getting through the door. The door has an integrity value of 40. If you reduce the integrity of the door to zero (or less) you have done sufficient damage for you to get through. You may use a ranged weapon, close quarter weapon, an attachment (example: cutting tool) or an explosive (or petard). Grenades may not be used in this situation.

Observe the following modifications for your choice of tool:

If you use a ranged weapon: You will automatically score a hit for each die you would normally roll in each round and you will cause the damage listed for your weapon only. For instance if you are using a *Twin pulse rifle* then each round you would cause 8 points of damage (2 automatic hits multiplied by 4 damage). Note: pistols will count as a ranged weapon in this task.

If you use a close quarter weapon: All 'to hit rolls' are automatic hits (no need to roll for them) but in addition to the damage you do with your weapon, add an additional dice roll worth of damage to the total. For instance if you are using an *electro razor*, you will cause 4 damage plus the result of one dice roll.

If you use an explosive: The damage done will be automatic and add the total of 2 dice to the tally.

If you use an attachment such as cutting tool: Make your roll to use your tool of choice. If you are successful: add the damage of the weapon (as if it were a CQ weapon), along with the result of one dice roll, along with 10 additional points. If you are unsuccessful, do the same, but do not add on the 10 additional points.

You may start your attempt to break through the door.

If you want to leave at any point, turn to 392.

After your first 'round', roll one die and take the action stated:

1. Turn to 475 then return to this reference.
2. Nothing happens
3. Turn to 680 then return to this reference.
4. Test your endurance. (See below)
5. Nothing happens
6. Turn to 890 then return to this reference.

If you roll a 4, you will need to test your endurance for this task. To do this for this particular task, roll 2 dice. If the total is equal to or less than your *endurance*, then continue with the task. If the total is greater than your *endurance* then deduct 2 *vitality* before continuing.

Continue to destroy the door, after each 'round' at it, roll one die and consult the list above.

If you reduce the integrity of the door to zero, you have made it through. Enter by turning to 781.

774.

You quickly leave the area, heading to the end of the corridor and then taking a right turn towards port side where you reach a junction. Write the word "scrape" on your mission sheet. Turn to 391.

775.

Time passes. [If you have the *Tech hoarder* ability, turn to 1004 now.]

Pulling down from a high shelf you find a *Positron diffuser* which you may add to your inventory as a miscellaneous item if you choose. Will you:

Continue looking, picking out another item that appears interesting?   Turn to 907.

Move over to the corner bench and take a look?   Turn to 463.

Check-out the toolbox on the floor?   Turn to 657.

Not spend any more time here and leave the room?   Turn to 743.

776.

'Somehow I don't believe you as I would have been notified directly,' he quips as he leaps up and pushes his chair into you. 'And you don't seem like the character I'd have any work with,' he snarls as he draws a short laser blade and leaps at you. You must fight him at close quarters.

Manufacturing foreman	CQ	5
	Vitality	17
	4+ to hit, 4 damage.	
	No defense.	

If you defeat the foreman, write the word "driver" on your mission sheet.

Check your mission sheet for any of the following words, turning to the associated reference accordingly. Note this reference as you will be returning here afterwards.

"Deter"   Turn to 368.
"Filter"   Turn to 442.

If you have neither of those words, nor the word "capacity" written down, write down the word "deter".

You may:
Search the room: Turn to 908.
Or return down the elevator and
Go into the lunch rooms: Turn to 883.
Head down the ramp to the lower level: Turn to 822.
Head towards the stern along the portside wall: Turn to 796.

777.

Seeing your struggle, an XBR guard that has just entered the hall jumps into the fight to help you out.

Helpful XBR guard	CQ	4
	Vitality	19
	5+ to hit, 3 damage.	
	No defense.	

Using the stats above for the guard, return to 863 to continue the fight, making it a 3 way battle. To determine who the LWS agent will attack, each round roll a die. On 3 or less, the agent will attack you; on a roll of 4 or more, the agent will attack the XBR guard.

778.

[If you are into the *final tier* of time remaining, turn to 1143 now.] Otherwise, turn to 1118.

779.

The only way you can see of getting the man's attention is to tap him on the shoulder. This startles him and he sharply removes the goggles. Not recognizing you and presumably for interrupting him he reacts in a distraught manner; 'What do you think you are doing?' he spits out. Taken aback you attempt to settle the man but he fires up even more, ordering you to 'get out of his face' as he puts it.

The raucous has the other crew members eyeing you with concern - enough so that you back away, leaving the tempered man alone and reaching the door. Turn to 565.

780.

Time passes. Browsing the items you find various attachments and parts which appear to be from other pieces of equipment or machinery. None of these items are useful to you and would only burden you down further. You decide to move on. Will you:

Take a look at the terminal if you have not already?   Turn to 844.
Leave?   Turn to 597.

781.

It may have been tough, but you made it into the ships armory. Before you are shelves and aisles of all manner of weapons and tech packed into a moderately sized room. You do not have the luxury of time however. Breaking into the armory is sure to stir up the nest of XBR personnel, and there are no other exits from this room. Quickly you scan the stocked items to grab an item or two of value.

Roll 2 dice. Compare the result to table 1 of the *discovered item tables* near the beginning of the book.

You may add the item to your inventory if you choose.

Repeat the process, this time using table 2 of the *discovered item tables*.

Instead of choosing one of the items, you may take either of the following once:

A Med pack or

2 High impact grenades.

If you do not have any armor you may also take a Ceramic plated vest.

After you have made your choices, roll one die. On a roll of 3 or less, turn to 929. On a roll of 4 or more, turn to 717.

782.

Pushing open the door to the suspended office, you find nobody in it. A cursory check of the room yields nothing of value to you. You quickly head down the elevator as the ship creaks and rumbles as it undergoes excessive structural stress. Reaching the bottom you leap off and choose a direction:

Head down the ramp to the lower level: Turn to 822.

Head towards the stern along the portside wall: Turn to 796.

783.

There is a list of workers here, all cataloged according to worker number and crew number. The list does not detail names, ages or other personal information as it is more for skills and division allocation.

Will you:

Search current and future manufacturing plans?   Turn to 738.

Look at the supply of raw materials?   Turn to 719.

Leave now?   Turn to 691.

784.

Returning to the room you find the bodies are still here as before. You decide not to stick around. Turn to 565.

785.

Part way along the corridor you stop dead on the spot. A strip which runs around the floor, walls and ceiling illuminates red and slowly pulses. Just in front of that warning light is a fine laser mesh. It is visible to you and is the reason for your abrupt halt. The laser mesh acts as a barrier - you know you won't be able to disable it and there is no way you can pass through it - unless in sliced up pieces. It is more than likely controlled remotely. Your only option is to head back to the junction. Will you:

Head toward port side?	Turn to 419.
Take the corridor in the direction of the stern?	Turn to 465.

786.

[If you have the *Got the lingo* ability, turn to 946 now.]

Looking for a way to redeem yourself, you attempt to fabricate something she will accept. Despite your best effort she is dismissive, seeing you as not being a scientist and not having sufficient reason for being in here. She insists you leave the laboratory. Will you:

Attack her?	Turn to 834.
Leave, taking the starboard exit?	Turn to 471.
Leave and head into the portside section?	Turn to 538.

787.

Responding to your actions, a group of 4 airborne drones round the corner at top speed heading in your direction. You'll need to take them down fast with some short range shooting.

Drone flock	Ra	5
	Vitality	20

3+ to hit, 3 damage.
5+ Agile flyer defense will negate all damage.

>For each reduction to the *vitality* of the drones by 5 (at 15, 10 and 5) increase the to hit roll of the drones by 1. In other words when the

drones have between 15 and 11 *vitality*, the drones' to hit roll will be 4 or more and so on.

After defeating the drones, write the word "block" on your mission sheet. Will you:

Use a cutting or siege tool if you have one?	Turn to 546.
Simply attempt to damage the door?	Turn to 664.
Leave it alone?	Turn to 675.

788.

You sprint ahead, reaching another slightly open doorway. You step through and see Sjonn ahead, at the end of this section of tunnel being slowed by having to open another door. The guy can certainly run you think to yourself while puffing. To stay on his tail you cannot rest but have to sprint yet again. Test your endurance by rolling two dice and adding your *endurance*. If the total is 13 or more, turn to 613 now.

If the total is lower than 13, perform the following procedure:

If you have the word "one" written down, change it to a "zero" now.

Otherwise if you have the word "two" written down, change it to a "one" now.

Otherwise, write the word "two" on your mission sheet. Now turn to 613.

789.

Face the three guards at close quarters, fighting each separately. Note that each guard will attack you once before you can attack your choice of guard once before repeating.

First guard	CQ	4
	Vitality	14
	5+ to hit, 4 damage.	
	No defense.	

Second guard	CQ	4
	Vitality	12

5+ to hit, 3 damage.
No defense.

Guard leader	CQ	4
	Vitality	16

4+ to hit, 4 damage.
No defense.

>The guards have you surrounded and as such you cannot flee from this battle.

If you defeat the guards, you may take any of the following items which they had on them: *laser pistol, electro razor* and a *high impact grenade.* Remove the word "clang" from your mission sheet and return to 332.

790.

Moving through the room you glance at some of the equipment and gauges in here. In the far corner of the room you notice a trapdoor in the floor. It would make sense if this was used to service the equipment here. Will you:

Rest for a moment?	Turn to 896.
Investigate the sub compartment?	Turn to 847.
Leave the room?	Turn to 447.
[SDN: Wreck the equipment?	Turn to 932.]

791.

You recall that the ramp is where you entered from earlier. It seems pointless to head back down - you are sure what you are looking for is to found on the level you are on. Will you:

Take a look in some of the rooms here?	Turn to 658.
Keep moving to the end of the corridor?	Turn to 763.
Head back into Sector F?	Turn to 397.

792.

Doing so as inconspicuously as possible you step across the crossover. Roll one die. On a roll of 1 or 2, if you have not done so before, write the word "cross" on your mission sheet. Regardless of your roll, you do not stop to look out over the facility, but instead reach the other side and now have two options before you:

Head further down port side: Turn to 961.

Head down a nearby ramp to the lower level: Turn to 822.

793.

Quickly you rummage through the draws and cabinets seeking anything which may be of use to you.

In one of the draws you find a pair of link pistols. You may take these as *Dual link pistols* if you choose. Turn to 691.

794.

Having dealt with the guards you hardly have time to be at ease as you see someone enter the decontamination chamber. You take cover behind a bench as the second door opens and a broad shouldered Confederacy agent steps inside the room. He will happily take you alive, but does not mind you being dead either.

Begin the battle as a short ranged fight. If you want to engage him at close quarters, you may do so by forgoing your turn to attack. In your following turn to attack, fight in Close Quarters and the agent will do the same for the rest of the battle.

Confederacy Agent	CQ	5	3+ to hit, 5 damage.
	Ra	6	3+ to hit, 4 damage.
	Vitality	28	
	5+ to reduce damage by 5 as defense		

>Whilst his *vitality* is above 18 and fighting a ranged combat, the agent will attempt to stun you rather than kill you. For any successful

hits, replace the damage done with the *stunned* lingering effect. If you are *stunned* again whilst still affected, upgrade the effect to the *shaken* lingering effect. If you are stunned whilst *shaken*, upgrade the effect to a *shocked* effect. If you are stunned whilst *shocked* you will not recover. The agent has brought you down and will inevitably capture you - a fate equivalent to your death.

>In the event of the agent rolling a 1 when rolling to hit you, he will forgo his attack and attempt to take several red capsules. Roll another die - if this roll is 4 or more, he succeeds - add 5 to his *vitality* (never exceeding his starting value of 28.) If the roll is 3 or less he loses the pills all over the floor.

>If the agent rolls a 6 when rolling to hit, in the next combat round he will charge at you, attempting to engage you at close quarters. In this case, you may take one free combat round of shooting at him or perform any alternative action. Then proceed as normal, with the rest of the battle as a close quarter encounter. He stands between you and the only exit, so this will be a fight to the death.

If you defeat the agent, you decide not to burden yourself with the agent's weapons as you know they are uniquely micro chipped, disabling their function for any non-agent and you do not have the means to re-engineer them on this ship.

Time passes. Write the word "seeker" on your mission sheet and turn to 957.

795.

Having taken only a few steps into the laboratory a female technician rushes by you, pausing as she does and stating emphatically, 'We need to get out of here now.' With that she continues on her way out quickly. From the other side of the room you can see a thick noxious cloud spreading out into the room. No doubt the gas is harmful and so you do not hesitate to take the advice of the scientist. Write the word "gaseous" on your mission sheet and turn to 398.

796.

You have reached the port/stern corner of the facility; offset from the corner is one of the entry/exit doors. Will you:

Head along the port side wall?	Turn to 961.
Head along the stern wall towards starboard?	Turn to 889.
Exit the room?	Turn to 488.

797.

Following the tunnel around, you can now see to the end through the dim lighting, noting the tunnel verges off to the left. Approaching the corner, you suddenly are on edge from hearing footsteps. You freeze. You listen intently. The steps are getting louder; whoever or whatever it is sounds like it is heading your way. Will you:

Wait and prepare to meet the individual?	Turn to 885.
Quickly head back and return to upper deck?	Turn to 764.

798.

Turning around you bolt back out into the corridor, reaching the corner at the end and turning right. You are stopped in your tracks however as there is a thick isolation door in front of you and it is securely closed, blocking your path. With only one option you turn back to face the agent, using the corner for cover.

Begin the battle as a short ranged fight. If you want to engage him at close quarters, you may do so by forgoing your turn to attack. In your following turn to attack, fight in Close Quarters and the agent will do the same for the rest of the battle.

Confederacy Agent	CQ	5	3+ to hit, 5 damage.
	Ra	6	3+ to hit, 4 damage.
	Vitality	28	

5+ to reduce damage by 5 as defense

>Throwing a grenade will do double damage. If you roll a 6 when throwing the grenade, add an additional 3 damage.

>Whilst his *vitality* is above 20 and fighting a ranged combat, the agent will attempt to stun you rather than kill you. For any successful hits, replace the damage done with the *stunned* lingering effect. If you are *stunned* again whilst still affected, upgrade the effect to the *shaken* lingering effect. If you are stunned whilst *shaken*, upgrade the effect to a *shocked* effect. If you are stunned whilst *shocked* you will not recover. The agent has brought you down and will inevitably capture you - a fate equivalent to your death.

>In the event of the agent rolling a 1 when rolling to hit you, he will forgo his attack and attempt to take several red capsules. Roll another die - if this roll is 4 or more, he succeeds - add 5 to his *vitality* (never exceeding his starting value of 28.) If the roll is 3 or less he fumbles and fails to retrieve the packet of pills.

>If the agent rolls a 6 when rolling to hit, in the next combat round he will charge at you, attempting to engage you at close quarters. In this case, you may take one free combat round of shooting at him or perform any alternative action. Then proceed as normal, with the rest of the battle as a close quarter encounter. He stands between you and any escape, so this will be a fight to the end.

If you defeat the agent, you decide not to burden yourself with the agent's weapons as you know they are uniquely micro chipped, disabling their function for any non-agent and you do not have the means to re-engineer them on this ship.

Time passes. Write the word "seeker" on your mission sheet and turn to 957.

799.

Squeezing through the entrance you carved for yourself, you find yourself in a small control room of some sort. Reading several descriptions you'd say the room is used for auxiliary control of the engine under emergency conditions. As you scan over the controls further, you notice a display which states the console is in lockdown. This could have been done remotely or it could be the result of you putting a hole in the door. Either way, without the means to unlock the console, there is nothing else here for you to do. Turn to 597.

800.

You wait silently in the darkness provided away from the signs outside the pens. A moment passes with the tension not subsiding in the slightest. With no signals whatsoever you start to move away. Roll a die. If you have the *Stealth* ability you may add 1 to the result. If the result is 4 or more, turn to 219. If the result is 3 or less, turn to 177.

801.

You have been hit by the high voltage array of the robot which puts you on the floor shaking uncontrollably in paralysis. Deduct 5 *vitality*. Reduce your *strength* and *agility* by 1 point each. The robot draws nearer and recharges its array. With what capability you have left, you manage to scramble behind a piece of cover before the robot can hit you again and permanently paralyze you. As the robot moves around searching, heaving yourself off the floor you try to get away while you still can. Will you:

Head towards the cabin?   Turn to 940.

Leave the area and return to upper deck via the ramp? Turn to 796.

802.

'Well I am unsure on this particular individual, but if I were to guess I would say he is one of the laborers working aboard the ship, probably in sector F. We have too many of them unfortunately. Now I must return to my work; I am sure other crew members can help you locate the man you are looking for.'

Leaving the scientist be, will you:

Head into the starboard section: Turn to 486.

Head into head portside section: Turn to 538.

803.

[If you have the word "shelf" written down, turn to 1029 now.]

Moving over to the other side of the room you push open the door with due caution. In this well lit room you see a kitchenette to one side and washing and cleaning facilities on the other. There are several cupboards lining the wash area which you decide to check for any chems. Roll one die.

On a roll of 1 turn to 872. On a roll of 2 or 3, turn to 898. On a roll of 4 or more, turn to 760.

804.

Greeting the pair of researchers they both do not reply but rather look you up and down discerningly. Though you have your weapons concealed, their concern over you is quite apparent. 'Unless you have authority from Rholiva, then you cannot be in here. You must leave,' one of them says sternly.

Will you:

Leave as ordered? Turn to 565.

Attack the crew? Turn to 741.

805.

Time passes. You have reached the starboard/stern corner of the facility. Here there are several large crates as well as two workbenches against the stern wall. You may either stop to look or keep moving.

Investigate pieces of equipment here that may be of interest?

Turn to 989.

Skirt the production line towards the bow? Turn to 920.

Head along the stern wall towards portside? Turn to 889.

806.

To get out of this sticky situation you tell him you have made a mistake and without waiting for a reply or explaining yourself you close the door behind you and whack the elevator controls to send you on your way. Reaching the floor, you keep moving. Now you may:

Go into the lunch rooms: Turn to 883.
Head down the ramp to the lower level: Turn to 822.
Head towards the stern along the portside wall: Turn to 796.

807.

Walking beside the production line you eventually reach a dead end as the production line snakes around you. The area is vacated of workers though there are still signs of life with various pieces of equipment lying around, some of which are in an unordered fashion as if crew had been working here recently. *Time passes* as you return back to the edge of the production line. Will you:

Head towards the corner starboard/stern?   Turn to 805.
Head towards port side?   Turn to 796.

808.

Escaping the scene you quickly head down the corridor, keeping a close look out for incoming security.

Check your mission sheet for any of the following words, turning to the associated reference accordingly. Note this reference as you will be returning here afterwards.

"Deter"   Turn to 368.
"Filter"   Turn to 442.

If you have neither of those words, nor the word "capacity" written down, write down the word "deter".

Now write the word "forest" on your mission sheet and turn to 710.

809.

Pounding away at the keypad you render it completely unusable and in pieces with sparks flying out of it. To your surprise, the door remains locked and no security seems to be activated.

You decide not to waste any more time here. Turn to 585.

810.

Trying to leave you realize you are in a lockdown chamber designed for security purposes. Fortunately the system is still allowing you to leave after a short programmed delay, probably due to your security clearance provided by the keypass. If you do not already have it written down, write the word "deter" on your mission sheet. Turn to 450.

811.

Time passes. Looking through the data stores there is much detailed information regarding experiments and research being carried out here. It is mostly highly scientific information and what you can make sense of does not seem relevant to you. The holographic matrix of elements seems to be a simulation of proteins and enzymes from what you can tell. Some documents being projected list in detail physical traits of some creature or organism the people here were looking at. Seemingly done in here, you make for the door. Turn to 569.

812.

Though you are quick to get out of the room you feel as if some of the gas is trapped in your lungs as you run. Deduct 2 *vitality* for some residual effects of the gas. Fortunately the robot does not pursue and there are no signs of any guards yet. You follow the ramp back to the level above and move quickly yet carefully along the port side wall. Turn to 796.

813.

You silence the corporal swiftly so that you can prove him wrong and continue with your task of getting in. Before you can make the smallest of progress however you are forced to look down the corridor when a metallic rumbling sound alerts you. Rounding the corner you see what looks like a silver plated ball rolling towards you. The skull-sized ball snakes from side to side - clearly not a grenade - and when it reaches you it abruptly stops. Knowing it spells trouble you shoot at it from a little more than arm's length away. The ball does not even get pushed back and the only sign of damage is a black smear on one of the plates. Seemingly trapped you try to prepare for what might happen - which you sense could be almost anything from this unfamiliar device. Attempting to grab it quickly, you realize it weighs a massive amount for its size. You cannot even pick it up, besides you do not know if it about to explode or what. Hissing loudly, the ball suddenly extends four vents on each side. You back away. Then a gas, thick and green begins being expelled from the vents rapidly. Poisonous gas! You cover your mouth and make a run for the junction at the end of the corridor. Roll one die and add your *agility*. If your total is 7 or less, add the *poisoned* lingering effect as you have taken in some of the gas.

Write the word "fresh" on your mission sheet.

You quickly leave the area, heading to the end of the corridor and then taking a right turn towards port side where you reach a junction. Write the word "iris" on your mission sheet. Turn to 391.

814.

Sampling some of the food and drink hits the spot. Wiping away your mouth you get back to the task at hand. Will you:

Enter into the adjoining room? Turn to 803.
Leave? Turn to 728.

815.

Entering into sector H, you are walking through a long stretch of corridor with no doors.

If you are into the *final tier* of time, turn to 1088. Otherwise, turn to 1047.

816.

Up ahead the corridor appears to be filled with a noxious gas escaping from the door at the end of the corridor. You cannot risk heading down there and decide it best to avoid the area. Turn to 553.

817.

Typing in the number combination you believe is correct, the keypad display lights up with "Entry denied". Fortunately no alarms have sounded, though you do not want to test it by entering two incorrect codes. Unless you have another plan here it seems if you are intent on getting into this room you will have to break in. Will you:

Try an explosive on the door?	Turn to 845.
Attempt to hack through the door?	Turn to 744.
Leave the door alone?	Turn to 597.

818.

If you have any of the following, you could ask Kinlac of them if you choose:

An RT data emulator:	Turn to 1025.
A micro blocker:	Turn to 1059.
An EM scanner:	Turn to 941.
A positron diffuser:	Turn to 1086.

If you have a damaged high speed laser cutter and would like to ask if he can repair it, turn to 1180.

If you have an unusual item you think Kinlac may be able to help you with, turn to 1276.

In the event you have none of these items you simply say you were just looking and will be on your way. Slightly disappointed Kinlac responds with a farewell and continues with his work. Turn to either 451 to leave the room or 383 to spend time looking at the shelves on the port side if you haven't already.

819.

You dash for the door. Roll two dice and add your *agility*. If the total is less than 12, turn to 828. If the total is 12 or more, turn to 875.

820.

Moving closer to him, he does now see that you are in his presence. You attempt to interact with him.

If you have the *Biohazard borrower* mission, turn to 887.
If you have the *Proto-swipe* mission, turn to 1036.
If you have the *Disrupt and extract* mission, turn to 1075.
Otherwise, turn to 1008.

821.

When you do finally enter the room you are discouraged to find a ladder leading to a hatch on the ceiling which is hanging open and Sjonn must have escaped through. You quickly climb the ladder to look, but there is no sign of the fugitive - he is long gone. You can only hope you will pick up his trail elsewhere. Remove the word "pursuit" from your mission sheet and replace it with the word "reverse". You decide to return to manufacturing and see what you can find there. Mark off two *time passes* as you make the trek back along the tunnel system and climb the ladder back to manufacturing. Atop of the hatch will you:

Move along the starboard wall towards the bow?	Turn to 856.
Head towards the stern corner?	Turn to 805.

822.

Time passes. [If you have the word "insist" written down, turn to 668 immediately.]

Stepping cautiously down the ramp, you suddenly notice movement through the visible wedge shaped gap opening up between levels. Roll one die. On a roll of 1, turn to 958 immediately.

On a roll of anything else, you reach the lower level without incident, finding the movement was merely part of the moving machinery. Looking around you see the production line still flowing around, though here it is relatively empty as the foundation parts for the robots and equipment are attached to the line. The room itself is smaller than the level above and only spans nearly twice your height. You have yet to notice anyone around - simply the motion of the line, machinery and the clunk of gears and belts. Will you:

Walk along the stern wall towards port?	Turn to 940.
Head along the conveyor line towards the bow?	Turn to 888.

823.

To push on the door, test your strength by rolling two dice and adding your *strength*. If the total is 11 or more, turn to 854. If the total is 10 or lower, turn to 729.

824.

Still no sign of a way in you notice the woman turn to look at you directly, eyeing you suspiciously. She looks at a device on her wrist and you guess she will be probably considering calling security about now.

Roll one die. If you roll 4 or more, turn to 1079.

If you roll 3 or less she makes use of the device she has with her: turn to 740.

825.

Fortunately as you have hacked the biometric scanning system of the ship, your entry will be considered valid.

The door opens and you enter. Turn to 781.

826.

The one nearest tries to verbally hurry a terminal which is in the process of transferring data. You see his crew number: 237. The other scientist, having just retrieved something from a draw turns to the nearer man. 'I'm out,' he says, signaling his intent to leave. You see his number: 241. You need to make a decision. Whichever target you choose, the other scientists are likely to start running as soon as you kill one of them. As these two scientists are close, you have the opportunity at the moment to take them both out. Will you:

Eliminate both scientists here? Turn to 264.

Take out the nearest scientist 237? Turn to 165.

Take out the furthest scientist 241? Turn to 1245.

Leave these two and look over the other side for Minkla?

Turn to 240.

827.

Pushing through your makeshift door you find yourself in a darkened room and thus have to shine your own light around to see what the room contains. To your dismay you find the room to be packed with aerial drones - all active and at their stations... suspended fortunately. There are more drones lining this small room than you have time to count. Will you:

Carefully see if there is anything of value to you in this room?

Turn to 904.

Leave this room cautiously and quietly?   Turn to 873.

828.

You sprint towards the door, pushing through the gap. Not only does the drone loosen off a shot at you, cutting into your back, a piece of the door cuts across your right arm. Deduct 5 *vitality*. You pull yourself through however and do not wait around to see if the drone pursues. You run down the corridor towards port side and round a corner. Turn to 460.

829.

[If you have the *Fugitive hunt* mission, turn to 960 now.]

Further up ahead of you the mobile platform stops and you see the driver make an addition to his cargo. Next he swings it around and heads back toward you, neither taking a straight line nor looking like he is paying that much attention. As he approaches you realize he is not slowing down and could potentially collide with you. Roll a die. If you roll 2 or less, the platform swerves dangerously close and you have to dive out of the way, grazing your arm on some side railing. Deduct 2 *vitality*. If you roll 3 or more, you are fortunate enough to dodge the mad driver without having to leap out of the way. The driver does not seem to care and continues on his way as if there was nothing to it. Seeing nothing of interest here and keen to stay out of the path of the platform driver you decide to head back and search elsewhere.

Will you:

Head towards the corner starboard/stern?   Turn to 805.

Head towards port side?   Turn to 796.

830.

You have reached port side perimeter of the platform you are on. Will you:

Walk around the perimeter platform towards the bow? Turn to 694.

Take the perimeter platform towards the stern?   Turn to 677.

831.

Without hesitation you turn on your heels and take off away from the robot. Roll two dice and add your *agility*. If you score 10 or more, then you have put sufficient distance between you, running up the ramp to the higher level. Turn to 796. If your total is 9 or less, the robot hits you in the back, electrically paralyzing you. Turn to 801.

832.

Part way along the tunnel you start to doubt your choice - there is certainly no sign Sjonn came this way. You turn and, perceiving what appears as a shadow moving you change direction, running hard to try to catch up.

If you have the word "two" written down, change it to the word "one". If you do not have the word "two" written down, then write it down now. Turn to 994.

833.

On your mission sheet, how much time do you have remaining?

If you are into the *final tier* of time remaining, turn to 1115. If you are still in the *first* or *second tiers*, turn to 984.

834.

She is unprepared for your attack and as such with your weapon to her throat you have her a moment from death. Sensing her impending doom she pleads for mercy.

[If you have the *Proto-swipe* mission, turn to 1041.]

[If you have the *Disrupt and extract* mission, turn to 1109.]

[If you have the *Biohazard borrower* mission, turn to 1135.]

Otherwise turn to 1084.

835.

Will you:

Move towards the door to other lab section?	Turn to 561.
Head towards the benches and exit on the port side?	Turn to 745.

836.

There is no sign of the fugitive here and you see no reason for him to return.

Head towards the corner starboard/stern?	Turn to 805.
Head towards port side?	Turn to 796.

837.

Attempting to make conversation with the woman, she seems withdrawn and after you ask her a simple question about the forest she politely but firmly asks you to leave. Will you:

Do as requested?	Turn to 1030.
Or persist in attempting to talk to her?	Turn to 740.

838.

You move further along the production line where you notice a door on the starboard side.

Head along the production line towards the stern:	Turn to 881.
Head along the production line towards the bow:	Turn to 910.
Exit manufacturing:	Turn to 465.

839.

You steer sharply, but it is not enough. The agent is quick: he slips to the side of the cart as you pass him and you see the momentary glint of a blade as he slashes you on the way past. Deduct 3 *vitality*. Reeling from the wound you pull up the cart and looking back, you see the agent taken out by a laser beam through his midriff, falling face first to the floor. Noticing a large crane is nearby and you haul yourself across to it, consolidating behind the provided cover. Turn to 346.

840.

Time passes. Returning to the lab scientist, you are faced with explaining to him the situation.

What will you tell him:

You seem to have misplaced your keypass?   Turn to 925.

You don't have a keypass?   Turn to 983.

841.

Fortune is with you as when the robot was interrupted and consequently destroyed, it left the terminal open and idling, meaning you can jump straight in and search for data. What will you look for?

Current and future manufacturing plans?   Turn to 963.

The supply of raw materials?   Turn to 901.

Labor workforce information?   Turn to 783.

842.

Roll 2 dice. If you roll 7 or less, turn to 1027. If you roll between 8 and 11 inclusive, turn to 1102. If you roll a 12, turn to 996.

843.

The connection could not be established. Worse than that however, your activities have been classed as suspicious and your location logged. The terminal is suspended indefinitely.

Add the word "swoop" to your mission sheet. If you have the word "flutter" written down, turn to 254.

If you do not have this word written down, you decide to leave quickly: turn to 743.

844.

Testing the power up sequence you find the terminal does not function properly and within a brief moment it shuts itself down. The terminal is clearly defective. Now will you:

Investigate some of the items on the shelves?   Turn to 780.
Leave?   Turn to 597.

845.

You are about to take out an explosive when a thought occurs to you. If you damage the door you are likely to damage the keypad, which may trigger a security breach just the same as entering the wrong code. The only other option may be to cut through the door avoiding the keypad if possible. Will you:

Cut through the door?   Turn to 744.
Ignore the door and move on?   Turn to 597.

846.

Fortunately you have not come into contact with any spores and have managed to get the vapor canister with spores inside out of the bag. Quickly you head for the exit, putting the canister into your inventory. Add *Contained Buitonixum spores* to your inventory. You quickly make for the exit. Turn to 866.

847.

Opening up the trapdoor you see that there is a ladder leading down one level to a tunnel heading towards the stern. You climb down the tunnel for a better look and see that the tunnel extends for some distance before ending with a closed door. Will you:

Head further into the tunnel?   Turn to 870.
Or head back to the room?   Turn to 891.

848.

Just as you are treading down the ramp, you instinctively turn back. At that moment a rough looking man leaps down at you with a chain intent on strangling you. He lands on top of you but you manage to cast him aside. He swings the chain around over his head and lashes out at you.

Line worker	CQ	4
	Vitality	17
	4+ to hit, 3 damage.	
	No defense.	

If you defeat the worker, remove the word "cross" from your mission sheet and ignore any instance to write it again. Now turn back to 940.

849.

In an effort to outrun the guards, roll 2 dice and add your *agility* score. If the total is 12 or more, you have managed to escape them, ducking into the teleport hub in the process. Remove the word "clang" from your mission sheet and turn to 400. If the total is 11 or less, one of the guards shoots you with a laser pistol before you can make it out the door. Deduct 2 *vitality*. The wound has slowed you temporarily necessitating your self-defense. Turn to 789.

850.

Reaching the cabin, which has one large shaded window on the bow side, you try the door to check accessibility. It seems the door swings open, but at present is held firmly closed magnetically. It appears likely you will set something off by opening the door, but believe it to be possible to push the door open with some strength. Will you:

Attempt to push the door open and enter?   Turn to 823.
Leave the area return to upper deck via the ramp?   Turn to 796.

851.

You are situated beside the first toroid in the room. Will you:

Head up the stairway towards the platform?   Turn to 864.

Follow the ringed walkway you are on around the toroidal structures?   Turn to 912.

Take one of the pathways to the perimeter platform?   Turn to 922.

Take a walkway towards the middle of the toroids?   Turn to 995.

852.

With your efforts you have attracted another dose of security. Two guards rush at you with prods designed to subdue you.

Crew control guards	CQ	4
	Vitality	22
	4+ to hit, 2 damage.	
	No defense.	

>The guards are attempting to bring you down with their instruments: prods capable of shocking you with high voltage sufficient to make your muscles unresponsive. If their hit is successful and damage is done to you, then roll one die. If you roll 2, 3 or 4 then you will suffer the *shocked* lingering effect. If you roll 5 or 6, then nothing happens as you avoid the electrical discharge. If you roll a 1 then make a note of it as well as suffering the *shocked* lingering effect. If you roll a 1 a second time when making the roll, turn to 953 immediately.

If you defeat the guards you may:

Keep trying to get through the door: Turn to 765.
Leave before more security arrives: Turn to 675.

853.

Investigating the dish with what appears to be a mould you find it to be lifeless and without value to you. Will you:

Attempt to open the substance repertory?	Turn to 1020.
Not spend time here and leave?	Turn to 967.

854.

Pushing with all your might you break the magnetic bind, flinging the door open. Inside you are surprised to find a large robot in the center of the room operating multiple controls at the same time. The room is lit up with numerous displays and gauges, all abuzz with activity. The robot does not cease its operations but announces directly to you;

'Entry unauthorized. Validate immediately.'

You have no response to this and within a couple of seconds a gas is released into the room from underneath the robot. The gas immediately fills your lungs and begins to saturate your blood with its toxin. Deduct 4 from your *vitality*. You'll have to act fast:

Attack the robot?	Turn to 914.
Get outside the room?	Turn to 985.
Flee the room and sub level entirely?	Turn to 812.

855.

Taking the right hand tunnel, you run a short distance down it, all the while looking for signs of Sjonn. There are none, which prompts you to take a glance over your shoulder, and you see a blur. It was him, passing through a door. You're heading the wrong way and will have to double back to chase after him.

Perform the following:

If you have the word "two" written down, change it to a "one" now.

Otherwise, write the word "two" on your mission sheet. Now turn to 788.

856.

Following the production line you sense you may be being watched. You pause for a moment, standing still beside one of the support beams for the line. A moment later you carefully move on. Will you:

Head toward the bow?   Turn to 881.
Head toward the stern?   Turn to 920.

857.

You have a nagging feeling there is something else in here, but you do not know what. Or perhaps you have just been so intent of finding things you mistakenly convinced yourself there should be something more. Will you:

Spend more time looking?   Turn to 969.
Move over to the corner bench and take a look?   Turn to 463.
Check out the toolbox on the floor?   Turn to 657.
Not spend any more time here and leave the room?   Turn to 743.

858.

Add the word "conduit" to your mission sheet. Roll 1 die. If you roll 4 or more, turn to 1098. If you roll 3 or less, turn to 1136.

859.

On his body you pick up a single *stimsert* which you may grab if you choose. Without hesitation you quickly leave the scene. Turn to 419.

860.

[If you have the word "havoc" written down, turn to 1176 now.] Otherwise turn to 1137.

861.

The staircase you are on continues upwards for quite some distance. Roll 2 dice and add your *endurance*. If you are carrying more than 5 items, deduct 1 from the total rolled. If the sum total is 12 or more, you push yourself to make it to the top without exhausting yourself. If the total is 11 or less, you must slow yourself down; *time passes*. Having reached the platform, you find yourself at the very top of the engine bay. The platform extends around the perimeter and inwards near the filaments themselves. There is various service apparatus here on the walls, the platform itself and even the ceiling just above your head. The filaments themselves originate from 3 ringed structures made of a smooth, flawless material.

[If you are aligned with the SDN, turn to 748.]

[If you are an LWS agent, turn to 1044.]

Otherwise you see no reason for being here and return down; turn to 851.

862.

Time passes. By the time you recover you realize Sjonn has escaped through the hatch in the ceiling and is probably long gone. Your only hope now will be to see if you can pick up his trail elsewhere.

Remove the word "pursuit" from your mission sheet and replace it with the word "reverse". You decide to return to manufacturing and see what you can find there. *Time passes* as you make the trek back along the tunnel system and climb the ladder back to manufacturing. At the top of the hatch will you:

Move along the starboard wall towards the bow?   Turn to 856.

Head towards the stern corner?   Turn to 805.

863.

Staying where you are, you note as XBR guards push forward along the hall, gaining new ground and taking up position behind a central container. Whilst watching this, you do not see from a side ramp an LWS agent entering into the hall from behind you. He sees you and immediately launches at you which you sense, spinning around just in time to face your attacker who has a distinctive scar that runs from his neck across his chest.

Scarred LWS agent	CQ	5
	Vitality	17

5+ to hit, 4 damage.

5+ to negate 4 damage as defense.

>If your *vitality* is reduced to less than the *vitality* of the agent at any time, turn to 777.

If you defeat the agent, turn to 916.

864.

Taking the stairway upwards you find it is a long haul as the stairs gradually wind their way towards the top of the engine bay. You reach a small platform when you feel something slippery underfoot. Roll for *chance*. If the result is 3 or lower, you have slipped on what seems to be some grease on the top step. As you graze yourself deduct 2 *vitality*. If the result is 4 or higher, you manage to maintain your footing.

Continuing, the stair case leads further upwards and towards the bow, though it vectors slightly after the platform you are on. Alternatively a walkway extends off the platform you are now on. Will you:

Continue up the snaking stairway?   Turn to 923.

Take the walkway onto the ridge on top of the toroids? Turn to 954.

865.

The lab scientist lays dead still on the laboratory floor, a large pool of blood surrounding him. Will you:

Head towards the door to other lab section?   Turn to 561.

Go towards the benches and exit on the port side?   Turn to 745.

866.

Write the word "laborious" on your mission sheet. Outside of the lab, will you:

Try the other room opposite the laboratory if you have not already?

Turn to 886.

Head back to the nearest junction in sector G?   Turn to 520.

867.

Time passes. Heading along the starboard perimeter there is no sign of Sjonn. You check behind pieces of equipment and look through the robots moving with the production line in case he has squeezed himself through. You start to move more frantically up the line with greater desperation to find him again, but the chances seem increasingly diminishing. Reaching the other entry/exit for manufacturing, you draw the conclusion you have lost him. Remove the word "pursuit" and then write the word "reverse" on your mission sheet. Turn to 881.

868.

You enable your *ghost processor*, allowing it to do its job. To see if it is successful, roll one die. If you roll 3 or more, turn to 972. If you roll a 1 or 2, turn to 1007.

869.

As Kinlac seems to have numerous items and tools in here and is capable of repairing things, you ask him if he has a cutting tool that you may either borrow or have - for a "maintenance" task of your own.

'Why yes I do,' he exclaims, before beginning to fumble around his shelves looking for something.

Eventually he finds what he is after. If you do not already have one and think one may be useful to you, Kinlac has a *micro torch* which you may take with you if you choose.

If you think Kinlac may be able to build or repair something for you, turn to 818. Otherwise turn to either 451 to leave the room or 383 to spend time looking at the shelves on the port side if you haven't already.

870.

Traveling down the tunnel you reach the door and turn the sealing valve to open it. Before you lies a long stretch of tunnel, but occupying your attention is a drone hovering a short distance down the tunnel. Fortunately it is a monitoring drone - here to check the pipes and equipment. It does however notice you and you sense that it may alert security as it performs a bio scan of you. You respond:

Quickly destroy the drone: Turn to 906.
Get out of the tunnel now: Turn to 891.

871.

Before you stands the bulk of the controller robot. It is designed to work the manufacturing facility. It is also designed to deal with intruders.

Manufacturing Controller	CQ	6
	Vitality	22
	4+ to hit, see below.	
	5+ to negate 3 damage as defense.	

>If the robot scores a hit on you, roll one die.

On a roll of 1, the robot has pierced you with a telescopic spike; deduct 5 *vitality* (defense allowed)

On a roll of 2 or 3, the robot has shocked you, deduct 2 *vitality* (defense allowed) and apply the *shocked* lingering effect.

On a roll of 4 or more, the robot attempts to crush you; deduct 3 *vitality* (defense allowed).

>The robot has a shielding system for defense - if you reduce the robot's *vitality* to 10 or less, the shields will no longer function: the robot has no defense for the rest of the combat.

>If you need to flee the combat, follow the fleeing rules and then run back to the level above by turning to 796.

If you manage to defeat the controller robot, turn to 724.

872.

Fortune is with you - on the top shelf in one of the cupboards you discover two doses of *adreno* which you may snatch up if you choose. With this find you decide to leave, heading back to the corridor. Write the word "shelf" on your mission sheet and turn to 728.

873.

Very carefully you step across to the door and slip through. Outside you breathe a sigh of relief as you realize the level of danger in that room and the fact you broke into it and survived. Slowing your heart rate back down you press on. Will you:

Head towards port, following the corner around towards the stern?

Turn to 460.

Continue along the corridor towards starboard?   Turn to 597.

874.

Despite altering some key registry values there appears to be no change to the system. The software is designed to be impermeable to alterations from terminals such as this one. It appears as though if the biometric data is to be changed at a terminal it will need to be done at a terminal with greater clearance. Now you may either finish up searching the terminal and leave by turning to 743 or spend more time seeking information by turning back to 972 and choosing again.

875.

Quick on your feet you sprint to the door and slip through. The drone still has time to take multiple shots at you, with one of those shots slicing across one of your calves. Deduct 3 *vitality*. You race off down the corridor towards port side where you hope the drone will not follow. Turn to 684.

876.

Thinking your claim to be incredulous, the technicians silently look at each other and then separate with a single slow step. Their awkward response quickly escalates the tension. You suspect their disbelief and as one raises a gadget on his wrist you reach for your weapon and step forward. Turn to 915.

877.

Beginning with the data stores you can see they are filed categorically. A holographic display provides a snapshot of each one when you hold it near. The trouble is that they all contain detailed scientific research data, which aside from being massive in scope is beyond you to see the overall picture of. You determine it may better serve you to talk with someone directly. Will you:

Greet the pair looking at documents?	Turn to 804.
Talk to the woman over in the corner?	Turn to 917.
Try to communicate with the man along the side wall?	Turn to 779.
Leave the room?	Turn to 565.

878.

Having just left the laboratory you are confronted by one of the crew; and it seems he has been searching for you. Fend off the corporal at close quarters:

XBR corporal	CQ	5
	Vitality	18

4+ to hit, 4 damage.
5+ to reduce damage by 2 as defense.

If you defeat the corporal, his weapon appears useless to you and a quick search shows he has nothing of interest on him. If you return to the previous reference you may ignore the dice roll for having either word "trend" or "ranked" written down; simply count the roll as a 1 and do not face the corporal again as he is now dead. Now turn to 565.

879.

Time passes. Write the word "vision" on your mission sheet and remove the word "learn".

Just as you are approaching the man he slides off his contraption and notices you. 'Yes?' he asks inquisitively. You respond by saying you'd simply like to ask a question.

'Well make it quick, I must return to my work,' he says with no real sign of urgency.

What will you ask?

Where can I find the infirmary?	Turn to 1046.
Where is the engine room?	Turn to 933.
How to get to the bridge?	Turn to 1147.
What is happening in here?	Turn to 1235.

880.

Though not wanting to talk you have convinced her your need to be here and ask her of the latest developments as if you were doing your duty of reporting the status to a superior crew member.

'Well no new developments at this stage. The uptake of the genetic transfer still has the previous issues, though we are making progress and hope to have positive results by the next deadline. You can tell the Captain that we will soon have a deployable and deadly hybrid so he can rest assured,' she states.

She now expects you to leave her in peace, which you do as you see she has divulged enough details. Add the word "skip" to your mission sheet and either:

Leave, and head into the starboard section:	Turn to 486.
Leave and head into the portside section:	Turn to 538.

881.

The clunk of the production line shunting forward echoes throughout the room. Following the line, will you:

Head toward the stern?	Turn to 856.
Head toward the bow?	Turn to 838.

882.

Less than ideally you decide to hack at each of the filament casings. With each strike an electrical discharge runs across your body, draining you of energy. You begin to feel the effect of the ionizing radiation at the same time. Having taken this damage already you step back as far as you can and begin firing at the casings. This too is less than helpful as the casings take the damage, and the filaments arc with every use of your weapon in their vicinity. The damage you have taken has weakened you dramatically and weakened your resolve also. Deduct 8 from your *vitality* and head back up by turning to 981.

883.

Time passes. Opening the door, you find the building to be unoccupied. You are in a main room which appears to function as an eating and rest facility and as you check the door at the far end, you find a washroom and other amenities. There appears to be little of value to you in here and a cursory check yields nothing. Now:

Take an elevator platform to the suspended office: Turn to 696.
Head down the ramp to the lower level: Turn to 822.
Head towards the stern along the portside wall: Turn to 796.

884.

Reaching the crossover you realize if you take this path you may be easily visible along the top of the ramp. It may not be the best idea to attract attention to yourself. Then again trying to duck through the production line which is the only other alternative could be a little tricky also. Will you:

Take the crossover to get across?   Turn to 792.
Take a chance getting through the production line directly?

Turn to 707.

885.

Time passes. You wait as the sound of the footsteps grow nearer. Weapon drawn, something rounds the corner and you are confronted with an armored man brandishing a pistol. Instinctively you strike him, knocking the pistol out of his hand, sending it skidding down the tunnel behind you. He quickly flicks out a copper colored blade and thrusts it towards you.

Lone escapee	CQ	5
	Vitality	16

4+ to hit, 4 damage.
5+ to negate 3 damage as defense.

>If the escapee scores a hit on you and inflicts damage, roll one die. If you score a 5 or 6, add the *corroding* lingering effect to your wound as his blade causes your flesh to disintegrate around the cut.
>You may flee back to the ladder at any time by following the procedure for fleeing and then turning to 764.
If you defeat the escapee, turn to 651.

886.

[If you have the word "seeker" written down, turn to 944 now.]
Entering the room the first thing you notice is a well-built man wearing a dark colored armor viewing several holographic displays. Aside from the displays the room is relatively bland and there are no other occupants. Seeing you enter he looks toward you and you suddenly realize he is a Confederation agent. Not only that; two of the displays have your face on them. He seems as surprised as you are that the both of you have met in such a fashion.
As he reaches for his weapon, make a split second decision:
Fight him: Turn to 964.
Flee: Turn to 798.

887.

Time passes. 'I am very busy, unless it is highly important then it can wait,' states the man stoutly. You begin to insist when he cuts you off with a wave of his arm and a gruff sound. After a moment of waiting in silence, the man looks at you and upon noticing you still standing there intently, he yields, though with condition.

'Better to help me than to just stand there. I need a Granular filter. If you can go and grab that for me from the store room, then I'll consider what you are after,' he says. Will you:

Seek the item he needs?	Turn to 934.
Refuse to do his bidding and move on?	Turn to 835.

888.

[If you have the word "overseer" written down, turn to 1013 now.]

Following the line toward the bow you are taken aback as a six wheeled robot veers around the corner and heads straight for you. It is a possibility it may see you as a threat, or it may simply be interested in performing its duty related to the manufacturing. Will you:

Fire at the robot with your weapon?	Turn to 747.
Attempt to run in the opposite direction?	Turn to 831.
Stand your ground?	Turn to 950.

889.

Walking along the stern perimeter you notice the production line snaking back in towards the middle of the room. Alongside the line is a mobile platform with a man atop heading away from you. Will you:

Follow the mobile platform inwards along the production line? Turn to 829.

Head towards the corner starboard/stern?	Turn to 805.
Head towards port side?	Turn to 796.

890.

You've been spotted by a plain clothed crew member - and he doesn't seem to like your presence:

Lower deck Crewman	CQ	4
	Vitality	20

4+ to hit, 4 damage.
No defense.

>If the crewman rolls a 1 when rolling to hit, in the next combat round he will roll 2 dice to hit instead of 1, each causing 4 damage if successful.

After the battle return to your previous reference.

891.

Returning to the room, will you:

Rest for a moment?	Turn to 896.
Leave the room?	Turn to 447.

[SDN: Wreck the equipment? Turn to 932.]

892.

This part of the laboratory is empty. The man you encountered earlier has left, taking with him any personal belongings. Will you:

Head towards the door to other lab section?	Turn to 561.
Go towards the benches and exit on the port side?	Turn to 745.

893.

You find the worker has nothing of value on him. Write the word "paid" on your mission sheet.

[If you have the *Collector of things* mission <u>and</u> have the word "bracelet" written on your mission sheet, turn to 993 now.]

Otherwise you may:

Head towards port and cross a ramp:	Turn to 884.
Head towards starboard side:	Turn to 838.

894.

The room appears to be empty. There are terminals in here which you may take a look at as well a sizeable holographic projection. As you near the display you see that it appears to be scientific data relating to genetics and biology. There does not appear to be anything else of interest in here.

Will you:

Try one of the terminals?	Turn to 956.
Leave the room?	Turn to 471.

895.

Taking a look around, the tunnel itself appears to be deserted. Seeing no value in being down here and treading seemingly endless tunnels, you decide to head back up Will you:

Move along the starboard wall towards the bow?	Turn to 856.
Head towards the stern corner?	Turn to 805.

896.

The short rest and the clear air you find rejuvenating. Restore up to 2 points to your *vitality*. Now will you:

Investigate the sub compartment?	Turn to 847.
Leave the room?	Turn to 447.

[SDN: Wreck the equipment? Turn to 932.]

897.

There is a long list of users whom are currently scanned in biometrically. The system provides an overview of what is currently happening regarding scans, however it does not seem to provide any means to make adjustments. If you have the *Collector of things* mission and want to attempt to alter the biometric data, turn to 1062. If this does not interest you or you feel it would be a waste of time, you may either finish up searching the terminal and leave by turning to 743 or spend more time seeking information by turning back to 972 and choosing again.

898.

Looking inside and around the area you can find nothing that will be helpful to you - chems yes but not the sort you could do with. Taking care not to spend too much time here you decide to leave, returning to the corridor. Write the word "shelf" on your mission sheet and turn to 728.

899.

Time passes. Waiting silently, scanning for any movement you notice nothing. You look around some of the closer crates and pieces of equipment but there is no sign of him. Beginning to think he is not here and getting away, will you:

Take the ladder down?   Turn to 980.

Move along the starboard wall towards the bow?   Turn to 856.

900.

Turn to the relevant reference for your mission:

Disrupt and extract	Turn to 1100.
Data thief	Turn to 1200.
Techno savage	Turn to 700.
Proto-swipe	Turn to 700.
Collector of things	Turn to 928.
Biohazard borrower	Turn to 833.
Fugitive hunt	Turn to 1258.

901.

The raw materials list is long and detailed. Supply is derived from numerous contractors, some of which operate without registration in order to avoid the watchful eyes of the Confederacy. Aside from this you find no relevant information and nothing unusual about the materials themselves. Now:

Search for current and future manufacturing plans?   Turn to 738.

Search for research and prototypes in progress?   Turn to 663.

Leave?   Turn to 691.

902.

Time passes.

[If you have the word "planted" written down and have a bomb/explosive to use, turn to 1069 now.]

Otherwise, will you:

Plant a bomb here if you have one?   Turn to 1006.

Attempt to damage the casings for each of the filaments?

Turn to 882.

Leave the area and head back up?   Turn to 981.

903.

Now will you:

Head towards starboard?   Turn to 520.

Take the corridor towards port side?   Turn to 728.

Try the door on the bow side labeled "G002"?   Turn to 517.

904.

Looking around, it is difficult to see anything that might interest you. The scores of drones dominate your view and their inky blackness do nothing to illuminate the room to help your search. Without warning one of the drones behind you has activated. It lifts off from its station in near silence and begins scanning you. You realize what is happening upon seeing the faint blue light running the length of your body. Will you:

Attack the drone while it is still scanning?   Turn to 931.

Make for the door?   Turn to 819.

905.

Time passes. Will you:

Take a look at the agitating machine that is running on the port side?   Turn to 1035.

Check out the liquid being stirred in a cylinder on the starboard side?   Turn to 1012.

906.

Before it has time to fly away you smash the drone into the wall, breaking it into multiple metal fragments. With the drone out of the way *time passes* as you continue along the tunnel for some distance. Probably only half way along the tunnel you are halted as you see something or *things* heading your way, and fast. Three small winged creatures are flying towards you at a rapid pace. Hardly a threat you think to yourself - until they open fire; they are part creature and part drone.

Talon hybrid drones	CQ	3	On 2 dice, 4+ to hit, 2 damage.
	Ra	4	On 2 dice, 4+ to hit, 3 damage.
	Vitality	18	

5+ agile winged creature as defense will negate all incoming damage.

>Begin this combat by fighting a round of long ranged combat, followed by a round of short range combat and then fighting the rest of the combat at close quarters. This represents the approach of the Talon hybrid drones with them firing at you and then attacking you with their claws when near enough.

>If you reduce the *vitality* of the drones to less than 10, then you may roll only one attack die for the drones to represent their reduced number.

>Due to their high speed, you cannot outrun the drones and thus cannot flee.

If you defeat the drones, you determine it best to head back before more show up. Write the word "purify" on your mission sheet and turn to 959.

907.

Another piece of equipment that you consider interesting and potentially useful is a *universal timer*. This you may take as a miscellaneous item if you choose.

[If you are NFA, turn to 857 now.]

You feel you have spent enough time going through someone else's stuff to find a treasure; now will you:

Move over to the corner bench and take a look?	Turn to 463.
Check out the toolbox on the floor?	Turn to 657.
Not spend any more time here and leave the room?	Turn to 743.

908.

Time passes. Quickly you look over the foreman's body. He has nothing on his person aside from a *short laser blade* which you may take if you choose. Searching the room you find the terminal he had been using has been disabled; it looks as though it required a physical connection to him whilst he was alive.

Located in one of the draws to his desk you find an *interface trigger* which you may add to your inventory if you choose as a miscellaneous item.

With nothing more to do here, you exit the room and take the elevator back down to the floor. Now will you:

Enter into the lunch rooms?	Turn to 883.
Take the ramp to the lower level?	Turn to 822.
Head towards the stern along the portside wall?	Turn to 796.

909.

Filling the room you find a thick grayish plume of noxious gas. It is slowly enveloping the room and will shortly envelop you if you stay. You begin to cough and splutter. Before suffering any further, you turn around and get out as quickly as possible, making it part way down the corridor. Add the word "gaseous" to your mission sheet and turn to 553.

910.

Heading towards the bow, after a short distance you reach the corner of the room and turn towards port side, following the production line. Further along, the production line is running from bow to stern again. This means you can either continue to follow the production line or follow the edge of the room towards port side, where there is a crossover ramp which acts as an overpass to the production line.

Will you:

Head down one of the production lines into the middle of the room? Turn to 975.

Move towards port and take the crossover? Turn to 884.

Head towards starboard side? Turn to 838.

911.

Your efforts have been insufficient: the fugitive has gotten too far ahead and has escaped from you.

Remove the word "pursuit" from your mission sheet and replace it with the word "reverse". You decide to return to manufacturing and see what you can find there. Mark off two *time passes* as you make the trek back along the tunnel system and climb the ladder back to manufacturing. Atop of the hatch will you:

Move along the starboard wall towards the bow? Turn to 856.

Head towards the stern corner? Turn to 805.

912.

You continue around the outer ring.

[If you have the word "planted" written down, turn to 987 now.]

Will you:

Keep heading around the ring? Turn to 981.

Take a walkway towards the middle of the toroids? Turn to 995.

Take the path to the perimeter platform? Turn to 694.

913.

Your choice has paid off; and in a short amount of time too. There is a small tool piece attached to the line coming towards you. You wait for it to arrive and then when the production pauses you duck underneath it, crossing the guidance rails and reaching the other side.

Before you is a ramp which will take you to the level below, or you have the option of moving towards the stern along the perimeter.

Head further down port side: Turn to 961.

Take the ramp to the lower level: Turn to 822.

914.

The cloud of gas thickens and although you strike out at the robot, your attacks are futile as the gas begins to take hold of you. Coughing and spluttering you scramble outside before the gas kills you. Deduct 3 *vitality* and turn to 985.

915.

As soon as you draw your weapon and advance upon them, the two lab scientists technicians go into panic mode. One scrambles to the left side of the room and the other to the right. The taller man on the left begins hurling flasks and any other small item he can grab hold of at you. The other technician has ducked down behind a bench and is holding his wrist watch, talking quickly but quietly, alerting someone to the situation. Shielding yourself as you rush the man on the left, you quickly cut him down as he attempts to make a run for it. Trying to locate the other man is not as easy as he scampers around several island benches. At that point the double doors open and two guards open fire upon you.

Roll one die. If you roll a 5 or a 6, one of their shots hits you, deduct 3 *vitality* if you fail to make a defense roll.

Instinctively you duck behind a bench to recuperate yourself, now you'll have to fight back; treat them as one enemy:

High ranked guards	Ra	5
	Vitality	35
	5+ to hit on 2 dice, 3 damage.	
	5+ to reduce damage by 3 as defense.	

If you defeat the guards:

Turn to 957 if you have the word "seeker" written down.

Turn to 794 if you do not.

916.

Victorious and relieved, the body of the agent lies at your feet. The agent was carrying a *short laser blade* which you may take if you choose. Additionally you may take an identity scan of the individual to aid in your mission. To do this, make a tally of identity scans on your mission sheet and add one to the total. Next you decide to move out to a central piece of cover to the aid of other XBR guards. Turn to 1064.

917.

The woman in the corner sees you approach her. She questions who gave you permission for being in here. Who will you say?

Corporal Samin?	Turn to 1116.
Colonel Smyth?	Turn to 1154.
The scientist Rholiva?	Turn to 1278.
Use the *Got the lingo* ability if you have it?	Turn to 1028.
Use the *Negotiator* ability if you have it?	Turn to 982.
Say you have no permission?	Turn to 1198.

918.

Though she is reluctant to talk with you, you convince her of a purpose here as a researcher. You step closer, noticing a name tag on her bench which reads "Rholiva". Asking her of the use of spores in weaponry, she responds by saying there are a number of known fungi and spores that are quite deadly in their own right.

'They could certainly be weaponized and our agents do use several types that I am aware of. But all infectious substances are contained in the appropriate laboratory, which on this level would be in sector H,' she says.

After a slight pause while you digest her comment, she adds:

'You seem to be in the wrong place,' indicating the exit. You may:

Threaten her for more information: Turn to 1135.
Head into the starboard section: Turn to 486.
Head into the portside section: Turn to 538.

919.

Time passes. Investigating the dish with what appears to be a mould you find it to lifeless and without value to you. Will you:

Look at another of the substances?   Turn to 952.
Attempt to open the substance repertory?   Turn to 1020.
Not spend time here and leave?   Turn to 967.

920.

Moving on you come across an access hatch to a ladder leading to the level below. Will you:

Take the ladder down?   Turn to 980.
Move along the starboard wall towards the bow?   Turn to 856.
Head towards the stern corner?   Turn to 805.

921.

You're in. The room appears to be a multi-office and living area. From the size and number of bunks you would say it housed 3 people. It is vacant at the moment so you decide to perform a cursory check for anything valuable. If you currently have no more unmarked time passed boxes on your mission sheet, turn to 270 now. Otherwise *time passes.* Write the word "strung" on your mission sheet.

It looks as though the room has been cleared out, though you are quick to find a *med pack* on one of the tables off to the side. If you'd like to keep looking, roll a die. For a 4 or more, turn to 152. For a 3 or less, turn to 230. If you feel you must keep moving and decide to leave now, return to 32.

922.

You return to the starboard perimeter. *Time passes.* Will you:

Take a walkway towards one of the toroidal structures?

Turn to 713.

Walk around the perimeter platform towards the bow? Turn to 694.

Head along the perimeter platform towards the stern? Turn to 677.

Leave the engine bay? Turn to 709.

923.

The stairway seems arduous as it sharply curls around, bringing you to another deviation. Will you:

Take the stairway towards starboard? Turn to 991.

Try the adjoining stairway heading towards the stern? Turn to 861.

924.

There is another terminal on the network you are currently accessing which has a long list of past and present research and development plans. You could spend far too long going through them and even then not learn anything of value. If you have the *Data thief* mission, turn to 1010 now.

If not you may either shutdown the terminal and leave the room by turning to 743 or you may return to 972 and choose another option.

925.

'Ah, yes I've done that a few times myself - they are so easy to lose,' he replies.

'Not to worry, just input this code,' he says with cheer. He recites a five digit number which you make a mental note of.

'It will log you in as me.'

You leave the lab and return to the store room and on the small keypad beside the scanner you input the code given to you. Turn to 705.

926.

Walking between two rows of the production line you notice up ahead an individual on a mobile platform traveling towards you with considerable speed. As the platform gets closer you are able to identify the driver; it is fugitive Sjonn! As you spot him he sees you, recognizing the armor of a Confederacy agent. Immediately he steers the platform towards you in an effort to hit you. Roll one die and add your *agility*. For each point below 10, deduct 1 *vitality* as he swipes you and you take a secondary hit from the fall to the ground. Down but not beaten you are back on your feet as you see Sjonn abandon the platform at the end of the production line and run towards starboard.

Write the word "pursuit" on your mission sheet.

You give chase reaching the end of the line and then dashing along the starboard perimeter. Whilst you can no longer see him, he must have rounded the corner of the room so you follow. Around the corner and breathing heavily from the sprint, there is no sign of the fugitive. He cannot be too far away yet, but you risk losing him to the expansiveness of the ship if you are not careful. Beside you near the corner are a number of crates, pieces of machinery and a workbench. Slightly ahead along the wall is a hatch and ladder leading below.

If you have the *tracker* ability, turn to 1152 to use it.

Will you:

Open the hatch and take the ladder down?	Turn to 980.
Move along the starboard wall towards the bow?	Turn to 867.
Wait a moment in case he is hiding nearby?	Turn to 899.

927.

Drinking the liquid proves fatal. Effectively the liquid acts like a glue for biological tissue, though it causes cells to rupture after the binding. You messed with an experiment in progress and became the experiment for what happens when ingested. You have failed your mission and died.

928.

To teleport off the ship, you will need to be verified by the biometric scanning system. To scan yourself now, turn to 1005, unless you know of an alternative.

929.

Searching through the armory shelves you are suddenly alarmed when the sounds of items crashing to the floor ricochets from another aisle. Someone else is inside the armory with you. Cautiously you walk to the end of the aisle and look towards where the noise originated. Barreling down the side aisle is a paunchy, grimy looking man wielding some newly acquired items straight off the shelf. Known as Mannek to his fellow XBR crew, he is the leading hand for the armory and was already disgruntled before you arrived. Spotting you he curses as he pulls the trigger of his high powered rifle.

Mannek Curln	Ra	5
	CQ	5
	Vitality	29

4+ to hit, 5 damage.

5+ to reduce damage by 3 as defense.

>After the first round of combat you may run at him and fight at close quarters for the rest of the battle if you choose. Alternatively you may use the shelves as cover and continue to fire at him at short range.

>If you reduce Mannek to 10 *vitality* or less, he will pop some pills and redouble his efforts. Roll one die and add the result to Mannek's *vitality*. For the rest of the battle, any roll to hit for Mannek that is a 1, he will reroll the die, but only rerolling once per combat round. Also, any successful defense rolls by Mannek will reduce 5 points of incoming damage.

>Since there is only one exit and Mannek has a clear shot to it, this will be a fight to the death.

If you defeat Mannek, turn to 986.

930.

As you draw your weapon the scientist almost jumps out of his coat in surprise. 'I should have known!' he shouts out, grabbing a running burner from the bench top to use as a weapon.

Lab scientist	CQ	4
	Vitality	15

5+ to hit, 3 damage, add the *burned* lingering effect. No defense.

>You may escape at any time by following the procedure to flee, writing the word "induct" on your mission sheet and turning to 835.

If you defeat the scientist, write the word "criteria" on your mission sheet and roll 1 die. If you roll a 1 or a 2, turn to 973 now. Otherwise, finding nothing of value here, you may either;

Go towards the door to the other lab section: Turn to 561.

Head towards the benches and exit on the port side: Turn to 745.

931.

Though the drone has not completely finished scanning, it reads your intention and unrecognized identity. Other drones have begun to activate. You strike down the scanning drone before it has a chance to attack you. But you have only served to awaken a nest of drones. More of them are activating as the first few draw their guns on you. You don't stand a chance of making it through the door nor taking them all down. There is no way you'll leave this room alive.

932.

Noting the purpose of the room you determine that damaging the equipment in here could serve to create havoc aboard the ship. Given your secondary mission you willfully hack at the pipes, wreck the gauges and smash up the equipment. If you have not already done so, begin a tally on your mission sheet of the damage you have done to the starship. Add 1 point for the damage done to this room. Write the word "purify" on your mission sheet. You now leave the room; turn to 447.

933.

'I hope you are going there to fix it,' he says with a chuckle to himself. 'It is in sector H...no wait sector J, yes that's it.' The man then proceeds to shuffle out the door and you follow suit. Turn to 565.

934.

You agree to the task of heading to the store room and retrieving a granular filter. When you are looking in the store, take note of the number of items that may be of value to you. When you return to talk to the scientist, instead of him trying to shrug you off, multiply the number of items by 10, and then add the total to the reference you are on at the time. Now you need to leave the area;

To go towards the door to the other lab section: Turn to 561.

To move towards the benches and exit on the port side: Turn to 745.

935.

If you have the word "pursuit" written down, turn to 951. If you do not have this word written down, turn to 895.

936.

Looking for doors along this corridor, you find none, until you near the end of the corridor, where you see two doors on opposite sides of the corridor. As you are considering either, a guard looks around the corner ahead from a seated position. Upon seeing you he leaps up, ready to attack as if suddenly called to duty. You will have to deal with him at short range:

Lazy guard   Ra   4

Vitality   16

4+ to hit, 3 damage.

No defense.

If you defeat the guard, you waste no time with the body, but instead choose a room:

Bow side room: Turn to 992.

Stern side room: Turn to 886.

937.

Now you have to get the vapor canister out of the bag without becoming exposed to any spores. The air within the bag *appears* to be spore free, but you cannot be sure due to how fine the spores actually are.

You will have to take a risk. As carefully as you can you cut open the bag around the vapor canister and attempt to take it out.

Choose one of the following references to turn to: 1021 or 846.

938.

The connection could not be established. There appears to be no definitive answer as to why and the terminal becomes suspended. You can no longer make use of the terminal now and have no idea on how long it will remain as it is.

Add the word "swoop" to your mission sheet. You decide to leave quickly: turn to 743.

939.

With the system running you watch in anticipation when suddenly the biometric software begins to glitch. The database is open to editing and not knowing how long before the glitches cause a reset, you go straight to your own identification information, deleting the restrictions and replacing them with complete access. Quickly you return the values in the indexing and seeking module back to their original values and the system stabilizes. You smile as it appears as though you have done it - you have removed your biometric restraints from the system. When dealing with any biometric scanner, add the number two hundred and twenty two to the reference you are on. You have made great progress and decide to shut down the terminal and make for the exit. Turn to 743.

940.

[If you have the word "cross" written down, turn to 848 now.]

Much of the operations in the area appear to be automated. Nearby a motorized machine adjusts a torso before attaching it to the production line. Further along towards port there lies a cabin which looks as though it may be a manager's office or similar. Other than that you cannot see anything else worth spending time investigating.

Approach the cabin and try to enter?   Turn to 850.

Leave the area and return to upper deck via the ramp? Turn to 796.

941.

'Do you also have a universal timer by any chance?' he asks.

'If so I can build you a Bio scanner. Maybe a little crude, but it will work.'

If you have a *universal timer* and plan to have him build the scanner, turn to 1199 now. Otherwise return to 818.

942.

Heading down the staircase, a loud whip-like crack splits the air beside you: the filaments have surged and your proximity to them makes you an opportune conductor. Roll one die. If you roll a 1 or a 2, then deduct 3 *vitality* as you take some of the power surge. If you roll higher than 2, with luck the surge has taken an alternate path, avoiding you.

You have reached a junction;

Take the staircase towards port wall: Turn to 970.

Take the adjoining staircase going down: Turn to 522.

943.

The terminal crashes during the process and looks to be unrecoverable. You have no choice but to abandon your hacking attempts. Write the word "swoop" on your mission sheet. You leave the room. Turn to 743.

944.

Peering into the room you notice it to be an office of sorts, currently vacated. It looks as though nothing of value to you has been left inside, so you decide not to waste any more time here.

To try the door on the other side of the corridor, turn to 992.

To head back towards sector G, turn to 520.

945.

Closer to the center of the engine bay you see the structure a mess: the toroids themselves have held up well, but much of the rest of the structure including the walkways and steps are twisted and torn. As there is nothing here for you, you decide to leave: turn to 730.

946.

[If you have the *Proto-swipe* mission, turn to 880.]

[If you have the *Biohazard borrower* mission and would like to ask her a question related to your mission, turn to 918.]

Despite doing your best to convince her of your need to be here and talk with her, she will not have any of it. Deeming you to have wandered in she instructs you to leave now. Will you:

Attack her?	Turn to 834.
Leave, taking the starboard exit?	Turn to 471.
Leave and head into the portside section?	Turn to 538.

947.

As you near him the man spots you and thinking you are armed, treats you as a threat and picks up a nearby pneumatic wrench to use as a weapon:

| *Production worker* | CQ | 4 |
| | Vitality | 15 |

4+ to hit, 2 damage.
No defense.

>Remember to roll on any of the appropriate battle tables.
If you defeat the worker, turn to 893.

948.

Your keypass needs to match your biometric identification to work. Since the keypass you have belongs to somebody else, you cannot combine the two - which is why they have such security. Return to 726 and try another option.

949.

You reach the foreman's office to find nothing has changed. His body lies still slumped on the floor, the aftermath of items scattered about the room. You may:

If you did not earlier spend some time searching the room:

Turn to 908.

Or return down the elevator and
Go into the lunch rooms: Turn to 883.
Head down the ramp to the lower level: Turn to 822.
Head towards the stern along the portside wall: Turn to 796.

950.

As the robot approaches it scans you in less than a second; you ready yourself, but not soon enough as it sends out numerous bolts of electricity intended to subdue you. Roll one die. If you roll 4 or more, you become paralyzed; turn to 801. If you roll 3 or less, fight the robot at close quarters.

Overseer robot	CQ	4
	Vitality	15

5+ to hit, 0 damage, see below.

4+ to negate 5 damage as defense.

The robot will attempt to paralyze you with a high voltage array. If the robot scores a hit on you, roll one die. If you roll 4 or more, turn to 801 immediately. If you have a *resilience* of 6 or more, the dice roll needs to be 5 or more, for you to become paralyzed (turn to 801). If you roll lower, continue as normal; the attempt to subdue you has failed.

If you defeat the robot:

If you are NFA, turn to 1055. If you are with any other faction, turn to 979.

951.

Reaching the bottom of the ladder you turn and see Sjonn further down the tunnel racing away. Dropping past the remaining steps you immediately give chase, following the tunnel towards the bow. You sprint hard as you have much catching up to do and you may not get another chance if you lose him. The tunnel curves toward portside and a thick metal door lies ajar. Sjonn is now out of sight and you run as quickly as you can towards the next junction. Test your agility by rolling two dice and adding your *agility* score. If the total is 11 or less, write down the word "two" on your mission sheet.

You reach the junction panting heavily. Still out of sight, there is no sign of the fugitive, but he could only have gone one of two ways. Will you:

Take the tunnel towards the bow?	Turn to 994.
Or towards the stern?	Turn to 832.

952.

A distinct whizzing sound suddenly steals your attention. Flying around inside the room is a winged drone about the size of your fist.

It is armed with a retractable spike and is designed to bring you down with a poisonous injection.

Paralysis drone	CQ	7
	Vitality	6

6 to hit, see below for effect.
No defense.

>Due to its high mobility, regardless of any abilities or your *CQ* score, any rolls to hit the drone cannot be lower than 5 or more.
>If the drone hits you, roll for defense. If you fail your roll, deduct 4 *vitality* and make a note you have become partially paralyzed.
>In the event the drone makes a successful strike while you are partially paralyzed, turn to 1 immediately.
>If you survive whilst partially paralyzed, deduct a further 3 *vitality*, and reduce both your *strength* and *agility* by 1 point temporarily until either you a treated with a med pack, a field medical surgeon, or your *vitality* is restored to full.

If you defeat the deadly drone, you may:
Choose a substance you have not looked at already:

The yellow powder:	Turn to 772.
The vials in the cabinet:	Turn to 1067.
The dish with the mould:	Turn to 853.

Alternatively:

Attempt to open the substance repertory:	Turn to 1020.
Not spend time here and leave:	Turn to 967.

953.

One of the guards has shocked you with high voltage and you are brought to your knees. You attempt to get back up to defend and at the same time the other guard hits you with his prod, electrifying you and totally rendering your body paralyzed. In this state it only takes a moment for the guards to bind you and take you away. Your mission ends here with your capture and subsequent death.

954.

The walkway leads you out to the top of one of the toroids. Here the walkway ends abruptly - there is nothing but some service equipment over the side of the walkway. You may:

Take a look at some of the equipment: Turn to 988.

Head back to the platform, taking the stairway heading upwards:
Turn to 923.

Return to the stairway and head downwards: Turn to 851.

955.

Your activities have been deemed suspicious by the system as it abruptly shuts down the terminal.

Add the word "swoop" to your mission sheet. If you have the word "flutter" written down, turn to 254.

If you do not have this word written down, you decide to leave quickly: turn to 743.

956.

Trying the first terminal you find that it has very limited access. It shows "Restricted network access. Security code V5." The terminal beside it is the same. It looks as though these terminals have been cut off from the rest of the network. You head to the exit. Turn to 471.

957.

Having dealt with your attackers you assess the situation, noting the second lab technician has escaped out the door during the battle.

On the bodies are a few items that may be of interest for you to grab: a *Punisher auto gun*; an *electro razor* and a *scatter grenade*.

Deciding to waste no more time you start searching the room to find anything of value so you can get out before more hostiles arrive.

Check out the equipment? Turn to 905.

Check out some of the substances? Turn to 1001.

Open up the substance repertory? Turn to 1020.

Leave the room? Turn to 866.

958.

Spotted through the wedge you see a humanoid robot walking past. You quickly recoil in order to avoid being seen. It is walking away now, though this takes time until eventually it disappears behind the production line on the far side of the room. *Time passes.* You may now act. Will you:

Walk along the stern wall towards port?	Turn to 940.
Head along the conveyor line towards the bow?	Turn to 888.

959.

On your way back you notice something stuffed between a pair of pipes up above your head. Will you:

Take a closer look and try to get it down?	Turn to 1092.
Not waste more time here?	Turn to 891.

960.

Which word do you have written down?

"Grasp"	Turn to 807.
"Pursuit" or "Reverse"	Turn to 836.
None of these?	Turn to 926.

961.

Moving along the port side perimeter you pass numerous pieces of machinery and equipment. Some of the machinery is connected directly to the production line whilst other pieces lie on the floor disconnected from anything else. Reaching almost mid-way you observe a small plain building set against the wall. Slightly further along, but attached to the wall and suspended several times your height up the wall is another small building. This you suspect may be a foreman's office overlooking the facility. Towards the bow the production line runs into an enclosure where you guess it goes down to the level below. Beside the line is a wide ramp for workers to traverse to get to the lower level. Will you:

Go into the building nearby?   Turn to 883.
Take an elevator platform to the suspended office?   Turn to 696.
Head down the ramp to the lower level?   Turn to 822.
Head towards the stern along the portside wall?   Turn to 796.

962.

'They are dangerous as the slightest amount in the air is enough to kill you,' he says seriously.

'On the other hand they will not survive long without a medium on which to survive. In other words, without the plant bud they will lose their dormancy and eventually die off unless suspended in a suitable carrier. To transport them anywhere would need to be done in a double sealed container - such as a carrier vapor container, and thank you for the filter, yes sector H it is,' he says, waving towards the door. This you feel is valuable information. Make a note of any of this information as well as the number 100, as when you encounter the spores and are looking to take them with you, you may need to do so very carefully. Now will you:

Go towards the door to other lab section?   Turn to 561.
Head towards the benches and exit on the port side?   Turn to 745.

963.

The manufacturing plans tell you nothing you did not take note of on the way in; they are building bio-synthetic robots which you are aware the XBR faction has been doing for some time now - in several of their installations or vessels. Future plans are almost non-existent; much of the same with a minor possible alteration or improvement.

[If you have the *Techno savage* mission, turn to 1058 now, remembering this reference.]

Will you:

Look up the supply of raw materials?   Turn to 719.
Take a look at any labor workforce information?   Turn to 663.
Leave now?   Turn to 691.

964.

Eye to eye you both charge at other true to the feud between your respective factions.

Confederacy Agent	CQ	5
	Vitality	28

3+ to hit, 4 damage.
5+ to reduce damage by 5 as defense.

>In the event of the agent rolling a 1 when rolling to hit you, he will forgo his attack and attempt an alternative action. Roll another die - if this roll is 4 or more, he will attempt to take a combat aid - add 5 to his *vitality* (never exceeding his starting value of 28.) If the roll is 3 or less he takes on a defensive stance: the next time you attack, if he is required to roll for defense then a successful roll will be 4+ instead of 5+.

If you defeat the agent, you decide not to burden yourself with the agent's weapons as you know they are uniquely micro chipped, disabling their function for any non-agent and you do not have the means to re-engineer them on this ship. Write the word "seeker" on your mission sheet.

The displays only show you unidentified areas and you perceive nothing else in the room of value.

Will you:

Try the door on the other side of the corridor?	Turn to 992.
Return to the nearest junction in sector G?	Turn to 520.

965.

If you have the *Disrupt and extract* mission, turn to 1095.
If you have the *Data thief* mission, turn to 1156.

966.

Time passes. There appears to be nothing out of the ordinary aside from the production assembly. You do notice a scrap compacting area in the far corner however. Will you:

Take a look at the compactor?   Turn to 1053.

Head towards the cabin?   Turn to 940.

Leave the area and return to upper deck via the ramp? Turn to 796.

967.

Just as you prepare to leave the door opens and a guard rushes in. Armed with a *corroder blade* he races toward you. Take a single short ranged shot at him if able, then begin the combat.

XBR Adjutant	CQ	4
	Vitality	20
	4+ to hit, 4 damage.	
	No defense.	

>If you take any damage from the Adjutant, add the lingering effect *corroding.*

If you defeat the guard turn to 1018.

968.

Slipping out of your hold, the woman breaks away from you and begins to flee. You are quick to respond, blocking the only exit through the containment field. In response she runs through the forest amongst the plants trying to get away, to at least hide and call security. You give chase, weapon drawn pursuing her around shrubs and trunks. You drag her to the ground and hold your weapon directly to her face as you give her one final chance to confess more of what she knows. She resists, squirms and tries anything she can and you are left with the merciless decision of silencing her permanently. With this little escapade *time passes.* Being unarmed there are no weapons on her body, but you do find an *executive keypass* which you may take if you choose. Add the item to your inventory as a miscellaneous item if you do. To use this particular keypass , subtract 321 from the reference you are on at the time when you attempt to scan it. If the reference you turn to flows and makes sense then your keypass will have worked. Quickly, before any security arrives you leave the room. Write the word "forest" on your mission sheet then turn to 710.

969.

Time passes. Roll one die. If you roll a 5 or a 6, turn to 1042. If you roll 4 or less, turn to 636.

970.

Having reached the port-side wall, you find there are no other paths from, here. The walkway ends with a large service panel on the side wall.

To return to the previous junction and take the staircase going down: Turn to 522.

To take the staircase going up: Turn to 981.

971.

Finally you manage to subdue Sjonn, holding him on the floor whilst you place some Confederacy arm locks on him, preventing him from doing anything further. He is beaten, and as such does not have anything to say but simply yields completely as you half drag him out of the room. The trek back to manufacturing is a long one as you continually have to prod the captured fugitive to move and he only regains walking properly about half way. Once back in manufacturing you continue to chaperon Sjonn back to the main teleport hub in sector E without any incident. Mark off <u>three</u> *time passes* on your mission sheet.

Write the word "grasp" on your mission sheet and erase the word "pursuit".

Now, after teleporting with Sjonn back to your ship and containing him there, you may either end your mission, or continue to investigate the happenings on the starship, even though you are not required to.

To end your mission: Turn to 1258.

To return to the starship: Turn to 400.

972.

Time passes. You now have free access to the terminal. Will you search for:

Crew data: Turn to 1002.

Ship layout data: Turn to 1019.

Manufacturing data: Turn to 1081.

Activity logs and biometrics: Turn to 897.

Reports and alarms: Turn to 1054.

Research and development data: Turn to 924.

Or alternatively end your searching and leave the room:

Turn to 743.

973.

Tucked away in an inside pocket you find the scientist's *keypass*. You may take this if you choose, adding it as a miscellaneous item. To use the keypass, next time you have the option to scan one, add 132 to the reference you are on. If the new reference makes sense and flows on, then your keypass has worked. Turn to 835.

974.

Climbing around ten steps of the staircase carefully, you reach a point where the staircase is particularly twisted and has a whole section of steps missing. Since the gap is too far to jump you attempt to pull yourself up along the twisted railings. Clambering up you reach for one of the railings when suddenly it tears from another beam as it structurally fails. You fall back to the steps below, landing awkwardly against the cold metal. Deduct 3 *vitality*. Seeing the attempt to climb the damaged stairs as futile, you consider an alternative:

Move past the toroid to the center of the engine bay: Turn to 945.
Leave the engine bay: Turn to 730.

975.

Time passes. [If you have the word "paid" written down, turn to 1073.]

Moving towards the center of the room, ahead of you is a stout man reaching for an item from a bench beside him. He does not seem to find what he is looking for amongst the scattered items and so returns to making adjustments to a part freshly built by the three dimensional printer close by him. There is no indication he has seen you yet, so you may have a chance to return to the perimeter of the room and either:

Head towards port and cross a ramp: Turn to 884.
Head towards starboard side: Turn to 838.
Or continue on the course you are on: Turn to 947.

976.

Nothing you try seems to alter the system in any way; it stands solid to any of your hacking attempts.

It appears as though if the biometric data is to be changed at a terminal it will need to be done at a terminal with greater clearance. Now you may either finish up searching the terminal and leave by turning to 743 or spend more time seeking information by turning back to 972 and choosing again.

977.

Just as you are leaving, halfway along the corridor you see - as he sees you - an XBR agent heading towards you, weapons drawn. He was coming for you, and now he has found you, with the plan of stopping you where you stand. Fight the first 3 combat rounds in short ranged combat, then switch to close quarter for the rest of the battle. If you choose to assault him straight up, then after the first combat round you can do so. In this case, the agent will be entitled to a free ranged attack at you whilst you make up the ground between the both of you, then continue the battle at close quarters.

XBR agent Deial	CQ	5	3 or more to hit, see below for damage
	Ra	5	On 2 dice, 4 or more to hit, see below
	Vitality	22	
	Agility	6	

5 or more to reduce damage by 3 as armor defense.

> Whether in close quarters or at range, the agent uses a type of needle pistol to attack you. These are specialist XBR weapons sometimes used by agents and the weapon itself will be uniquely identified with this particular agent. Whenever a successful hit is achieved by the agent, roll one die:

1-2 will cause 2 damage.

3 will cause 3 damage

4 or more will cause 3 damage and add the *poisoned* lingering effect.

>If you want to try to flee from the agent, you will have to out run him. To do this roll a die and add your *agility* and do the same for the agent. If your total is higher, you have a chance to escape. The agent will now get one free ranged attack at you. If you survive this, roll 2 dice and add your *agility*. If this total is higher than the total of the agent's *agility* plus one die roll, you have lost him. Turn to 565.

Otherwise if you defeat the agent, turn to 1129.

978.

Time passes. Waiting patiently the agitator eventually stops. The container easily slides out and you place it on the bench nearby. At the bottom of the container you can see in greater detail the plant bud whilst the rest of the container is filled with a dense rotating cloud of very fine particles. The container appears to be too bulky to take with you. Unless you know of something else to try, will you:

Open the container?   Turn to 1033.
Not take the risk and leave it alone?   Turn to 1014.

979.

Amongst the scrap pieces you discover a *universal timer* which you may add to your inventory as a miscellaneous item if you choose.
Write the word "overseer" on your mission sheet. Will you:
Head towards the cabin?   Turn to 940.
Leave the area and return to upper deck via the ramp? Turn to 796.

980.

[If you have the *Fugitive hunt* mission, turn to 935 now.]
[If you have the word "pipes" written down, turn to 759.]
Climbing down the ladder you reach the bottom and take a glance around. A tunnel stretches out running from bow to stern. Towards the stern, only a few steps away is a solid metal door. As it is nearby you test it to see your options. You find the door to be securely locked. Will you:
Follow the tunnel towards the bow?   Turn to 797.
Not waste any more time here and return up the ladder to the upper deck?   Turn to 920.

981.

You are now close to the third toroid in the room. Will you:
Take the staircase leading down?   Turn to 942.
Continue around the outer ring?   Turn to 851.
Take a walkway towards the middle of the toroids?   Turn to 995.
Take the path to the perimeter platform?   Turn to 677.

982.

Informing her you are Confederacy and are here on an investigation, she this time requests you leave. Showing your colors in response you also remind her it is an offense to hinder an authorized investigation by a Confederacy agent. To this she backs down from her stance disapprovingly and allows you to ask her a question. What will you ask?

Of new technology aboard the ship?   Turn to 1121.

Of research being done here?   Turn to 1048.

983.

'What do you mean you don't have one?' he exclaims in surprise.

'You would have been issued one when you started here. I suggest you sort that out - now I must get back to my work,' he says as he turns to continue with what he was doing.

Write the word "induct" on your mission sheet. Now will you:

Attack him?   Turn to 930.

Move towards the door to other lab section?   Turn to 561.

Head towards the benches and exit on the port side?   Turn to 745.

984.

To teleport off ship you will need to be scanned. [If you have a *Bio-mimic* device, turn to 1217 now.]

Stepping up to the biometric scanner, it scans up and down your body, taking only a moment before illuminating red, indicating use of the off ship teleporters has been denied. Smashing the controls won't help either; if anything you might disable the tele pad permanently. It looks as though you will need find an alternative to getting off this ship. You decide to leave the teleport hub. Will you:

Take the port side exit?   Turn to 497.

Take the starboard side exit?   Turn to 363.

985.

Quick on your feet you leap outside of the room to avoid breathing any more of the toxic gas. Catching your breath and allowing the gas to disperse, you are ready to take on the robot. Turn to 871 to head back into the room and take on the robot. Alternatively if you'd rather leave while still breathing, turn to 796 to return to the upper deck of the manufacturing facility.

986.

Roll 1 die. If you roll 4 or more, turn to 1130. If you roll 3 or less, turn to 1173.

987.

Before you have time to fully realize what is happening, a bomb, or multiple bombs explode, causing the filaments to 'break' and the result is the energy contained in what is left of them dissipates in a tremendous explosion which rips through the entire engine bay, completely frying you in the process. Your life and mission have ended.

988.

Time passes. [If you have the *Collector of things* mission, turn to 1039 now.]

Amongst the service equipment you find nothing of value, throwing a piece back down in dissatisfaction at the time wasted. Now:

Head back to the platform, taking the stairway heading upwards: Turn to 923.

Return to the stairway and head downwards: Turn to 851.

989.

[If you have the *Survey and defend* mission <u>and</u> have the word "decide" written down, turn to 1108 now.]

Looking around you see numerous pieces of equipment - some large and some small, mostly stacked and ordered. Roll for *chance*. If the result is 3 or less, you have brushed past a thermal tank for a shearing device which is idling. Add the *burned* lingering affect or simply deduct 2 *vitality* if you already have this affliction. If the result is 4 or more you fortunately do not make contact with the tank. Deciding to move on, will you:

Skirt the production line towards bow?   Turn to 920.

Head along the stern wall towards portside?   Turn to 889.

990.

Now you realize having broken into the security room for this level is really going to stir things up. There is no other way out of this room so you could be easily trapped or overpowered when your next hostile arrives. You also expect they won't simply send a guard or two when they do; it will be something severe.

Of interest to you is the weapons cabinet and the terminal which is still on and useable.

You can open up the weapons cabinet and quickly grab any or all of the following:

Laser pistol
Modified laser pulse rifle
Med pack
2 High impact grenades
Will you:

Make use of the terminal?	Turn to 646.
Leave now?	Turn to 774.

991.

Heading across to the starboard side, the stair reaches a door on the wall. The door is solid and from the position it is in would access the level on the ship above the one you were on. It has no handle and looks as though it is meant as a one way into the engine bay from the other side. Trying to hack through the door from the awkward position of the stairs seems too time consuming and an explosive is likely to damage the stairs joined to the door. You realize there must be other ways to the level above around the place which may be a smarter move. You decide on one of your other options:

To take the adjoining stairway:	Turn to 861.
Or you may head down the stairs:	Turn to 851.

992.

[If you have the word "laborious" written down, turn to 766 now.]

[If you have the word "quarantine" written down, turn to 1074 now.]

The door opens automatically for you and although there appears to be an identity scanner on the side wall, you pass it without anything seemingly happening. After being delayed by passing through a decontamination chamber you find yourself in a large, openly spaced laboratory. Around the edge of the room lie numerous machines most of which sit on the bench top. Some are in operation, either whirring away or lights flashing, while other pieces of equipment lie idle.

Two lab technicians in sealed suits are working in the far corner of the room and upon noticing your entry and since you do not have uniform or safety gear, one of them asks through an amplified speaker your reason for being here. How will you respond?

Tell them you are here to pick up a substance for another lab worker?   Turn to 755.

Tell them you are searching the area for any LWS agents?

Turn to 876.

Attack them?   Turn to 915.

993.

Looking around for something suitable to provide the magnetic field you think will be needed, you come across a disused part laying on the floor. The part is an electro magnet used to shunt pieces from the production line in and out for modifications. The test will be to see if it working or not. It has its own energy accumulator so you activate it even though it is not installed as it is meant to be. Good fortune - the unit appears to be working fine. There is only one way to find out if this will work you think, so you increase the field to maximum and hold your wrist and the bracelet within the field. Aside from the humming, nothing dramatic happens. Pulling your arm out, you take a look at the bracelet. The display is now a jumbled mess, it seems to be corrupted. Taking the next step you find a vice to put the bracelet in and tighten it up. The bracelet begins to elongate under the pressure and then eventually cracks. With that you grab a tool from nearby to pry open the bracelet by increasing the split until the bracelet is open enough for you to release your hand. Finally you are clear of that dreaded thing. Remove the word "bracelet" from your mission sheet and add 1 to your *chance* score. Now:

Head towards port and cross a ramp: Turn to 884.
Head towards starboard side: Turn to 838.

994.

Running up the tunnel you reach a door that is ajar and push it open with unquenchable force. Stepping through you see Sjonn once again - running further ahead down the tunnel. Seeing him spurs you on, but you fail to notice the trap he had set near the door. You are tripped up by a carefully placed wire wrapped around piping at ankle height and you hit the floor with a crushing thud. Deduct 2 *vitality*. Worse however, pulling yourself back up is you have missed seeing which way he turned at the junction up ahead.

Sprinting to the junction you stop to look for him both ways. Nothing - no movement to see and the din of the ship and machinery running ruins any chance of hearing. Test your perception by rolling two dice and adding your *perception* score. If the total is 14 or more, turn to 682.

If the total is lower than 14, you'll need to choose a direction fast:
Go left: Turn to 788.
Or go right: Turn to 855.

995.

Time passes. [If you have the word "planted" written down, turn to 987 now.]

You are approaching the middle of the bay, directly between the three filaments. The closer you get, the more you notice the filaments affecting you with a strong electrical field that surrounds them. Roll two dice and pick the highest and deduct the value from your *vitality*. Fortunately the affect is short lived and does not leave any residual effects. You keep moving. Choose a direction:

To the first toroid	Turn to 851.
To the second toroid	Turn to 912.
To the third toroid	Turn to 981.

996.

Fortune is with you. The officer here has a *keypass* which you may take if you choose. This will count as a light miscellaneous item. To use the keypass when the opportunity is available, add 132 to the reference you are on at the time. If the text flows and makes sense then your keypass has worked. With this find you decide to leave the room. Now will you:

| Investigate the room if you have not already? | Turn to 811. |
| Leave now? | Turn to 569. |

997.

'Ah you've returned,' exclaims the scientist enthusiastically. If you do not have a granular filter with you, then he refuses to help - turn to 835 now. Otherwise he snaps up the granular filter from your hands (remove it from your inventory) and continues with his work. A moment passes where you begin to think he may have forgotten about you. Then he looks up and asks you what you need.

You mention to him that you are looking for some toxic spores - for a research project you are working on.

'Ah well we only have a few here, but the most potent of those would be the Buitonixum spores which are in the lab in sector H. Straight from the bud of a Generum Kinareg plant. They could certainly be used as a bio weapon which we are looking into at present. They'd be too dangerous to keep in here,' he says.

Will you ask him:

| Why are the spores so potentially dangerous? | Turn to 962. |
| Why would anybody want to use them as a weapon? | Turn to 1052. |

Or thank him for his help and leave:

| Heading towards the door to other lab section: | Turn to 561. |
| Heading towards the benches and exit on the port side: | Turn to 745. |

998.

Mustering everything you have left you manage to cease coughing, hold your breath and sprint towards the exit. Hoping that the laboratory has not already gone into lockdown by the time you get there, you reach the door and hit the release pad. The door opens then closes behind you and you sigh with relief taking in a gulp of clean air. Some pain in your lungs persists (deduct 2 *vitality*) but you have come through the ordeal alive. Your attacker however has escaped, identity unknown.

Write the word "quarantine" on your mission sheet and return to sector G. Turn to 520.

999.

You have done sufficient damage to the starship to complete your secondary mission.

Write the word "havoc" on your mission sheet. Check your mission sheet for any of the following words, turning to the associated reference accordingly. Note this reference as you will be returning here afterwards.

"Deter"   Turn to 1104.
"Filter"   Turn to 1037.

If you have neither of those words, nor the word "capacity" written down, write down the word "deter".

Now return to your previous reference.

1000.

Falling into the atmosphere of one of the moons of Phaeadron, the doomed starship descends into self-destruction. One of the last systems to fail; the artificial gravity field shuts down as the physical structure of the starship begins to tear apart catastrophically. The ship splits into fragments as the gravity pull and heat generated twists and buckles the ship beyond what it can withstand. Even if you survive being ripped apart with the ship or escape one of many ensuing explosions, you cannot survive in the freezing and breathless upper atmosphere of Beutohn.

1001.

Of the substances that are around that might be of interest, you can see a yellow powder in a small tray on the bench; two types of liquid in numerous vials in a refrigerated cabinet and a sealed petrification dish containing some type of mould. Will you take a closer look at:

The yellow powder?	Turn to 772.
The vials in the cabinet?	Turn to 1049.
The dish with the mould?	Turn to 919.
Or	
Ignore these and try the substance repertory?	Turn to 1020.
Not spend time here and leave?	Turn to 967.

1002.

Looking up crew data you find the majority of data entries are missing. Whether they are being deleted or this terminal is failing to access the database correctly you cannot be sure. Either way the search did not provide any insight. You may either finish up searching the terminal and leave by turning to 743 or spend more time seeking information by turning back to 972.

1003.

Threatening her with a slow and painful demise, you push for information.

'He is on the ship but I do not know where - he only comes down here sometimes - I mean rarely sometimes,' she stammers.

'What do you mean, *down here*?' you query back.

'As in the level above us, level four - he works there,' she confesses.

You start to prod her for more information, but she sees your relentlessness and fears for her life, making a desperate effort to escape your hold. Roll one die. If you roll 3 or more, turn to 1111. If you roll a 1 or a 2, turn to 968.

1004.

You see it. Tucked away behind a worn relay set you find a *Phyclo generator* which you may take with you if you choose by adding it as a miscellaneous item on your mission sheet. Now will you:

Continue looking, picking out another item that appears interesting?	Turn to 907.
Move over to the corner bench and take a look?	Turn to 463.
Check out the toolbox on the floor?	Turn to 657.
Not spend any more time here and leave the room?	Turn to 743.

1005.

Time passes. You wait for a short moment whilst the scanner runs up and down your body. A light surrounding the scanner suddenly lights up red and it is clear you have been blocked by the system from using the teleporter to leave the ship. It will not matter if you smash the controls, you'll have to leave and look for an alternative. Will you:

Take the port side exit?	Turn to 497.
Take the starboard side exit?	Turn to 363.

1006.

An explosive or bomb here would likely do severe damage to the filaments. To prevent any possibility of reigniting the filaments, two bombs exploding simultaneously at both ends of the filaments would be required. The actual placing of the bombs is also a little tricky. The challenge is to place it close to the filaments for maximum damage, but at the same time you do not want to get too close as to absorb some of the ionizing radiation. If you have an explosive or bomb (grenades or petards do not count) and want to use it here, remove it from your inventory and roll one die. If you roll a 1 or a 2, deduct 3 *vitality* for the dose of short term ionizing radiation. If you plant a bomb or explosive, write the word "planted" on your mission sheet as you carefully set the timer. You now head back up. Turn to 981.

1007.

On this occasion your *ghost processor* has failed you in attempting to break into the system. It has however, stayed true to avoiding being detected. You'll need to try something else. Will you:

Look at what data is openly accessible? Turn to 265.

Attempt to remove restrictions to the ships network? Turn to 380.

Attempt to update the platform to make the terminal perform better? Turn to 537.

Attempt to connect directly to another terminal? Turn to 659.

Leave the room? Turn to 743.

1008.

'Can you not see I am in the middle of this,' exclaims the man and nodding towards the apparatus that fills the bench in front of him. You try to interject but he will not have any part of it.

Will you:

Attack the man? Turn to 930.

Move towards the door to other lab section? Turn to 561.

Head towards the benches and exit on the port side? Turn to 745.

1009.

Fight the corporal:

Bitter XBR corporal	CQ	5
	Vitality	25
	5+ to hit, 3 damage.	
	5+ to reduce damage by 2 as defense.	

If you defeat the man, *time passes* as you search his body, finding nothing of value to you.

You may:

Try the door on port side labeled "F006":   Turn to 632.

Head along the corridor towards the bow where you can see a junction: Turn to 391.

Head along the corridor towards the stern: Turn to 551.

1010.

These plans may prove to be imperative to your mission. You immediately take an imprint of the data. In the moment the data is transferred you note one development plan in particular. It involves the weaponization of a hybrid species developed from a recent xeno discovery mission. The idea you were already aware of XBR seeking to achieve - the utilization of alien specimens to improve their weapons and systems. But in this case the particular xeno specimen and latest hybridization techniques appears as though it is set to produce some extraordinary results. Write the word "break" on your mission sheet. With this newfound knowledge you shut down the terminal and make for the exit. Turn to 743.

1011.

As you walk slowly you ask her about any technology that is being developed on the ship. She takes her time responding and when she does, tells of robot manufacturing that may be retrofitted with different weapons and gear depending on their deployment. This level of technology is nothing new to you and you are aware the XBR faction have been manufacturing robots for some time now, as do many other organizations. As you encourage her to spill more details she continues, telling of what the robots may be capable of and that they are their best development yet. At the same time as she talks you notice her fiddling with a gadget on her wrist.

Moments later, cutting short her talk, an XBR Corporal steps into the room; and he has you in his sights. He rushes at you with an immense fist intent on pounding you.

XBR Corporal Jaogan	CQ	5
	Vitality	18

4+ to hit, 6 damage.

5+ to reduce damage by 2 as defense.

>Jaogan will attempt to break your skull with his hefty weapon: If he scores a hit and inflicts damage on you in any combat round, then roll 2 dice and add your *strength*. If the total is less than or equal to Jaogan's current *vitality*, then he will begin crushing you whilst he has a grip on you. Deduct another point from your *vitality* and feel the pain.

>As he blocks the doorway you will have to defeat him to leave.

If you defeat the Corporal, you may take his *hammer fist* if you choose.

Looking back towards the forest, there is no sign of the woman. Where she went or how she escaped you have no idea. Turn to 1030.

1012.

If you choose to take the liquid in its container with you, add *cyan liquid* to your inventory as a miscellaneous item. If you decide to drink the liquid at any time, turn to 927. Next, will you:

Take a look at some of the substances?	Turn to 1001.
Open up the substance repertory?	Turn to 1020.
Leave the room?	Turn to 866.

1013.

Returning to the area you find the wreckage of the robot as it was before. You see that the area appears to be clear of anything that might interest you. Will you:

Search the area?	Turn to 966.
Head towards the cabin?	Turn to 940.
Leave the area and return to the upper deck via the ramp?	
	Turn to 796.

1014.

You decide to leave alone what could be a potentially hazardous substance. Will you:

Check out some of the substances?	Turn to 1001.
Open up the substance repertory?	Turn to 1020.
Leave the room?	Turn to 866.

1015.

The uncontrollable coughing persists and you can barely move as a result. Deduct 3 *vitality* as the pain becomes horrendous. With the room going into lockdown, you must make it to the exit else you will be trapped inside and will surely die. Roll one die and add 10. If your *vitality* is less than the total, turn to 1032. If your *vitality* is equal to or greater than the total, turn to 998.

1016.

[If you have the word "coast" written down, turn to 1139 now.]

As you enter the room you are confronted by a rough looking man on his way out. Upon seeing you he draws a copper colored blade and aggressively slashes at you.

Utility worker	CQ	4
	Vitality	22
	4+ to hit, 4 damage, add *corroding* as a lingering effect.	
	No defense.	

>If you defeat the worker, you may take his *corroder blade* if you choose. *Time passes* as you look around the room. You find it is largely a mess as if the contents of boxes and containers have all been upturned onto the floor. It is a mess you do not have time to sort through. You quickly leave. Add the word "coast" to your mission sheet and turn to 711.

1017.

Whilst the updating is taking place the terminal blocks any network access. Will you:

Try again?	Turn to 955.
Continue to wait for the update to finish?	Turn to 601.
Or attempt to crash the update now?	Turn to 943.

1018.

From the guard you may take his *corroder blade* if you choose. On the way out the chamber runs through a purging procedure. As you wait for the delay before you can leave, *time passes.* Turn to 866.

1019.

Searching for the ships layout data, good fortune is with you: There are complete blueprints of the entire level. It is a mass of information to take in, so you note those areas you consider most important:

An armory and security room in sector F on the bow side; a large manufacturing area in sector F; an infirmary, central teleport hub and navigation room in sector E; Laboratory and research rooms in sector G; a data storage room in sector G; the engine bay and controls in sector J. You also note there are terminals in the infirmary, laboratory, manufacturing, security, research and navigation rooms. You may either finish up searching the terminal and leave by turning to 743 or spend more time seeking information by turning back to 972.

1020.

Time passes. You move to the back of the room where a transparent door with a keypad on the side is situated. The room is locked and you will need to input the correct code to enter.

If you know the code, type it in now by adding it to this reference.

You dare not use an explosive or try to hack your way inside for fear of releasing dangerous substances due to collateral damage. If you have no other ideas then you will need to look for an alternative if you are intent on entering the repertory. Turn to 866.

1021.

As you cut open the bag you begin to feel a rasping sensation at the back of your throat. You immediately reel backwards pulling the vapor canister out at the same time. A cough and blood spatters across a bench top. You scramble to the exit. Roll one die, add 3 to the result and deduct the total from your *vitality*. If you are still alive, you are fortunate as you just had contact with a single spore and managed to survive it. What you now have in your possession is obviously deadly if that is what just one spore can do. Add *Contained Buitonixum spores* to your inventory as you leave the room. Turn to 866.

1022.

Entering into the engine bay you find the filaments which would normally drive the ship are down and the place could easily be categorized as a wreck. Three large toroids on the level you are on seem to be intact, however you also find the stair structure and many of the walkways which cross the room on multiple levels are damaged severely. Will you:

Attempt to climb the broken stairs?   Turn to 974.
Move past the nearest toroid to the center of the engine bay?

Turn to 945.

Leave the engine bay?   Turn to 730.

1023.

Time passes. Your device functions well: the scanner panel lights green and the door opens.

Inside you meet with two guards whom were intently occupied with monitoring screens. Fight them both as a single unit.

Security room guards	CQ	5
	Vitality	20
	4+ to hit, 3 damage.	
	No defense.	

>If you reduce the *vitality* of the guards to 10 or less, increase the to hit roll of the remaining guard to 5+.

If you defeat the guards, turn to 990.

1024.

The ship shakes. Sending shockwaves through the vessel a series of explosions break out on the level above, tearing a hole in the ceiling above you. The force of the blast is enough to knock you to the floor, slamming you into a side wall. Deduct 3 *vitality*. Dazed and battered, you slowly manage to pull yourself up and press on. *Time passes*. You can see nothing through the hole aside from the odd spark.

Write down the word "stall" on your mission sheet. Turn to 903.

1025.

'Ah this is an interesting little gadget you have,' he says excitedly as you hand him the emulator.

'It's a Real time data emulator,' he says proudly.

'Yes I know what it is,' you reply. 'Can you make something with it?'

'Well maybe, see it could be used in quite a few different ways...what did you have in mind?'

You begin to wonder.

Do you have a *Phyclo generator*? If so, turn to 1237 now. If not then you are not sure how the device can be used and Kinlac is not sure how you intend to use the item to know what else he may need. Return to 818.

1026.

A quick inspection of the guards reveal a few items of interest. You may take one of their *laser pistols* if you choose. Now return to 590.

1027.

Looking through the crew members clothes you find one of them has an unusual item in their pocket. It is a *rotating lens diode* which you may take if you choose as a miscellaneous item. Now will you:

Investigate the room if you have not already?   Turn to 811.
Leave now?   Turn to 569.

1028.

You tell her you have no permission but quickly follow it up with a convincingly tall tale of your need to ask her something for your own documentation. Though skeptical she grants you your request, allowing you to ask her a question. What will you ask?

Of new technology aboard the ship?   Turn to 1121.
Of the substance LF-7?   Turn to 1192.
Of research being done here?   Turn to 1048.

1029.

The room is as it was before. You waste no more time here. Turn to 728.

1030.

Write the word "forest" on your mission sheet and then make for the door by turning to 710.

1031.

Beyond the door you find the corridor swings around towards starboard. You find a door on your left leading into a decontamination chamber and are confident it is the right way to go. Turn to 93.

1032.

Try as you do, there is not enough strength left within you to reach the door in time. The laboratory goes into lockdown and the air is vented from the room. You only manage to make it part of the way before collapsing for the last time on the cold smooth floor. Your mission and life ends here.

1033.

As you break the seal on the container you realize with horror what you have done. Immediately the spores begin spreading into the air and you cannot avoid breathing even the smallest of doses. Within seconds the effects of the toxic spores become obvious as you collapse on the way to the exit, your mind goes blank and your body convulses. You managed to find the biohazardous substance your contractor was after, however you did not prepare adequately for the danger of exposure. You have failed your mission and died.

1034.

You face the guard;

XBR Guard	CQ	4
	Vitality	18
	4+ to hit, 4 damage.	
	No defense.	

If you defeat the guard, you may take his *short laser blade* if you choose. Remove the word "deter" from your mission sheet. Return to 523 and continue reading that reference.

1035.

As it is running at a steady rate you cannot see exactly what is in the agitator, though you notice at the bottom a portion of a plant of some sort which you have never seen before. The agitator appears to be running on a countdown timer with a short while to go. It does not seem like a smart idea to break the machine and you cannot tell how it is powered.

Will you wait for the agitator to finish so you can access the contents? Turn to 978.

Take a look at the liquid in the cylinder on the other side?

Turn to 1012.

1036.

After an initial greeting, you decide to ask him directly of the latest projects under development. Waving his hand rather dismissively, the scientist tells you to check with Rholiva, the head scientist here.

Will you:

Move towards the door to other lab section? Turn to 561.

Head towards the benches and exit on the port side? Turn to 745.

1037.

Replace the word "filter" with the word "capacity" on your mission sheet and return to 999.

1038.

Knowing the spores are airborne and you've completed the transfer with two sealed containers, you take the contamination bag over to a large tub and quickly fill it with water. Once the bag is submerged you cut a small hole, allowing the bag to fill with water. Next you quickly cut the bag at the end where the carrier vapor canister is and using some gloves from nearby, grab the vapor canister out and head for the exit. Wasting no more time here you place the canister in your pack and head for the exit. Add *Contained Buitonixum spores* to you inventory and turn to 866.

1039.

You find in a service panel a *micro blocker* which you may add to your inventory as a miscellaneous item if you choose. Will you:

Head back to the platform, taking the stairway heading upwards?

Turn to 923.

Return to the stairway and head downwards? Turn to 851.

1040.

Lying on the floor beside the terminal is the body of one of the crew. Checking him you find he has not been dead long. You decide to run a scan on him to see if he is relevant to the Confederacy. There are no records on him, so you decide it best to leave the body and the room. *Time passes* as you head to the exit, returning to the corridor. Turn to 597.

1041.

You demand from her information regarding any new developments aboard the ship. With her life in the balance, she confesses what she knows;

'You are probably looking for new technology but there is nothing new here. We are however developing a new hybrid species. Something we can use to enhance our agents...it is still in early development....you cannot steal biology.'

She has a point and you have no reason to doubt her. This is certainly a turn of events. Originally the Syndicate sought new technology. It was said to be something cutting edge, hence the need for an assault. But something has gone wrong. Not only is there no cutting edge technology aboard this ship, the XBR faction has in development something that could give them supremacy over all the other factions. Write the word "skip" on your mission sheet.

Having extracted all you can from her and realizing this incident cannot be known of, you finish her off. Turn to 1084.

1042.

Even with the extra effort looking through all the items with meticulous attention you come up empty handed. You determine there is nothing more here. Will you:

Move over to the corner bench and take a look?	Turn to 463.
Check out the toolbox on the floor?	Turn to 657.
Not spend any more time here and leave the room?	Turn to 743.

1043.

Safely out of the engine bay, the explosives detonate, causing extensive damage and more importantly shutting down the engine filaments. The ship has no main thrust without the filaments functioning. You try your com-link in an effort to report what has just happened. There is no response. Maybe the signal is jammed. Your doubts about this mission are growing and encountering a rogue agent leaves some pertinent unanswered questions. For now you will have to persist however. Turn to 730.

1044.

Out on the platform near the filaments you spot a hooded individual fidgeting with a device of some sort. You draw your weapon to shoot at him but he hits you with a disarmament device which causes you to drop your gun which you can only watch as it falls to the platform below. You realize you are up against an agent. He launches at you:

SDN Agent	CQ	7
	Vitality	26

4+ to hit, 6 damage.
4+ to reduce damage by 4 as defense.

>If you reduce the agent's *vitality* to 10 or less at any point, turn to 1097.
>If the SDN agent rolls a 1 when he rolls to hit, then increase his chance to defend in the next round by replacing his defense with an evasive maneuver which will negate all incoming damage on a roll of 2 or more for that combat round only.
>After 3 rounds of combat, turn to 1097.

1045.

It is just an ordinary compactor which, unless you have some items to discard into for crushing is of no value to you. Will you:

Head towards the cabin?   Turn to 940.

Leave the area and return to the upper deck via the ramp?

Turn to 796.

1046.

'What; are you injured?' asks the man. Not waiting for a response; 'It is in sector E, just take the teleporter,' he says looking you up and down to see you are not bleeding. With that you leave the room with the man not far behind, also leaving. Turn to 565.

1047.

[If you have the word "ferry" written down, turn to 1162.]

There is something down the end of the corridor. As you move further you can make it out. At the end of the corridor a guard is stationed with a double barreled laser mounted on a tripod. He sits behind the shielding, his gun aimed directly at you. Will you:

Continue along this corridor?   Turn to 1182.

Not take the risk and head back?   Turn to 608.

1048.

'I cannot tell you of that without clearance, not that there is anything to tell you wouldn't already know since you are aboard an XBR starship.'

Not allowing for any more questions, she orders you to leave. Will you:

Leave as ordered?   Turn to 565.

Attack the crew?   Turn to 741.

1049.

Time passes. Opening the cabinet you take a look inside. Although the vials for both types of liquid are neatly labeled with their contents, their long chemical names mean nothing to you. There are some other sealed jars with liquids on the bottom shelf which you had not noticed earlier but you have no idea of their contents. Will you:

Look at another of the substances?   Turn to 952.
Attempt to open the substance repertory?   Turn to 1020.
Not spend time here and leave?   Turn to 967.

1050.

Roll 1 die. If you roll 4 or more, turn to 1066. If you roll 3 or less, turn to 1080.

1051.

'Ok put it here then,' Kinlac says with enthusiasm whilst clearing some space on another bench. 'Now leave it with me,' he says as he looks through a draw of parts. Write the word "mend" on your mission sheet. Now return to 818 and select another option.

1052.

'Ah well the usual reasons I guess. As long as it is not some rebel group making a bomb out of them or something - who knows where they would drop that,' he answers.

'Thank you for the filter, yes sector H it is,' he adds, waving towards the door. Will you:

Go towards the door to other lab section?   Turn to 561.
Head towards the benches and exit on the port side?   Turn to 745.

1053.

If you have the word "starman" written down, turn to 1101. If you do not have this word written down, turn to 1045.

1054.

Current reports only give limited information regarding the LWS attack - neither stating the full extent of damage or casualties. The level below is on high security alert whilst the one you are on has a moderate security alert issued. Damage to the side of the ship is listed as severe, though it is also shown to be repairable. The LWS assault itself is listed as contained. Monitoring for all activity on this level for crew members has also been increased and you find the issuance of a previous announcement for crew to limit activity to essential tasks only. Now you may either finish up searching the terminal and leave by turning to 743 or spend more time seeking information by turning back to 972 and choosing again.

1055.

Amongst the scrap pieces you discover a *multi sensor* which you may add to your inventory as a miscellaneous item if you choose. Thinking to yourself what the sensor could be used for, you have an idea, but to make it work, you'll also need a spring of some sort to build the item. When you think you have both components, turn to 18, remembering the reference you are on to attempt to put the device together. Write the word "overseer" on your mission sheet. Will you:

Head towards the cabin?   Turn to 940.

Leave the area and return to the upper deck via the ramp?

Turn to 796.

1056.

Fortunately you are quick enough to pull him off the tele pad and prevent him from escaping. Return to 1161 and continue the fight; if you have the *Wrestler* ability you may deduct 2 *vitality* from him as you throw him off the pad and into a wall.

1057.

[If you have the word "recover" written down, turn to 301 now.]
Time passes.

[If you have the word "Melea" written down, turn to 213.] If you do not have this word on your mission sheet, turn to 1260.

1058.

Something doesn't add up. This mission was to retrieve new technology aboard this starship. Yet no new technology is here. Could our commanders have made such a mistake? How or from where did they source their intelligence knowledge? Your mind races with such questions; the main manufacturing terminal which you are accessing now would be the most likely place to find information regarding any such new technology. But there is none. There must be more to this picture you think. You try your com-link. No signal, nothing. You'll have to continue as you are. Write the word "pup" on your mission sheet. Return to the previous reference.

1059.

'Hmmm,' he says long and slowly. 'Well if you get me a *universal timer* and an *interface trigger* I reckon I could make you something you'd like,' he says.

'What will it do?' you ask unsure of what he plans to build.

'It'll mess things up,' he says. 'Not permanently, just for a while; enough for a good laugh,' he says.

If you manage to find all three items and return to this room and meet with Kinlac again you may have him build the item for you. Instead of showing him the *micro blocker* again, simply turn directly to 1189. Return to 818.

1060.

Realizing you are walking down a long stretch of corridor into a sector you are unfamiliar with, you could also be a great distance from any teleporters you determine. As the ship rocks from the pull of the moon, you decide it best to head back given the severity of the situation. Turn to 520.

1061.

Now that he has turned around, you see the crew number of the scientist at the door. It is 229. He speaks to the man approaching him who just entered.

'The door won't open. We'll have to go through the operating room,' he exclaims.

'Doesn't matter, we need to get moving,' responds the other scientist as he moves swiftly across the room. You catch a glimpse of his crew number: 237. The scientists are moving apart, with one heading towards the door to the operating room while the one that just entered towards the stern. You need to make a decision. Whichever target you choose, the others are likely to start running as soon as you kill one of them. There are also the other scientists over towards the stern. Will you:

Take out the scientist 229 heading towards the operating room?

Turn to 1245.

Take out the scientist 237 as he heads toward the stern side of the room? Turn to 1091.

Let the situation play out further and sneak around the room?

Turn to 1298.

1062.

Time passes. Searching for a way in, you try every trick you know of to try to hack the system in order to be able to alter the biometric data. Roll one die and add your *sci* and *tech* scores. If the total is 10 or more, turn to 1113. If the total is 9 or less, turn to 976.

1063.

Turn to 1245.

1064.

Time passes. There looks to be a sufficient gap in the firing - albeit only brief; you dash across the floor to the cover of a long bulk transport container around shoulder height. Alongside you are 2 XBR guards, each taking shots when they can with their pistols.

You sneak a fast glance over the container. There appears to be three LWS agents. Two of them are behind a cargo cart which sits off center down near the entry of the loading bay, whilst the third is off to the side hiding behind a beam which forms an alcove in the side of the wall. There could be others that you have yet to see also. Using the corner of the container for cover, fend off the invading agents as best you can:

Multiple LWS agents	Ra	5
	Vitality	42

5+ to hit, 4 damage.
5+ armor negates 4 damage as defense.

>The agents are bunkered in as well as wearing sophisticated armor - they will be tough to beat.

>Although there are 3 agents potentially attacking you each round, you have both the cover of the container and the XBR guards taking some of the punishment on your side, reducing the chance of you taking damage. This is all taken into account with the values above. If you do take damage in a combat round, then you may stay down behind cover - in the next round, an XBR guard will in effect fight for you with the following stats:

XBR guard ally	Ra	4
	Vitality	18

4+ to hit, 3 damage.
No defense.

>If this XBR guard dies at any point and you subsequently take damage, you may sit the other round out - simply pass the round as you will not attack and the LWS agents will not be firing at you in that round.

>If you need to use a med pack in any combat round then you have the option in that round to have the XBR guard if still alive to fight for you.

>If you have a grenade to throw and want to do so, turn to 1148.

After either surviving 8 rounds of combat or killing the agents, turn to 1243.

1065.

Whilst searching the door opens and a large man wearing worn clothes enters. He sees you and immediately reacts to your intrusive activities by leaping across at you and attempting to strangle you.

You must fend the crew member off you. Fight this close quarter combat unarmed: your rolls to hit will be 5 or more to inflict 2 damage. Your *CQ* score relative to the Utility worker's *CQ* score may still change the to hit roll in the usual fashion.

Utility worker	CQ	5
	St	6
	Vitality	18
	5+ to hit, 2 damage.	
	No defense.	

> If the Utility worker rolls a 3 to hit, he will grab you in a strangle hold which you will need to get out of. Ignore any defense rolls for this attack; instead roll one die and add your *resilience*. Now roll one die and add the Utility worker's *strength* (6). If the total for the worker is greater than your total, then deduct 4 *vitality*.

>If you roll a 6 when rolling to hit him, you may (if you choose) attempt to wrestle him to the ground and pummel him from there. To do this, roll 2 dice. If the total is equal to or higher than your *strength* you fail to grapple him and do no damage to him either. If the total is less than your *strength*, you have succeeded: You will inflict 4 damage this round of combat and may make a free attack on him (perform another combat round with you attacking) whilst he is down. If you roll a 6 a second time whilst he is down, simply do 4 damage only.

>If you have the *Strong arm* ability then you may reroll the dice when testing your strength in attempting to wrestle him to the ground.

>If you have the *wrestler* ability you may use it twice in this combat.

Once you have shown the worker he is now out of a job, you may either finish up searching the terminal and leave by turning to 743 or spend more time seeking information by turning back to 972.

1066.

Upon the body of the agent, you find a *laser pistol* and a *scatter grenade* which you may take with you if you choose. Remove the word "decide" from your mission sheet and replace it with the word "proceed". Now will you:

Skirt the production line towards the bow?	Turn to 920.
Head along the stern wall towards portside?	Turn to 889.

1067.

Opening the cabinet you take a look inside. Although the vials for both types of liquid are neatly labeled with their contents, their long chemical names mean nothing to you. There are some other sealed jars with liquids on the bottom shelf which you had not noticed earlier but you have no idea of their contents.

Will you:

Attempt to open the substance repertory?	Turn to 1020.
Not spend time here and leave?	Turn to 967.

1068.

Time passes. A tense moment passes as you stay locked in your concealed position. You slowly steal a glance both ways along the corridor. The gunman remains. No sign of the agent. There has to be a way, but for now you decide to head back into sector G. Write the word "ferry" on your mission sheet and turn to 398.

1069.

Still on schedule, you plant the second bomb, set the timer and then move quickly out of the engine bay.

Write the word "fatal" on your mission sheet and remove the word "planted."

If you have not already done so, begin a tally on your mission sheet of the damage you have done to the starship. Add 3 points for the destroying the engine filaments. If you have accumulated 5 or more points, turn to 999, before returning to this reference and continuing.

If you have not yet done 5 or more points worth of damage, make a note to turn to 999 as soon as you do, remembering the reference you are on at the time. Turn to 730.

1070.

An alarm grabs your attention. It is continuous and cannot be ignored as it whirs in conjunction with pulsing red lights running the length of the corridor and beyond. Taking another sneak peak along the corridor you are surprised to find the gunman has gone. Now is your chance, you rush up the corridor, reaching the end. Peering around the corner there is no sign of any hostiles. Just before the corner are two doors on opposite sides. Will you try:

The bow side room?	Turn to 992.
The stern side room?	Turn to 886.

1071.

Rounding the corner from the junction at the end of the corridor you spot an LWS agent. He sees you too drawing a pistol and taking aim.

LWS agent	Ra	5
	CQ	5
	Vitality	22

5+ to hit, 3 damage.
5+ to reduce damage by 4 as defense.

>if you throw a grenade, then double the damage inflicted.

>At any point you may charge at the agent. He will be entitled to one free ranged attack at you, then after that, continue the rest of the battle at close quarters.

If you defeat the agent, turn to 1103.

1072.

Taking a massive running leap across, you clear the pool and roll through the landing to safety on the far side. Moving on you reach a junction and decide to head left. Then you find a door on your right which clearly leads into a decontamination chamber. You decide to enter. Turn to 93.

1073.

The body of the worker lays on the floor from earlier, much of the blood now dry. Now will you:

Head towards port and cross a ramp: Turn to 884.
Head towards starboard side: Turn to 838.

1074.

The laboratory has been securely locked down. It does not seem like a smart decision to consume a lot of time in an attempt to break into a potentially contaminated area. You decide to return to the nearest junction. Turn to 520.

1075.

As they are both scientists, you consider if he knows Tuo Minkla and put forth the question to him.

'I know him, but he works on level 4, I hardly see him really.'

You ask him how you can get to level 4, to which he responds:

'Either take the teleport or walk there through sector J. Now I must get back to my work thank you.'

Now wanting to be left alone you don't think you will get any more information out of him.

Will you:

Attack the man?   Turn to 930.
Move towards the door to the other lab section?   Turn to 561.
Head towards the benches and exit on the port side?   Turn to 745.

1076.

The uniformed man pauses as he sees you, before panicking after noticing you are armed and then drawing his own weapon:

Director of Operations	CQ	4
	Vitality	19
	4+ to hit, 3 damage	
	No defense.	

If you defeat the crew member, turn to 208.

1077.

Punching in the code, the door shunts open as the side panel illuminates green. You step inside to a small booth which acts as an airlock. After the door closes and the air is purged from the room, the opposite door opens allowing you to enter. Inside the cool temperate repertory you are surrounded by shelves lined with all manner of transparent containers, jars and vials. All have some sort of labeling on them, some printed, others scribbled.

To your left just slightly you notice a large container with three plant buds sitting at the bottom of it. The label on the container reads "Buitonixum spores". You are confident this is what you are after.

At that moment a laser beam shatters the transparent door of the repertory as well as a single vial to your side, fortunately missing you. Instinctively you duck and move to a corner out of sight from the woman that shot at you. From the broken vial a pale green liquid seeps and you wonder in that moment if it is toxic. That may be one of your problems as being in the small room of the repertory you are pinned with no other exit.

A tense moment of silence passes as you consider your options, looking up to the shelf with the spores as well as the green liquid moving across the floor.

Growing impatient, your attacker fires two more shots into the room to stir things up and hopefully flush you out. Several containers shatter with one of them sending a splattering of a clear liquid your way. Tiny droplets touch your skin bringing a painful reaction at each point. You have become *infected* with a toxic substance. Add the lingering effect and deduct 2 *vitality* as the infection begins to take hold.

Realizing it is simply too dangerous to stay inside here you roll your way out hoping for some cover from the benches. As you do so an alarm begins to sound and a whooshing sound of vented air fills the room.

An automated announcement bellows out:

'Contamination alert. Purge in process. Evacuate immediately.'

The other of the containers that was destroyed released a vapor which must have triggered the alarm you surmise. Now the lab is going into lockdown. Looking over the bench you spot your attacker making for the exit. Seeing you she haphazardly sprays several shots in your direction and across the room causing all sorts of damage.

Looking again you can see she is in the decontamination chamber now and you take the opportunity to go back to the repertory to try to get the spores. Reaching the door you see more shattered containers than before, including the container with the spores. Although the air in the room is rapidly being sucked out you dare not enter the contaminated area and there is no hope recovering the spores anyway. You start to make your way to the exit but begin coughing uncontrollably. Between the coughing and the air being sucked out of the room you are struggling to keep moving.

Roll one die and add your *resilience* and your *endurance*.

If the total is 13 or more, turn to 998. If the total is 12 or less, turn to 1015.

1078.

Knowing that you must be very careful not to become exposed to the spores you look around for a way of how to transfer them to a container. If you have a carrier vapor canister with you, turn to 1261.

Otherwise turn to 1157.

1079.

You find it. On the other side of the room is a panel on the wall which you are confident will open up an entrance into the forest. As you move closer to the panel the woman stands to attention, now discerning your intention. But her hesitation may prove to be her downfall. Activating the switch to open up an entry through the field you rush inside and grab the woman in a vice like grip with your weapon close by. 'I am unarmed,' she pleads, which you ignore and instead begin interrogating her.

If you have the *Disrupt and extract* mission, turn to 1003. If you have the *Data thief* mission, turn to 1238.

1080.

Upon the body of the agent, you find a *laser pistol* and a *high impact grenade* and a *stimsert* which you may take with you if you choose. Remove the word "decide" from your mission sheet and replace it with the word "proceed". Now will you:

Skirt the production line towards the bow?	Turn to 920.
Head along the stern wall towards portside?	Turn to 889.

1081.

There is little information regarding manufacturing aside from details which hold no value to you, such as power usage requirements and equipment supply information. Roll for *chance*: If the result is 4 or more, turn to 1065. If the result is 3 or less, turn to 1141.

1082.

You try the elevator but it seems to be disabled or at least not functioning. The doors remain closed temporarily until finally responding by opening back up. You have a moment to catch your breath or perform a major or minor alternative action as *time passes*.

If you have not already, you may take an identity scan of the agent by turning to 1131.

Otherwise, you attempt to duck back to the next alcove: turn to 1291.

1083.

Roll a die. If you have the *Stealth* ability you may reroll the die once. If you choose you may also add your *chance* score to the result. If you do this, deduct 1 point from your *chance* score afterwards. If the end result is 4 or more, turn to 317. If the result is 3 or less, turn to 200.

1084.

With a swift move you make the death quick and near painless. The quiet is short lived however as a guard rushes in to find you standing over the body. Either she must have alerted him or he has just managed to be on the scene. Whichever it is he now blocks the exit and is intent on doing his duty.

XBR Guard	CQ	5
	Vitality	18
	4+ to hit, 3 damage.	
	No defense.	

If you defeat the guard you find his weapon is damaged and therefore useless to you and he has no other valuable items on him. You figure it is best to leave the area now. Write the word "trend" on your mission sheet. You quickly exit via the starboard door; turn to 471.

1085.

The agent, badly wounded looks to flee the fight. Roll 1 die. If your *perception* is 6 or more, add 1 to the result. If the total is 4 or more, you prevent him from escaping; return to 1212 and finish him off. If the total is 3 or less, turn to 1273.

1086.

'Yes I have been after one of these,' he says. 'Would you be willing to trade it?'

'How much?' you ask.

'Fifty creds,' he replies.

Hesitant you are about to try to push the price up when he blurts out: 'All I have at the moment.'

He looks at you eager to claim his new item for one of the many projects he has been working on.

Will you accept his offer?   Turn to 1127.

Turn the offer down and keep the item?   Turn to 818.

1087.

Just as you are about to move another agent spots you from a distance and shoots at you with his laser pistol. Resolve this as a ranged combat consisting of three rounds.

Worn LWS agent	Ra	5
	Vitality	14
	5+ to hit, 4 damage.	
	5+ armor negates 4 damage as defense.	

>The agent is heavily fatigued, giving you a chance to take him down quickly. If you defeat the agent in less than three rounds, turn to 1291.

>If you are forced to pull back and the enemy agent is still alive, then he will have one free shot at you before you escape: resolve an extra attack against you.

By the end of the third round, you take your chances ducking down to the next alcove: turn to 1291.

1088.

[If you have the word "crash" written down, turn to 1060 now.]
Else,

If you are allied with the LWS, turn to 1047.
If you have the *Biohazard borrower* mission, turn to 936.
If you are part of the Confederacy, turn to 1159.
Otherwise, turn to 1201.

1089.

Time passes. With fortune you find a sealable bag in a draw nearby. It fits over both containers with just enough room to spare. Placing both items inside you proceed with the transfer. So far so good. Now, you have to remove the smaller container with the spores without any contact. Roll one die. If you roll a 1, turn to 1297. If you roll 2 or more, turn to 1122.

1090.

Time passes. Pressing him for information, the agent does not budge. He simply grins at you with a bloody smile and says 'You are wasting both of our time 'fed.'

You twist his arm further behind his back and make another demand for the reason behind the attack.

Though his arm makes a sickening breaking sound and he is in terrible pain he still refuses to give in.

'Finish it,' he spits out.

That you do, silencing him permanently. Turn to 1226.

1091.

A single shot cuts down the scientist. Immediately the other men rush for the exits or scurry out of sight. Previously unaware of his presence, an XBR agent on the far side of the room raises his head above a cooling instrument. He fires at your location after he spots you. Add the word "slam" to your mission sheet and turn to 144.

1092.

Time passes as you scale the side wall in order to see what it is. It looks to be a small bag, which you grab hold of as you drop back down to the floor. Opening the bag and letting out a musty smell you find a small set of tools which appear to be quite aged. Along with the tools is a slim-disc with the number 1981 etched on it. It you think either of these items are of any value to you, add either to your inventory as a miscellaneous item. Now turn to 891.

1093.

The drone seems to be getting the better of you and your allies. There are only two XBR guards remaining, crouched down on the edge of the ramp at the end of the hall; that is, until an XBR agent rushes down the ramp armed with a grenade launcher. Not pausing for a moment the agent takes aim at the drone and sends two well-placed grenades into the machine; the resultant explosions ripping the drone apart, causing the metal body to veer forward as it crashes directly into the XBR forces mangling flesh and metal alike. The agent you see is no more and your allies are near all expended. Turn to 1165.

1094.

The ship rattles and a great pounding is felt from the floor through your legs. You can tell the starship is failing and fast, you need to get off the ship at all costs. Another automated message resonates through the corridor, instructing evacuation. Return to 523.

1095.

Putting the question to her as you slowly move around the room, you ask of the scientist Tuo Minkla.

'I cannot tell you where he is as I do not know,' she replies. On one hand she may not actually know where he is and may have very little to do with him. On the other she may be avoiding giving details.

If you want to covertly try to find a way past the containment field while keeping her distracted with conversation, then turn to 1170. Alternatively you may leave by turning to 1030.

1096.

Searching the body of the agent yields a few items. His close combat weapon is an XBR design and has some sort of biometric lock on it, so you decide to leave that alone. His gun you may take however: it is a *twin pulse rifle*. The agent also carried a *high impact explosive* which you may take. Replace the word "capacity" with the word "filter". Turn to 728.

1097.

Just when you think you have gained the upper hand against the agent he manages to knock you off your feet with a spinning kick and with that takes the opportunity to set up an escape. In an elite display of acrobatics the SDN agent throws a line down from a hand railing and uses this to swing down to a lower level. Barely back on your feet by the time you look down he has set up another line and began dropping all the way to a floor below. Instinctively you look at what the agent was messing with and notice it is a bomb. Not only that, it is on a timer and there is not much time left.

If you have the *explosives expert* ability, and plan to try to use it to diffuse the bomb, turn to 1124 now.

Otherwise you have no choice but to run as diffusing the bomb is out of the question.

You dash down the stairs as fast as you can, skipping steps and sliding along rails where you can to speed the trip up and picking up your weapon from the next platform. If you are still in this room when the bomb goes off, you are quite certain you will not survive. As you rush for the exit, perform the following test twice:

Test your agility by rolling two dice and adding your *agility*. If the result is 10 or more, you have passed. If the result is 9 or less you have failed the test. If you fail either test, turn to 987.

Otherwise, write the words "havoc" and "fatal" on your mission sheet and turn to 1043.

1098.

Stepping heavily with a consistent thud is a large XBR Corporal approaching you from down the corridor. His approach appears menacing though he should know you have authority being here and intend to help. Will you:

Do nothing and let him past?	Turn to 1185.
Greet the man?	Turn to 1223.
Attack the Corporal?	Turn to 1287.

1099.

The agent is still an aggressor aboard the ship of a rival faction without due permission and for that you are acting within your duty when you swiftly execute him. To fulfill your mission you may also take an identity scan of the agent. If you do so, add 1 to the tally of identity scans created on your mission sheet. You head over to the exit. Turn to 649.

1100.

With no impedances you teleport off the doomed starship to the only available co-ordinate lock-on at the time; a neutral supply vessel en route to Beutohn. It is safety none the less and you know you can teleport to Phaeadron upon landing. Turn to 223.

1101.

The scrap compactor itself is nothing amazing - you see a large box like structure in which scrap pieces that are not picked straight up off the line normally may be thrown into. The scrap is not stored inside the box though. Instead, after being initially squashed the scrap is sent down a chute into a room on the other side of the wall. The room is not accessed here aside from a maintenance hatch on the side of the box. If you want to enter the access hatch for the simple sake of curiosity, turn to 1149. Else you can head towards the cabin: turn to 940, or return to the upper deck: turn to 796.

1102.

It turns out the crew members have nothing of value on them. Now will you:

Investigate the room if you have not already?　　Turn to 811.

Leave now?　　Turn to 569.

1103.

The agent dead, you look over his body. You discover a *stimsert* and a *laser pistol* which you may take if you choose. Additionally you may take an identity scan of the agent - if you do, add one to an identity scan tally written on your mission sheet. Remove the word "concede" from your mission sheet and replace it with the word "decide". Now will you:

Stick to the main passage and head towards port side? Turn to 391.

Keep to the main passage and move towards starboard side?

　　Turn to 614.

Take the side passage towards bow?　　Turn to 450.

1104.

Replace the word "deter" with the word "filter" on your mission sheet, return to 999 and ignore the query for having the word "filter" on your mission sheet.

1105.

If you have the word "stall" written down, turn to 903. Otherwise:

If you have the word "constant" written down, turn to 1024. If you do not have the word "constant" written down, roll 1 die. If you roll 1 or 2, turn to 1216. If you roll 3 or more, turn to 1188.

1106.

Write the word "last" on your mission sheet. Turn to 1225.

1107.

As the scientists are unarmed and within a short range you shoot them down easily with a single shot well trained for each. After executing the scientists there is a moment of pause. Falsely thinking the room is now clear, you are forced to dive for cover as a torrent of laser fire beams through your immediate surroundings. Roll 3 dice. For each 4 or more, suffer 3 damage, though you may roll for defense. If you have the *Evasion* ability, you may reroll up to two of the to hit rolls once. Write the word "analog" on your mission sheet and turn to 144.

1108.

As you near the crates and work equipment an agent whom was hiding stands up, believing he is about to be discovered and fires at you with his laser pistol. The shot hits you in the shoulder - deduct 3 *vitality* unless you can negate this with a successful defense roll.

LWS agent	Ra	6
	CQ	5
	Vitality	18

5+ to hit, 3 damage.
5+ to reduce damage by 4 as defense.

>You may use the cover of the crates and equipment to get closer to the agent, fighting him at close quarters. You may start any combat round <u>after the second round</u> at close quarters and continue the rest of the battle at close quarters with no penalty.

>If you reduce the agent's *vitality* to 5 or less and intend to interrogate him, turn to 1179.

If you kill the agent, turn to 1050.

1109.

Pressing her hard for any info regarding the scientist Minkla, she yields in the hope you will spare her by telling you what she knows.

'He is not on this level. He works on level 4 - the level above. But you won't be able to get there due to the attack. The sector is isolated and teleporting has been restricted.'

If this is true you think, you will either have to find a way to get through or disable the isolation. Learning all you can from her, you finish her off. Turn to 1084.

1110.

An unusual approach to the situation, you decide to hop your way across the pool. You do so, ensuring one foot only ever enters the pool. Aside from a few tingles you make it to the other side without being electrocuted as there was no path for the current to flow. Add 1 to your *chance* score. Moving on you reach a junction and decide to head left. Then you find a door on your right which clearly leads into a decontamination chamber. You decide to enter. Turn to 93.

1111.

She tries, managing to slip out of your hold, but does not get far in her attempt to breakaway. You cut her down, denying her escape. Unarmed there are no weapons on her body, but you do find an *executive keypass* which you may take if you choose. Add the item to your inventory as a miscellaneous item if you do. To use this particular keypass , subtract 321 from the reference you are on at the time when you attempt to scan it. If the reference you turn to flows and makes sense then your keypass will have worked. Quickly, before any security arrives you leave the room. Write the word "forest" on your mission sheet then turn to 710.

1112.

Deciding not to waste time with the two unidentified men, you press on with your mission. Will you:

Try the door on port side labeled "F006"?   Turn to 632.

Head along the corridor towards the bow where you can see a junction?   Turn to 391.

Take the corridor towards the stern?   Turn to 551.

1113.

You seem to have found a niche in the indexing and seeking module of the software. Attempting to sabotage the program, you are not sure if this will work, as you will have to see when it runs again as to how effective you were if at all. Roll one die. If you roll 1-2, turn to 939. If you roll 3-4, turn to 874. If you roll 5-6, turn to 976.

1114.

Time passes. While you still can, you sneak back to the next - and last - alcove recessed into the wall. You make it without taking any fire and take up a new position behind a large beam. The LWS agents advance. Behind the main group you see a couple more tailing towards the other end of the hall. With only two XBR guards remaining, you see that your team is out numbered. As they near, the guards and yourself are spotted and start taking fire. You shoot back, but cannot match their firepower. Take two instances of incoming fire: On 2 dice, 5+ to hit, 3 damage. You may roll for defense against any damage incurred. After you have performed the above attack (twice), turn to 1271.

1115.

As instructions have been issued for everyone to evacuate the ship, the biometrics has been disabled for off ship teleportation. It looks as though you cannot teleport directly to Phaeadron at present as you would have liked to, but there is a neutral supply ship not far off heading to Beutohn. It will have to do, given the circumstances. You activate the teleporter which in a near instant whisks you away. Turn to 1119.

1116.

'I have no idea who that is if such a person exists. You had better leave,' she states harshly. Will you:

Leave as ordered?	Turn to 565.
Attack the crew?	Turn to 741.

1117.

You wait for longer, taking peaks every so often at the gunman. He is not budging. You wonder if he is a robot. *Time passes.* You check again. He remains the same; totally motionless. Will you:

Continue to wait?	Turn to 1140.
Abandon the attempt to get to the end of the corridor?	Turn to 520.

1118.

There is a com-link on the wall nearby which you use to establish communication with the crew of the bridge.

'The captain will see you now, please step into the teleporter,' is the response back from one of the crew. Returning to the bridge, you find the Captain mulling over several holographic displays towards the rear of the room. The other crew members are busy operating controls or analyzing their own displays. The captain sees your entry and asks of your report.

You respond by saying you helped successfully defend against the LWS attackers, although there may be a few still loose, the threat has been suppressed. You add that you have information on individual agents and that with video footage from the ships surveillance - if the captain would be considerate enough to share it - you will have plenty of evidence to bring before the council.

'Yes of course,' replies the captain, gesturing towards one of the crew members. You step over to the crew member - a short woman with long hair whom is transferring the video data to a data store. Upon completion she hands you the small data store which you place in your pocket as the captain, watching closely bids you farewell.

Write the word "footage" on your mission sheet. You step into the teleporter to jump back to your own ship. Turn to 1222.

1119.

The supply ship appears to be already filled with a few other crew members who obviously jumped ship also. Seemingly quite happy to take you on board, one of the few crew of the supply ship encourages you on board and finds a small cargo room for you to rest in for the duration of the trip.

If you have *spores* in your inventory, turn to 320.

If you are not carrying spores of any sort, turn to 193.

1120.

Opening the door a cloud of smoke billows out and you cannot help but cop a face full of the black smog. Deduct 2 *vitality*. Inside, the room is filled with an inky darkness; the only light emanating from flames and sparks to the side. You can barely enter into the room and are quickly forced to leave to avoid choking. You pull back to the corridor. Turn to 903.

1121.

'Look, I know little of that as that is not what I am here for. We are developing our technology if that is what you are asking, but there are no breakthroughs that I know of.'

Not allowing for any more questions, she orders you to leave. Will you:

Leave as ordered?	Turn to 565.
Attack the crew?	Turn to 741.

1122.

There are spores which have become airborne during the transfer and with the opening of the bag they are released into the air around you. The highly toxic substance spreads, with only a few minute spores making contact with your skin. Roll 2 dice and add 3. Deduct the total from your *vitality*. If you manage to survive this, you may add *Buitonixum spores* to your inventory. Whilst you may have what you need, the ordeal is not over. You cough up some blood on the way to the exit; turn to 866.

1123.

Remove the explosive from your inventory. Roll 2 dice and add the damage value of your explosive which will be on the item description. If the total is 13 or more, the blast cleanly rips apart the door and you can get through: turn to 1031. If the total is 12 or less, the door has only been partially destroyed, you will have to cut it open further and bend back some of the metal in order to squeeze through. Roll a die and add your CQ score. If the result is 8 or more, turn to 1031. If the result is 7 or less, turn to 1283.

1124.

Knowing the intricacies of explosives well, you do not hesitate to remove the casing on the bomb and take a look. It appears as nothing exceptional is involved with this one - the usual tampering circuit, but you have a work around for that too. A small battery you carry allows you to retain a voltage on the tampering circuit whilst you disconnect the timer from the explosive and... The bomb is diffused...or so you thought: there is a secondary timer. This one is further delayed for if the first timer fails or somebody happens to disable it as you have done. This timer seems molded to the explosive material itself. You are capable of removing it, but not here without specialist tools and in the amount of time remaining. You will have to leave it and get out. Fortunately, there will be sufficient time for you to make it down to the exit, though you will still need to do so quickly. You start on the stairs down, grabbing your weapon from the platform below and continuing until you reach the exit. Write the words "havoc" and "fatal" on your mission sheet and turn to 1043.

1125.

Time passes. Remove the word "proceed" from your mission sheet. The agent proves to be resistant to your attempts to extract information. He grapples with you, attempting to clutch your throat (deduct 1 *vitality*) as you question him.

'It makes no difference now,' he says defiantly.

Placing the agent in a crushing hold, you order him to detail the reason for the attack.

'Then tell me anyway and maybe I will let you live,' you reply.

Seeing his inescapable position he finally yields;

'Our mission was to extract new technology. Not just the latest and greatest. We were told it was something capable of changing the balance dramatically. But it turns out there was no such thing - just XBR and their alien experiments.'

His information sheds new light on the situation and has provided recorded evidence for the LWS intent. Write the word "astray" on your mission sheet.

Now will you let the agent live: Turn to 1262.
Or end his life: Turn to 1099.

1126.

The door opens and you find yourself in another small cubicle for washing yourself off, which you do so with a quick rinse. The next room is like the other one you passed through, lined with suits on the wall. If you are wearing a sealed suit you take it off here. There is only one other exit to the room, which you open, bringing you to a low lit corridor. Amidst the near continual shaking of the ship you reach an intersection, where you make an easy decision to head left as you can see the ramp that will take you to the next level. Turn to 159.

1127.

He gladly makes the trade with you by scanning each other's cred chips to complete the transaction. Add 50 creds to your tally and remove the *positron diffuser* from your inventory. Return to 818.

1128.

Time passes as you wait. Roll one die. If you roll a 2, turn to 1193. If you roll anything else, turn to 1289.

1129.

You dare not try to take his pistol, but on his body you do find a single *stimsert* as well as one dose of *adreno* which you may take if you like. *Time passes.* Turn to 649.

1130.

Looking over Mannek's body you find he has on him a bottle of *brutenide* tablets. There is still enough left for one dose which you may take if you choose. As you are already armed you leave his rifle behind which is rather bulky anyway.

You head back out into the corridor and reach the nearest junction. Turn to 419.

1131.

You take the opportunity inside the cover of the elevator to capture the identity of the agent for your records. On your mission sheet, make a tally of the identity scans you have and add 1 to the total.

As the LWS forces are likely advancing outside in the hall, you look to pull back to the next alcove in order not to get swept up in their assault. Turn to 1291.

1132.

The corporal ignores your actions and moves straight towards you, in doing so he covertly draws an electrified blade. Taking you by surprise, he thrusts the blade into your side:

'Confeds on our ship...got their dirty noses in everything,' he sneers. Turn to 1009.

1133.

You stand frozen, hiding in the shadows. A moment passes with you watching intently. You suspect whatever the thing is may still be near the end of the aisle. Will you:

Keep moving toward the end of the aisle?   Turn to 341.

Head back and try to get through along another aisle? Turn to 220.

1134.

Time passes. You wait for just a moment to see what happens. After some more exchanging of what to do in the situation the group of scientists move over behind the panel towards the restricted area. They all head through a door in the corner. With the scientists out of sight, will you:

Head over to the door the scientists were having trouble with?

Turn to 1083.

Let a moment pass and then enter the restricted area? Turn to 1284.

1135.

Pushing her against the wall with your weapon pressed against her, you demand information regarding the spores you are looking for. She stammers out an answer:

'They will be in the lab in sector H...in the repertory.'

'Not enough,' you reply dryly.

'You'll need the number for the door. It's 57.'

'Keep going,' you insist.

'That's it. Everything is labeled, what else do you want?'

Having exhausted her of information you drop the offense. Will you:

Finish her off?   Turn to 1084.

Let her live?   Turn to 1239.

1136.

Clambering out from the teleport room down the corridor two plain clothed individuals suddenly freeze as they spot you. One of them reveals a laser pistol, slinging off several shots at you. Roll 3 dice. For each 4 or more, deduct 3 *vitality*, though you may make a defense roll. Whilst you instinctively take cover, the two men begin running in the opposite direction in an effort to escape. Will you:

Chase after them?   Turn to 1194.

Ignore them and let them flee?   Turn to 1112.

1137.

Up ahead, approximately half way along the corridor you see a mesh of some sort blocking the path. As you near it, you see that it is a laser grid, intended to act as a blockade to anyone trying to get past. You test it with a piece of wrapper, which it slices the end off. It would do the same to you - slicing you to pieces - if you to try and pass through. It appears there is no way to damage the lasers themselves as they emanate from recesses in the floor, walls and ceiling. There is also a black strip near shoulder width which you notice runs around beside the grid. This you would say is for disabling explosives and other devices. It is clear you are not meant to pass this point and unless you can find another way should seek out an alternative path. Returning to the previous junction, will you:

Take the corridor towards port side?   Turn to 597.

Take the corridor towards the stern?   Turn to 730.

1138.

As you approach the start of the aisle, the ship abruptly shakes, unsettling your balance and hopefully the balance of the alien. You take the chance whilst the current burst of shaking is taking place to sprint up one of the other aisles, hoping to get closer to the far side. As the shaking subsides you slow your movement again to reduce the likelihood of detection. Roll a die. If you roll 4 or more, turn to 192. If you roll 3 or less, turn to 544.

1139.

Entering into the room you find it is as it was before; including the dead utility worker on the floor. *Time passes* as you exit the utility storage room. Turn to 711.

1140.

[If you are now into the *final tier* of time remaining, turn to 1070.]

[If you are still in the *first tier* of time remaining, turn to 1247.]

You wait some more. *Time passes.* Another peak; still nothing. No movement, no change. He is still ready to gun you down if you advance. Will you:

Continue to wait?   Turn to 1172.

Abandon the attempt to get to the end of the corridor? Turn to 520.

1141.

You hear footsteps outside the room and freeze momentarily. They fade as somebody passes by and with quiet relief you continue. If you have finished searching the terminal and plan to leave, turn to 743 or you may spend more time seeking information by turning back to 972.

1142.

[If you have not done so already, turn to 1234 before returning here.]

Roll a die. Apply up to 2 of the following modifications to the roll: If your *chance* score is +2, add 1 to the roll. If you have half or less of your maximum *vitality*, add 1. If you have any of the following words: "hollow", "learn" or "starman", add 1 to the roll. If the end result is 4 or more, turn to 1219. Otherwise, turn to 1137.

1143.

Using a com-link on the side wall you try to establish a connection. There is no response from the bridge. You do not know if the system is down or the crew are pre-occupied. Either way time is running short, the starship is destabilizing. Will you:

Teleport to sector F? Turn to 525.

Teleport to sector G? Turn to 539.

Continue to try to use the com-link to contact the bridge?

Turn to 1295.

Exit the teleport room? Turn to 684.

1144.

You line yourself up and begin the dash across. As soon as you step into the water you feel a jolt travel through your body, electrocuting you, causing your muscles to twitch involuntarily. The spasms cause you to slip and you slide the rest of the way across the pool, but not before receiving several more painful jolts. Deduct 5 *vitality*. Across the other side you manage to roll out of the pool so you can recover. *Time passes*. When you are back on your feet again, you keep moving though somewhat shaken up. Another junction has you thinking yet again. You head towards portside where you soon reach a door on your right. It leads into a decontamination chamber and you decide to enter it. Turn to 93.

1145.

If you can topple over one of the bulky instrumentation housing cabinets nearby, it may cascade onto other equipment, causing enough chaos to get in his way or injure him, but more importantly buying you some time to get to an exit. To give this a shot, roll two dice. Add your *agility* and *strength* to sprint to the cabinet and push it over. If the result is 15 or more, you have succeeded. Turn to 1270. If the end result is 14 or less, return to 144. There is only one other cabinet beside the first, so you may attempt this feat again only once more; failing that you are out of options and must fight to the death or be gunned down trying to flee.

1146.

Remove the word "linger" from your mission sheet. Having defeated the droid you are now free to continue without such a hindrance.

To continue along the corridor on the starboard side of this sector, turn to 730. To continue along the corridor on the port side outside of the teleport room, turn to 684.

1147.

'Just take the teleporter,' he responds. 'Don't tell me it is in lockout again,' he adds. Obviously not wanting to communicate any further he picks up his things and leaves the room and you decide to do the same. Turn to 565.

1148.

If you can hit the cargo cart with a grenade, you may be able to take out two of the agents. Deduct your grenade from your inventory and then roll to hit as normal, adding 1 to the dice roll. If you score a hit, triple the damage of the grenade and then add the result of one extra dice roll to the total damage done. If you are using a cluster grenade, there is no additional benefit to doing so in this situation - treat the damage as 3 and follow the procedure above.

If you miss with your grenade, there is still a likelihood you will inflict damage - take the damage your grenade does and add 1 dice roll to determine the damage done. Now return to 1064 and continue the fight.

1149.

Time passes. You open the hatch and crawl through the short tunnel. At the end you open another hatch and reach a small platform, allowing you to stand upright. You are in a mid-sized room with the platform you are on running around the outside. In the middle, where the scrap chute feeds into is a crushing machine used to compact scrap to a much smaller size. If you were to fall in there whilst the machine was running, you too would become very painfully compact. You walk around the platform to the other side. Passing through a doorway leading out of the room brings you to a sealed door. This looks to be a dead end, aside from another door on your right. Opening this door with an ordinary door handle, you find it is a very small room or more like a closet used by maintenance workers. There is a bag on one of the shelves that catches your attention. Inside the bag you find a few items that may be helpful. Roll 2 dice and compare the result to your choice of table from the three *discovered item tables* near the beginning of the book. You may take this item if you choose, along with your choice of either a *stun pistol* OR a *manta stinger.* There is also a slim-disc with the number 1963 imprinted on it. If you think the disc could be of any value to you, turn to 147. If you are content with your findings, turn to 95.

1150.

With the biometric database editing you performed earlier, the system has no issue with you teleporting off ship. Unable to jump to Phaeadron directly at present, you are able to lock onto a small neutral supply ship heading towards Beutohn. Only a moment later, after returning to materiality you step off a tele pad inside the supply ship. A man greets you immediately;

'Enter; are you injured at all?' Asks the man waving you towards him near the exit.

'We've taken a few crew abandoning the ship already. Here, you can rest in here,' he says, showing you to a small room, normally used for cargo.

You enter into the room and plan to do as the man suggested - rest - while the supply ship safely takes you to Beutohn. Turn to 118.

1151.

Write the word "east" on your mission sheet. Turn to 1225.

1152.

Your skills and senses indicate he would not have stopped or slowed down at this stage. So he is unlikely hiding. Taking a brief moment you scan ahead and see no movement aside from the machinery.

That only leaves one other option. Will you:

Open the hatch and take the ladder down?	Turn to 980.
Move along the starboard wall towards the bow?	Turn to 867.
Wait a moment in case he is hiding nearby?	Turn to 899.

1153.

You sneak around towards the stern, past a bank of instruments and taking up position behind a work bench. There are three scientists you can see. They are spread out and moving quickly, preparing to leave. Will you:

Take out scientist 231?	Turn to 94.
Take out the scientist 237?	Turn to 1091.
Take out the furthest scientist 241?	Turn to 224.
Wait to see what happens?	Turn to 136.

1154.

'I have no idea who that is if such a person exists. You had better leave,' she states harshly.

Will you:

Leave as ordered?	Turn to 565.
Attack the crew?	Turn to 741.

1155.

The last aisle has specimen pens on one side only. The perimeter wall has no pens, but instead houses various pieces of equipment and storage compartments. As such this aisle is even darker than the others as there is only illumination from the signs above the specimen pens on one side. Roll for *chance*. If the result is 4 or more, turn to 204. If the result is 3 or less, turn to 444.

1156.

Moving alongside the containment field as you make conversation with the woman, you are interrupted by an aural message from SDN Control: "The individual in your vicinity is to be interrogated and executed". With that command you determine you will need to get past the containment field and look for a way in whilst you distract the woman with a vague query on research progress. Turn to 1170.

1157.

You begin searching the room for a suitable container. Finding a small container under a bench on the opposite side of the room, you quickly tip out the contents and bring it back. Now for the tricky part of getting the spores into the container. How will you do it?

Look for a space or bag in which you can perform the transfer?

Turn to 1089.

Not waste time and just do the transfer quickly while holding your breath?   Turn to 1251.

1158.

You are in a tough situation. If you try to run from where you are, the agent is highly likely to cut you down. If you want to try throwing a grenade if you have one, turn to 135. If you want to see if you can change cover, turn to 1272. Otherwise, return to 144 and continue the fight.

1159.

As you are heading down the corridor a uniformed man rushes up to you from further down the corridor. 'You must leave now agent - the ship is falling into the atmosphere of Beutohn. You'll be killed if you stay,' he urges. 'This way,' he exclaims as he grabs you by the arm, turning you around to follow him back to sector G. You follow him back along the corridor where he begins looking inside rooms for others. Write the word "crash" on your mission sheet and turn to 710.

1160.

You suddenly halt as you spot a dark shape at the end of the aisle. It looks like you have company. Will you:

Head directly at the thing and take it on?	Turn to 253.
Turn and run back along the aisle?	Turn to 1256.

1161.

Arriving in sector G, you are taken by surprise when you see an LWS agent in the room. You're not sure if he is entering or exiting, but seek to stop him just the same. The agent, also unprepared by your timely entry tries to fend you off.

Veteran LWS agent	CQ	6
	Vitality	23

4+ to hit, 4 damage.
5+ to reduce damage by 4 as defense.

>At the end of each combat round in which the agent has 15 *vitality* or less, roll 1 die. If the result of the roll is a 6, turn to 1210 immediately.

>If you reduce the agent to 8 or less *vitality* and intend to interrogate him, turn to 1190.

If you defeat the agent, turn to 1226.

1162.

Fortune is with you: there is no sign of the gunman at the end of the corridor as before. You quickly take the opportunity to advance along the long stretch of passage. Reaching the end, you peer around the corner finding no sign of any hostiles. Just before the corner are two doors on opposite sides.

Will you try:

The bow side room?	Turn to 992.
The stern side room?	Turn to 886.

1163.

You make it to the door and open it. With the scientists arguing they do not notice your activity. Inside is a short room with one wall lined with full contamination suits. The sign on the other wall indicates in bold lettering: "Restricted: full protection must be worn beyond this point."

Will you:

Don one of the fully sealed suits?   Turn to 299.

Move fast into the operating rooms without protection?

Turn to 1196.

1164.

You have budged open the door enough for you to squeeze through. The corridor veers toward starboard and you reach a large door on your left which leads into a decontamination chamber which you decide to enter. Turn to 93.

1165.

Further down the hall you see LWS agents continuing to push forward. A group of four or more appear to be storming down the center, ignoring any cover, guns at the ready. The smoke from the wreckage is clearing, you need to act:

To pull back behind to next alcove: Turn to 1114.

To stay where you are and shoot: Turn to 1202.

1166.

Approaching from the bow, a guard spots you and quickly advances:

XBR guard   CQ   4
            Vitality   18
            5+ to hit, 3 damage.
            No defense.

>If you need to flee at any point, then do so after resolving the guard's free attack on you and then turning to 1228.

If you defeat the guard, turn to 1254.

1167.

Inside the short rectangular room you have to wait while the exit remains temporarily locked. The room is a decontamination room and automatically runs through a purging process. *Time passes* while the air is cleared and your body scanned. Eventually the door unlocks and you can freely leave. The room ahead is a specimen holding room. Dimly lit and expansive in size, there are transparent containers spaced around the room, most illuminated showing their contents of unusual and alien creatures. You do not have time to browse however; you trek straight up the middle to the door on the far side. Roll for *chance*. If the result is 4 or more, turn to 167. If the result is 3 or less, turn to 131.

1168.

Moving up the ramp at a quick pace, you turn a full 180 degrees before reaching the floor of the fourth level. You reach a corridor spanning bow to stern and check that it is clear.

If you are allied with the LWS, turn to 297.

If you are an SDN agent, turn to 356.

1169.

Through the narrow gaps of the containers you push, intent to escape the killer drone. Squeezing through you reach a dead end - the containers butt up against the corridor wall. Feeling defeated, until you push against the end container and find it moves relatively easily as there is nothing beyond it. The medium sized container falls out of the way and you pull yourself out of the narrow gap. There is no way the drone is following you now. The containers themselves are all sealed, but nearby, behind a few cylinders on the side of the tunnel you spot something unusual. It is a case which appears to be locked.

The lock is small enough - you smash it to pieces with your weapon. Fortune is with you; inside the case you find a stash of items somebody was hiding here. There is a *shock pistol, fists of flame* and two *scatter grenades.* You may take any or all of these items if you choose.

The corridor extends a short distance more before ending at a door. There is also an opening in the floor with a ladder leading to a tunnel below. The door you find is locked and the confined space would make trying to blast through hazardous. You opt for the ladder, taking it down to the tunnel below. Following the tunnel, you are eager to get back out of this service passage and find a teleporter or some way off this ship. Reaching a junction, you decide to head right, where you eventually reach another junction. Again, not having any idea where you are and simply choosing a direction based only on where you think you might be, you head right again. Fortune is still with you for up ahead is a ladder leading up and out of the tunnel. Swiftly taking the ladder up you unlock and push open the hatch at the top, climbing into the corridor above. Heading along the corridor, you soon discover you are in sector G as you reach a junction, entering from starboard side. Turn to 520.

1170.

This is a test of both your ability to recognize a way to defeat the field as well as your ability to avoid having your intentions realized by the woman. Roll one die and add your *perception*. If you have the Stealth ability, add 1 to the total. If the total result is 9 or more, turn to 1079. If the total is 8 or less, turn to 824.

1171.

Without incident you continue on your current path, moving carefully as you do so. Ahead you can see the entrance to the loading bay with the two fields partly obscuring your vision out into space. Turn to 1072.

1172.

Holding position, you suddenly see movement in the other direction at the junction in sector G. It is a Confederacy agent! You quickly duck hoping he hasn't seen you. If the agent attacks you, you could be between a rock and a hard place with the agent on one side and the gunman on the other and no way out. Stealing a glance from your hiding position you the see the agent did not spot you. He is a little further down the corridor looking inside a room - probably for the likes of you. You are in a dangerous situation and as such consider leaving any idea of getting into sector H for now or finding another way in. You can either move out to get away from both the agent and gunman or take your chances where you are.

To head back to the nearest junction then head towards the stern:

Turn to 398.

To remain where you are: Turn to 1068.

1173.

Looking over Mannek's body you find he has on him two *stimserts* which you may take if you choose. As you are already armed you leave his rifle behind which is rather bulky anyway.

You head back out into the corridor and reach the nearest junction. Turn to 419.

1174.

Still no reply from the bridge. The ships shakes with a deep thunder. Will you:

Teleport to sector F?   Turn to 525.

Teleport to sector G?   Turn to 539.

Continue to try to use the com-link to contact the bridge?

Turn to 1128.

Exit the teleport room?   Turn to 684.

1175.

Time passes. Again you flee from the droid, easily outrunning the machine and reaching a corridor towards the stern side. Turn to 395.

1176.

If you are into the *final tier* of time remaining on your mission sheet, turn to 1219. If you are still in the *second tier*, but have 3 or less unmarked boxes within the *second tier*, turn to 1142. Otherwise, turn to 1137.

1177.

Pushing the door open you step inside the room which you discover is vacant. Quickly closing the door you look for something to jam against it to act as a barricade. A waist high cabinet will suffice; you tip it into position. For a moment there is no sign of the drone and you think you have escaped...until a laser beam pierces the door around head height and begins cutting through. This drone is intent on killing you and from this room there is nowhere else to go. You will have to face it as the laser beam nears completion of a cut-out in the door for which the drone will fit through. Use the *vitality* of the drone which you have noted down and continue the battle with the following stats:

Ra of 5, On 2 dice, 3+ to hit, 3 damage, 5+ to negate 5 damage armor for defense. The drone will make only the one type of attack for the rest of the battle and you may begin attacking first since you have the upper hand of being ready for when it enters the room. If you defeat the drone, you return to the corridor in which the encounter began. Turn to 355.

1178.

Passing by several banks of instruments you crouch behind a bench with a large blocky analyzer sitting on top. From here you can monitor most of the stern side of the lab. You can see two scientists not far away talking to each other quickly about organizing themselves to evacuate. Will you:

Move across to the storage aisles to look from there? Turn to 1259.

Try to identify the two scientists you can see here?   Turn to 1181.

1179.

Holding the agent by his suit with a barrel against his cheek you press him for info.

'What are you doing here,' you throw at him.

He barely looks at you through half closed eyes and says nothing.

'Why have you attacked this ship,' you yell in his ear.

'Had nothing else to do 'fed,' he squeezes out with a smirk.

You press your barrel into him harder.

'Last chance,' you reply.

'You talk too much, I would have pulled the trigger by now,' he says with eyes closed.

Seeing as he is not going to talk, you are left with the only option but to finish him off. Turn to 1050.

1180.

'Ah this little one,' he says as you reveal the cutter to him. 'I had been meaning to get round to it. Tell you what, I'll get straight onto it if you come back in a little while it will be as good as new.'

Will you:

Tell him you don't have the luxury of time?   Turn to 1231.

Agree for him to fix it and return later?   Turn to 1051.

1181.

Time passes. You peer out from your hiding place, waiting for the chance to catch a glimpse of some way to identify the scientists or see what they do. As the pair talk quickly to each other, their movements increase in pace also. If you have the word "east" written down, turn to 1241. If you have the word "last" written down, turn to 826.

1182.

[If you have the *Biohazard borrower* mission, turn to 1240.]

Stationed there with orders to prevent anyone passing, he does not hesitate to open fire. Roll 3 dice. For each, 4 or more, his gun will inflict 3 damage on you if you do not make a successful defense roll. With such a hefty weapon firing at you from the far end of the corridor you don't stand a chance. You'll need to find another way. You head back to the previous junction. Turn to 520.

1183.

Dashing around a corner you look for an opportunity to hide. There appears to be none - unless you can try to conceal yourself behind a support beam on the side of the corridor. It looks to be a tough squeeze which you'll need to achieve quickly. Roll two dice. If you have the *Contortion* ability you may add 4 to the result. If the total is 9 or more, turn to 207. If the total is 8 or less, turn to 1212.

1184.

Still waiting and looking every so often down the corridor, nothing changes. You hear movement back in sector G - somebody moving from one room to another, but the corridor you are in remains silent. Mark off <u>eight</u> *time passes* on your mission sheet. With this amount of time spent hiding here and making no progress at all, you decide it best to either return later or find another way around if there is one. Turn to 520.

1185.

It seems the corporal is intent on getting somewhere so you put yourself to the side and neither greeting him nor showing any emotion allow him to pass. If you are down to the *final tier* of time remaining, turn to 1132. If not, turn to 1279.

1186.

Passing by several large instrument banks, you pause to peer over an island bench to see more of this side of the room. Roll a two dice and add your *perception*. If you have the *Keen eyes* ability you may reroll one of the dice once only. If the result is 12 or more, turn to 1230. If the result is 11 or less, turn to 425.

1187.

In one of the draws you discover 3 doses of *adreno*. It looks as though there is nothing else left in the room. Add the word "weave" to your mission sheet. Now will you:

Try the first door if you have not already?	Turn to 30.
Keep moving?	Turn to 3.

1188.

Write down the word "constant" on your mission sheet. Just as you are passing a room on the bow side, an XBR corporal bursts out of the room, straight into you. Immediately pushing you hard, you have no choice but to push back to avoid toppling over. The corporal, already aggravated takes the response as aggression and decides to hit back with a fist. You'll need to deal with the corporal:

Aggressive XBR Corporal	CQ	5
	Vitality	18

4+ to hit, 3 damage (after 1st combat round).
5+ to reduce damage by 2 as defense.

>For the first combat round, fight the battle unarmed (On one die, roll 5 or more to hit, 2 damage). Afterwards you may use your close quarter weapon and the corporal will use the hit and damage values listed above.

If you defeat the corporal, a cursory check of his body reveals he was carrying nothing useful to you. *Time passes.* Turn to 903.

1189.

'I'll need a little time here,' he says as you hand him all three components.

'I will wait,' you reply. And wait you do as it seems to take longer than you would like even though the short man works quickly with his nimble fingers. Mark off two *time passes* while you wait and watch him work.

'And we're done,' he finally exclaims, holding the little device up high.

'Watch!' he says excitedly. He places the device near a meter readout on one of his benches. When he switches the device on, the readout appears jumbled and incomprehensible until he turns the device off again. He looks at you and smiles.

You thank him for his work. Remove the three components and replace them with a *memory scrambler*. Return to 818.

1190.

Through bleeding teeth the agent spits out his defiance.

'I just need some info,' you say firmly.

If you have the *Negotiator* ability, turn to 1252.

Otherwise roll 1 die. If you roll 3 or more, turn to 1125. If you roll 2 or less, turn to 1090.

1191.

'I'm not sure what that is or what you plan to do with it,' responds Kinlac as you show him. Return to 818 and select another option.

1192.

'If it is a hazardous substance and we have anything to do with it, then it will be in one of the hazardous material handling laboratories. Which on this level there is one in sector H.'

Not allowing for any more questions, she orders you to leave. Will you:

Leave as ordered?   Turn to 565.

Attack the crew?   Turn to 741.

1193.

Finally you get through, though the response is urgent and not what you expected:

'Report back to the bridge - you need to leave the ship now.' With that you step into the teleporter which takes you to the bridge in an instant. The captain immediately approaches you.

'There is no time agent, you must leave now - conditions are getting worse,' he says directing you towards a main teleporting pad; one capable of sending you off ship.

'I hope you report what you have found and the council declares this vicious attack an act of war,' he says sharply.

'I will fulfill my duty,' you respond solemnly, just as the teleporter begins to dematerialize you. Turn to 1222.

1194.

Taking up pursuit around the first corner and to the end of that corridor, the two men continue to flee, the one of them, trailing behind the other loosening off some laser beams to try to shake you off. Roll 3 dice. For each 5 or more, deduct 3 *vitality*, though you may make a defense roll. Ducking inside manufacturing, it looks as though they may lose you amongst the machinery and equipment in there. Will you:

Pursue them into manufacturing?   Turn to 1246.

Let them go?   Turn to 465.

1195.

As soon as you begin trying to help her Melea reopens her eyes and speaks again: 'Leave me, I'm fading fast. Just go, get to the teleport hub on level 5.' She raises her arm slightly, revealing to you the extent of her wounds. They are much more severe than you initially thought. In reality she is dying and won't last long. No number of med packs will treat the extensive wounds and to try to carry her would slow you down far too much. Remove the word "Melea" from your mission sheet. Turn to 1265.

1196.

Time is critical and with the ship in peril you move fast through the door, then a tiny room and into the operating room. You are struck by a pungent odor but quickly cover your nose to at least avoid the smell. The operating room is divided into four smaller rooms and you head straight to the rear to find a door there, ignoring the carcass on the side bench and instruments left unattended. In the room beyond you see workbenches on one side and a collection of small carrying carts on the other. An involuntary cough and then you begin to feel nauseous. It may not have been the smartest choice to enter the area unprotected after all. Deduct 3 vitality and add the *infected* lingering effect. In addition, until the infection is cleared, reduce your *endurance* and *close quarter* scores by 1 point each. You head straight to the starboard exit, turn to 1126.

1197.

Write the word "trawl" on your mission sheet and decide which available sector you will teleport to:

Sector E:	Turn to 416.
Sector F:	Turn to 525.
Sector G:	Turn to 539.

1198.

'Then out the door,' she states coldly. Will you:

Leave as ordered?	Turn to 565.
Attack the crew?	Turn to 741.

1199.

Handing him both items he immediately set out o build the scanner. It takes time even though he is quick joining the modules together and adding only a few loose pieces from around his workshop. *Time passes.*

'And we're done!' he finally says holding the little device up high. Thanking him for his work, you may add a *bio scanner* to your inventory removing the two components. Now return to 818.

1200.

Without any trouble you teleport off the doomed starship. Where to is not an SDN ship or outpost, but to a neutral supply vessel en route to Beutohn. It is safety none the less and you know you can teleport to Phaeadron upon landing if needed.

Using the code words you have written down, can you create the word "breakdown"? If so, turn to 338. If you can make up only part of this word, turn to 108. If you cannot make up even part of this word, turn to 191.

1201.

You are part way along the corridor when you need to stop. A few steps up ahead you notice something on the floor. There are more of them evenly spaced further along the corridor also. You've seen them before. They are proximity mines. Another step closer could have been your last. Even if you had a way of disabling these dangerous devices, it would take far too long to diffuse them all. You'll need to find another way. Turn to 520.

1202.

Standing ground you fire into the group which has dispersed somewhat, but advances just the same. You hit one agent and put him on the floor in pain and from that his allies direct their fire towards you. Resolve the following attack against you: On 2 dice, 5+ to hit, 3 damage. You may roll for defense against any damage. You immediately crouch behind cover, completely out of sight. You are simply out gunned. Next you see an XBR guard firing and again, the squad retaliates, killing the guard outright. With their attention drawn elsewhere, you decide to pull back rather than face being gunned down. Turn to 1114.

1203.

You throw your grenade down the length of the corridor. Despite your best effort it ends up nowhere near the gunman and he remains undeterred behind his shielding. Will you:

Continue to wait?   Turn to 1117.

Abandon the attempt to get to the end of the corridor? Turn to 520.

1204.

Another deep, droning creak and the shaking of something exploding elsewhere on the ship. As the alarm continues to sound, it is clear the ship is disintegrating faster. You'll need to get a move on if you are to escape this dire situation. Roll 1 die. If you roll a 5, turn to 127. Otherwise return to 590 and continue the reference from where you left off.

1205.

Roll a die. If you roll a 1, turn to 1195. If you roll anything else, turn to 540.

1206.

The droid you encountered earlier is patrolling the corridor and upon identifying you opens fire. Roll 2 dice. For each 5 or more, suffer 4 damage, allowing for a defense roll. Now you must face this fearsome robot. If you had previously damaged the droid, it has repaired itself in the meantime.

Armed Droid	Ra	5
	Vitality	28

5+ to hit, 4 damage.

4+ to negate 4 damage as armor for defense.

>If you choose to throw a grenade at the droid, the grenade will do double base damage for a successful hit. The droid will still roll for defense against the attack.

>If you want to flee this combat (or choose to avoid taking on the droid altogether), you may disengage without any penalty as the droid is comparatively slow to react. Simply turn straight to 1175 before any new combat round.

Should you manage to defeat the droid, turn to 1146.

1207.

The blip on your visual display is now quite close to you. Looking down the corridor towards stern you would say that the signal is emanating from the first of two rooms along there. You call out over the audio channel but still nothing returns. Will you:

Ignore the signal and head towards the bow?   Turn to 345.

Head towards the stern and try the first room on the right?

Turn to 1057.

Head towards the stern and try the second door on the right?

Turn to 46.

1208.

The call might have been startling, but now you are completely vigilant as you hear heavy thumping footsteps - and they are getting louder as something approaches. At the far end of the aisle you see a black shape flash by, it is too difficult to tell if it entered the same aisle as the one you are in. You need to make a decision. Will you:

Hold up for the moment?   Turn to 800.

Keep moving along the aisle?   Turn to 250.

1209.

As you reach the junction, you are confronted by a droid standing in the corridor heading towards port side. It only takes a moment to denounce you as an intruder and open fire with a powerful laser attached to its right arm. Roll 2 dice. If either scores a 5 or 6, deduct 4 *vitality*, unless you can make a successful defense roll. Write the word "expire" on your mission sheet.

You may either take on the droid or turn and run:

Armed Droid	Ra	5
	Vitality	28

5+ to hit, 4 damage.
4+ to negate 4 damage as armor for defense.

>If you choose to throw a grenade at the droid, the grenade will do double base damage for a successful hit. The droid will still roll for defense against the attack.

>If you want to flee this combat (or choose to avoid taking on the droid altogether), you may disengage without any penalty as the droid is comparatively slow to react. Simply turn straight to 1282 before any new combat round.

Should you manage to defeat the droid, turn to 1221.

1210.

After knocking you down to the floor, the agent attempts to get onto a teleport pad and teleport out of the room. Roll one die. If you have the *Enhanced leap* ability, you attempt to leap onto the pad to stop him: deduct 2 from the dice roll. If the result of the roll is 3 or more, turn to 1233. Otherwise, turn to 1056.

1211.

Remove the explosive from your inventory. Roll a die and add the result to the damage value of the type of explosive you are using. If you are trying to use a micro petard on this door, deduct 2 from the total. If the end total is 8 or more, the explosion is sufficient and the hole left is large and clean enough for you to get through; turn to 194. If the end total is 7 or less, you have done enough damage, but will have to spend time cutting away some of the metal for you to squeeze through. In this case mark off a *time passed* box on your mission sheet and turn to 194.

1212.

The agent has caught you; you are forced to face him at close quarters.

XBR agent Nethit	CQ	5
	Vitality	27
	On 2 dice, 5+ to hit, 5 damage.	
	5+ to negate 3 damage as defense.	

>If the agent rolls a double 6 when attacking you, he hits you with an unusual weapon you have not seen before. In this case, make a single defense roll if you can and if you fail that roll, add the *infected* lingering effect. If you become *infected* then ignore this ability for the rest of the combat for any further double 6 rolls.

>You cannot flee this combat, you will have to defeat the agent.

If you reduce the agent to less than 10 *vitality*, turn to 1085.

If you manage to kill the agent, turn to 274.

1213.

Prying open the control box mounted on the wall, you quickly find the source of the problem. Part of the circuit is fried. You can however form a quick bypass which will open the door temporarily though the circuit itself will remain damaged. Working quickly, the door opens and you slip through before the door closes again. Turn to 1167.

1214.

Time passes. Taking the corridor towards the bow, you encounter a tricky situation. A head you see a large pool of what appears to be water on the floor. You can see the ripples pulse across the pool as the ship shakes every so often. What makes this situation difficult however is toward the other side you can see a damaged ambient energy accumulator from a piece of broken equipment sitting in the water and sparking furiously. That means the water will be electrified. You notice the hole above you in the ceiling where more water drips down, expanding the pool. You will need a way to get past. Will you:

Try to run through the pool in order to get past?   Turn to 1144.

Hop your way across?   Turn to 1110.

Take a running leap at it?   Turn to 1274.

1215.

Edging closer to the far corner of the room, you are now crouched behind an island bench with a large hologram projected above it simulating a number of biological processes. To your left nearer the corner is a translucent panel, behind that a window that you cannot clearly see through from your vantage point to a restricted operating area. On the opposite side of the bench you are behind, though further away at the side of the room you can hear the source of the quarreling. You can see only one of the scientists there listening to another speak; the rest are obscured visually due to instruments and equipment.

'Why won't the manual override work?' asks one of the scientists.

'Let's just go through the operating rooms,' interjects another.

'We can't, they haven't been sanitized,' argues a third.

'Well let's just suit up then,' responds the second scientist.

Time passes. It looks as though the group is trying to exit the laboratory but are experiencing some difficulty. Will you:

Sneak over to the restricted area and try to exit through the operating rooms?   Turn to 1286.

Attack the group of scientists and try the exit they are currently blocking?   Turn to 1107.

Wait a moment to see what happens?   Turn to 1134.

Head back around towards the stern-port side of the lab?

Turn to 1186.

1216.

Write down the word "constant" on your mission sheet. Bursting out of the door near you is a uniformed woman, stumbling several steps before collapsing on the floor. Rushing over to evaluate her condition, you find her unconscious. From the door which is not fully sealed smoke is pouring through the gaps. The woman needs help otherwise she will go down with the ship. You rush around the corridor, looking for a solution or someone to help out. Fortunately after taking two corridors you meet a man just leaving another room. You hammer out the dire situation and although he is reluctant initially he is soon convinced and follows you back to the scene. With his help *time* passes as you both carry the woman to the teleporter for this sector where the helpful crew member jumps with her to the bridge as you watch from the doorway. Turn to 649.

1217.

Activating your trusty *Bio-mimic* device, you fool the scanner into recognizing you as someone you are not, enabling the off ship tele pads to work for you. You are certainly glad you went to the trouble to build such a device. Manipulating the controls for the teleporter it seems that jumping directly to Phaeadron is not possible at the moment, so you begin a search of other possible teleport locks.

Your fortune continues as a supply ship en route to Beutohn is available for teleportation entry. It is a neutral vessel and it is on the move; that will do you think to yourself as you begin the process of teleporting. Turn to 1119.

1218.

Roll a die. If the result is 4 or more, turn to 1294. If the result is 3 or less, turn to 1288.

1219.

[If you have not done so already, turn to 1234 before returning here.]

The corridor appears to be clear. You begin heading along the long stretch when all of a sudden the ship lurches and shakes abruptly. You keep your footing and brace yourself by pushing against one of the walls. When the rattling subsides you move rapidly towards the end of the corridor where you see a ramp heading upwards. Will you:

Take the ramp up to level 4?   Turn to 1168.
Return to the previous junction?   Turn to 670.

1220.

Remove the word "deter" from your mission sheet. Now will you:
Take time searching their bodies?   Turn to 1249.
Leave the area immediately?   Turn to 590.

1221.

Reduced to a pile of scrap metal, the droid is no more, allowing you to continue on your way.

At the junction you can:
Go towards portside: Turn to 699.
Head towards the bow taking a right hand corner at the end:
                                                Turn to 585.
Take the corridor in the direction of the stern: Turn to 684.

1222.

Safely back aboard your own ship, you can only watch as the XBR starship is pulled into the atmosphere of Beutohn, one of the three moons of Phaeadron. It disintegrates into countless pieces and no doubt some of those pieces are the human remains of those that did not make it off in time.

After taking a moment to compose yourself you establish a connection with your commander using your holo-view. After providing a detailed account of occurrences aboard the starship, your commander thinks it over.

'Send through the files you have agent,' he says gruffly.

You do this with a few swift gestures, initializing the process.

'We will assess the information and draw our conclusions as soon as possible. For now agent, suspend your previous task and get some rest while we deal with the situation; you may be needed again shortly.

His face then disappears from the holo-view.

If you have the word "astray" written down and at least 2 identity scans, turn to 86.

Otherwise, turn to 201.

1223.

Though you greet the man in an attempt to relieve any tension, as the broad shouldered corporal reaches you he shows no sign of friendliness. If you are down to the *final tier* of time remaining, turn to 1132. If not, turn to 1279.

1224.

You are about half way along the aisle with no sign of the thing that is lurking in the room with you. Roll a die and add your *perception*. If you have the *Keen eyes* ability you may reroll the die once. If the result is 8 or more, turn to 112. If the result is 7 or less, turn to 123.

1225.

According to the information you have, inside this large laboratory is the most likely place Minkla will be. Hopefully he is in here and has yet to evacuate; he would not be the only one if so. Your task requires you to identify him, steal the data regarding his current research and then eliminate him without being traceable. You consider these three aspects of your mission as you decide how to proceed.

To assess the room will you:

Head down one of the short material storage aisles nearby?

Turn to 1259.

Scout around the portside wall towards the stern?　Turn to 1178.

1226.

Remove the word "proceed" from your mission sheet. Now that the agent is dead you can move on with the task at hand. You may also take an identity scan of the agent before you leave. If you do so, add 1 to the tally of identity scans created on your mission sheet. You head over to the exit. Turn to 649.

1227.

You take a look outside the hatch very cautiously. There is nothing immediately outside the door. Pressing the hatch closed again, you take a moment to make your decision. The walls rattle as the ship undergoes more turbulence. You decide you cannot wait. Turn to 260.

1228.

Seizing the opportunity you turn and run as fast as you can from the guard. Rounding two corners you are out of sight of the guard and so quickly find a room to hide in.

Time passes. Ducking inside, you are in the teleport room for this sector. You have to make a decision whether to jump or to wait in the hope the guard does not enter the room:

To teleport jump to another sector: Turn to 1197.
To wait until the guard enters or passes: Turn to 1290.

1229.

You begin heading along one of the aisles, moving carefully as you go. The dim lighting of the room is helpful in that it makes you difficult to see, but it also makes seeing anything else just as tough. Suddenly a strange animal call from the nearest specimen pen puts you on edge. Roll a die. If you roll 4 or more, turn to 1208. If you roll 3 or less, turn to 216.

1230.

Over towards the starboard side, mostly obscured by a floor to wall spectroscopic analyzer you spot an armored individual. He appears to be moving minimally, occupied with watching something else which you cannot see. What will you do:

Wait to see if he leaves or what happens?   Turn to 187.

Open fire?   Turn to 154.

Try to sneak further around behind him?   Turn to 124.

1231.

'No point being impatient about it,' grumbles Kinlac, turning back to his tinkering.

'Leave it on the bench over there,' he says half pointing to a very limited amount of clear space on a nearby bench.

'I'll get to it when I get to it.' You can either take the cutter with you or leave it on the bench. Return to 818 and either make another enquiry or select an option to leave the area.

1232.

The drone crashes to the floor, spinning itself further into pieces. You have done well to bring down a deadly machine. You may add up to 1 point to your *chance* score. Now turn to 1165.

1233.

The agent is too quick for you, activating the tele pad and jumping before you have a chance to stop him. By the time you work out which sector he teleported to, he will be long gone. *Time passes.* Picking yourself up and brushing yourself off, you have no choice but to get on with it. Remove the word "proceed" from your mission sheet. You head over to the exit. Turn to 649.

1234.

Without warning an alarm sounds. At the same time small lights at intervals along the walls pulse a deep red. The alarm is neither deafening nor blinding, but it is enough to grab your attention. You suspect the ship is in some serious trouble - then your thoughts are answered when you hear an automated message emitted from speakers in the ceiling.

'Critical condition alert: All technical personnel to perform emergency repair. All other personnel to perform emergency evacuation procedure,' you hear the voice say, just as the ship shakes and thumps, testing your steadiness. It looks as though the ship will not hold up for too much longer as its structural integrity begins to falter.

If you have not already, write down the following words: "hollow" and "fatal". Return to your previous reference.

1235.

'What do you think is going on in here? This is research! Did you miss the induction?' Replies the man. 'But if you must know, we are looking into the merging of three species in order to improve the genetics of our agents. It's the specimen HK-01 that has them all excited,' he says, looking you in the eyes. Leaning down the man then proceeds to take his items and leave the room; you decide to do the same. Turn to 565.

1236.

In the corner of the room you notice a long rugged box. You quickly open it and peer inside. There is a *paroxysm flail*; a weapon normally confiscated from rebels and non-faction aligned individuals which you may take if you choose. Add the word "weave" to your mission sheet. Now will you:

Try the first door if you have not already?   Turn to 30.

Keep moving?   Turn to 3.

1237.

You show him the generator you have.

'Well, I don't know where you got this from, but you don't usually see these anymore!'

'Can they work together?' You ask.

'Sure they can and now I know what might be your kind of thing,' he replies.

'Ah but I will also need an *interface trigger* module for it to work.'

Do you have an *interface trigger*? If so, turn to 1299 now. If you do not have this item, if you happen to find one later on, return to this room, meet with Kinlac and then you may turn directly to 1299 rather than showing him the data emulator again. Return to 818.

1238.

Threatening her with a slow and painful demise, you push for information. She is resistant to tell you anything of the data kept on this ship. You push harder, making her bleed a little and proving you are willing to hurt or kill. Defiant, she claims ignorance which does not seem likely for her ranked position. You are not beaten however as you have one final trick you can use. Recently you have been issued with a microchip implant which will allow you temporary limited access into another individuals memories. It requires contact with the other person and is something still in development by SDN control. You determine it a worthy test and activate it now. For a moment you lose awareness and a blinding white light fills your vision, though you are not sure if it is in the room or just in your own mind. As fast as it arrived it leaves and you return to consciousness of your surroundings. At the same time with your intent of seeking data from the ship, you suddenly recall memories, not your own relating to this. You see a data vault filled with data stores. There is a secure room for select data. You see yourself, or more accurately the hand of the woman inputting a code to open the secure vault... you note the numbers... 1, 7, 0 as the hand inputs them. Then you feel an acute pain inside your head. Deduct the result of 1 rolled die from your *vitality*. Meanwhile, as you lost awareness and then dealt with the subsequent pain, the woman makes a desperate attempt to break free. Roll one die. If you roll 3 or more, turn to 1111. If you roll a 1 or a 2, turn to 968.

1239.

Leaving her be, you turn to walking away when you are struck from behind by a blunt object. Deduct 3 *vitality*. She looks at you angrily, hoping her attack would have knocked you out. But she was mistaken and now you decide it best to end her suffering. Turn to 1084.

1240.

You really don't stand a chance against the gunman. If you decide to turn back, heading to the previous junction, you may do so by turning to 520. If you are determined to enter in sector H and are willing to wait it out or devise some sort of plan, turn to 1269.

1241.

The one nearest scurries around looking for something either on the benches or in a draw. You see his crew number: 235. The other scientist, having just retrieved something from a draw turns to the nearer man. 'I'm out,' he says, signaling his intent to leave. You see his number: 241. You need to make a decision. Whichever target you choose, the other scientists are likely to start running as soon as you kill one of them. As these two scientists are close, you have the opportunity at the moment to take them both out. Will you:

Eliminate both scientists here?   Turn to 224.

Take out the nearest scientist 235?   Turn to 1063.

Take out the furthest scientist 241?   Turn to 1245.

Leave these two and look over the other side for Minkla?

                                                 Turn to 240.

1242.

[If you have the word "strung" written down, return to 32 and choose again rather than reenter the room.]

An uncommon type of keypass is required for this door. If you have one, use it here otherwise you may either spend time trying to break into this room; turn to 1267, or choose an alternative; turn to 32.

1243.

When you look back over the cover again, you spot a syndicate agent bringing up the rear with a heavy pulse rifle mounted on his shoulder. Realizing your vulnerability you do not hesitate in the moment to make a dive in the direction of the back of the hall, rolling and tumbling as you do. At that moment two high energy pulses rip apart the container you were just using as cover, sending pieces through the air at deadly velocities. Scrambling, you find the nearest cover behind a support beam on the port side of the hall. There is an elevator behind you that you notice so you hit the button to call it or open the door - you figure you may need it. Next you see several XBR guards come down a main ramp at the back of the hall, but only to meet a burst of pulsed energy which divides the group in two, as well as carving chunks out of two of the guards, leaving them reeling on the floor. The others still standing leap to the nearest cover they can find.

Will you:

Hold position?   Turn to 1277.
Pull back to the next alcove segment in the wall?   Turn to 1087.

1244.

You run hard, determined to put some distance between you and the creature. You pick an aisle and utilize the dark spots to stay out of sight as you slow to cautious single steps. There is no sign of the alien at present. Roll a die. If the result is a 3 or a 4 or more, turn to 304. If the result is anything else, turn to 544.

1245.

The scientist hits the floor dead from your well placed shot. The other scientists go into panic mode either ducking for cover or bolting to the closest exit. There is another individual in the room you were previously unaware of. On the far side towards the stern an XBR agent stands up, having witnessed what you have just done. He has an idea of your location, sending a torrent of laser fire into the instruments and equipment surrounding you. You are under attack and will need to fight back. Add the word "fountain" to your mission sheet and turn to 144.

1246.

Time passes. Entering into the room, you see no signs of the two men. Either they have found an effective hiding place or have run around the production line somewhere. You decide to check the nearby pieces of equipment to see if they are hiding close by, but nothing is to be found. Rather than waste more time here you return to the corridor and press on. Turn to 465.

1247.

You wait a while longer. Taking a peak, there is still no difference with the gunman. This is definitely a standoff. Will you:

Continue to wait for as long as it takes?   Turn to 1184.

Abandon the attempt to get to the end of the corridor? Turn to 520.

1248.

Difficult to see in the darkness you find there is a medical cabinet beside you. Will you:

Grab some supplies while you can?   Turn to 1218.

Ignore it and keep moving?   Turn to 1160.

1249.

Time passes. Roll a die. If the result is 4 or more, turn to 389. If the result is 3 or less, turn to 1026.

1250.

Inputting a teleport lock onto the attack ship, you successfully teleport off the XBR starship. Back aboard the attack ship you head to the helm where you can obtain reports on the overall situation. The ship itself has distanced itself from the XBR starship to remain out of sight and out of danger. The read outs indicate the XBR starship is perilously being pulled down by the gravity of Beutohn. It also looks as though you are the first to return, though there are still a few remaining on the ship according to the status monitoring. Without hesitation you contact Commander Ashkin. Upon hearing your report that despite extensive searching there is no technology aboard as the mission had planned for, he makes the call for any remaining agents to be pulled out of the ship. Though there has been no success with the mission, the commander remains detached despite the heavy casualties sustained. Without providing further information on the mission or any future plans, he ends the communication.

For now, neglecting needed rest you continue to monitor the fate of the XBR starship and the status of your comrades. The XBR ship does not take long to be pulled down into the moon and disintegrates in the process; flashes of light can be seen in the upper atmosphere as explosions take place. As for the other agents, it looks as though a few have returned through the teleporter. Add 250 creds to your credit tally. Turn to 197.

1251.

Holding your breath you have a go at transferring the contents across. Only when some of the spores become airborne and then make contact with your skin do you realize you do not simply have to breathe them in to suffer the ill effects of these deadly spores. Your skin starts to wither away and turn a sickly green around each minute spore that makes contact. In horror you reel backwards, but nothing can be done: within seconds you lose consciousness and hit the floor. You have failed your mission and died a terrible death.

1252.

Time passes. Resisting you at first, you drill him for information.

'Surely you must know,' he taunts.

Placing the agent in a crushing hold, you order him to detail the reason for the attack.

'Our mission was to extract new technology. Not just the latest and greatest. We were told it was something capable of changing the balance dramatically. But it turns out it was just a run around - just XBR and their alien pets and the likes of you...'

His information sheds new light on the situation and has provided recorded evidence for the LWS intent. Write the word "astray" on your mission sheet.

What you did not notice however as he was talking to you was with one of his hands he has just pulled out the pin of a grenade that is on his belt. Without hesitation you throw him against the wall and leap out of the room as fast as you can. You escape the brunt of the blast but fragments of metal bounce off the corridor wall and lodge into you calves. Deduct 2 *vitality*. Add the word "curb" to your mission sheet. Picking yourself back up and peering into the teleport room you see it is a mess of torn metal and broken equipment. As for the agent, you can only recognize pieces of his body spread across the room.

Remove the word "proceed" from your mission sheet. In the corridor you may now:

Head towards starboard side:	Turn to 523.
Make your way to the port side junction:	Turn to 553.

1253.

Time passes. It looks as though someone has really ransacked the room, taking anything of value. But not one particular thing; on the wall is a cabinet with medical supplies. It is locked, so it may be likely whoever looted the room could not get it open in time. It is an easy enough task for you however to destroy the small lock with your weapon. There is enough supplies in the cabinet to form 2 full *med packs*. Add the word "reel" to your mission sheet. Exiting the room will you:

Try the second door if you have not already?	Turn to 510.
Keep moving along the corridor?	Turn to 3.

1254.

It looks as though the laser pistol the guard used is irreparably damaged. He has on him nothing else worth taking. Write the word "trawl" on your mission sheet. Will you:

Try the door on port side labeled "Engine bay"?   Turn to 770.
Continue along the corridor towards the bow?   Turn to 670.
Head along the corridor towards the stern?   Turn to 711.

1255.

Though there may have been other important data that you could have gathered, you have done well enough to satisfy your mission and to aid in SDN plans. Add 200 creds to your total and turn to 82.

1256.

You turn and you run. As you start to do so you notice the heavy pounding footsteps of whatever it is that is now after you. You reach the end of the aisle and run across to choose another aisle to lose your pursuer. Roll a die. If you roll a 1 or a 2, turn to 180. If you roll anything else, turn to 246.

1257.

You are making great headway on the agent as you round another corner, almost out of sight from the agent as he enters the corridor you are leaving. Roll 2 dice and add your *endurance*. If you have the *Ultra runner* ability, you may add 3 to the total. If the total is 12 or more, turn to 1264. If the total is 11 or less, turn to 1212.

1258.

Safely back aboard your ship, you take a moment to rest and recuperate yourself. You may restore your *vitality* to maximum and remove any lingering effects you have. Then, dutifully you establish a connection with your commander.

'Glad you made it off that doomed starship,' he opens with upon seeing your face.

'Me too,' you reply before giving a brief account of what happened and the outcome for your mission.

'Your work is much appreciated as always agent. But it is far from done. The council is currently evaluating the Syndicate attack and will have a decision shortly. If the result is as I expect it to be, then we will be launching a pre-emptive strike on one of their bases. If that is the case and since you are nearby, I may call upon you to assist the team. But for now, rest up and we will communicate later.'

With that the commander's face disappears from your holo-view.

You catch some much needed rest.

You will have the option of participating in the strike.

If you do, continue your adventure as a Confederacy agent in book 2 of the **Bionic Agent** series: *Vault of carnage*. If you decline the mission, you may finish delivering the supplies before returning to Phaeadron. In this case, continue your life as a Confederacy agent with book 3...

If you have the word "grasp" written down on your mission sheet, then turn to 199. If you do not have this word written down, turn to 1300.

1259.

Taking up position at the end of one of the short storage aisles, you survey the part of the room you are able to see. Towards the starboard-bow corner there is a translucent panel, behind which appears to be a windowed room. Across towards starboard you see a scientist facing a door, looking as though he is trying to manually open the door, but without any success. Will you:

Wait here and try to identify the scientist you can see? Turn to 289.

Head back and scout around the portside wall towards the stern to look there?   Turn to 1178.

1260.

Write the word "recover" on your mission sheet. The double doors open automatically for you and once inside you realize you are in a small training facility of some sort. The place is a mess and you notice two bodies on the floor and another slumped up against one of the walls. Walking up closer to the one slumped against the wall you notice it is an allied agent but from one of the other teams. You recognize his face though you hardly know him. He is conscious and he looks at you through one eye but is having trouble breathing with more than one hole through his lungs. 'Don't bother helping. I'm too shot up,' he spits out.

'What about the mission?' You ask.

'That scumbag Ashkin screwed us. No tech here. Nothin'. Nobody to pick us up. Just a damn mess. You have to get off this ship. Get the rats.'

With that he closes his eye and splutters up some more blood. Though you'd like to help you see the futility of the situation. Urgency moves you to the exit. Turn to 715.

1261.

You know you need to find a way to transfer the spores to the canister. With some good fortune you find a contamination bag which allows you to put both items in and perform the transfer safely within the closed bag, into the carrier vapor canister, bud and all.

If you have a *Bio* score of 4 or more, turn to 1038. If your *Bio* score is 3 or less, turn to 937.

1262.

As he is unarmed and near death he is hardly a threat and since he gave testimony which is valuable to you, you release your grip on him. The agent, a little surprised, moves away cautiously and steps onto one of the tele pads. A moment later he is gone. You head over to the exit. Turn to 649.

1263.

You slam the readout panel as it fails to find a destination to lock onto. A series of explosions rips through the vessel. These begin the inevitable destruction, as the ship splits and the artificial gravity fails, throwing you to the wall. Despite making it to the teleport hub, you cannot find a lock in time and so have nowhere to jump to, resulting in the doomed starship becoming your grave, though a grave with no remains as it burns up into countless fragments in the upper atmosphere.

1264.

You have escaped the agent for now: with the agent out of sight, you look to enter a room in order to lose him. Replace the word "capacity" with the word "filter".

To enter into a research room: Turn to 616.
To enter into a laboratory: Turn to 448.
To enter into the teleport room: Turn to 453.

1265.

Melea has expended most of her gear; she is out of medical supplies or grenades and her armor is shot to bits. A *laser pulse rifle* lies by her side which you may take if you choose. You leave her as she loses consciousness, focused on getting off the ship alive. Leave the room and turn to 715.

1266.

The corridor is clear. Hearing yelling from within a room to your side, you decide to keep moving and head straight to the end of the corridor quickly. Turn to 1275.

1267.

You'll need to be quick in cutting through the door. If you have a tool to break through such as a *high speed laser cutter* or a *siege ram,* roll to get through as per the details for the item you are using. In this instance, you may reroll one die, once. If you are successful, turn to 1280. If not, you still get through, though it takes longer than hoped; mark off a *time passed* box on your mission sheet and turn to 1280. If you do not have the right tool for the job or after the first attempt want to abandon the break-in, return to 32 and choose an alternate option.

1268.

Time passes. You move past several rooms on your way with no sign of anyone. Sensing your time growing short, you race to the end of the corridor where you encounter another junction. A sign gives minimal help by pointing the way to level 5 towards the bow. If you have the word "Melea" written down, turn to 1207. Otherwise make your choice of direction:

Head towards the bow?   Turn to 345.

Head towards the stern?   Turn to 251.

1269.

You step back a short distance to position yourself in a small alcove in the side of the corridor. You are out of sight from the gunman, though you can take peaks to see what he may be doing. Looking the other way you can see a short distance to the nearest junction in sector G. For now you don't have any plan to get by the gunman so you begin to wait. *Time passes.* Thinking to yourself, it would probably be near impossible to get a direct hit with a grenade at such a distance within the confines of the corridor. You could however give it a shot if you choose.

To throw a grenade if you have one: Turn to 1203.

To continue to wait: Turn to 1117.

To abandon the attempt to get to the end of the corridor:

Turn to 520.

1270.

The cabinet topples over, hitting a mobile piece of apparatus in line, sending it forward into the agent. As bits off the apparatus crash to the floor and the agent scrambles to recuperate, you make a dash for the door. Inside is a short room with one wall lined with full contamination suits. The sign on the other wall indicates in bold lettering: "Restricted: full protection must be worn beyond this point."

Will you:

Don one of the fully sealed suits?   Turn to 299.

Move fast into the operating rooms without protection?

Turn to 1196.

1271.

Seeing only one option here, you make a dash for the ramp out of the hall. Roll one die. If you roll a 1, you take a hit - deduct 2 *vitality*. Otherwise you are quick enough - and their shots are sloppy enough - that you make it up the ramp and out of sight. This is a fight for the XBR faction, you are here to help. Though there are no guards remaining, you are confident on a ship this size the XBR are not beaten yet.

Write the word "concede" on your mission sheet. Continuing up as it changes direction twice, you further the distance between yourself and the invaders. Reaching the top of the ramp, you are in a corridor with an option to head either into sector E towards port side or sector F towards starboard.

You decide to take the corridor towards starboard. Turn to 397.

1272.

To see how you fair ducking across to behind an analyzer machine, roll 2 dice. For each 4 or more, suffer 3 damage. You may roll for defense to negate the damage. Repeat the process again. If you have an *agility* of 4 or less, repeat the process a third time. If you survive the incoming fire, you can either fire back at him: return to 144 and continue, or you can look for an alternative: turn to 99.

1273.

The agent is swift despite being injured; he dashes around the corridor and out of sight faster than you can run. You are fortunate to have fended him off. Replace the word "capacity" with the word "filter" and turn to 453.

1274.

A running leap might work; provided you make it all the way across you think. Roll 2 dice. This is a jumping task so if you have the *Enhanced leap* ability, you may reroll either dice once, accepting the second roll. For each point your *agility* is <u>above</u> 5 you may add 1 to the total. If the end result is 7 or more, turn to 1072. If the end result is 6 or less, turn to 371.

1275.

At the end of the corridor there is a closed door. The door is solid and acts to seal off this section. You hit the button on the side wall to manually open it but nothing happens. The door is controlled remotely. *Time passes.* You'll need to find a way through. Will you:

Use an explosive if you have one?   Turn to 1211.

Try to hack the circuit to force the door to open?   Turn to 325.

1276.

If you have a pair of items that you are looking to decode, turn to 330. If you have something else, turn to 1191.

1277.

Time passes. When the elevator doors open up, they catch your attention and you peer inside. Just as you do, you notice out of your peripheral vision an LWS agent charging at you. The enemy hits you with such force the both of you end up on the floor inside the elevator. Scrambling to your feet you meet the man head on, inside this large cargo elevator. Fight your attacker in close combat:

LWS agent   CQ   5

Vitality   16

4+ to hit, 3 damage.

5+ armor negates 4 damage as defense.

>You will need to defeat this agent in order to leave.

If you dispatch the agent you may take his *electro razor* if you choose. Now will you:

Activate the elevator to head to another level?   Turn to 1082.
Take an identity scan of the agent?   Turn to 1131.
Get out of the elevator and pull back to the next alcove in the hall?
    Turn to 1291.

1278.

'Well she would have let me know beforehand - that is not like her,' responds the woman. In her momentary confusion, you take the opportunity to insist you are only after some information and then proceed to ask a question:
What will you ask?
Of new technology aboard the ship?   Turn to 1121.
Of research being done here?   Turn to 1048.

1279.

As the corporal passes he turns in your direction and gives you a disgusted look, as if intentionally to show his hatred. Letting him disappear down the end of the corridor *time passes* as you decide what to do next. You may:
Try the door on port side labeled "F006":   Turn to 632.
Head along the corridor towards the bow where you can see a junction: Turn to 391.
Head along the corridor towards the stern: Turn to 551.

1280.

Turn to 921.

1281.

From up ahead you see a guard heading straight for you. He sees you in plain sight and immediately grows suspicious. Several steps closer and he is convinced you're not meant to be here. He calls out to you as he reaches for a pistol. You have no time to try to persuade him and he is blocking your path.

Resolve a single attack against you as the guard fires a shot. He will hit on a 3 or more and will inflict 3 damage, though you may roll for defense. After this you rush at the guard and take him on at close quarters. You may strike first in this combat.

XBR Guard	CQ	5
	Vitality	15
	4+ to hit, 4 damage.	
	No defense.	

If you defeat the guard, you find nothing you could do with on him; turn to 1275.

1282.

Time passes. As the droid can stride quickly but not run as fast as you can, you manage to avoid the droid relatively easily. It is however still patrolling in the sector. Write the word 'linger" on your mission sheet.

Head towards either starboard: Turn to 597.
Or towards stern: Turn to 395.

1283.

Time passes as you have to open up the mangled door so that you can fit through. Eventually the job is done. Turn to 1031.

1284.

You make it to the door and open it. Inside you find yourself in a short room with one wall lined with full contamination suits. The sign on the other wall indicates in bold lettering: "Restricted: full protection must be worn beyond this point."

Will you:
Put on one of the fully sealed suits?   Turn to 299.
Move quickly into the operating rooms without protection?

            Turn to 1196.

1285.

Another rumble and you have to steady yourself as the ship twists and contorts. The alarm continually reminds you of the critical situation. Cutting through the air, buzzing towards you from port side is a swift flying security drone.

Attack drone	Ra	5
	Vitality	8

4+ to hit, 4 damage.
5+ Agile flyer defense will negate all damage.

Shoot down the drone before it shoots you.

If you defeat the drone, replace the word "filter" on your mission sheet with the word "deter". Now return to 523 and continue reading the reference from where you left off.

1286.

Aiming to get out of here as soon as possible, you decide to find and make use of the door to the operating rooms. Roll a die to test if you make it to the door without being noticed. If you have the *Stealth* ability, add 1 to the roll. If your *chance* score is at -2, deduct 1 from the roll. If the result is 3 or more, turn to 1163. If the result is 2 or less, turn to 641.

1287.

Sensing the corporal resents the fact a Confederacy agent is aboard an XBR starship and may be harboring considerable hatred, you initiate conflict. Turn to 161 now, then after reading that reference, turn to 1009.

1288.

Taking the opportunity you grab out the supplies and load yourself up with them. You may add a *med pack* to your inventory. Just as you are grabbing the last item however, a glucose monitoring tool falls down from one of the shelves, banging against both the floor and another cabinet. It is a sure give away so you decide to duck back and get into another aisle before anything arrives at the scene. Roll a die. If you roll a 4 or a 5, turn to 26. If you roll anything else, turn to 1256.

1289.

No response from the bridge. You are starting to feel on edge given the accelerating rate of deterioration of the ship. You step outside the teleport room to see if there are any crew members around that might be of help - but there is no sign of anyone. Turn to 684.

1290.

Fortunately the guard passes with his reverberating footsteps easily heard as he runs by. You wait a short while longer to be sure he will be gone. Write the word "trawl" on your mission sheet and exit into the corridor by turning to 684.

1291.

To the safety of the next alcove you pull back, knowing you do not want to be stranded as the attacking faction pushes toward the rear of the hall. XBR forces are still attempting to keep the LWS at bay, though you see your allies losing ground to the fewer but more advanced attackers. Being tech driven, there is clearly no shortage of armaments with the LWS - evident by an approaching aerial drone large enough to span the width of two doors in circumference. Below its circular fan are three small turrets, each capable of locking onto a different target. The drone flies up towards the end of the hall and opens up with all barrels blazing.

Several XBR guards as well as you take incoming fire from the drone, which hovers in a central position dishing out damage across a 180 degree arc. Roll 1 die. If you roll 3 or less, resolve 1 attack against you (1 die, 5+ to hit, 4 damage); if you roll 4 or more, resolve 2 attacks against you. You may roll for defense against these attacks as in combat. Then proceed into the battle:

Heavy assault drone Ra   5

                     Vitality   30

                     On 2 dice, 5+ to hit, 4 damage.

                     5+ Armor plating negates 6 damage as defense.

>Fight for five rounds of combat. Each round, roll for a collective attack against the drone by XBR forces. In other words in each round, the drone will attack; you will attack; the XBR will attack. The drones' attacks are directed at you and the XBR guards though you only need to resolve those attacks at you which are factored into the stats above - if the drone were attacking only you with all three turrets, you would be dealing with the full killing capacity of it.

                XBR allies Ra   4

                            On 2 dice, 4+ to hit, 3 damage.

If you bring down the drone by reducing its *vitality* to zero in 5 combat rounds or less, turn to 1232.

At the end of the fifth combat round, turn to 1093.

1292.

The door on the stern side appears to be securely locked. You decide to try the starboard door before spending time breaking through. Turn to 1126.

1293.

Searching the body of the agent yields a few items. His close combat weapon is an XBR design and has some sort of biometric lock on it, so you decide to leave that alone. His gun you may take however: it is a *twin pulse rifle*. The agent also had on him two *stimserts* which you may take. Replace the word "capacity" with the word "filter". Turn to 728.

1294.

You begin by grabbing what supplies you can quickly. Add two *stimserts* as well as 3 doses of *adreno*. In your haste to grab items you could use, a pair of medical shears drops to the floor and sounding an obvious clang which will surely give your position away. Leaving the cabinet, you duck back and get into another aisle before anything arrives at the scene. Roll a die. If you roll a 2 or a 5, turn to 26. If you roll anything else, turn to 1256.

1295.

Time passes as you wait. Roll one die if you roll a 4, turn to 1193. If you roll anything else, turn to 1174.

1296.

Roll a die. If the result is 4 or more, turn to 1151. If the result is 3 or less, turn to 1106.

1297.

By luck or by skill you have managed to make the transfer and you are both still alive and feeling okay. Add *Buitonixum spores* to your inventory. Quickly now you leave the room with your cargo. Turn to 866.

1298.

You sneak around towards the stern, past a bank of instruments and taking up position behind a work bench. You see the scientist 237 nearby start accessing a terminal. Further across towards the starboard another scientist is collecting something from a draw. His number is 241. A third scientist is on his way out. Your opportunities are running out. Will you:

Take out the nearest scientist 237?   Turn to 165.
Take out the furthest scientist 241?   Turn to 1245.
Wait to see what happens?   Turn to 136.

1299.

'Ok, leave me in peace while I get the job done,' he says as he collects the modules from you. You take a seat in the corner and wait patiently. After having to make adjustments on the emulator to make it compatible he finishes the task - relatively quickly, yet longer than preferable for you. Mark off two *time passes.*

'And we're done,' he says with his trademark smile. 'You'll have to test it in the field, but if I haven't put it together backwards it should fool any biometric scanner,' he says handing you the device.

Remove the three components from your inventory and add a *Bio-mimic device* to your inventory.

For such good fortune add 1 to your chance score also. Now return to 818.

1300.

Epilogue:

With the **Bionic Agent** series you may use your current character to continue to play future missions without having to start a new character for each book. In this sense you will further improve your character, upgrade weapons and ultimately shape the course of events. This aspect of the series of books means continuity of storyline and the part you play in the fate of your faction and the population as a whole. If your character does die, you can either start afresh, either from the first book in this series or simply start again with the book you are reading. If you are intent on using the same character the whole way through the series to get the most out of your adventure, then you may also have a backup copy of your character at the end of each book. This means if you die in any book, you can start that particular book again with the character as they were from completing your previous book. If you do this, simply transfer your mission sheet to a new one, and keep the old one for any 'resurrections' of your character.

Now that you have completed *Starship deadfall,* there are certain code words you may have written down which will be applicable in future books. If you have any of the following words written down, they are to be kept on your mission sheet (until instructed to remove) for future missions. To keep them, write them in the bottom section of the code words box on your mission sheet.

Keep these words:

Fracture

Frozen

Research

Scar

Breakdown

Anarchy

You may remove all other words.

As for items, you must choose which you will keep. There are many items in the books, more than anyone can carry. Some items may be useful later or sold for a profit; others will be completely worthless and only burden you. Remember you can discard items at any time outside of battle or at the end of your mission.

The only stats you may change are your *vitality* - restore it to maximum. The rest remain as they are. You may also remove any lingering effects, though if you have any other special conditions or injuries, these remain with you. You may also clear all time remaining check boxes. For completing *Starship deadfall*, you may add 2 points to any stat(s) of your choice out of *Vitality, CQ, Ra, St, Ag, Pe, En* or *Re*. You may add 1 point to any intelligence stat out of *Sci, Tech* or *Bio*. Finally, you may select an additional ability of your choice or you may randomize a compatible ability if you created a randomized character for instance.

It is not necessary to read *every* book in the **Bionic Agent** series though you do need to read them in order. Book 2 is an *optional* book. This means you may skip book 2 and go straight to book 3 if you so choose. To get the most out of the storyline and bolster your character as much as possible however it would be beneficial to follow on with book 2.

If you are continuing onto book 2: *Vault of carnage*, then you will be heading straight there.

If you are returning to Phaeadron for book 3, then you may visit a supply shop when you arrive. In this case see the shop following this reference. It is not necessary to visit the shop however as there will be multiple opportunities to buy and sell in book 3 whilst on Phaeadron. You may now visit the trade shop at the back of the book if you choose. Note there will be opportunities for trade in the next book also.

TRADE:

The following 'shop' acts as a conglomerate of items available to you from sellers at the present time. You may purchase any item listed for the credit amount shown. At this point, it is suggested you give priority to what you need, such as a basic CQ and Ra weapon and medical supplies.

BUY:	
Knuckle lasers	100
Skewer launcher	100
Micro torch	150
Laser pistol	100
Laser pulse rifle (LPR)	200
Breaker gun	180
Shock pistol	200
Dual auto pistols	200
Dual link pistols	320
Punisher auto gun	400
Stun pistol	350
Twin pulse rifle	500
Laser blaster	700
Grenade launcher	600
Volatile liquid sprayer	620
Shock mace	100
Short laser blade	100
Electro razor	100
Hammer fist	200
Manta stinger	220
Paroxysm flail	280
Fists of flame	450

Dart vest	450
Med pack	100
Stimsert	60
High impact grenade	50
Scatter grenade	40
High impact explosive	50
Proximity explosive	80
Demolisher bomb	80
Micro petard	40
Combat armor	100
Ceramic plated vest	100
Coated multi alloy suit	100
Reconstructing synthesized polymer suit	100
Xeno exo suit	100
Siege ram	300
Utility socket	100
Shoulder utility socket	120
Continuous high speed laser cutter	150
Heavy rock breaker	200
Battering hammer	250

If you are looking to sell any items - no more than one of each will be accepted for the given credit amount:

SELL:	
Laser pistol	70
Breaker gun	120
Upgraded dual auto pistols	180
Modded LPR	200
Magnetic disc sling	350
Short laser blade	50
Electro razor	50
Corroder blade	100
Siege ram	200
Continuous high speed laser cutter	100
Utility socket	50

www.ingramcontent.com/pod-product-compliance
Lightning Source LLC
Chambersburg PA
CBHW070540030726
47505CB00001B/108